# THE RCA LIFECYCLE MADRIKH

# מדריך למחזור החיים

# MADRIKH

מאת
הרב ראובן פנחס בולקא

הוצאת
**הסתדרות הרבנים דאמריקא**

# THE RCA LIFECYCLE

*by*

Rabbi Reuven P. Bulka

*Published by the*

**Rabbinical Council of America**

---

**THE RCA LIFECYCLE MADRIKH**


305 Seventh Avenue
New York, N.Y. 10001
(212) 807-7888

---



ISBN: 0-89906-587-2

Printed in the United States of America by
Noble Book Press Corp., New York, N.Y.

# ☙ *Table of Contents*

# Introduction

Within Rabbinic circles, there has long been a felt need for a new Madrikh. This is in no way to be construed as a slight of Hyman Goldin, the author of the original Rabbinic guide, The Madrikh. His guide was and remains an excellent work, the standard by which to measure any new venture of this type.

Times have changed, and new realities have made for new needs to be addressed, such as having a celebration to name a girl, bat mitzvah, adoption, among others. Goldin cannot be faulted for not having these in his Madrikh; they were not standard events in his time.

Many Rabbis have expressed a preference for a leaner Madrikh, more compact and focused. Others have put forth ideas of what a new Madrikh should contain. If we were to put all these ideas into the Madrikh, it would be a thick, and effectively unusable volume, at least for the intended purpose of helping the Rabbi in times of most frequent need.

With due trepidation at the prospect of not addressing the Rabbis' needs adequately, I have set out to offer a slimmed down volume, called THE RCA LIFECYCLE MADRIKH, because this Madrikh contains material dealing only with lifecycle events.

The categories of this volume are Baby Naming for a girl, Berit, Pidyon HaBen, Adoption, Conversion, Bat Mitzvah, Pre-Nuptial and Arbitration Agreements, Tenaim, Marriage and Sheva Berakhot, Visiting the Sick, Changing of Name, Dying, the Funeral, Birkat HaMazon in a House of Mourn-

and Dedicating the Memorial Monument — no more, no less. These are the lifecycle events, the times when the guiding hand of a Rabbi are most needed.

With so many halakhic guides available today, this volume contains very little in the form of halakhic decisions. Instead, the focus is on the text and context of the specific occasions, and on helping the Rabbi to properly discharge Rabbinic obligations. Much attention has been given to offering a coherent, contemporary translation of the original texts, attempting to balance accuracy with easy readability. The English transposition of the Hebrew follows Sephardic pronunciation and there is an open space at the end of each section for insertion of other pertinent material.

A special feature of this Madrikh are two laminated inserts enclosed in a pouch inside the front cover. One is for the wedding ceremony, and the other is for the funeral service.

Many have helped to make this Madrikh a reality. **HaRav Gedaliah Schwartz,** our venerated RCA Av Bet Din, gave his most invaluable insights to assure the halakhic propriety of the Madrikh.

The RCA executive Vice-President, **Rabbi Binyamin Walfish,** was always available, with sage counsel and energetic willingness to help, as was his successor, **Rabbi Steven Dworken.**

**Rabbi Moshe Gorelik,** diligently carrying out his mandate as RCA President, kept pushing for me to complete this Madrikh, aware of and sensitive to the demand for this work. The help of incumbent President **Rabbi Rafael Grossman** is likewise acknowledged.

Many Rabbis contributed material which was helpful in developing this Madrikh. My gratitude, and assuredly the gratitude of all our colleagues, the beneficiaries of this Madrikh, goes to **Rabbi Elazar Muskin, Rabbi Joseph Radinsky, Rabbi Abner Weiss,** and **Rabbi Moshe Yeres** for their enhancing this volume.

Gratitude is also expressed to the **Orthodox Caucus** and **Rabbi Mordechai Willig** for their vital role in formulating the Pre-Nuptial and Arbitration Agreements, to address the pressing aguna problem. These documents have been endorsed by the Rabbinical Council of America, and their being signed for the wedding will hopefully become standard procedure.

Down the road, we plan a second companion text to this one, which will contain many more topic areas, dealing with the host of occasions not covered in this volume, and containing other pertinent material for Rabbis, including halakhot and homiletic matter.

I close this short introduction with the fervent hope that this volume will be helpful to my Rabbinical colleagues as they endeavor to serve their congregational families with the surpassing excellence for which they continually strive.

*Reuven P. Bulka*

**About the Author**

Reuven P. Bulka is the Rabbi of Congregation Machzikei Hadas in Ottawa, Ontario, Canada, and chairs the Rabbinical Council of America Publications Committee. A prolific author, this is his 25th book.

## ◆ Baby Naming

*The birth of a girl is as great a joy as the birth of a boy. However, the immediate imperatives for the family following the birth of a girl are not as time-pressured. Many are relieved that the only pressing need is to give the girl her name. The name can be bestowed on the first day of Torah reading after birth, on the first or second Shabbat, or even a month after birth.*
*The naming follows the call of the father to the Torah.*

## BABY NAMING

A special prayer on behalf of the mother and her newborn daughter is recited. The essential text is from Iggerot Mosheh to Orah Hayyim, Volume 4, #67.

**מִי שֶׁבֵּרַךְ** אֲבוֹתֵינוּ אַבְרָהָם יִצְחָק וְיַעֲקֹב מֹשֶׁה אַהֲרֹן דָּוִד וּשְׁלֹמֹה, הוּא יְבָרֵךְ אֶת הָאִשָּׁה הַיּוֹלֶדֶת (שם האם) בַּת (שם אמה) עִם בִּתָּהּ הַנּוֹלְדָה לָהּ לְמַזָּל טוֹב, בַּעֲבוּר שֶׁבַּעְלָהּ עָלָה לַתּוֹרָה. בִּשְׂכַר זֶה הַקָּדוֹשׁ בָּרוּךְ הוּא יִמָּלֵא רַחֲמִים עָלֶיהָ לְהַחֲלִימָהּ וּלְרַפְּאוֹתָהּ וּלְהַחֲזִיקָהּ וּלְהַחֲיוֹתָהּ, וְיִשְׁלַח לָהּ מְהֵרָה רְפוּאָה שְׁלֵימָה מִן הַשָּׁמַיִם לְכָל אֵבָרֶיהָ וְגִידֶיהָ בְּתוֹךְ שְׁאָר חוֹלֵי יִשְׂרָאֵל, רְפוּאַת הַנֶּפֶשׁ וּרְפוּאַת הַגּוּף, (בשבת או יום טוב מוסיפים שַׁבָּת/יוֹם טוֹב הִיא מִלִּזְעוֹק) הַשְׁתָּא בַּעֲגָלָא וּבִזְמַן קָרִיב. וְאֶת בִּתָּהּ הַנּוֹלְדָה לָהּ לְמַזָּל טוֹב לְאוֹרֶךְ יָמִים וְשָׁנִים; יִקָּרֵא שְׁמָהּ בְּיִשְׂרָאֵל (שם הילדה) בַּת (שם האב; אם מבחינה הלכתית אין אב להבת קוראים לה על שם אמה), וְיִזְכּוּ אָבִיהָ וְאִמָּהּ (אם מבחינה הלכתית אין אב להבת, אומרים וְתִזְכֶּה אִמָּהּ) לְגַדְּלָהּ לְתוֹרָה, לְחוּפָּה, וּלְמַעֲשִׂים טוֹבִים, וְנֹאמַר אָמֵן.

Following the conclusion of the services, it is appropriate to have a festive meal, or some repast, to celebrate the giving of the name.

## BABY-NAMING CELEBRATION

In addition to bestowing the name during the course of the Torah reading, one may also call a special gathering of family and friends for the express purpose of celebrating the special joy of the birth, through expressions of gratitude and embracing of responsibility, and again bestowing the name. This is done after due time has been given for the mother to recover, gain some strength, and thus participate in the event.

What follows is one of many possible formats for this gathering.

תהלים קכז

**שִׁיר הַמַּעֲלוֹת,** לִשְׁלֹמֹה, אִם יהוה לֹא יִבְנֶה בַיִת, שָׁוְא עָמְלוּ בוֹנָיו בּוֹ, אִם יהוה לֹא יִשְׁמָר עִיר, שָׁוְא שָׁקַד שׁוֹמֵר. שָׁוְא לָכֶם מַשְׁכִּימֵי קוּם, מְאַחֲרֵי שֶׁבֶת

## BABY NAMING

A special prayer on behalf of the mother and her newborn daughter is recited. The essential text is from Iggerot Mosheh to Orah Hayyim, Volume 4, #67.

**מִי שֶׁבֵּרַךְ** *May God, Who has blessed our patriarchs Avraham, Yitzhak and Yaakov, Mosheh, Aharon, David and Shelomoh, bless* (mother's Hebrew name) *daughter of* (mother's mother's Hebrew name), *who has given birth, together with her daughter who has been born to her in good fortune and for which her husband has come up to the Torah. In merit of this, may the Holy One, Blessed is God, be filled with compassion for her to restore her health, to heal her, to strengthen her, and to revitalize her. May God send her a complete recovery from heaven for all her organs and veins, among the other sick people in Israel, a recovery of the spirit and a recovery of the body* — (on Shabbat or Yom Tov add: *because it is Shabbat/Yom Tov we cannot cry out*), *yet may the recovery be speedily and in due time; and (may God bless) her daughter who has been born to her in good fortune for length of days and years; let her name in Israel be called* (baby's Hebrew name) *daughter of* (father's Hebrew name; if child has no halakhic father, mother's name is inserted here). *May her [father and]* (omit if child has no halakhic father) *mother merit raising her to Torah, the marital canopy, and good deeds, and let us respond, Amen.*

Following the conclusion of the services, it is appropriate to have a festive meal, or some repast to celebrate the giving of the name.

## BABY-NAMING CELEBRATION

In addition to bestowing the name during the course of the Torah reading, one may also call a special gathering of family and friends for the express purpose of celebrating the special joy of the birth, through expressions of gratitude and embracing of responsibility, and again bestowing the name. This is done after due time has been given for the mother to recover, gain some strength, and thus participate in the event.

What follows is one of many possible formats for this gathering.

Psalm 127

**שִׁיר הַמַּעֲלוֹת** *A song of ascents of Shelomoh. If the Lord will not build the house, then they that build it labor in vain; if the Lord will not watch over the city, then the watchman's diligence is in vain. It is meaningless for you that rise early and sit up late,*

אֹכְלֵי לֶחֶם הָעֲצָבִים, כֵּן יִתֵּן לִידִידוֹ שֵׁנָא. הִנֵּה נַחֲלַת יהוה בָּנִים, שָׂכָר פְּרִי הַבָּטֶן. כְּחִצִּים בְּיַד גִּבּוֹר, כֵּן בְּנֵי הַנְּעוּרִים. אַשְׁרֵי הַגֶּבֶר אֲשֶׁר מִלֵּא אֶת אַשְׁפָּתוֹ מֵהֶם, לֹא יֵבֹשׁוּ, כִּי יְדַבְּרוּ אֶת אוֹיְבִים בַּשָּׁעַר.

תהלים קכח

**שִׁיר הַמַּעֲלוֹת,** אַשְׁרֵי כָּל יְרֵא יהוה, הַהֹלֵךְ בִּדְרָכָיו. יְגִיעַ כַּפֶּיךָ כִּי תֹאכֵל, אַשְׁרֶיךָ וְטוֹב לָךְ. אֶשְׁתְּךָ כְּגֶפֶן פֹּרִיָּה בְּיַרְכְּתֵי בֵיתֶךָ, בָּנֶיךָ כִּשְׁתִלֵי זֵיתִים, סָבִיב לְשֻׁלְחָנֶךָ. הִנֵּה כִי כֵן יְבֹרַךְ גָּבֶר יְרֵא יהוה. יְבָרֶכְךָ יהוה מִצִּיּוֹן, וּרְאֵה בְּטוּב יְרוּשָׁלָיִם, כֹּל יְמֵי חַיֶּיךָ. וּרְאֵה בָנִים לְבָנֶיךָ, שָׁלוֹם עַל יִשְׂרָאֵל.

The last two verses can be sung in Hebrew by the assembled. The name, having already been bestowed at a previous Torah reading occasion, is then reaffirmed.

**מִי שֶׁבֵּרַךְ** אֲבוֹתֵינוּ אַבְרָהָם יִצְחָק וְיַעֲקֹב, הוּא יְבָרֵךְ אֶת הָאִשָּׁה הַיּוֹלֶדֶת (שם האשה) בַּת (שם אביה) וְאֶת בִּתָּהּ הַנּוֹלָדָה לָהּ בְּמַזָּל טוֹב, לְאוֹרֶךְ יָמִים וְשָׁנִים, וְנִקְרָא שְׁמָהּ בְּיִשְׂרָאֵל (שם הילדה) בַּת (שם האב; אם מבחינה הלכתית אין אב להבת קוראים לה על שם אמה), וְיִזְכּוּ אָבִיהָ וְאִמָּהּ (אם מבחינה הלכתית אין אב להבת, אומרים וְתִזְכֶּה אִמָּהּ) לְגַדְּלָהּ לְתוֹרָה, לְחוּפָּה, וּלְמַעֲשִׂים טוֹבִים, וְנֹאמַר אָמֵן.

The mother, wearing a new dress, may then recite the following berakhah:

**בָּרוּךְ** אַתָּה יהוה אֱלֹהֵינוּ מֶלֶךְ הָעוֹלָם, שֶׁהֶחֱיָנוּ וְקִיְּמָנוּ וְהִגִּיעָנוּ לַזְּמַן הַזֶּה.

Here the parents may deliver a Devar Torah, which should include an explanation of the baby's name, and why that name was chosen. A fitting Devar Torah may then be delivered by the Rabbi.

*who eat the bread of disappointment; indeed God gives rest to God's beloved. Behold — children are a heritage of the Lord: the fruit of the womb is a reward. As arrows in the hand of a mighty one, so are the children of one's youth. Praiseworthy is the one who has filled the quiver with them; they shall not be shamed when they contend with adversaries in the gate.*

Psalm 128

**שִׁיר הַמַּעֲלוֹת** *A song of ascents. Praiseworthy is everyone who is in awe of the Lord, who follows in the Lord's ways. When you eat from the labor of your hands, you are praiseworthy and it is well for you. Your wife shall be like a fruitful vine in the innermost parts of your home; your children shall be like olive shoots around your table. Behold — so is the one who is in awe of the Lord blessed. May the Lord bless you from Zion and may you see the goodness of Yerushalayim all the days of your life. And may you see children for your children, harmony be upon Israel.*

The last two verses can be sung in Hebrew by the assembled. The name, having already been bestowed at a previous Torah reading occasion, is then reaffirmed.

**מִי שֶׁבֵּרַךְ** *May God, Who has blessed our patriarchs Avraham, Yitzhak and Yaakov, bless* (mother's Hebrew name) *daughter of* (mother's father's Hebrew name) *who has given birth, and her daughter, who has been born to her in good fortune for length of days and years, and her name is Israel has been called* (baby's Hebrew name) *daughter of* (father's Hebrew name; if child has no halakhic father, mother's name is inserted here). *May her [father and]* (omit if child has no halakhic father) *mother merit raising her to Torah, the marital canopy, and good deeds, and let us respond, Amen.*

The mother, wearing a new dress, may then recite the following berakhah:

**בָּרוּךְ** *Blessed are You, Lord our God, Ruler of the Universe, Who has given us life and sustained us, enabling us to reach this moment.*

Here the parents may deliver a Devar Torah, which should include an explanation of the baby's name, and why that name was chosen. A fitting Devar Torah may then be delivered by the Rabbi.

The parents then recite the Shema, which at once affirms faith and acceptance of parental responsibility to transmit Torah traditions to the child.

דברים ו:ד־ט

**שְׁמַע יִשְׂרָאֵל, יהוה אֱלֹהֵינוּ, יהוה אֶחָד:**

בָּרוּךְ שֵׁם כְּבוֹד מַלְכוּתוֹ לְעוֹלָם וָעֶד. – In an undertone

**וְאָהַבְתָּ** אֵת יהוה ׀ אֱלֹהֶיךָ, בְּכָל־לְבָבְךָ, וּבְכָל־נַפְשְׁךָ, וּבְכָל־מְאֹדֶךָ. וְהָיוּ הַדְּבָרִים הָאֵלֶּה, אֲשֶׁר ׀ אָנֹכִי מְצַוְּךָ הַיּוֹם, עַל־לְבָבֶךָ. וְשִׁנַּנְתָּם לְבָנֶיךָ, וְדִבַּרְתָּ בָּם, בְּשִׁבְתְּךָ בְּבֵיתֶךָ, וּבְלֶכְתְּךָ בַדֶּרֶךְ, וּבְשָׁכְבְּךָ וּבְקוּמֶךָ. וּקְשַׁרְתָּם לְאוֹת ׀ עַל־יָדֶךָ, וְהָיוּ לְטֹטָפֹת בֵּין ׀ עֵינֶיךָ. וּכְתַבְתָּם עַל־מְזֻזוֹת בֵּיתֶךָ, וּבִשְׁעָרֶיךָ.

The assembled join in singing:

**סִמָּן טוֹב וּמַזָּל טוֹב יְהֵא לָנוּ וּלְכָל יִשְׂרָאֵל, אָמֵן.**

It is appropriate to culminate the bestowal of the name with a festive meal.

The parents then recite the Shema, which at once affirms faith and acceptance of parental responsibility to transmit Torah traditions to the child.

Deuteronomy 6:4-9

***Hear, O Israel, the Lord is our God, only the Lord.***

In an undertone— *Blessed is the Name of God's honored Dominion forever.*

וְאָהַבְתָּ *You shall love the Lord your God with all your heart and with all your soul and with all your might. These words, which I instruct you this day, take to heart. Teach them diligently to your children and make them your essential conversation when you are at home and when you are on the way, when you lie down and when you are awake. Bind them as a sign on your hand and make them as frontlets on your forehead. Inscribe them on the doorposts of your home and on your gates.*

The assembled join in singing:

***May there be a good sign and good fortune***
***for us and for all Israel, Amen.***

It is appropriate to culminate the bestowal of the name with a festive meal.

## ◆ *Berit Milah — Covenantal Circumcision*

*Circumcision, the act of covenantal affirmation (Berit) for a newborn son, should take place on the eighth day following birth, preferably as early in the morning as possible, and ideally immediately after the morning Shaharit service.*

*On occasion, because of medical problems, the Berit must be delayed, perhaps for months. In such instances, the baby should be given its name earlier, and then appropriate prayers for its recovery should be recited.*

*If the eighth day after a natural (as opposed to Caesarian or induced) birth is a Shabbat or Yom Tov, the Berit takes place either prior to the Musaf service (if one can bring the child to the Bet Knesset), or immediately after the Musaf service (if for whatever reason, including absence of an eruv, one cannot bring the child to the Bet Knesset).*

*If the eighth day following a Caesarian section or induced birth is a Shabbat or Yom Tov, the Berit takes place on the first ordinary day following the Shabbat or Yom Tov. For multiple births, each covenantal ceremony, with all the blessings, is done separately.*

*It is customary to have a couple, called Kvater and Kvaterin, bring the newborn to the site of the Berit.*

## BERIT MILAH — COVENANTAL CIRCUMCISION

When the infant is brought in, the entire assemblage greets him:

# בָּרוּךְ הַבָּא

The mohel then says:

**וַיְדַבֵּר** יהוה אֶל מֹשֶׁה לֵּאמֹר. פִּינְחָס בֶּן אֶלְעָזָר בֶּן אַהֲרֹן הַכֹּהֵן הֵשִׁיב אֶת חֲמָתִי מֵעַל בְּנֵי יִשְׂרָאֵל, בְּקַנְאוֹ אֶת קִנְאָתִי בְּתוֹכָם, וְלֹא כִלִּיתִי אֶת בְּנֵי יִשְׂרָאֵל בְּקִנְאָתִי. לָכֵן אֱמֹר, הִנְנִי נֹתֵן לוֹ אֶת בְּרִיתִי שָׁלוֹם.

The baby is placed upon a specially designated chair — called the Throne of Eliyahu — by the father or one of the prominent guests, whereupon the mohel says:

**זֶה** הַכִּסֵּא שֶׁל אֵלִיָּהוּ הַנָּבִיא, זָכוּר לַטּוֹב. לִישׁוּעָתְךָ קִוִּיתִי יהוה. שִׂבַּרְתִּי לִישׁוּעָתְךָ יהוה, וּמִצְוֹתֶיךָ עָשִׂיתִי. אֵלִיָּהוּ מַלְאַךְ הַבְּרִית, הִנֵּה שֶׁלְּךָ לְפָנֶיךָ, עֲמוֹד עַל יְמִינִי וְסָמְכֵנִי. שִׂבַּרְתִּי לִישׁוּעָתְךָ יהוה. שָׂשׂ אָנֹכִי עַל אִמְרָתֶךָ, כְּמוֹצֵא שָׁלָל רָב. שָׁלוֹם רָב לְאֹהֲבֵי תוֹרָתֶךָ, וְאֵין לָמוֹ מִכְשׁוֹל. אַשְׁרֵי תִּבְחַר וּתְקָרֵב יִשְׁכֹּן חֲצֵרֶיךָ —

והנאספים עונים: נִשְׂבְּעָה בְּטוּב בֵּיתֶךָ, קְדֹשׁ הֵיכָלֶךָ.

The child is then placed on the lap of the sandak, the person honored with holding the baby during circumcision. When the mohel is ready to perform the circumcision, the baby's father says:

**הִנְנִי** מוּכָן וּמְזֻמָּן לְקַיֵּם מִצְוַת עֲשֵׂה שֶׁצִּוַּנִי הַבּוֹרֵא יִתְבָּרַךְ, לָמוּל אֶת בְּנִי.

If the father is not performing the circumcision, he verbally appoints the mohel as his agent to circumcise his son, by saying:

**הִנְנִי** מְמַנֶּה אוֹתְךָ לִהְיוֹת שְׁלוּחִי לָמוּל אֶת בְּנִי.

## ✥ BERIT MILAH – COVENANTAL CIRCUMCISION ✥

When the infant is brought in, the entire assemblage greets him:

***Blessed is the one who has come!***

The mohel then says:

**וַיְדַבֵּר** *The Lord spoke to Mosheh, saying: Pinhas son of Elazar son of Aharon the Kohen, removed My wrath from upon the Children of Israel, when he zealously showed his passion for Me among them, so that I did not annihilate the Children of Israel in My passion. Therefore say, 'Behold! I give him My covenant of peace.'*

The baby is placed upon a specially designated chair – called the Throne of Eliyahu – by the father or one of the prominent guests, whereupon the mohel says:

**זֶה** *This is the Throne of Eliyahu the Prophet, who is remembered meritoriously.*

*For Your salvation do I long, Lord. I hoped for Your salvation, Lord, and I fulfilled Your commandments. Eliyahu messenger of the covenant, behold yours is now before you; stand at my right and support me. I hoped for Your salvation, Lord. I rejoice over Your word, like one who finds abundant treasures. There is abundant peace for the lovers of Your Torah, and there is no stumbling block for them. Praiseworthy is the one You choose and draw near to dwell in Your Courts.*

All present respond:

**נִשְׂבְּעָה** *May we be sated by the goodness of Your House, Your Holy Sanctuary.*

The child is then placed on the lap of the sandak, the person honored with holding the baby during circumcision. When the mohel is ready to perform the circumcision, the baby's father says:

**הִנְנִי** *Behold, I am prepared and ready to fulfill the affirmative precept that the Creator, Blessed is God, has commanded me, to circumcise my son.*

If the father is not performing the circumcision, he verbally appoints the mohel as his agent to circumcise his son, by saying:

**הִנְנִי** *I hereby delegate you as my agent, to act on my behalf in circumcising my son.*

The mohel then joyously proclaims:

**אָמַר** הַקָּדוֹשׁ בָּרוּךְ הוּא לְאַבְרָהָם אָבִינוּ, הִתְהַלֵּךְ לְפָנַי וֶהְיֵה תָמִים. הִנְנִי מוּכָן וּמְזֻמָּן לְקַיֵּם מִצְוַת עֲשֵׂה שֶׁצִּוָּנוּ הַבּוֹרֵא יִתְבָּרַךְ לָמוֹל. (אם האב בעצמו מל, אומר: שֶׁצִּוַּנִי הַבּוֹרֵא יִתְבָּרַךְ לָמוֹל אֶת בְּנִי).

Just before performing the circumcision, the mohel recites:

**בָּרוּךְ** אַתָּה יהוה אֱלֹהֵינוּ מֶלֶךְ הָעוֹלָם, אֲשֶׁר קִדְּשָׁנוּ בְּמִצְוֹתָיו, וְצִוָּנוּ עַל הַמִּילָה. (All – אָמֵן)

After the removal of the outer skin, and prior to the uncovering of the crown, the father (or, if the father is not present, the sandak) recites:

**בָּרוּךְ** אַתָּה יהוה אֱלֹהֵינוּ מֶלֶךְ הָעוֹלָם, אֲשֶׁר קִדְּשָׁנוּ בְּמִצְוֹתָיו, וְצִוָּנוּ לְהַכְנִיסוֹ בִּבְרִיתוֹ שֶׁל אַבְרָהָם אָבִינוּ.

All respond, loudly and joyfully:

**אָמֵן. כְּשֵׁם שֶׁנִּכְנַס לַבְּרִית,**
**כֵּן יִכָּנֵס לְתוֹרָה, וּלְחֻפָּה, וּלְמַעֲשִׂים טוֹבִים.**

When the circumcision is completed, the baby is handed for holding to one of the guests whom the family desires to honor, while the following prayers (including the giving of the name) are recited. The honor of reciting them may be given to one person, or may be divided between two people. If so, the first person pronounces the two blessings over a full cup of wine and the second person recites the prayer during which the baby is given his name.

**בָּרוּךְ** אַתָּה יהוה אֱלֹהֵינוּ מֶלֶךְ הָעוֹלָם, בּוֹרֵא פְּרִי הַגָּפֶן. (All – אָמֵן)

**בָּרוּךְ** אַתָּה יהוה אֱלֹהֵינוּ מֶלֶךְ הָעוֹלָם, אֲשֶׁר קִדַּשׁ יְדִיד מִבֶּטֶן, וְחֹק בִּשְׁאֵרוֹ שָׂם, וְצֶאֱצָאָיו חָתַם בְּאוֹת בְּרִית קֹדֶשׁ. עַל כֵּן בִּשְׂכַר זֹאת, אֵל חַי, חֶלְקֵנוּ צוּרֵנוּ, צַוֵּה לְהַצִּיל יְדִידוּת שְׁאֵרֵנוּ מִשַּׁחַת. לְמַעַן בְּרִיתוֹ אֲשֶׁר שָׂם בִּבְשָׂרֵנוּ. בָּרוּךְ אַתָּה יהוה, כּוֹרֵת הַבְּרִית. (All – אָמֵן)

The mohel then joyously proclaims:

**אָמַר** *The Holy One, Blessed is God, said to Avraham, our father, 'Walk before Me and be complete.' Behold I am prepared and ready to fulfill the affirmative commandment that the Creator, Blessed is God, has commanded us, to circumcise* (if the father is the mohel, he says: *has commanded me, to circumcise my son).*

Just before performing the circumcision, the mohel recites:

**בָּרוּךְ** *Blessed are You, Lord our God, Ruler of the Universe, Who has sanctified us with the Godly commandments and has commanded us regarding circumcision.* (All— *Amen)*

After the removal of the outer skin, and prior to the uncovering of the crown, the father (or, if the father is not present, the sandak) recites:

**בָּרוּךְ** *Blessed are You, Lord our God, Ruler of the Universe, Who has sanctified us with the Godly commandments, and has commanded us to usher him into the covenant of our patriarch Avraham.*

All respond, loudly and joyfully:

***Amen. Just as he has entered into the covenant, so may he enter into Torah, the marital canopy, and good deeds.***

When the circumcision is completed, the baby is handed for holding to one of the guests whom the family desires to honor, while the following prayers (including the giving of the name) are recited. The honor of reciting them may be given to one person, or may be divided between two people. If so, the first person pronounces the two blessings over a full cup of wine and the second person recites the prayer during which the baby is given his name.

**בָּרוּךְ** *Blessed are You, Lord our God, Ruler of the Universe, Who creates the fruit of the vine.* (All— *Amen)*

**בָּרוּךְ** *Blessed are You, Lord our God, Ruler of the Universe, Who sanctified the beloved one from the womb and placed the Godly imprint in his flesh, and sealed his offspring with the sign of the holy covenant. Therefore, in recognition of this, O Living God, our Portion, our Rock, may You issue the command to rescue the beloved soul of our posterity from calamity, for the sake of God's covenant that God has placed in our flesh. Blessed are You, Lord, Who establishes the covenant.* (All— *Amen)*

## GIVING THE NAME

**אֱלֹהֵינוּ** וֵאלֹהֵי אֲבוֹתֵינוּ, קַיֵּם אֶת הַיֶּלֶד הַזֶּה לְאָבִיו וּלְאִמּוֹ (אם אין לבן אב או אם מדלגים „לאביו" או „ולאמו" ואם אין לו אב ואם, אומרים לְיִשְׂרָאֵל), וְיִקָּרֵא שְׁמוֹ בְּיִשְׂרָאֵל (שם הילד) בֶּן (שם האב; אם מבחינה הלכתית אין אב להבן, קוראים לו על שם אמו). יִשְׂמַח הָאָב בְּיוֹצֵא חֲלָצָיו, וְתָגֵל אִמּוֹ בִּפְרִי בִטְנָהּ.

אם האב בעצמו נותן את השם יאמר:

יְהִי רָצוֹן שֶׁאֶשְׂמַח בְּיוֹצֵא חֲלָצַי וְתָגֵל אִמּוֹ בִּפְרִי בִטְנָהּ.

ליתום מהאב יאמר:

יִשְׂמַח הָאָב בְּגַן עֵדֶן בְּיוֹצֵא חֲלָצָיו וְתָגֵל אִמּוֹ בִּפְרִי בִטְנָהּ.

ליתום מהאם יאמר:

יִשְׂמַח הָאָב בְּיוֹצֵא חֲלָצָיו וְתָגֵל אִמּוֹ בְּגַן עֵדֶן בִּפְרִי בִטְנָהּ.

ליתום מהאב ומהאם יאמר:

יִשְׂמַח הָאָב בְּגַן עֵדֶן בְּיוֹצֵא חֲלָצָיו וְתָגֵל אִמּוֹ בְּגַן עֵדֶן בִּפְרִי בִטְנָהּ.

**כַּכָּתוּב:** יִשְׂמַח אָבִיךָ וְאִמֶּךָ, וְתָגֵל יוֹלַדְתֶּךָ. וְנֶאֱמַר: וָאֶעֱבֹר עָלַיִךְ וָאֶרְאֵךְ מִתְבּוֹסֶסֶת בְּדָמָיִךְ (הנאספים אומרים ואח"כ אומר נותן השם, בשעה שנותנים טפת יין להתינוק) **וָאֹמַר לָךְ בְּדָמַיִךְ חֲיִי, וָאֹמַר לָךְ בְּדָמַיִךְ חֲיִי.** וְנֶאֱמַר: זָכַר לְעוֹלָם בְּרִיתוֹ, דָּבָר צִוָּה לְאֶלֶף דּוֹר. אֲשֶׁר כָּרַת אֶת אַבְרָהָם, וּשְׁבוּעָתוֹ לְיִשְׂחָק. וַיַּעֲמִידֶהָ לְיַעֲקֹב לְחֹק לְיִשְׂרָאֵל בְּרִית עוֹלָם. וְנֶאֱמַר. וַיָּמָל אַבְרָהָם אֶת יִצְחָק בְּנוֹ, בֶּן שְׁמֹנַת יָמִים, כַּאֲשֶׁר צִוָּה אֹתוֹ אֱלֹהִים. (נותן השם אומר, וכל הקהל עונים) **הוֹדוּ לַיהוה כִּי טוֹב, כִּי לְעוֹלָם חַסְדּוֹ.** (נותן השם אומר, וכל הקהל עונים) **הוֹדוּ לַיהוה כִּי טוֹב, כִּי לְעוֹלָם חַסְדּוֹ.** (שם הילד) בֶּן (שם האב; אם מבחינה הלכתית אין אב להבן, קוראים לו על שם אמו) זֶה הַקָּטָן גָּדוֹל יִהְיֶה.

**כְּשֵׁם שֶׁנִּכְנַס לַבְּרִית, כֵּן יִכָּנֵס לְתוֹרָה, וּלְחֻפָּה, וּלְמַעֲשִׂים טוֹבִים. אָמֵן.**

## GIVING THE NAME

**אֱלֹהֵינוּ** *Our God and the God of our ancestors, preserve this child for his [father and]* (skip if child has no father) *mother (*skip if child has no mother; if child has neither parent, say, *for Israel), and may his name in Israel be called* (baby's Hebrew name) *son of* (father's Hebrew name; if child has no halakhic father, mother's name is inserted here). *May the father rejoice in the issue of his loins and may his mother exult in the fruit of her womb.*

If the father is giving the name, he says:

*May it be God's will that I rejoice in the issue of my loins and may his mother exult in the fruit of her womb.*

If the child's father is deceased, say:

*May the father rejoice in Paradise in the issue of his loins and may his mother exult in the fruit of her womb.*

If the child's mother is deceased, say:

*May the father rejoice in the issue of his loins and may his mother exult in Paradise in the fruit of her womb.*

If both the child's parents are deceased, say:

*May the father rejoice in Paradise in the issue of his loins and may his mother exult in Paradise in the fruit of her womb.*

**כַּכָּתוּב** *as it is written: 'May your father and mother rejoice and may she who gave birth to you exult.' And it is said: 'Then I passed by you and saw you wallowing in your blood,* (first said by the assembled and repeated by the mohel as a drop of wine is placed in the child's mouth) ***and I said to you: "Via your blood, live!" and I said to you: "Via your blood, live."*** *' And it is said: 'God remembered the Divine covenant forever; the word of the Divine command for a thousand generations, that God struck with Avraham and vowed to Yitzhak. Then God established it for Yaakov as a statute, for Yisrael as an everlasting covenant.' And it is said: 'Avraham circumcised his son Yitzhak at the age of eight days as God had commanded him.'* (This phrase is said twice by the giver of the name and repeated twice by the assembled:) ***Give thanks to the Lord for the Lord is good; The Lord's lovingkindness is everlasting. Give thanks to the Lord for the Lord is good; The Lord's lovingkindness is everlasting.*** *May this little one* (baby's Hebrew name) *son of* (father's Hebrew name; if child has no halakhic father, mother's name is inserted here) *become great.*

***Just as he has entered the covenant, so may he enter into Torah, the marital canopy, and good deeds. Amen.***

The one who recited the blessings drinks some wine.
The mohel then blesses the child:

**מִי שֶׁבֵּרַךְ** אֲבוֹתֵינוּ אַבְרָהָם יִצְחָק וְיַעֲקֹב, הוּא יְבָרֵךְ אֶת הַיֶּלֶד הָרַךְ הַנִּימּוֹל (שם הילד) בֶּן (שם האם) וְיִשְׁלַח לוֹ רְפוּאָה שְׁלֵמָה, בַּעֲבוּר שֶׁנִּכְנַס לַבְּרִית. וּכְשֵׁם שֶׁנִּכְנַס לַבְּרִית כֵּן יִכָּנֵס לְתוֹרָה, וּלְחֻפָּה, וּלְמַעֲשִׂים טוֹבִים, וְנֹאמַר אָמֵן.

תפלה למוהל ולאב

**רִבּוֹנוֹ** שֶׁל עוֹלָם, יְהִי רָצוֹן מִלְּפָנֶיךָ, שֶׁיְּהֵא חָשׁוּב וּמְרֻצֶּה וּמְקֻבָּל לְפָנֶיךָ, כְּאִלּוּ הִקְרַבְתִּיהוּ לִפְנֵי כִּסֵּא כְבוֹדֶךָ. וְאַתָּה, בְּרַחֲמֶיךָ הָרַבִּים, שְׁלַח עַל יְדֵי מַלְאָכֶיךָ הַקְּדוֹשִׁים נְשָׁמָה קְדוֹשָׁה וּטְהוֹרָה

המוהל אומר:
לְ(שם הילד) בֶּן (שם האב; אם מבחינה הלכתית אין אב להבן, קוראים לו על שם אמו)

האב אומר:
לִבְנִי
(שם הילד)

הַנִּמּוֹל עַתָּה לִשְׁמְךָ הַגָּדוֹל, וְשֶׁיִּהְיֶה לִבּוֹ פָּתוּחַ כְּפִתְחוֹ שֶׁל אוּלָם, בְּתוֹרָתְךָ הַקְּדוֹשָׁה, לִלְמֹד וּלְלַמֵּד, לִשְׁמֹר וְלַעֲשׂוֹת. וְתֵן לוֹ אֲרִיכוּת יָמִים וְשָׁנִים, חַיִּים שֶׁל יִרְאַת חֵטְא, חַיִּים שֶׁל עֹשֶׁר וְכָבוֹד, חַיִּים שֶׁתְּמַלֵּא מִשְׁאֲלוֹת לִבּוֹ לְטוֹבָה. אָמֵן, וְכֵן יְהִי רָצוֹן.

The conclusion of the Berit is followed by a festive meal.

## BIRKAT HAMAZON FOLLOWING A BERIT

תהלים קכו

**שִׁיר הַמַּעֲלוֹת,** בְּשׁוּב יהוה אֶת שִׁיבַת צִיּוֹן, הָיִינוּ כְּחֹלְמִים. אָז יִמָּלֵא שְׂחוֹק פִּינוּ וּלְשׁוֹנֵנוּ רִנָּה, אָז יֹאמְרוּ בַגּוֹיִם, הִגְדִּיל יהוה לַעֲשׂוֹת עִם אֵלֶּה. הִגְדִּיל יהוה לַעֲשׂוֹת עִמָּנוּ, הָיִינוּ שְׂמֵחִים. שׁוּבָה יהוה אֶת שְׁבִיתֵנוּ, כַּאֲפִיקִים בַּנֶּגֶב. הַזֹּרְעִים בְּדִמְעָה בְּרִנָּה יִקְצֹרוּ. הָלוֹךְ יֵלֵךְ וּבָכֹה נֹשֵׂא מֶשֶׁךְ הַזָּרַע, בֹּא יָבֹא בְרִנָּה, נֹשֵׂא אֲלֻמֹּתָיו.

The one who recited the blessings drinks some wine.
The mohel then blesses the child:

**מִי שֶׁבֵּרַךְ** *May God, Who blessed our patriarchs Avraham, Yitzhak, and Yaakov, bless the tender, circumcised child* (baby's Hebrew name) *son of* (mother's Hebrew name) *and grant him a complete recovery as he has entered the covenant. Just as he has entered the covenant, so may he enter into Torah, the marital canopy, and good deeds. And let us respond, Amen.*

The mohel and father then recite the following prayer:

**רִבּוֹנוֹ** *Master of the Universe, may it be Your will that he be worthy, favored, and acceptable before You as if I had offered him before the throne of Your glory. May You, in Your abundant mercy, send through Your holy angels a holy and pure soul to*

mohel says: (baby's Hebrew name) *son of* (father's Hebrew name; if child has no halakhic father, the mother's name is inserted here)

father says: *my son* (baby's Hebrew name) *son of* (father's Hebrew name;)

*who has just been circumcised for the sake of Your Great Name, and may his heart be as open to Your holy Torah as the entrance to the Sanctuary, to learn and to teach, to observe and to fulfill. Bestow upon him length of days and years, a sin-fearing life, a life of abundance and honor, a life in which his heartfelt wishes are filled for the good. Amen, and thus may it be Your will.*

The conclusion of the Berit is followed by a festive meal.

## BIRKAT HAMAZON FOLLOWING A BERIT

Psalm 126

**שִׁיר הַמַּעֲלוֹת** *A song of ascents. When the Lord returns the captives of Zion, we will be like dreamers. Then our mouths will be filled with laughter and our tongues with song; then it will be said among the nations, 'The Lord has done great things for them.' The Lord did great things for us, we were happy. Lord, return our captives, like streams in the desert. Those who sow in tears shall reap in joy. The one who cries in carrying the bag of seed will return in joy, carrying the grain sheaves.*

Some add the following:

**תְּהִלַּת** יהוה יְדַבֶּר פִּי, וִיבָרֵךְ כָּל בָּשָׂר שֵׁם קָדְשׁוֹ לְעוֹלָם וָעֶד. וַאֲנַחְנוּ נְבָרֵךְ יָהּ, מֵעַתָּה וְעַד עוֹלָם, הַלְלוּיָהּ. הוֹדוּ לַיהוה כִּי טוֹב, כִּי לְעוֹלָם חַסְדּוֹ. מִי יְמַלֵּל גְּבוּרוֹת יהוה, יַשְׁמִיעַ כָּל תְּהִלָּתוֹ.

## THE INVITATION

If a minyan is present, this zimun is recited by the leader with a full cup of wine in hand. The words in brackets are omitted in the absence of a *minyan.*

המזמן– רַבּוֹתַי נְבָרֵךְ.

המסובין– יְהִי שֵׁם יהוה מְבֹרָךְ מֵעַתָּה וְעַד עוֹלָם.

המזמן– יְהִי שֵׁם יהוה מְבֹרָךְ מֵעַתָּה וְעַד עוֹלָם.
נוֹדֶה לְשִׁמְךָ בְּתוֹךְ אֱמוּנַי, בְּרוּכִים אַתֶּם לַיהוה.

המסובין– **נוֹדֶה לְשִׁמְךָ בְּתוֹךְ אֱמוּנַי, בְּרוּכִים אַתֶּם לַיהוה.**

המזמן– בִּרְשׁוּת אֵל אָיוֹם וְנוֹרָא, מִשְׂגָּב לְעִתּוֹת בַּצָּרָה, אֵל נֶאְזָר בִּגְבוּרָה, אַדִּיר בַּמָּרוֹם יהוה.

המסובין– **נוֹדֶה לְשִׁמְךָ בְּתוֹךְ אֱמוּנַי, בְּרוּכִים אַתֶּם לַיהוה.**

המזמן– בִּרְשׁוּת הַתּוֹרָה הַקְּדוֹשָׁה, טְהוֹרָה הִיא וְגַם פְּרוּשָׁה, צִוָּה לָנוּ מוֹרָשָׁה, מֹשֶׁה עֶבֶד יהוה.

המסובין– **נוֹדֶה לְשִׁמְךָ בְּתוֹךְ אֱמוּנַי, בְּרוּכִים אַתֶּם לַיהוה.**

המזמן– בִּרְשׁוּת הַכֹּהֲנִים הַלְּוִיִּם אֶקְרָא לֵאלֹהֵי הָעִבְרִיִּים, אֲהוֹדֶנּוּ בְּכָל אִיִּים, אֲבָרְכָה אֶת יהוה.

המסובין– **נוֹדֶה לְשִׁמְךָ בְּתוֹךְ אֱמוּנַי, בְּרוּכִים אַתֶּם לַיהוה.**

המזמן– בִּרְשׁוּת מָרָנָן וְרַבָּנָן וְרַבּוֹתַי, אֶפְתְּחָה בְּשִׁיר פִּי וּשְׂפָתַי, וְתֹאמַרְנָה עַצְמוֹתַי, בָּרוּךְ הַבָּא בְּשֵׁם יהוה.

המסובין– **נוֹדֶה לְשִׁמְךָ בְּתוֹךְ אֱמוּנַי, בְּרוּכִים אַתֶּם לַיהוה.**

המזמן– בִּרְשׁוּת מָרָנָן וְרַבָּנָן וְרַבּוֹתַי, נְבָרֵךְ [אֱלֹהֵינוּ] שֶׁאָכַלְנוּ מִשֶּׁלּוֹ.

המסובין– בָּרוּךְ [אֱלֹהֵינוּ] שֶׁאָכַלְנוּ מִשֶּׁלּוֹ וּבְטוּבוֹ חָיִינוּ.

המזמן– בָּרוּךְ [אֱלֹהֵינוּ] שֶׁאָכַלְנוּ מִשֶּׁלּוֹ וּבְטוּבוֹ חָיִינוּ.
בָּרוּךְ הוּא וּבָרוּךְ שְׁמוֹ.

Some add the following:

תְּהִלַּת *Let my mouth declare the praise of God, so that all humanity will bless God's holy Name for all eternity. And we will bless God, and henceforth and forever sing God's praises. Give thanks to the Lord, for the Lord is good; the Lord's lovingkindness is everlasting. Who can adequately express the mighty deeds of the Lord, or make known all the Lord's praise?*

## THE INVITATION

If a minyan is present, this zimun is recited by the leader with a full cup of wine in hand. The words in brackets are omitted in the absence of a *minyan*.

Leader – *Distinguished Assembled, let us bless.*

Assembled – *Blessed is the Name of the Lord henceforth and forever!*

Leader – *Blessed is the Name of the Lord henceforth and forever! We give thanks to Your Name among my faithful; blessed are you to the Lord.*

Assembled – ***We give thanks to Your Name among my faithful; blessed are you to the Lord.***

Leader – *With permission of the Almighty — fearful and awesome, Refuge in times of trouble, the Almighty girded with strength, Mighty on high is the Lord.*

Assembled – ***We give thanks to Your Name among my faithful; blessed are you to the Lord.***

Leader – *With permission of the holy Torah, it is pure and explicit, commanded to us as a heritage, by Mosheh, servant of the Lord.*

Assembled – ***We give thanks to Your Name among my faithful; blessed are you to the Lord.***

Leader – *With permission of the Kohanim of the Levitic tribe, I call upon the God of the Hebrews, I will thank God unto all islands, I will give blessing to the Lord.*

Assembled – ***We give thanks to Your Name among my faithful; blessed are you to the Lord.***

Leader – *With permission of the noble and distinguished people present, I open my mouth and lips in song, and my bones shall proclaim, 'Blessed is the one who comes in the Name of the Lord.'*

Assembled – ***We give thanks to Your Name among my faithful; blessed are you to the Lord.***

Leader – *With the permission of the distinguished people present, let us bless [our God] of Whose bounty we have eaten.*

Assembled – *Blessed be [our God] of Whose bounty we have eaten and through Whose goodness we live.*

Leader – *Blessed be [our God] of Whose bounty we have eaten and through Whose goodness we live. Blessed is God and Blessed is God's Name.*

**בָּרוּךְ** אַתָּה יהוה אֱלֹהֵינוּ מֶלֶךְ הָעוֹלָם, הַזָּן אֶת הָעוֹלָם כֻּלּוֹ, בְּטוּבוֹ, בְּחֵן בְּחֶסֶד וּבְרַחֲמִים. הוּא נֹתֵן לֶחֶם לְכָל בָּשָׂר, כִּי לְעוֹלָם חַסְדּוֹ, וּבְטוּבוֹ הַגָּדוֹל, תָּמִיד לֹא חָסַר לָנוּ, וְאַל יֶחְסַר לָנוּ מָזוֹן לְעוֹלָם וָעֶד. בַּעֲבוּר שְׁמוֹ הַגָּדוֹל, כִּי הוּא אֵל זָן וּמְפַרְנֵס לַכֹּל, וּמֵטִיב לַכֹּל, וּמֵכִין מָזוֹן לְכָל בְּרִיּוֹתָיו אֲשֶׁר בָּרָא. ❖ בָּרוּךְ אַתָּה יהוה, הַזָּן אֶת הַכֹּל. (All– אָמֵן)

**נוֹדֶה** לְּךָ יהוה אֱלֹהֵינוּ, עַל שֶׁהִנְחַלְתָּ לַאֲבוֹתֵינוּ אֶרֶץ חֶמְדָּה טוֹבָה וּרְחָבָה. וְעַל שֶׁהוֹצֵאתָנוּ יהוה אֱלֹהֵינוּ מֵאֶרֶץ מִצְרַיִם, וּפְדִיתָנוּ מִבֵּית עֲבָדִים, וְעַל בְּרִיתְךָ שֶׁחָתַמְתָּ בִּבְשָׂרֵנוּ, וְעַל תּוֹרָתְךָ שֶׁלִּמַּדְתָּנוּ, וְעַל חֻקֶּיךָ שֶׁהוֹדַעְתָּנוּ, וְעַל חַיִּים חֵן וָחֶסֶד שֶׁחוֹנַנְתָּנוּ, וְעַל אֲכִילַת מָזוֹן שָׁאַתָּה זָן וּמְפַרְנֵס אוֹתָנוּ תָּמִיד, בְּכָל יוֹם וּבְכָל עֵת וּבְכָל שָׁעָה.

בחנוכה מוסיפים:

**(וְ)עַל** הַנִּסִּים וְעַל הַפֻּרְקָן וְעַל הַגְּבוּרוֹת וְעַל הַתְּשׁוּעוֹת וְעַל הַמִּלְחָמוֹת שֶׁעָשִׂיתָ לַאֲבוֹתֵינוּ בַּיָּמִים הָהֵם בַּזְּמַן הַזֶּה.

**בִּימֵי** מַתִּתְיָהוּ בֶּן יוֹחָנָן כֹּהֵן גָּדוֹל חַשְׁמוֹנָאִי וּבָנָיו, כְּשֶׁעָמְדָה מַלְכוּת יָוָן הָרְשָׁעָה עַל עַמְּךָ יִשְׂרָאֵל, לְהַשְׁכִּיחָם תּוֹרָתֶךָ, וּלְהַעֲבִירָם מֵחֻקֵּי רְצוֹנֶךָ. וְאַתָּה בְּרַחֲמֶיךָ הָרַבִּים, עָמַדְתָּ לָהֶם בְּעֵת צָרָתָם, רַבְתָּ אֶת רִיבָם, דַּנְתָּ אֶת דִּינָם, נָקַמְתָּ אֶת נִקְמָתָם. מָסַרְתָּ גִבּוֹרִים בְּיַד חַלָּשִׁים, וְרַבִּים בְּיַד מְעַטִּים, וּטְמֵאִים בְּיַד טְהוֹרִים, וּרְשָׁעִים בְּיַד צַדִּיקִים, וְזֵדִים בְּיַד עוֹסְקֵי תוֹרָתֶךָ. וּלְךָ עָשִׂיתָ שֵׁם גָּדוֹל וְקָדוֹשׁ בְּעוֹלָמֶךָ, וּלְעַמְּךָ יִשְׂרָאֵל עָשִׂיתָ תְּשׁוּעָה גְדוֹלָה וּפֻרְקָן כְּהַיּוֹם הַזֶּה. וְאַחַר כֵּן בָּאוּ בָנֶיךָ לִדְבִיר בֵּיתֶךָ, וּפִנּוּ אֶת הֵיכָלֶךָ, וְטִהֲרוּ אֶת מִקְדָּשֶׁךָ, וְהִדְלִיקוּ נֵרוֹת בְּחַצְרוֹת קָדְשֶׁךָ, וְקָבְעוּ שְׁמוֹנַת יְמֵי חֲנֻכָּה אֵלּוּ, לְהוֹדוֹת וּלְהַלֵּל לְשִׁמְךָ הַגָּדוֹל.

**בָּרוּךְ** *Blessed are You, Lord our God, Ruler of the Universe, Who sustains the entire world in Godly goodness, with grace, lovingkindness, and compassion. God gives sustenance to all flesh, for God's lovingkindness is everlasting, and in bountiful goodness God has never failed us, and may God never fail to sustain us for all eternity. For the sake of God's great Name, for God sustains and provides for all, and does good for all and prepares provision for all the creatures that God created. Blessed are You, Lord, Who sustains all.* (All – *Amen)*

**נוֹדֶה** *We extend thanks to You, Lord our God, for having given to our ancestors the heritage of a lovely, good, and spacious land; for Your having brought us out, Lord our God, from the land of Egypt, and having redeemed us from the house of bondage; for Your covenant that You sealed in our flesh; for Your Torah which You taught to us; for Your statutes which You made known to us; for the life, grace, and loving-kindness You have graciously bestowed upon us; and for the provision of food through which You sustain and provide for us constantly, every day, every occasion, and every hour.*

On Hanukah add:

**(וְ)עַל הַנִּיסִים** *(And) we thank You for the miracles, for the redemption, for the mighty deeds and deliverances, and for the battles which You carried out for our ancestors in those days, at this season.*

**בִּימֵי מַתִּתְיָהוּ** *In the days of the Hasmonean, Matityahu son of Yohanan, the Great Kohen, and his sons, when a wicked Hellenic government rose up against Your people Israel to make them forget Your Torah and divert them from fulfilling the laws of Your will. You in Your great mercy stood by them in the time of their distress; You championed their cause, defended their rights and avenged their wrong. You delivered the strong into the hands of the weak, the many into the hands of the few, the impure into the hands of the pure, the wicked into the hands of the righteous, and the arrogant into the hands of those who occupy themselves with Your Torah. You made a great and holy Name for Yourself in Your world, and for Your people Israel You performed a great deliverance unto this day. Thereupon Your children came to the shrine of Your House, cleansed Your Temple, purified Your Sanctuary, kindled lights in Your holy Courts, and designated these eight days of Hanukah for giving thanks and praise to Your great Name.*

בפורים מוסיפים:

**(וְ)עַל** הַנִּסִּים וְעַל הַפֻּרְקָן וְעַל הַגְּבוּרוֹת וְעַל הַתְּשׁוּעוֹת וְעַל הַמִּלְחָמוֹת שֶׁעָשִׂיתָ לַאֲבוֹתֵינוּ בַּיָּמִים הָהֵם בַּזְּמַן הַזֶּה.

**בִּימֵי** מָרְדְּכַי וְאֶסְתֵּר בְּשׁוּשַׁן הַבִּירָה, כְּשֶׁעָמַד עֲלֵיהֶם הָמָן הָרָשָׁע, בִּקֵּשׁ לְהַשְׁמִיד לַהֲרֹג וּלְאַבֵּד אֶת כָּל הַיְּהוּדִים, מִנַּעַר וְעַד זָקֵן, טַף וְנָשִׁים, בְּיוֹם אֶחָד, בִּשְׁלוֹשָׁה עָשָׂר לְחֹדֶשׁ שְׁנֵים עָשָׂר, הוּא חֹדֶשׁ אֲדָר, וּשְׁלָלָם לָבוֹז. וְאַתָּה בְּרַחֲמֶיךָ הָרַבִּים הֵפַרְתָּ אֶת עֲצָתוֹ, וְקִלְקַלְתָּ אֶת מַחֲשַׁבְתּוֹ, וַהֲשֵׁבוֹתָ לּוֹ גְּמוּלוֹ בְּרֹאשׁוֹ, וְתָלוּ אוֹתוֹ וְאֶת בָּנָיו עַל הָעֵץ.

**וְעַל הַכֹּל** יהוה אֱלֹהֵינוּ אֲנַחְנוּ מוֹדִים לָךְ, וּמְבָרְכִים אוֹתָךְ, יִתְבָּרַךְ שִׁמְךָ בְּפִי כָּל חַי תָּמִיד לְעוֹלָם וָעֶד. כַּכָּתוּב, וְאָכַלְתָּ וְשָׂבָעְתָּ, וּבֵרַכְתָּ אֶת יהוה אֱלֹהֶיךָ, עַל הָאָרֶץ הַטֹּבָה אֲשֶׁר נָתַן לָךְ. ❖ בָּרוּךְ אַתָּה יהוה, עַל הָאָרֶץ וְעַל הַמָּזוֹן. (All – אָמֵן)

**רַחֵם** יהוה אֱלֹהֵינוּ עַל יִשְׂרָאֵל עַמֶּךָ, וְעַל יְרוּשָׁלַיִם עִירֶךָ, וְעַל צִיּוֹן מִשְׁכַּן כְּבוֹדֶךָ, וְעַל מַלְכוּת בֵּית דָּוִד מְשִׁיחֶךָ, וְעַל הַבַּיִת הַגָּדוֹל וְהַקָּדוֹשׁ שֶׁנִּקְרָא שִׁמְךָ עָלָיו. אֱלֹהֵינוּ אָבִינוּ רְעֵנוּ זוּנֵנוּ פַּרְנְסֵנוּ וְכַלְכְּלֵנוּ וְהַרְוִיחֵנוּ, וְהַרְוַח לָנוּ יהוה אֱלֹהֵינוּ מְהֵרָה מִכָּל צָרוֹתֵינוּ. וְנָא אַל תַּצְרִיכֵנוּ יהוה אֱלֹהֵינוּ, לֹא לִידֵי מַתְּנַת בָּשָׂר וָדָם, וְלֹא לִידֵי הַלְוָאָתָם, כִּי אִם לְיָדְךָ הַמְּלֵאָה הַפְּתוּחָה הַקְּדוֹשָׁה (נ״א הַגְּדוּשָׁה) וְהָרְחָבָה, שֶׁלֹּא נֵבוֹשׁ וְלֹא נִכָּלֵם לְעוֹלָם וָעֶד.

On Purim add:

**(וְ)עַל הַנִּסִּים** *(And) we thank You for the miracles, for the redemption, for the mighty deeds and deliverances, and for the battles which You carried out for our ancestors in those days, at this season.*

**בִּימֵי מָרְדְּכַי** *In the days of Mordekhai and Esther, in Shushan the Persian capital, when the evil Haman rose up against them and sought to destroy, slay and wipe out all the Jews, young and old, infants and women, in one day, the thirteenth of the twelfth month, which is Adar, and to plunder their possessions. You in Your great mercy nullified his counsel, blunted his plan, and rebounded his designs upon his own head, and they hanged him and his sons upon the gallows.*

**וְעַל הַכֹּל** *For all this, Lord our God, we thank You and bless You; may Your Name be blessed in the mouths of all the living, constantly, for all eternity, according to that which is written: 'You shall eat and be satisfied, and shall bless the Lord, your God, for the good land that God gave to you.' Blessed are You, Lord, for the land and for the sustenance.* (All – *Amen)*

**רַחֵם** *Please have compassion, Lord our God, on Israel Your people, on Yerushalayim Your city, on Zion the dwelling of Your glory, on the royal house of David Your anointed one, and on the great and holy House through which Your Name is called. Our God, our Parent, our Shepherd, sustain us, provide for us, support us and relieve us, by granting us, Lord our God, speedy relief from all our troubles. Please, Lord our God, do not make us dependent on gifts of flesh and blood, nor upon their loans, but on Your hand — full, open, hallowed (abundant), and generous; that we not be shamed and not disgraced for all eternity.*

בשבת מוסיפים:

**רְצֵה** וְהַחֲלִיצֵנוּ יהוה אֱלֹהֵינוּ בְּמִצְוֹתֶיךָ, וּבְמִצְוַת יוֹם הַשְּׁבִיעִי הַשַּׁבָּת הַגָּדוֹל וְהַקָּדוֹשׁ הַזֶּה. כִּי יוֹם זֶה גָּדוֹל וְקָדוֹשׁ הוּא לְפָנֶיךָ, לִשְׁבָּת בּוֹ וְלָנוּחַ בּוֹ בְּאַהֲבָה כְּמִצְוַת רְצוֹנֶךָ. וּבִרְצוֹנְךָ הָנִיחַ לָנוּ יהוה אֱלֹהֵינוּ, שֶׁלֹּא תְהֵא צָרָה וְיָגוֹן וַאֲנָחָה בְּיוֹם מְנוּחָתֵנוּ. וְהַרְאֵנוּ יהוה אֱלֹהֵינוּ בְּנֶחָמַת צִיּוֹן עִירֶךָ, וּבְבִנְיַן יְרוּשָׁלַיִם עִיר קָדְשֶׁךָ, כִּי אַתָּה הוּא בַּעַל הַיְשׁוּעוֹת וּבַעַל הַנֶּחָמוֹת.

בראש חדש ויום טוב מוסיפים:

**אֱלֹהֵינוּ** וֵאלֹהֵי אֲבוֹתֵינוּ, יַעֲלֶה, וְיָבֹא, וְיַגִּיעַ, וְיֵרָאֶה, וְיֵרָצֶה, וְיִשָּׁמַע, וְיִפָּקֵד, וְיִזָּכֵר זִכְרוֹנֵנוּ וּפִקְדוֹנֵנוּ, וְזִכְרוֹן אֲבוֹתֵינוּ, וְזִכְרוֹן מָשִׁיחַ בֶּן דָּוִד עַבְדֶּךָ, וְזִכְרוֹן יְרוּשָׁלַיִם עִיר קָדְשֶׁךָ, וְזִכְרוֹן כָּל עַמְּךָ בֵּית יִשְׂרָאֵל לְפָנֶיךָ, לִפְלֵיטָה לְטוֹבָה לְחֵן וּלְחֶסֶד וּלְרַחֲמִים, לְחַיִּים וּלְשָׁלוֹם בְּיוֹם

| לראש חדש | לפסח | לשבועות |
|---|---|---|
| רֹאשׁ הַחֹדֶשׁ | חַג הַמַּצּוֹת | חַג הַשָּׁבֻעוֹת |
| לראש השנה | לסוכות | לשמיני עצרת/שמחת תורה |
| הַזִּכָּרוֹן | חַג הַסֻּכּוֹת | הַשְּׁמִינִי חַג הָעֲצֶרֶת |

הַזֶּה. זָכְרֵנוּ יהוה אֱלֹהֵינוּ בּוֹ לְטוֹבָה, וּפָקְדֵנוּ בוֹ לִבְרָכָה, וְהוֹשִׁיעֵנוּ בוֹ לְחַיִּים. וּבִדְבַר יְשׁוּעָה וְרַחֲמִים, חוּס וְחָנֵּנוּ וְרַחֵם עָלֵינוּ וְהוֹשִׁיעֵנוּ, כִּי אֵלֶיךָ עֵינֵינוּ, כִּי אֵל מֶלֶךְ חַנּוּן וְרַחוּם אָתָּה.

❖ **וּבְנֵה** יְרוּשָׁלַיִם עִיר הַקֹּדֶשׁ בִּמְהֵרָה בְיָמֵינוּ. בָּרוּךְ אַתָּה יהוה, בּוֹנֵה בְרַחֲמָיו יְרוּשָׁלָיִם. אָמֵן. (All – אָמֵן)

**בָּרוּךְ** אַתָּה יהוה אֱלֹהֵינוּ מֶלֶךְ הָעוֹלָם, הָאֵל אָבִינוּ מַלְכֵּנוּ אַדִּירֵנוּ בּוֹרְאֵנוּ גּוֹאֲלֵנוּ יוֹצְרֵנוּ קְדוֹשֵׁנוּ קְדוֹשׁ יַעֲקֹב, רוֹעֵנוּ רוֹעֵה יִשְׂרָאֵל, הַמֶּלֶךְ הַטּוֹב וְהַמֵּטִיב לַכֹּל, שֶׁבְּכָל יוֹם וָיוֹם הוּא הֵטִיב, הוּא מֵטִיב, הוּא יֵיטִיב לָנוּ. הוּא גְמָלָנוּ הוּא גוֹמְלֵנוּ הוּא יִגְמְלֵנוּ לָעַד, לְחֵן וּלְחֶסֶד וּלְרַחֲמִים וּלְרֶוַח הַצָּלָה וְהַצְלָחָה, בְּרָכָה וִישׁוּעָה נֶחָמָה פַּרְנָסָה וְכַלְכָּלָה

On Shabbat, the following paragraph is added:

**רְצֵה** *May it please You, Lord our God, to invigorate us through Your commandments, and through the commandment of the seventh day, this great and holy Shabbat. For this day is great and holy before You, to rest and relax thereon, in love, according to Your commanded desire. And by Your favor, allow for us, Lord our God, that there be no distress, grief, or lament on our day of rest. Let us experience, Lord our God, the consolation of Zion Your city, and the building of Yerushalayim the city manifesting Your holiness; for You are the Master of salvations and the Master of consolations.*

On Rosh Hodesh, the festivals, or Rosh HaShanah, the following paragraph is added:

**אֱלֹהֵינוּ** *God and the God of our ancestors, may there ascend, come, reach, be noted, favored, heard, acknowledged, and remembered before You the remembrance and recollection of us, the remembrance of our ancestors, the remembrance of the anointed, son of David Your servant, the remembrance of Yerushalayim the city manifesting Your holiness, and the remembrance of Your entire people the house of Israel; for deliverance, for goodness, for grace, lovingkindness and compassion, for life and tranquility,*

for Rosh Hodesh — *on this Rosh Hodesh day.*

for Pesah – *on this festival of Matzot.*

for Shavuot – *on this festival of Shavuot.*

for Sukkot – *on this festival of Sukkot.*

for Shemini Atzeret & Simhat Torah – *on the eighth day, this festival of Atzeret.*

for Rosh HaShanah – *on this day of Remembrance.*

*Remember us on it, Lord our God, for good; recall us on it for blessing; and save us on it for life. As to the matter of salvation and compassion, have pity and be gracious to us, have compassion on us and save us, as our eyes are directed toward You; for You are a gracious, compassionate God and Ruler.*

**וּבְנֵה** *And build Yerushalayim, the holy city, speedily, in our time. Blessed are You, Lord, Who in Godly compassion builds Yerushalayim. Amen.* (All – *Amen*)

**בָּרוּךְ** *Blessed are You, Lord our God, Ruler of the Universe, the God Who is our Parent, our Ruler, our Sovereign, our Creator, our Redeemer, our Fashioner, our Holy One, the Holy One of Yaakov; our Shepherd, the Shepherd of Israel, the Ruler Who is good and does good for all, Who every day has done good, does good, and will continue to do good for us. God was bountiful to us, is bountiful to us, and will forever be bountiful to us with grace, lovingkindness, compassion, and relief, rescue and success, blessing and salvation, comfort, provision and support,*

❖ וְרַחֲמִים וְחַיִּים וְשָׁלוֹם וְכָל טוֹב, וּמִכָּל טוּב לְעוֹלָם אַל יְחַסְּרֵנוּ. (אָמֵן –All)

**הָרַחֲמָן** הוּא יִמְלוֹךְ עָלֵינוּ לְעוֹלָם וָעֶד. הָרַחֲמָן הוּא יִתְבָּרַךְ בַּשָּׁמַיִם וּבָאָרֶץ. הָרַחֲמָן הוּא יִשְׁתַּבַּח לְדוֹר דּוֹרִים, וְיִתְפָּאַר בָּנוּ לָעַד וּלְנֵצַח נְצָחִים, וְיִתְהַדַּר בָּנוּ לָעַד וּלְעוֹלְמֵי עוֹלָמִים. הָרַחֲמָן הוּא יְפַרְנְסֵנוּ בְּכָבוֹד. הָרַחֲמָן הוּא יִשְׁבּוֹר עֻלֵּנוּ מֵעַל צַוָּארֵנוּ, וְהוּא יוֹלִיכֵנוּ קוֹמְמִיּוּת לְאַרְצֵנוּ. הָרַחֲמָן הוּא יִשְׁלַח לָנוּ בְּרָכָה מְרֻבָּה בַּבַּיִת הַזֶּה, וְעַל שֻׁלְחָן זֶה שֶׁאָכַלְנוּ עָלָיו. הָרַחֲמָן הוּא יִשְׁלַח לָנוּ אֶת אֵלִיָּהוּ הַנָּבִיא זָכוּר לַטּוֹב, וִיבַשֶּׂר לָנוּ בְּשׂוֹרוֹת טוֹבוֹת יְשׁוּעוֹת וְנֶחָמוֹת.

If the meal is held in a private home, add the following.
For a female, substitute the words in brackets from Shulkhan Arukh Orah Hayyim 201:1:

**יְהִי רָצוֹן** שֶׁלֹּא יֵבוֹשׁ (תֵבוֹשׁ) וְלֹא יִכָּלֵם (תִכָּלֵם) בַּעַל (בַּעֲלַת) הַבַּיִת הַזֶּה, לֹא בָעוֹלָם הַזֶּה וְלֹא בָעוֹלָם הַבָּא, וְיַצְלִיחַ (וְתַצְלִיחַ) בְּכָל נְכָסָיו (נְכָסֶיהָ), וְיִהְיוּ נְכָסָיו (נְכָסֶיהָ) מוּצְלָחִים וּקְרוֹבִים לָעִיר, וְאַל יִשְׁלוֹט שָׂטָן בְּמַעֲשֵׂה יָדָיו (יָדֶיהָ), וְאַל יִזְדַּקֵּק לְפָנָיו (לְפָנֶיהָ) שׁוּם דְּבַר חֵטְא וְהִרְהוּר עָוֹן, מֵעַתָּה וְעַד עוֹלָם.

**הָרַחֲמָן** הוּא יְבָרֵךְ בַּעַל בְּרִית הַמִּילָה, וְאֶת אִשְׁתּוֹ הַיּוֹלֶדֶת, וְאֵת בְּנָם הָרַךְ הַנִּמּוֹל, וְאֶת הַמָּל בְּשַׂר הָעָרְלָה, וְאֶת הַסַּנְדָּק, וְאֵת כָּל הַמְּסוּבִּין כָּאן, אוֹתָם וְאֶת כָּל אֲשֶׁר לָהֶם, אוֹתָנוּ וְאֵת כָּל אֲשֶׁר לָנוּ, כְּמוֹ שֶׁנִּתְבָּרְכוּ אֲבוֹתֵינוּ אַבְרָהָם יִצְחָק וְיַעֲקֹב בַּכֹּל, מִכֹּל, כֹּל. כֵּן יְבָרֵךְ אוֹתָנוּ כֻּלָּנוּ יַחַד בִּבְרָכָה שְׁלֵמָה, וְנֹאמַר אָמֵן.

**בַּמָּרוֹם** יְלַמְּדוּ עֲלֵיהֶם וְעָלֵינוּ זְכוּת, שֶׁתְּהֵא לְמִשְׁמֶרֶת שָׁלוֹם. וְנִשָּׂא בְרָכָה מֵאֵת יהוה, וּצְדָקָה מֵאֱלֹהֵי יִשְׁעֵנוּ. וְנִמְצָא חֵן וְשֵׂכֶל טוֹב בְּעֵינֵי אֱלֹהִים וְאָדָם.

*compassion, life, and tranquility, and all that is good; and may we never lack of all that is good.*

**הָרַחֲמָן** *May the Compassionate One rule over us for all eternity. May the Compassionate One be blessed in the heavens and on earth. May the Compassionate One be praised for all generations, glorified through us forever, to ultimate times, and honored through us forever, to all eternity. May the Compassionate One provide for us in dignity. May the Compassionate One break off the oppressive yoke from our necks, and lead us proudly to our land. May the Compassionate One bestow abundant blessing on this home, and on this table, upon which we have eaten. May the Compassionate One send to us the prophet Eliyahu, who is remembered for good, and may he bring us good tidings of salvations and comforts.*

If the meal is held in a private home, add the following,
from Shulhan Arukh Orah Hayyim, 201:1:

**יְהִי רָצוֹן** *May it be God's will that our host not be shamed or humiliated in this world or in the world to come; may our host be successful in all dealings; may those dealings be successful and close to the city; may no untoward impediment have power over our host's handiwork, and may no semblance of sin or iniquitous thought attach itself to our host from this time on and forever.*

**הָרַחֲמָן** *May the Compassionate One bless the father who carried out the Berit, his wife who gave birth, their tender circumcised child, the one who cut the flesh of circumcision, the sandak, and all those gathered here, them and all that is theirs, ourselves and all that is ours, just as our patriarchs Avraham Yitzhak and Yaakov were blessed in all, from all, and with all. So may God bless us all together, with complete blessing, and let us respond, Amen.*

**בַּמָּרוֹם** *On high may they seek out merit for them and for us, that shall be a safeguard of tranquility. Let us obtain blessing from the Lord and charitableness from the God of our salvation. And let us find grace and true understanding in the eyes of God and humankind.*

A person (or persons) is honored with reciting the following prayers aloud.
Someone other than the father should recite the following stanza:

**הָרַחֲמָן** הוּא יְבָרֵךְ אֲבִי הַיֶּלֶד וְאִמּוֹ, וְיִזְכּוּ לְגַדְּלוֹ וּלְחַנְּכוֹ וּלְחַכְּמוֹ, מִיּוֹם הַשְּׁמִינִי (אם הברית אחרי יום השמיני אומרים: מִיּוֹם הַזֶּה) וָהָלְאָה יֵרָצֶה דָמוֹ, וִיהִי יהוה אֱלֹהָיו עִמּוֹ. (All – אָמֵן)

לתאומים או יותר:

**הָרַחֲמָן** הוּא יְבָרֵךְ אֲבִי הַיְלָדִים וְאִמָּם וְיִזְכּוּ לְגַדְּלָם וּלְחַנְּכָם וּלְחַכְּמָם, מִיּוֹם הַשְּׁמִינִי (אם עושים הברית אחרי יום השמיני אומר: מִיּוֹם הַזֶּה) וָהָלְאָה יֵרָצֶה דָמָם, וִיהִי יהוה אֱלֹהֵיהֶם עִמָּם. (All – אָמֵן)

אם מבחינה הלכתית אין אב להבן אומר:

**הָרַחֲמָן** הוּא יְבָרֵךְ אֶת אֵם הַיֶּלֶד וְתִזְכֶּה לְגַדְּלוֹ וּלְחַנְּכוֹ וּלְחַכְּמוֹ, מִיּוֹם הַשְּׁמִינִי (אם עושים הברית אחרי יום השמיני, אומר: מִיּוֹם הַזֶּה) וָהָלְאָה יֵרָצֶה דָמוֹ, וִיהִי יהוה אֱלֹהָיו עִמּוֹ. (All – אָמֵן)

יכבדו איש זולת הסנדק לומר פסקא זו:

**הָרַחֲמָן** הוּא יְבָרֵךְ בַּעַל בְּרִית הַמִּילָה, אֲשֶׁר שָׂשׂ לַעֲשׂוֹת צֶדֶק בְּגִילָה, וִישַׁלֵּם פָּעֳלוֹ וּמַשְׂכֻּרְתּוֹ כְּפוּלָה, וְיִתְּנֵהוּ לְמַעְלָה לְמָעְלָה. (All – אָמֵן)

**הָרַחֲמָן** הוּא יְבָרֵךְ רַךְ הַנִּמּוֹל לִשְׁמוֹנָה (אם הברית אחרי יום השמיני אומר: בִּזְמַנּוֹ), וְיִהְיוּ יָדָיו וְלִבּוֹ לָאֵל אֱמוּנָה, וְיִזְכֶּה לִרְאוֹת פְּנֵי הַשְּׁכִינָה, שָׁלֹשׁ פְּעָמִים בַּשָּׁנָה. (All – אָמֵן)

לתאומים או יותר:

**הָרַחֲמָן** הוּא יְבָרֵךְ הַנִּמּוֹלִים לִשְׁמוֹנָה (אם הברית אחרי יום השמיני, אומר: בִּזְמַנּוֹ), וְיִהְיוּ יְדֵיהֶם וְלִבּוֹתָם לָאֵל אֱמוּנָה, וְיִזְכּוּ לִרְאוֹת פְּנֵי הַשְּׁכִינָה, שָׁלֹשׁ פְּעָמִים בַּשָּׁנָה: (All – אָמֵן)

A person (or persons) is honored with reciting the following prayers aloud. Someone other than the father should recite the following stanza:

**הָרַחֲמָן** *May the Compassionate One bless the father and mother of the child; may they merit to raise him, to educate him, and to make him wise, from the eighth day* (if the *Berit* takes place after the eighth day, substitute: *from this day*) *onward may his sacrifice be accepted, and may the Lord, his God, be with him.* (All – *Amen*)

For twins or more:

**הָרַחֲמָן** *May the Compassionate One bless the father and mother of the children; may they merit to raise them, to educate them, and to make them wise, from the eighth day* (if the Berit takes place after the eighth day, substitute: *from this day*) *onward may their sacrifice be accepted, and may the Lord, their God, be with them.* (All – *Amen*)

If the child has no halakhic father, say the following:

**הָרַחֲמָן** *May the Compassionate One bless the mother of the child; may she merit to raise him, to educate him, and to make him wise, from the eighth day* (if the Berit takes place after the eighth day, substitute: *from this day*) *onward may his sacrifice be accepted, and may the Lord, his God, be with him.* (All – *Amen*)

Someone other than the sandak should recite the following stanza:

**הָרַחֲמָן** *May the Compassionate One bless the master of the circumcision covenant, who rejoiced to do justice with glee; may his deed be rewarded, and his recompense doubled, and may God place him ever higher.* (All – *Amen*)

**הָרַחֲמָן** *May the Compassionate One bless the tender circumcised at eight days* (if the Berit takes place after the eighth day, substitute: *in the appropriate time*); *may his strength and heart be a trust to God, and may he merit to receive the Divine Presence, three times a year.* (All – *Amen*)

For twins or more:

**הָרַחֲמָן** *May the Compassionate One bless the tender circumcised at eight days* (if the Berit takes place after the eighth day, substitute: *in the appropriate time*); *may their strength and heart be a trust to God, and may they merit to receive the Divine Presence, three times a year.* (All – *Amen*)

יכבדו איש זולת המוהל לומר פסקא זו:

**הָרַחֲמָן** הוּא יְבָרֵךְ הַמָּל בְּשַׂר הָעָרְלָה, וּפָרַע וּמָצַץ דְּמֵי הַמִּילָה, אִישׁ הַיָּרֵא וְרַךְ הַלֵּבָב עֲבוֹדָתוֹ פְּסוּלָה, וְאִם שְׁלָשׁ אֵלֶּה לֹא יַעֲשֶׂה לָהּ. (All – אָמֵן)

**הָרַחֲמָן** הוּא יִשְׁלַח לָנוּ מְשִׁיחוֹ הוֹלֵךְ תָּמִים, בִּזְכוּת חֲתַן לַמּוּלוֹת דָּמִים, לְבַשֵּׂר בְּשׂוֹרוֹת טוֹבוֹת וְנִחוּמִים, לְעַם אֶחָד מְפֻזָּר וּמְפֹרָד בֵּין הָעַמִּים. (All – אָמֵן)

**הָרַחֲמָן** הוּא יִשְׁלַח לָנוּ כֹּהֵן צֶדֶק אֲשֶׁר לֻקַּח לְעֵילוֹם, עַד הוּכַן כִּסְאוֹ כַּשֶּׁמֶשׁ וְיָהֲלוֹם, וַיָּלֶט פָּנָיו בְּאַדַּרְתּוֹ וַיִּגְלוֹם, בְּרִיתִי הָיְתָה אִתּוֹ הַחַיִּים וְהַשָּׁלוֹם. (All – אָמֵן)

לשבת

הָרַחֲמָן הוּא יַנְחִילֵנוּ יוֹם שֶׁכֻּלּוֹ שַׁבָּת וּמְנוּחָה לְחַיֵּי הָעוֹלָמִים.

לראש חודש

הָרַחֲמָן הוּא יְחַדֵּשׁ עָלֵינוּ אֶת הַחֹדֶשׁ הַזֶּה לְטוֹבָה וְלִבְרָכָה.

ליום טוב

הָרַחֲמָן הוּא יַנְחִילֵנוּ יוֹם שֶׁכֻּלּוֹ טוֹב.

לראש השנה (יש אומרים תפילה זו עד יום הכפורים)

הָרַחֲמָן הוּא יְחַדֵּשׁ עָלֵינוּ אֶת הַשָּׁנָה הַזֹּאת לְטוֹבָה וְלִבְרָכָה.

לסוכות

הָרַחֲמָן הוּא יָקִים לָנוּ אֶת סֻכַּת דָּוִיד הַנֹּפֶלֶת.

**הָרַחֲמָן** הוּא יְזַכֵּנוּ לִימוֹת הַמָּשִׁיחַ וּלְחַיֵּי הָעוֹלָם הַבָּא. [בחול – מַגְדִּל] [בשבת, יו"ט ור"ח – מִגְדּוֹל] יְשׁוּעוֹת מַלְכּוֹ וְעֹשֶׂה חֶסֶד לִמְשִׁיחוֹ לְדָוִד וּלְזַרְעוֹ עַד עוֹלָם. עֹשֶׂה שָׁלוֹם בִּמְרוֹמָיו, הוּא יַעֲשֶׂה שָׁלוֹם עָלֵינוּ וְעַל כָּל יִשְׂרָאֵל, וְאִמְרוּ אָמֵן.

**יְראוּ** אֶת יהוה קְדֹשָׁיו, כִּי אֵין מַחְסוֹר לִירֵאָיו. כְּפִירִים רָשׁוּ וְרָעֵבוּ, וְדֹרְשֵׁי יהוה לֹא יַחְסְרוּ כָל טוֹב.

Someone other than the mohel should recite the following stanza:

**הָרַחֲמָן** *May the Compassionate One bless him who cut the flesh of circumcision, and uncovered and extracted the bloods of circumcision; the service of the coward and the faint-hearted is unfit, and if he does not perform upon it these three acts.* (All – *Amen*)

**הָרַחֲמָן** *May the Compassionate One send us God's anointed who goes with purity, in the merit of the groom bloodied for the sake of circumcision, to proclaim good tidings and consolations, to the one nation dispersed and splintered among the nations.*
(All – *Amen*)

**הָרַחֲמָן** *May the Compassionate One send us the righteous Kohen who was taken into hiding, until God's throne is established bright as sun and diamond, he who covered his face with his cloak and enwrapped himself, My covenant was with him for life and peace.* (All – *Amen*)

On Shabbat, the following sentence is added:

*May the Compassionate One bequeath to us a day of complete rest and contentedness in eternal life.*

On Rosh Hodesh, the following sentence is added:

*May the Compassionate One renew this month for us, for good and for blessing.*

On Festival days, the following sentence is added:

*May the Compassionate One bequeath to us a day that is wholly good.*

On Rosh HaShanah, the following sentence is added (some add this until Yom Kippur):

*May the Compassionate One renew this year for us, for good and for blessing.*

On the seven days of Sukkot, the following sentence is added:

*May the Compassionate One re-establish David's fallen tabernacle for us.*

**הָרַחֲמָן** *May the Compassionate One deem us worthy of the Messianic days and the life of the world to come.* [Weekdays – *God, Who magnifies the deliverances of God's king*] [Shabbat, Yom Tov, and Rosh Hodesh – *God, Who is a tower of deliverances to God's king*], *and does lovingkindness for God's anointed, for David and his posterity forever. The Effector of harmony in God's heights, may God effect harmony for us and for all Israel, and let us say, Amen.*

**יְראוּ** *Let the Lord's holy ones be in awe of the Lord, for those who are in awe of the Lord feel no deficiency. Young lions may experience poverty and hunger, but those who seek the Lord will not lack any good.*

הוֹדוּ לַיהוה כִּי טוֹב, כִּי לְעוֹלָם חַסְדּוֹ. פּוֹתֵחַ אֶת יָדֶךָ, וּמַשְׂבִּיעַ לְכָל חַי רָצוֹן. בָּרוּךְ הַגֶּבֶר אֲשֶׁר יִבְטַח בַּיהוה, וְהָיָה יהוה מִבְטַחוֹ. נַעַר הָיִיתִי גַּם זָקַנְתִּי, וְלֹא רָאִיתִי צַדִּיק נֶעֱזָב, וְזַרְעוֹ מְבַקֶּשׁ לָחֶם. יהוה עֹז לְעַמּוֹ יִתֵּן, יהוה יְבָרֵךְ אֶת עַמּוֹ בַשָּׁלוֹם.

The leader recites:

**בָּרוּךְ** אַתָּה יהוה אֱלֹהֵינוּ מֶלֶךְ הָעוֹלָם, בּוֹרֵא פְּרִי הַגָּפֶן.

(All – אָמֵן)

The leader, having consumed more than a revi'it (3.3 fluid ounces), then recites the following concluding blessing:

**בָּרוּךְ** אַתָּה יהוה אֱלֹהֵינוּ מֶלֶךְ הָעוֹלָם, עַל הַגֶּפֶן וְעַל פְּרִי הַגֶּפֶן, וְעַל תְּנוּבַת הַשָּׂדֶה, וְעַל אֶרֶץ חֶמְדָּה טוֹבָה וּרְחָבָה, שֶׁרָצִיתָ וְהִנְחַלְתָּ לַאֲבוֹתֵינוּ, לֶאֱכוֹל מִפִּרְיָהּ וְלִשְׂבּוֹעַ מִטּוּבָהּ. רַחֵם נָא יהוה אֱלֹהֵינוּ עַל יִשְׂרָאֵל עַמֶּךָ, וְעַל יְרוּשָׁלַיִם עִירֶךָ, וְעַל צִיּוֹן מִשְׁכַּן כְּבוֹדֶךָ, וְעַל מִזְבְּחֶךָ וְעַל הֵיכָלֶךָ. וּבְנֵה יְרוּשָׁלַיִם עִיר הַקֹּדֶשׁ בִּמְהֵרָה בְיָמֵינוּ, וְהַעֲלֵנוּ לְתוֹכָהּ, וְשַׂמְּחֵנוּ בְּבִנְיָנָהּ, וְנֹאכַל מִפִּרְיָהּ, וְנִשְׂבַּע מִטּוּבָהּ, וּנְבָרֶכְךָ עָלֶיהָ בִּקְדֻשָּׁה וּבְטָהֳרָה.

בשבת – וּרְצֵה וְהַחֲלִיצֵנוּ בְּיוֹם הַשַּׁבָּת הַזֶּה.

בראש חודש – וְזָכְרֵנוּ לְטוֹבָה בְּיוֹם רֹאשׁ הַחֹדֶשׁ הַזֶּה.

בפסח – וְשַׂמְּחֵנוּ בְּיוֹם חַג הַמַּצּוֹת הַזֶּה.

בשבועות – וְשַׂמְּחֵנוּ בְּיוֹם חַג הַשָּׁבֻעוֹת הַזֶּה.

בראש השנה – וְזָכְרֵנוּ לְטוֹבָה בְּיוֹם הַזִּכָּרוֹן הַזֶּה.

בסוכות – וְשַׂמְּחֵנוּ בְּיוֹם חַג הַסֻּכּוֹת הַזֶּה.

בשמיני עצרת ושמחת תורה – וְשַׂמְּחֵנוּ בְּיוֹם הַשְּׁמִינִי חַג הָעֲצֶרֶת הַזֶּה.

כִּי אַתָּה יהוה טוֹב וּמֵטִיב לַכֹּל,° וְנוֹדֶה לְּךָ עַל הָאָרֶץ וְעַל פְּרִי הַגָּפֶן. בָּרוּךְ אַתָּה יהוה, עַל הָאָרֶץ וְעַל פְּרִי הַגָּפֶן.

°If the wine used is from Israel, the blessing concludes as follows:

וְנוֹדֶה לְּךָ עַל הָאָרֶץ וְעַל פְּרִי גַפְנָהּ. בָּרוּךְ אַתָּה יהוה, עַל הָאָרֶץ וְעַל פְּרִי גַפְנָהּ.

*Give thanks to the Lord for the Lord is good; the Lord's lovingkindness is everlasting. You open Your hand, and satisfy the desire of all the living. Blessed is the person who trusts in the Lord, the Lord will be that one's security. I was once young and have also grown older, but have never seen a righteous person forlorn, with the offspring begging for sustenance. The Lord will give strength to the Lord's people, the Lord will bless the Lord's people with tranquility.*

The leader recites:

**בָּרוּךְ** *Blessed are You, Lord our God, Ruler of the Universe, Who creates the fruit of the vine.* (All – *Amen*)

The leader, having consumed more than a revi'it (3.3 fluid ounces), then recites the following concluding blessing:

**בָּרוּךְ** *Blessed are You, Lord our God, Ruler of the Universe, for the vine and for the fruit of the vine, for the produce of the field, and for the lovely, good, and spacious land that You desired and bequeathed to our ancestors, to eat of its fruits and to be sated from its goodness. Please have compassion, Lord our God, on Israel Your people, on Yerushalayim Your city, on Zion the dwelling of Your glory, on Your altar and on Your abode. And build Yerushalayim, the holy city, speedily, in our time; bring us up into it, make us happy in its being built, let us eat of its fruits and be sated from its goodness, and let us bless You upon it in holiness and purity.*

On Shabbat – *And may it please You to invigorate us on this Shabbat day.*

On Rosh Hodesh – *And remember us for good on this Rosh Hodesh day.*

On Pesah – *And gladden us on this festival of Matzot.*

On Shavuot – *And gladden us on this festival of Shavuot.*

On Rosh HaShanah – *And remember us for good on this day of Remembering.*

On Sukkot – *And gladden us on this festival of Sukkot.*

On Shemini Atzeret and Simhat Torah – *And gladden us on the eighth day, this festival of Atzeret.*

*For You, God, are good and do good for all, °and we thank You for the land and for the fruit of the vine. Blessed are You, Lord, for the land and for the fruit of the vine.*

° If the wine used is from Israel, the blessing concludes as follows:

*and we thank You for the land and for the fruit of its vine. Blessed are You, Lord, for the land and for the fruit of its vine.*

## ◆ Pidyon HaBen
## Redemption of the Firstborn

*The pidyon of the first issue of the mother's womb takes place on the thirty-first day after birth.*

*The money used for the redemption should have silver content or value of at least 100 grams. Five silver dollars may not contain sufficient silver.*

*The pidyon can also be effected with a silver object (cup, bowl, tray) that has the prescribed silver content.*

## PIDYON BY THE FATHER

The *pidyon* takes place after the assembled have washed their hands, recited the following berakhot, and eaten some bread:

**בָּרוּךְ** אַתָּה יהוה אֱלֹהֵינוּ מֶלֶךְ הָעוֹלָם, אֲשֶׁר קִדְּשָׁנוּ בְּמִצְוֹתָיו, וְצִוָּנוּ עַל נְטִילַת יָדָיִם.

**בָּרוּךְ** אַתָּה יהוה אֱלֹהֵינוּ מֶלֶךְ הָעוֹלָם, הַמּוֹצִיא לֶחֶם מִן הָאָרֶץ.

The father then brings the child, bedecked in jewelry gently surrounding him, and places the child on the table in front of the seated Kohen.

האב עומד ואומר לכהן:

**זֶה,** בְּנִי בְּכוֹרִי, הוּא פֶּטֶר רֶחֶם לְאִמּוֹ (אם אין הבן כאן, אומר: יֵשׁ לִי בֵּן בְּכוֹר וְהוּא פֶּטֶר רֶחֶם לְאִמּוֹ). וְהַקָּדוֹשׁ בָּרוּךְ הוּא צִוָּה לִפְדּוֹתוֹ. שֶׁנֶּאֱמַר: וּפְדוּיָו מִבֶּן חֹדֶשׁ תִּפְדֶּה, בְּעֶרְכְּךָ, כֶּסֶף חֲמֵשֶׁת שְׁקָלִים בְּשֶׁקֶל הַקֹּדֶשׁ, עֶשְׂרִים גֵּרָה הוּא. וְנֶאֱמַר: קַדֶּשׁ לִי כָל בְּכוֹר, פֶּטֶר כָּל רֶחֶם בִּבְנֵי יִשְׂרָאֵל, בָּאָדָם וּבַבְּהֵמָה; לִי הוּא.

הכהן שואל את האב:

**מַאי** בָּעִית טְפֵי, לִיתֵּן לִי בִּנְךְ בְּכוֹרְךְ שֶׁהוּא פֶּטֶר רֶחֶם לְאִמּוֹ, אוֹ בָּעִית לִפְדּוֹתוֹ בְּעַד חָמֵשׁ סְלָעִים כִּדְמִחֻיַּבְתָּא מִדְּאוֹרַיְתָא?

והאב משיב לכהן ואומר:

**חָפֵץ** אֲנִי לִפְדּוֹת אֶת בְּנִי, וְהֵילָךְ דְּמֵי פִדְיוֹנוֹ כִּדְמִחֻיַּבְנָא מִדְּאוֹרַיְתָא.

ובעוד שהוא מחזיק את המטבעות או החפצים בידו קודם שיתנם לכהן מברך:

**בָּרוּךְ** אַתָּה יהוה אֱלֹהֵינוּ מֶלֶךְ הָעוֹלָם, אֲשֶׁר קִדְּשָׁנוּ בְּמִצְוֹתָיו, וְצִוָּנוּ עַל פִּדְיוֹן הַבֵּן. (All– אָמֵן)

**בָּרוּךְ** אַתָּה יהוה אֱלֹהֵינוּ מֶלֶךְ הָעוֹלָם, שֶׁהֶחֱיָנוּ וְקִיְּמָנוּ וְהִגִּיעָנוּ לַזְּמַן הַזֶּה. (All– אָמֵן)

## PIDYON BY THE FATHER

The *pidyon* takes place after the assembled have washed their hands, recited the following berakhot, and then eaten some bread:

**בָּרוּךְ** *Blessed are You, Lord our God, Ruler of the Universe, Who has sanctified us with the Godly commandments, and has commanded us concerning the washing of the hands.*

**בָּרוּךְ** *Blessed are You, Lord our God, Ruler of the Universe, Who brings forth sustenance from the earth.*

The father then brings the child, bedecked in jewelry gently surrounding him, and places the child on the table in front of the seated Kohen.
The father, standing, declares to the Kohen:

**זֶה** *This, my first-born son, is the first issue of his mother's womb* (if the child is not present, the father says instead: *I have a first-born son and he is the first issue of his mother's womb*), *and the Holy One, Blessed is God, has commanded to redeem him, as it is said: 'And those who must be redeemed, from the age of a month are you to redeem, according to your estimate, five silver shekels in the shekel of the Sanctuary, which is twenty gerah.' And it is said: 'Sanctify unto Me every first-born, the first issue of every womb among the Children of Israel, both of human and of animal; it is Mine.'*

The Kohen asks the father:

**מַאי** *Which do you prefer: to give away your first-born son, who is the first issue of his mother's womb, or do you prefer to redeem him for five shekels as you are required by the Torah?*

The father replies to the Kohen:

**חָפֵץ** *I desire to redeem my son, and I hereby present you with the cost of his redemption as I am required by the Torah.*

With the redemption money or objects in his hand,
the father recites the following blessings:

**בָּרוּךְ** *Blessed are You, Lord our God, Ruler of the Universe, Who has sanctified us with the Godly commandments, and has commanded us regarding the redemption of the son.* (All – *Amen*)

**בָּרוּךְ** *Blessed are You, Lord our God, Ruler of the Universe, Who has given us life and sustained us, enabling us to reach this moment.* (All – *Amen*)

ונותן מיד המטבעות או החפצים לכהן, והכהן מברך מיד על כוס מלא יין:

**בָּרוּךְ** אַתָּה יהוה אֱלֹהֵינוּ מֶלֶךְ הָעוֹלָם, בּוֹרֵא פְּרִי הַגָּפֶן. (All– אָמֵן)

והכהן טועם מן היין ומוליך את הכסף או החפצים בידו על ראש הבן ואומר:

**זֶה** תַּחַת זֶה, זֶה חִלּוּף זֶה, זֶה מָחוּל עַל זֶה, וְיִכָּנֵס זֶה הַבֵּן לְחַיִּים, לְתוֹרָה וּלְיִרְאַת שָׁמָיִם. יְהִי רָצוֹן שֶׁכְּשֵׁם שֶׁנִּכְנַס לְפִדְיוֹן, כֵּן יִכָּנֵס לְתוֹרָה, וּלְחֻפָּה, וּלְמַעֲשִׂים טוֹבִים, וְנֹאמַר אָמֵן.

אם אין הבן לפניהם יאמר הכהן:

**זֶה** תַּחַת בִּנְךָ, זֶה חִלּוּף בִּנְךָ, זֶה מָחוּל עַל בִּנְךָ. יָצָא זֶה לַכֹּהֵן וְיִכָּנֵס בִּנְךָ לְחַיִּים לְתוֹרָה וּלְיִרְאַת שָׁמָיִם. יְהִי רָצוֹן שֶׁכְּשֵׁם שֶׁנִּכְנַס לְפִדְיוֹן, כֵּן יִכָּנֵס לְתוֹרָה וּלְחֻפָּה וּלְמַעֲשִׂים טוֹבִים. וְנֹאמַר אָמֵן.

הכהן נותן את ידו על ראש הבן ומברכו, ואומר:

**יְשִׂמְךָ** אֱלֹהִים כְּאֶפְרַיִם וְכִמְנַשֶּׁה. יְבָרֶכְךָ יהוה וְיִשְׁמְרֶךָ. יָאֵר יהוה פָּנָיו אֵלֶיךָ וִיחֻנֶּךָּ. יִשָּׂא יהוה פָּנָיו אֵלֶיךָ, וְיָשֵׂם לְךָ שָׁלוֹם. כִּי אֹרֶךְ יָמִים וּשְׁנוֹת חַיִּים וְשָׁלוֹם יוֹסִיפוּ לָךְ. יהוה יִשְׁמָרְךָ מִכָּל רָע, יִשְׁמֹר אֶת נַפְשֶׁךָ.

ומחזיר את הילד לאביו.

The festive meal in celebration of the pidyon continues, followed by Birkat HaMazon (After-Meal Thanks).

## PIDYON BY A BET DIN

When a child is orphaned or has no halakhic father, the Rabbinical Court may redeem the child on a conditional basis, using the Court's money. The conditional redemption is made with the following stipulation: אִם הַבֵּן יִגְדַּל וְיִפְדֶּה עַצְמוֹ, הֲרֵי מָעוֹת הַלָּלוּ מַתָּנָה לַכֹּהֵן, וְאִם לֹא יִפְדֶּה עַצְמוֹ כְּשֶׁיִּגְדַּל, הֲרֵי הֵן מֵעַתָּה מַתָּנָה לִבְכוֹר זֶה עַל מְנַת שֶׁיִּפְדֶּה עַצְמוֹ (ש"ות חמדת שלמה, יורה דעה, סימן לב) — *If the child, upon reaching maturity, will redeem himself, then this money is a gift to the Kohen, and if the child does not redeem himself upon reaching maturity, then the money is a gift to this first-born, from now, for the express purpose of redeeming himself* (Responsa Hemdat Shelomoh Y.D §32).

The father then gives the money or object to the Kohen,
who then takes a full cup of wine and recites:

**בָּרוּךְ** *Blessed are You, Lord our God, Ruler of the Universe, Who creates the fruit of the vine.* (All – *Amen*)

Then, after sipping some wine, while swinging the money or objects
in a circular motion over the infant's head, the Kohen says:

**זֶה** *This is instead of that, this is in exchange for that, this is pardoned because of that, and may this son enter into life, into Torah and into awe of Heaven. May it be God's will that just as he entered into redemption, so may he enter into Torah, the marital canopy, and good deeds, and let us respond, Amen.*

If the infant is not present, the Kohen says the following instead:

**זֶה** *This is instead of your son, this is in exchange for your son, this is pardoned because of your son. This has gone to the Kohen and may your son enter into life, into Torah and into awe of Heaven. May it be God's will that just as he entered into redemption, so may he enter into Torah, the marital canopy, and good deeds, and let us respond, Amen.*

The Kohen places his right hand on the infant's head and blesses him:

**יְשִׂמְךָ** *May God establish you as Ephrayim and Menasheh. May the Lord bless you and safeguard you. May the Lord shine the Godly countenance upon you and be gracious to you. May the Lord bestow favor upon you and grant you tranquility. For lengthy days and years of life and tranquility shall God add for you. The Lord will protect you from every harm; the Lord will guard your life.*

The Kohen then returns the infant to his father.

The festive meal in celebration of the pidyon continues,
followed by Birkat HaMazon (After-Meal Thanks).

## PIDYON BY A BET DIN

When a child is orphaned or has no halakhic father, the Rabbinical Court may redeem the child on a conditional basis, using the Court's money. The conditional redemption is made with the following stipulation: אִם הַבֵּן יִגְדַּל וְיִפְדֶּה עַצְמוֹ, הֲרֵי מָעוֹת הַלָּלוּ מַתָּנָה לַכֹּהֵן, וְאִם לֹא יִפְדֶּה עַצְמוֹ כְּשֶׁיִּגְדַּל, הֲרֵי הֵן מֵעַתָּה מַתָּנָה לִבְכוֹר זֶה עַל מְנַת שֶׁיִּפְדֶּה עַצְמוֹ (ש"ות חמדת שלמה, יורה דעה, סימן לב) – *If the child, upon reaching maturity, will redeem himself, then this money is a gift to the Kohen, and if the child does not redeem himself upon reaching maturity, then the money is a gift to this first-born, from now, for the express purpose of redeeming himself* (Responsa Hemdat Shelomoh Y.D §32).

The *pidyon* takes place after the assembled have washed their hands, recited the following berakhot, and then eaten some bread:

**בָּרוּךְ** אַתָּה יהוה אֱלֹהֵינוּ מֶלֶךְ הָעוֹלָם, אֲשֶׁר קִדְּשָׁנוּ בְּמִצְוֹתָיו, וְצִוָּנוּ עַל נְטִילַת יָדָיִם.

**בָּרוּךְ** אַתָּה יהוה אֱלֹהֵינוּ מֶלֶךְ הָעוֹלָם, הַמּוֹצִיא לֶחֶם מִן הָאָרֶץ.

בית דין אומר לכהן:

**זֶה** הַבֵּן בְּכוֹר, הוּא פֶּטֶר רֶחֶם לְאִמּוֹ, וְהַקָּדוֹשׁ בָּרוּךְ הוּא צִוָּה לִפְדּוֹתוֹ, שֶׁנֶּאֱמַר: וּפְדוּיָו מִבֶּן חֹדֶשׁ תִּפְדֶּה, בְּעֶרְכְּךָ, כֶּסֶף חֲמֵשֶׁת שְׁקָלִים בְּשֶׁקֶל הַקֹּדֶשׁ, עֶשְׂרִים גֵּרָה הוּא. וְנֶאֱמַר: קַדֶּשׁ לִי כָל בְּכוֹר, פֶּטֶר כָּל רֶחֶם בִּבְנֵי יִשְׂרָאֵל, בָּאָדָם וּבַבְּהֵמָה; לִי הוּא. וַאֲנַחְנוּ מוּכָנִים לִפְדּוֹתוֹ, אַחֲרֵי שֶׁאֵין לוֹ אָב לִפְדּוֹתוֹ, וְהִגִּיעַ זְמַן הַפִּדְיוֹן.

והכהן שואל:

**מַאי** בָּעֵית טְפֵי, אַתֶּם בֵּית דִּין, לִתֵּן בֵּן הַבְּכוֹר שֶׁהוּא פֶּטֶר רֶחֶם לְאִמּוֹ, אוֹ בָּעֵית לִפְדּוֹתוֹ בְּעַד חָמֵשׁ סְלָעִים.

בית דין משיב:

**חֲפֵצִים** אָנוּ לִפְדּוֹת אֶת הַבְּכוֹר הַזֶּה, וְהֵילָךְ דְּמֵי פִדְיוֹנוֹ.

With the redemption money or objects in hand, a member of the Bet Din recites the following blessings:

**בָּרוּךְ** אַתָּה יהוה אֱלֹהֵינוּ מֶלֶךְ הָעוֹלָם, אֲשֶׁר קִדְּשָׁנוּ בְּמִצְוֹתָיו, וְצִוָּנוּ עַל פִּדְיוֹן הַבְּכוֹר. (All – אָמֵן)

It is preferable that a Bet Din member have on a new piece of clothing, to which to apply the following blessing:

**בָּרוּךְ** אַתָּה יהוה אֱלֹהֵינוּ מֶלֶךְ הָעוֹלָם, שֶׁהֶחֱיָנוּ וְקִיְּמָנוּ וְהִגִּיעָנוּ לַזְּמַן הַזֶּה. (All – אָמֵן)

The *pidyon* takes place after the assembled have washed their hands, recited the following berakhot, and then eaten some bread:

**בָּרוּךְ** *Blessed are You, Lord our God, Ruler of the Universe, Who has sanctified us with the Godly commandments, and has commanded us concerning the washing of the hands.*

**בָּרוּךְ** *Blessed are You, Lord our God, Ruler of the Universe, Who brings forth sustenance from the earth.*

The Bet Din says to the Kohen:

**זֶה** *This first-born child is the first issue of his mother's womb; and the Holy One, Blessed is God, has commanded to redeem him, as it is said: 'And those who must be redeemed, from the age of a month are you to redeem, according to your estimate, five silver shekels in the shekel of the Sanctuary, which is twenty gerah.' And it is said: 'Sanctify unto me every first-born, the first issue of every womb among the Children of Israel, both of human and of animal; it is Mine.' We are prepared to redeem him, since this child has no father to redeem him, and the time to redeem him has arrived.*

The Kohen asks:

**מַאי** *Which do you prefer: For you, Bet Din, to give away the first-born child, who is the first issue of his mother's womb, or do you prefer to redeem him for five shekels as required by the Torah?*

Bet Din replies:

**חֲפֵצִים** *We desire to redeem this first-born, and hereby you are presented with the cost of his redemption.*

With the redemption money or objects in hand, a member of the Bet Din recites the following blessings:

**בָּרוּךְ** *Blessed are You, Lord our God, Ruler of the Universe, Who has sanctified us with the Godly commandments, and has commanded us regarding the redemption of the first-born.*

(All— *Amen*)

It is preferable that a Bet Din member have on a new piece of clothing, to which to apply the following blessing:

**בָּרוּךְ** *Blessed are You, Lord our God, Ruler of the Universe, Who has given us life and sustained us, enabling us to reach this moment.*

(All— *Amen*)

חברי הבית דין נותנים המטבעות או החפצים לכהן,
והכהן מברך מיד על כוס מלא יין:

**בָּרוּךְ** אַתָּה יהוה אֱלֹהֵינוּ מֶלֶךְ הָעוֹלָם, בּוֹרֵא פְּרִי הַגָּפֶן.
(אָמֵן – All)

After sipping some wine, the kohen swings the money or objects in a circular motion over the infant's head, and says:

**זֶה** תַּחַת זֶה, זֶה חִלּוּף זֶה, זֶה מָחוּל עַל זֶה, וְיִכָּנֵס זֶה הַבֵּן לְחַיִּים, לְתוֹרָה וּלְיִרְאַת שָׁמָיִם. יְהִי רָצוֹן שֶׁכְּשֵׁם שֶׁנִּכְנַס לְפִדְיוֹן, כֵּן יִכָּנֵס לְתוֹרָה, וּלְחֻפָּה, וּלְמַעֲשִׂים טוֹבִים, וְנֹאמַר אָמֵן.

The Kohen places his right hand on the infant's head and blesses him:

**יְשִׂמְךָ** אֱלֹהִים כְּאֶפְרַיִם וְכִמְנַשֶּׁה. יְבָרֶכְךָ יהוה וְיִשְׁמְרֶךָ. יָאֵר יהוה פָּנָיו אֵלֶיךָ וִיחֻנֶּךָּ. יִשָּׂא יהוה פָּנָיו אֵלֶיךָ, וְיָשֵׂם לְךָ שָׁלוֹם. כִּי אֹרֶךְ יָמִים וּשְׁנוֹת חַיִּים וְשָׁלוֹם יוֹסִיפוּ לָךְ. יהוה יִשְׁמָרְךָ מִכָּל רָע, יִשְׁמֹר אֶת נַפְשֶׁךָ.

The festive meal in celebration of the pidyon continues, followed by Birkat HaMazon (After-Meal Thanks).

## PIDYON THROUGH AN AGENT

On the rare occasion when the father cannot himself effect the pidyon, he may delegate an agent, including his wife, to act in his stead. This procedure should be employed only if there is no way that the father can be present.
The *pidyon* takes place after the assembled have washed their hands, recited the following berakhot, and eaten some bread:

**בָּרוּךְ** אַתָּה יהוה אֱלֹהֵינוּ מֶלֶךְ הָעוֹלָם, אֲשֶׁר קִדְּשָׁנוּ בְּמִצְוֹתָיו, וְצִוָּנוּ עַל נְטִילַת יָדָיִם.

**בָּרוּךְ** אַתָּה יהוה אֱלֹהֵינוּ מֶלֶךְ הָעוֹלָם, הַמּוֹצִיא לֶחֶם מִן הָאָרֶץ.

השליח אומר לכהן:

**זֶה** הַבֵּן בְּכוֹר, הוּא פֶּטֶר רֶחֶם לְאִמּוֹ, וְהַקָּדוֹשׁ בָּרוּךְ הוּא צִוָּה לִפְדּוֹתוֹ, שֶׁנֶּאֱמַר: וּפְדוּיָו מִבֶּן חֹדֶשׁ

The Bet Din gives the money or the object to the Kohen,
who then takes a full cup of wine and recites:

**בָּרוּךְ** *Blessed are You, Lord our God, Ruler of the Universe, Who creates the fruit of the vine.* (All— *Amen*)

After sipping some wine, the Kohen swings the money or objects
in a circular motion over the infant's head, and says:

**זֶה** *This is instead of that, this is in exchange for that, this is pardoned because of that, and may this son enter into life, into Torah, and into awe of Heaven. May it be God's will that just as he entered into redemption, so may he enter into Torah, the marital canopy, and good deeds, and let us respond, Amen.*

The Kohen places his right hand on the infant's head and blesses him:

**יְשִׂמְךָ** *May God establish you as Ephrayim and Menasheh. May the Lord bless you and safeguard you. May the Lord shine the Godly countenance upon you and be gracious to you. May the Lord bestow favor upon you and grant you tranquility. For lengthy days and years of life and tranquility shall God add for you. The Lord will protect you from every harm; the Lord will guard your life.*

The festive meal in celebration of the pidyon continues,
followed by Birkat HaMazon (After Meal Thanks).

## PIDYON THROUGH AN AGENT

On the rare occasion when the father cannot himself effect the pidyon, he may delegate an agent, including his wife, to act in his stead. This procedure should be employed only if there is no way that the father can be present.
The *pidyon* takes place after the assembled have washed their hands,
recited the following berakhot, and eaten some bread:

**בָּרוּךְ** *Blessed are You, Lord our God, Ruler of the Universe, Who has sanctified us with the Godly commandments, and has commanded us concerning the washing of the hands.*

**בָּרוּךְ** *Blessed are You, Lord our God, Ruler of the Universe, Who brings forth sustenance from the earth.*

The father's agent says to the Kohen:

**זֶה** *This first-born child is the first issue of his mother's womb; and the Holy One, Blessed is God, has commanded to redeem him, as it is said: 'And those who must be redeemed, from the age of a month*

תִּפְדֶּה, בְּעֶרְכְּךָ, כֶּסֶף חֲמֵשֶׁת שְׁקָלִים בְּשֶׁקֶל הַקֹּדֶשׁ, עֶשְׂרִים גֵּרָה הוּא. וְנֶאֱמַר: קַדֶּשׁ לִי כָל בְּכוֹר, פֶּטֶר כָּל רֶחֶם בִּבְנֵי יִשְׂרָאֵל, בָּאָדָם וּבַבְּהֵמָה, לִי הוּא. וַאֲנִי הַשָּׁלִיחַ מֵאֲבִי הַיֶּלֶד הַבְּכוֹר הַזֶּה שֶׁהִגִּיעַ זְמַן פִּדְיוֹנוֹ.

והכהן שואל:

**מַאי** בָּעֵית טְפֵי, אַתָּה הַשָּׁלִיחַ בְּשֵׁם הַמְשַׁלֵּחַךְ, לִתֵּן בֵּן הַבְּכוֹר שֶׁהוּא פֶּטֶר רֶחֶם לְאִמּוֹ, אוֹ בָּעֵית לִפְדּוֹתוֹ בִּשְׁלִיחוּת אֲבִי הַבְּכוֹר בְּעַד חָמֵשׁ סְלָעִים כְּדִמְחֻיָּב הַמְשַׁלֵּחַךְ מִדְּאוֹרַיְתָא?

והשליח משיב:

**חָפֵץ** אֲנִי לִפְדּוֹת אֶת הַבְּכוֹר בִּשְׁלִיחוּת אֲבִי הַבְּכוֹר הַזֶּה, וְהֵילָךְ דְּמֵי פִדְיוֹנוֹ מִן הַמְשַׁלֵּחַ כְּדִמְחֻיָּב מִדְּאוֹרַיְתָא.

With the redemption money or objects in hand, the agent recites the following blessings:

**בָּרוּךְ** אַתָּה יהוה אֱלֹהֵינוּ מֶלֶךְ הָעוֹלָם אֲשֶׁר קִדְּשָׁנוּ בְּמִצְוֹתָיו, וְצִוָּנוּ עַל פִּדְיוֹן בְּכוֹר. (All– אָמֵן)

It is preferable that the agent have on a new piece of clothing, to which to apply the following blessing:

**בָּרוּךְ** אַתָּה יהוה אֱלֹהֵינוּ מֶלֶךְ הָעוֹלָם, שֶׁהֶחֱיָנוּ וְקִיְּמָנוּ וְהִגִּיעָנוּ לַזְּמַן הַזֶּה. (All– אָמֵן)

השליח נותן מיד את המטבעות או החפצים לכהן והכהן מברך מיד על כוס מלא יין:

**בָּרוּךְ** אַתָּה יהוה אֱלֹהֵינוּ מֶלֶךְ הָעוֹלָם, בּוֹרֵא פְּרִי הַגָּפֶן. (All– אָמֵן)

After sipping some wine, the kohen swings the money or objects in a circular motion over the infant's head, and says:

**זֶה** תַּחַת זֶה, זֶה חִלּוּף זֶה, זֶה מָחוּל עַל זֶה, וְיִכָּנֵס זֶה הַבֵּן לְחַיִּים, לְתוֹרָה, וּלְיִרְאַת שָׁמָיִם. יְהִי רָצוֹן שֶׁכְּשֵׁם שֶׁנִּכְנַס לְפִדְיוֹן, כֵּן יִכָּנֵס לְתוֹרָה, וּלְחֻפָּה, וּלְמַעֲשִׂים טוֹבִים, וְנֹאמַר אָמֵן.

*are you to redeem, according to your estimate, five silver shekels in the shekel of the Sanctuary, which is twenty gerah.' And it is said: 'Sanctify unto me every first-born, the first issue of every womb among the Children of Israel, both of human and of animal; it is Mine.' I am the agent of this first-born child's father, and the time to redeem him has arrived.*

The Kohen asks:

**מַאי** *Which do you prefer: For you, the agent, in the name of the one who delegated you, to give away the first-born child, who is the first issue of his mother's womb, or do you prefer to redeem him as the agent of the first-born's father for five shekels as required of the one who delegated you by the Torah?*

The agent replies:

**חָפֵץ** *I desire to redeem the first-born as the agent of this first-born's father, and I hereby present you with the cost of his redemption, from the one who delegated me, as required by the Torah.*

With the redemption money or objects in hand,
the agent recites the following blessings:

**בָּרוּךְ** *Blessed are You, Lord our God, Ruler of the Universe, Who has sanctified us with the Godly commandments and has commanded us regarding the redemption of the first-born.* (All— *Amen*)

It is preferable that the agent have on a new piece of clothing,
to which to apply the following blessing:

**בָּרוּךְ** *Blessed are You, Lord our God, Ruler of the Universe, Who has given us life and sustained us, enabling us to reach this moment.* (All— *Amen*)

The agent then gives the money or the objects to the Kohen,
who takes a full cup of wine and recites:

**בָּרוּךְ** *Blessed are You, Lord our God, Ruler of the Universe, Who creates the fruit of the vine.* (All— *Amen*)

After sipping some wine, the Kohen swings the money or objects
in a circular motion over the infant's head, and says:

**זֶה** *This is instead of that, this is in exchange for that, this is pardoned because of that, and may this son enter into life, into Torah, and into awe of Heaven. May it be God's will that just as he entered into redemption, so may he enter into Torah, the marital canopy, and good deeds, and let us respond, Amen.*

The Kohen places his right hand on the infant's head and blesses him:

**יְשִׂמְךָ** אֱלֹהִים כְּאֶפְרַיִם וְכִמְנַשֶּׁה. יְבָרֶכְךָ יהוה וְיִשְׁמְרֶךָ. יָאֵר יהוה פָּנָיו אֵלֶיךָ וִיחֻנֶּךָּ. יִשָּׂא יהוה פָּנָיו אֵלֶיךָ, וְיָשֵׂם לְךָ שָׁלוֹם. כִּי אֹרֶךְ יָמִים וּשְׁנוֹת חַיִּים וְשָׁלוֹם יוֹסִיפוּ לָךְ. יהוה יִשְׁמָרְךָ מִכָּל רָע, יִשְׁמֹר אֶת נַפְשֶׁךָ.

The festive meal in celebration of the pidyon continues,
followed by Birkat HaMazon (After Meal Thanks):

## PIDYON OF ONE WHO REDEEMS HIMSELF

When the father and the Bet Din, for whatever reasons, failed to redeem the son, the child must redeem himself after he has attained the age of thirteen years and one day (Bar-Mitzvah). The text of the pidyon is as follows.

The *pidyon* takes place after the assembled have washed their hands,
recited the following berakhot, and eaten some bread:

**בָּרוּךְ** אַתָּה יהוה אֱלֹהֵינוּ מֶלֶךְ הָעוֹלָם, אֲשֶׁר קִדְּשָׁנוּ בְּמִצְוֹתָיו, וְצִוָּנוּ עַל נְטִילַת יָדָיִם.

**בָּרוּךְ** אַתָּה יהוה אֱלֹהֵינוּ מֶלֶךְ הָעוֹלָם, הַמּוֹצִיא לֶחֶם מִן הָאָרֶץ.

הבכור אומר לכהן:

**אֲנִי** בְּכוֹר פֶּטֶר רֶחֶם, וְהַקָּדוֹשׁ בָּרוּךְ הוּא צִוָּה לִפְדּוֹת אֶת הַבְּכוֹר (אם מת אביו, מוסיף: וּבַעֲוֹנוֹתַי מֵת אָבִי קֹדֶם זְמַן פִּדְיוֹנִי), וַאֲנִי נִשְׁאַרְתִּי בְּחִיּוּב לִפְדּוֹת עַצְמִי, דִּכְתִיב בְּכוֹר בָּנֶיךָ תִּפְדֶּה, וְקָרֵינַן תִּפָּדֶה, רוֹצֶה לוֹמַר שֶׁאֶפְדֶּה אֶת עַצְמִי. וַהֲרֵינִי מוּכָן וּמְזֻמָּן לְקַיֵּם מִצְוַת הַשֵּׁם.

והכהן שואל:

**מַאי** נִיחָא לָךְ, יַת גַּרְמָךְ אוֹ דְמֵי פִּדְיוֹנָךְ דְּמִחַיַּבְתְּ לִי בְּפוּרְקָנָךְ?

והבכור משיב:

**יַת** גַּרְמִי, וְהֵא לָךְ דְּמֵי פִּדְיוֹנִי.

The Kohen places his right hand on the infant's head and blesses him:

**יְשִׂמְךָ** *May God establish you as Ephrayim and Menasheh. May the Lord bless you and safeguard you. May the Lord shine the Godly countenance upon you and be gracious to you. May the Lord bestow favor upon you and grant you tranquility. For lengthy days and years of life and tranquility shall God add for you. The Lord will protect you from every harm; the Lord will guard your life.*

The festive meal in celebration of the pidyon continues, followed by Birkat HaMazon (After Meal Thanks).

## PIDYON OF ONE WHO REDEEMS HIMSELF

When the father and the Bet Din, for whatever reasons, failed to redeem the son, the child must redeem himself after he has attained the age of thirteen years and one day (Bar-Mitzvah). The text of the pidyon is as follows.

The *pidyon* takes place after the assembled have washed their hands, recited the following berakhot, and eaten some bread:

**בָּרוּךְ** *Blessed are You, Lord our God, Ruler of the Universe, Who has sanctified us with the Godly commandments, and has commanded us concerning the washing of the hands.*

**בָּרוּךְ** *Blessed are You, Lord our God, Ruler of the Universe, Who brings forth sustenance from the earth.*

The first-born says to the Kohen:

**אֲנִי** *I am a first-born, first issue of the womb, and the Holy One, Blessed is God, has commanded to redeem the first-born;* (If the father has passed away, the first-born adds the following: *Unfortunately my father died before the time of my redemption*) *and it remains as my obligation to redeem myself, as it is written: 'your first-born son you shall redeem. . .,' which we read as 'shall be redeemed;' that is to say, that I must redeem myself. Behold I am ready and prepared to fulfill God's command.*

The Kohen asks:

**מַאי** *Do you prefer yourself, or the amount that you are required to pay for your redemption?*

The first-born responds:

**יַת** *I prefer myself, and here is my redemption amount.*

ומברך:

**בָּרוּךְ** אַתָּה יהוה אֱלֹהֵינוּ מֶלֶךְ הָעוֹלָם, אֲשֶׁר קִדְּשָׁנוּ בְּמִצְוֹתָיו, וְצִוָּנוּ עַל פִּדְיוֹן בְּכוֹר. (All– אָמֵן)

**בָּרוּךְ** אַתָּה יהוה אֱלֹהֵינוּ מֶלֶךְ הָעוֹלָם, שֶׁהֶחֱיָנוּ וְקִיְּמָנוּ וְהִגִּיעָנוּ לַזְּמַן הַזֶּה. (All– אָמֵן)

The first-born then gives the money or the objects to the Kohen, who recites the following blessing over a full cup wine:

**בָּרוּךְ** אַתָּה יהוה אֱלֹהֵינוּ מֶלֶךְ הָעוֹלָם, בּוֹרֵא פְּרִי הַגָּפֶן. (All– אָמֵן)

After sipping some wine, the Kohen, redemption money or objects in hand, moves with his hand in a circular motion over the first-born's head, saying:

**זֶה** תַּחַת זֶה, זֶה חִלּוּף זֶה, זֶה מָחוּל עַל זֶה. יָצָא זֶה לַכֹּהֵן, וְאַתָּה תִּכָּנֵס לְחַיִּים, לְתוֹרָה, וּלְיִרְאַת שָׁמָיִם. יְהִי רָצוֹן שֶׁכְּשֵׁם שֶׁנִּכְנַסְתָּ לְפִדְיוֹן, כֵּן תִּכָּנֵס לְתוֹרָה, וּלְחֻפָּה, וּלְמַעֲשִׂים טוֹבִים, וְנֹאמַר אָמֵן.

The Kohen places his right hand on the first-born's head and blesses him:

**יְשִׂמְךָ** אֱלֹהִים כְּאֶפְרַיִם וְכִמְנַשֶּׁה. יְבָרֶכְךָ יהוה וְיִשְׁמְרֶךָ. יָאֵר יהוה פָּנָיו אֵלֶיךָ וִיחֻנֶּךָּ. יִשָּׂא יהוה פָּנָיו אֵלֶיךָ, וְיָשֵׂם לְךָ שָׁלוֹם. כִּי אֹרֶךְ יָמִים וּשְׁנוֹת חַיִּים וְשָׁלוֹם יוֹסִיפוּ לָךְ. יהוה יִשְׁמָרְךָ מִכָּל רָע, יִשְׁמֹר אֶת נַפְשֶׁךָ.

The festive meal in celebration of the pidyon continues, followed by Birkat HaMazon (After Meal Thanks).

The first-born recites the following blessings:

**בָּרוּךְ** *Blessed are You, Lord our God, Ruler of the Universe, Who has sanctified us with the Godly commandments and has commanded us regarding the redemption of the first-born.* (All— *Amen*)

**בָּרוּךְ** *Blessed are You, Lord our God, Ruler of the Universe, Who has given us life and sustained us, enabling us to reach this moment.* (All— *Amen*)

The first-born then gives the money or the objects to the Kohen, who recites the following blessing over a full cup of wine:

**בָּרוּךְ** *Blessed are You, Lord our God, Ruler of the Universe, Who creates the fruit of the vine.* (All— *Amen*)

After sipping some wine, the Kohen, redemption money or objects in hand, moves with his hand in a circular motion over the first-born's head, saying:

**זֶה** *This is instead of that, this is in exchange for that, this is pardoned because of that. This has gone to the Kohen, and you should enter into life, into Torah, and into awe of Heaven. May it be God's will that just as you entered into redemption, so may you enter into Torah, the marital canopy, and good deeds, and let us respond, Amen.*

The Kohen places his right hand on the first-born's head and blesses him:

**יְשִׂמְךָ** *May God establish you as Ephrayim and Menasheh. May the Lord bless you and safeguard you. May the Lord shine the Godly countenance upon you and be gracious to you. May the Lord bestow favor upon you and grant you tranquility. For lengthy days and years of life and tranquility shall God add for you. The Lord will protect you from every harm; The Lord will guard your life.*

The festive meal in celebration of the pidyon continues, followed by Birkat HaMazon (After Meal Thanks).

## ◂§ Conversion Adoption

*When a Jewish couple adopts a child of non-Jewish parentage, the youngster enters the covenantal community via conversion adoption. This conversion adoption is finalized 'al daat Bet Din.' The Rabbinical Court, after being satisfied that the parents will raise the child in a proper Jewish environment, fully consistent with Jewish law, formalizes the entry of the child into the Jewish community.*

*Conversion Adoption should be carried out only in conjunction with an authorized Bet Din. The office of the RCA will be pleased to provide a list of these Rabbinical Courts.*

*What follows is the procedure for the actual conversion adoption ceremony.*

# CONVERSION ADOPTION

## MALES

If the child is a male, it is circumcised in the presence of the Bet Din. At that time, the following blessing is recited by the mohel:

**בָּרוּךְ** אַתָּה יהוה אֱלֹהֵינוּ מֶלֶךְ הָעוֹלָם, אֲשֶׁר קִדְּשָׁנוּ בְּמִצְוֹתָיו, וְצִוָּנוּ לָמוֹל אֶת הַגֵּרִים. (All– אָמֵן)

If the child had already been circumcised, then only a token covenantal extraction, called 'hatafat dam berit,' is made, and no berakhah is recited.

After the circumcision, the following berakhot are recited over a full cup of wine:

**בָּרוּךְ** אַתָּה יהוה אֱלֹהֵינוּ מֶלֶךְ הָעוֹלָם, בּוֹרֵא פְּרִי הַגָּפֶן. (All– אָמֵן)

**בָּרוּךְ** אַתָּה יהוה אֱלֹהֵינוּ מֶלֶךְ הָעוֹלָם אֲשֶׁר קִדְּשָׁנוּ בְּמִצְוֹתָיו וְצִוָּנוּ לָמוֹל אֶת הַגֵּרִים וּלְהַטִּיף מֵהֶם דַּם בְּרִית, שֶׁאִלְמָלֵא דַּם בְּרִית לֹא נִתְקַיְּמוּ שָׁמַיִם וָאָרֶץ, שֶׁנֶּאֱמַר: אִם לֹא בְרִיתִי, יוֹמָם וָלַיְלָה, חֻקּוֹת שָׁמַיִם וָאָרֶץ לֹא שָׂמְתִּי. בָּרוּךְ אַתָּה יהוה, כּוֹרֵת הַבְּרִית. (All– אָמֵן)

The one who recited the blessings then drinks from the cup of wine.

After recovery from circumcision, the male convert is immersed in the mikveh, by a representative of the presiding Bet Din. The father may be the one appointed by the Bet Din to do this. Prior to immersion, the Rabbinical Court once again gains the assurance of the child's parents, that immersion will be followed by the parents' raising the child toward full adherence to Jewish belief and practice. If the child is able, he recites the following berakhah after immersion. If the child is too young to recite this blessing, it is not recited at all.

**בָּרוּךְ** אַתָּה יהוה אֱלֹהֵינוּ מֶלֶךְ הָעוֹלָם, אֲשֶׁר קִדְּשָׁנוּ בְּמִצְוֹתָיו, וְצִוָּנוּ עַל הַטְּבִילָה.

Following immersion, the convert is welcomed with a special prayer which includes the bestowal of a Jewish name:

**אֱלֹהֵינוּ** וֵאלֹהֵי אֲבוֹתֵינוּ קַיֵּם אֶת הַיֶּלֶד לְיִשְׂרָאֵל וְיִקָּרֵא שְׁמוֹ בְּיִשְׂרָאֵל (שם הילד) בֶּן אַבְרָהָם אָבִינוּ. הוֹדוּ לַיהוה כִּי טוֹב כִּי לְעוֹלָם חַסְדּוֹ. זֶה הַקָּטָן גָּדוֹל יִהְיֶה, וְיִכָּנֵס לְתוֹרָה, לְחוּפָּה, וּלְמַעֲשִׂים טוֹבִים, אָמֵן.

# CONVERSION ADOPTION

## MALES

If the child is a male, it is circumcised in the presence of the Bet Din. At that time, the following blessing is recited by the mohel:

**בָּרוּךְ** *Blessed are You, Lord our God, Ruler of the Universe, Who has sanctified us with the Godly commandments, and has commanded us to circumcise converts.* (All– *Amen*)

If the child had already been circumcised, then only a token covenantal extraction, called 'hatafat dam berit,' is made, and no berakhah is recited.

After the circumcision, the following berakhot are recited over a full cup of wine:

**בָּרוּךְ** *Blessed are You, Lord our God, Ruler of the Universe, Who creates the fruit of the vine.* (All– *Amen*)

**בָּרוּךְ** *Blessed are You, Lord our God, Ruler of the Universe, Who has sanctified us with the Godly commandments and has commanded us to circumcise converts and to draw from them the covenantal blood, for without the blood of the covenant heaven and earth could not be sustained, as it is said: 'Were it not for My covenant, day and night, and the laws that maintain heaven and earth I would not have implemented.' Blessed are You, Lord, Who establishes the covenant.* (All– *Amen*)

The one who recited the blessings then drinks from the cup of wine.

After recovery from circumcision, the male convert is immersed in the mikveh, by a representative of the presiding Bet Din. The father may be the one appointed by the Bet Din to do this. Prior to immersion, the Rabbinical Court once again gains the assurance of the child's parents, that immersion will be followed by the parents' raising the child toward full adherence to Jewish belief and practice. If the child is able, he recites the following berakhah after immersion. If the child is too young to recite this blessing, it is not recited at all.

**בָּרוּךְ** *Blessed are You, Lord, our God, Ruler of the Universe, Who has sanctified us with the Godly commandments, and has commanded us concerning immersion.*

Following immersion, the convert is welcomed with a special prayer which includes the bestowal of a Jewish name:

**אֱלֹהֵינוּ** *Our God, and the God of our ancestors, preserve this individual for Israel, and may his name be called in Israel* (child's Hebrew name) *son of Avraham Avinu. Give thanks to the Lord, for the Lord is good; the Lord's lovingkindness is everlasting. May this child become great, and enter into Torah, the marital canopy, and good deeds, Amen.*

## FEMALES

For the female convert, the main component of the conversion adoption procedure is immersion in the mikveh. Prior to immersion, the Rabbinical Court must be assured that the child's parents will raise the child toward full adherence to Jewish belief and practice. The child is immersed by a representative of the presiding Bet Din. Here too, the father may be the one appointed by the Bet Din to do this. If the child is able, she recites the following berakhah after immersion. If the child is too young to recite this blessing, it is not recited at all.

**בָּרוּךְ** אַתָּה יהוה אֱלֹהֵינוּ מֶלֶךְ הָעוֹלָם, אֲשֶׁר קִדְּשָׁנוּ בְּמִצְוֹתָיו, וְצִוָּנוּ עַל הַטְּבִילָה. (All– אָמֵן)

Following immersion, the convert is welcomed with a special prayer which includes the bestowal of a Jewish name:

**אֱלֹהֵינוּ** וֵאלֹהֵי אֲבוֹתֵינוּ קַיֵּם אֶת הַיַּלְדָּה לְיִשְׂרָאֵל וְיִקָּרֵא שְׁמָהּ בְּיִשְׂרָאֵל (שם הילדה) בַּת אַבְרָהָם אָבִינוּ. הוֹדוּ לַיהוה כִּי טוֹב כִּי לְעוֹלָם חַסְדּוֹ. זוֹ הַקְּטַנָּה גְּדוֹלָה תִּהְיֶה, וְתִכָּנֵס לְתוֹרָה, לְחוּפָּה, וּלְמַעֲשִׂים טוֹבִים, אָמֵן.

Following the completion of the conversion procedure for both males and females, it is fitting for the child's parents to recite the Shema (p. 66), which speaks of the obligation to transmit the Torah tradition to one's children.

The finalization of conversion of both males and females is a joyous event, and should be celebrated in an appropriate, religiously meaningful fashion, such as by a Kiddush in shul or at home, accompanied by fitting words of Torah by the parents and the Rabbi. It is vital to assure that the child, upon reaching the age of responsibility (thirteen years and a day for boys, twelve years and a day for girls), be made aware of the conversion process entered into on the child's behalf. The child must then be given the opportunity to decide whether or not to reaffirm that commitment.

## FEMALES

For the female convert, the main component of the conversion adoption procedure is immersion in the mikveh. Prior to immersion, the Rabbinical Court must be assured that the child's parents will raise the child toward full adherence to Jewish belief and practice. The child is immersed by a representative of the presiding Bet Din. Here too, the father may be the one appointed by the Bet Din to do this. If the child is able, she recites the following berakhah after immersion. If the child is too young to recite this blessing, it is not recited at all.

**בָּרוּךְ** *Blessed are You, Lord our God, Ruler of the Universe, Who has sanctified us with the Godly commandments, and has commanded us concerning immersion.* (All— *Amen*)

Following immersion, the convert is welcomed with a special prayer which includes the bestowal of a Jewish name:

**אֱלֹהֵינוּ** *Our God, and the God of our ancestors, preserve this individual for Israel, and may her name be called in Israel* (child's Hebrew name) *daughter of Avraham Avinu. Give thanks to the Lord, for the Lord is good; the Lord's lovingkindness is everlasting. May this child become great, and enter into Torah, the marital canopy, and good deeds, Amen.*

Following the completion of the conversion procedure for both males and females, it is fitting for the child's parents to recite the Shema (p. 67), which speaks of the obligation to transmit the Torah tradition to one's children.

The finalization of conversion of both males and females is a joyous event, and should be celebrated in an appropriate, religiously meaningful fashion, such as by a Kiddush in shul or at home, accompanied by fitting words of Torah by the parents and the Rabbi. It is vital to assure that the child, upon reaching the age of responsibility (thirteen years and a day for boys, twelve years and a day for girls), be made aware of the conversion process entered into on the child's behalf. The child must then be given the opportunity to decide whether or not to reaffirm that commitment.

## ◈ Conversion

*Conversion to Judaism is a long journey. It involves learning the fundamentals of Judaism, the principles and the practices, leading to a genuine, complete, unconditional embrace of Judaism in its totality.*

*Conversion should be carried out only in conjunction with an authorized Bet Din. The office of the RCA will be pleased to provide a list of these Rabbinical Courts.*

*What follows is the procedure for the actual conversion ceremony.*

# CONVERSION

If the prospective convert is a male, he is circumcised in the presence of the Bet Din. At that time, the following blessing is recited by the mohel:

**בָּרוּךְ** אַתָּה יהוה אֱלֹהֵינוּ מֶלֶךְ הָעוֹלָם, אֲשֶׁר קִדְּשָׁנוּ בְּמִצְוֹתָיו, וְצִוָּנוּ לָמוּל אֶת הַגֵּרִים. (All– אָמֵן)

If the convert had already been circumcised, then only a token covenantal extraction, called 'hatafat dam berit,' is made, and no berakhah is recited. After the circumcision, the following berakhot are recited over a full cup of wine:

**בָּרוּךְ** אַתָּה יהוה אֱלֹהֵינוּ מֶלֶךְ הָעוֹלָם בּוֹרֵא פְּרִי הַגָּפֶן. (All– אָמֵן)

**בָּרוּךְ** אַתָּה יהוה אֱלֹהֵינוּ מֶלֶךְ הָעוֹלָם אֲשֶׁר קִדְּשָׁנוּ בְּמִצְוֹתָיו וְצִוָּנוּ לָמוּל אֶת הַגֵּרִים וּלְהַטִּיף מֵהֶם דַּם בְּרִית, שֶׁאִלְמָלֵא דַם בְּרִית, לֹא נִתְקַיְּמוּ שָׁמַיִם וָאָרֶץ שֶׁנֶּאֱמַר: אִם לֹא בְרִיתִי יוֹמָם וָלַיְלָה, חֻקּוֹת שָׁמַיִם וָאָרֶץ לֹא שָׂמְתִּי. בָּרוּךְ אַתָּה יהוה, כּוֹרֵת הַבְּרִית. (All– אָמֵן)

The one who recited the blessings then drinks from the cup of wine

After recovery from circumcision, the male convert is immersed in the mikveh.

For the female convert, the main component of the conversion procedure following her embrace of Jewish belief and practice is immersion in the mikveh. Just prior to immersion, the Rabbinical Court once again seeks the assurance of the convert (whether male or female) that immersion will be followed by full adherence to Jewish belief and practice. The immersion takes place in the presence of the Bet Din, who give special attention to not compromising the dignity of the immersing convert. The convert must be completely surrounded by the waters of the mikveh, but can do this in a loosely fitting garment or covering that simultaneously preserves dignity and fulfills the halakhic requirements.

After immersion in the mikveh, the following blessing is recited by the convert:

**בָּרוּךְ** אַתָּה יהוה אֱלֹהֵינוּ מֶלֶךְ הָעוֹלָם, אֲשֶׁר קִדְּשָׁנוּ בְּמִצְוֹתָיו, וְצִוָּנוּ עַל הַטְּבִילָה. (All– אָמֵן)

Following immersion, the convert is welcomed with a special prayer which includes the bestowal of a Jewish name. This prayer is cited in Nahalat Zevi by HaRav Gedalyah Felder, p. 46.

# CONVERSION

If the prospective convert is a male, he is circumcised in the presence of the Bet Din. At that time, the following blessing is recited by the mohel:

בָּרוּךְ *Blessed are You, Lord our God, Ruler of the Universe, Who has sanctified us with the Godly commandments, and has commanded us to circumcise converts.* (All– *Amen*)

If the convert had already been circumcised, then only a token covenantal extraction, called 'hatafat dam berit,' is made, and no berakhah is recited. After the circumcision, the following berakhot are recited over a full cup of wine:

בָּרוּךְ *Blessed are You, Lord our God, Ruler of the Universe, Who creates the fruit of the vine.* (All– *Amen*)

בָּרוּךְ *Blessed are You, Lord our God, Ruler of the Universe, Who has sanctified us with the Godly commands and has commanded us to circumcise converts and to draw from them the covenantal blood, for without the blood of the covenant, heaven and earth could not be sustained, as it is said, 'Were it not for My covenant, day and night, and the laws that maintain heaven and earth I would not have implemented.' Blessed are You, Lord, Who establishes the covenant.* (All– *Amen*)

The one who recited the blessings then drinks from the cup of wine

After recovery from circumcision, the male convert is immersed in the mikveh.

For the female convert, the main component of the conversion procedure following her embrace of Jewish belief and practice is immersion in the mikveh. Just prior to immersion, the Rabbinical Court once again seeks the assurance of the convert (whether male or female) that immersion will be followed by full adherence to Jewish belief and practice. The immersion takes place in the presence of the Bet Din, who give special attention to not compromising the dignity of the immersing convert. The convert must be completely surrounded by the waters of the mikveh, but can do this in a loosely fitting garment or covering that simultaneously preserves dignity and fulfills the halakhic requirements.

After immersion in the mikveh, the following blessing is recited by the convert:

בָּרוּךְ *Blessed are You, Lord our God, Ruler of the Universe, Who has sanctified us with the Godly commands, and has commanded us concerning immersion.* (All– *Amen*)

Following immersion, the convert is welcomed with a special prayer which includes the bestowal of a Jewish name. This prayer is cited in Nahalat Zevi by HaRav Gedalyah Felder, p. 46.

For males:

**אֱלֹהֵינוּ** וֵאלֹהֵי אֲבוֹתֵינוּ הַצְלַח נָא לַגֵּר הַזֶּה הַנִּקְרָא שְׁמוֹ בְּיִשְׂרָאֵל (שמו) בֶּן אַבְרָהָם אָבִינוּ, וּמְשׁוֹךְ עָלָיו חַסְדֶּךָ. וּכְשֵׁם שֶׁזִּכִּיתָ אוֹתוֹ לְהִסְתּוֹפֵף וְלַחֲסוֹת תַּחַת כְּנָפֶיךָ, כֵּן תִּטַּע בְּלִבּוֹ אַהֲבָתְךָ וְיִרְאָתְךָ וְתִפְתַּח לִבּוֹ בְּתוֹרָתֶךָ. וְתַדְרִיכֵהוּ בִּנְתִיב מִצְווֹתֶיךָ וְלַעֲשׂוֹת רְצוֹנְךָ לְמַעַן יִמְצָא חֵן בְּעֵינֶיךָ. אָמֵן, כֵּן יְהִי רָצוֹן.

For females:

**אֱלֹהֵינוּ** וֵאלֹהֵי אֲבוֹתֵינוּ, הַצְלַח נָא לַגִּיּוֹרֶת הַזֹּאת הַנִּקְרָא שְׁמָהּ בְּיִשְׂרָאֵל (שמה) בַּת אַבְרָהָם אָבִינוּ וּמְשׁוֹךְ עָלֶיהָ חַסְדֶּךָ. וּכְשֵׁם שֶׁזִּכִּיתָ אוֹתָהּ לְהִסְתּוֹפֵף וְלַחֲסוֹת תַּחַת כְּנָפֶיךָ, כֵּן תִּטַּע בְּלִבָּהּ אַהֲבָתְךָ וְיִרְאָתְךָ וְתִפְתַּח לִבָּהּ בְּתוֹרָתֶךָ. וְתַדְרִיכֶהָ בִּנְתִיב מִצְווֹתֶיךָ וְלַעֲשׂוֹת רְצוֹנְךָ לְמַעַן תִּמְצָא חֵן בְּעֵינֶיךָ. אָמֵן, כֵּן יְהִי רָצוֹן.

It is fitting that following the completion of the conversion procedure, a male convert should don Tallit and Tefillin. Both male and female converts should recite the Shema (p. 66) faith affirmation.

The finalization of the conversion is a joyous event, and should be celebrated in an appropriate, religiously meaningful fashion, such as by a Kiddush in shul or at home, accompanied by fitting words of Torah by the convert and the supervising Rabbi.

For males:

**אֱלֹהֵינוּ** *Our God, and the God of our ancestors, assure the continuing success of this convert whose name is called in Israel* (convert's Hebrew name) *son of Avraham Avinu and spread over him Your lovingkindness. Just as You have caused him to merit standing on the threshold and being protected under Your wings, so may You plant within him the love and awe of God, and open his heart in Your Torah. Guide him in the path of Your commandments and to actualize Your will in order to find favor in Your eyes. Amen — thus may it be God's will.*

For females:

**אֱלֹהֵינוּ** *Our God, and the God of our ancestors, assure the continuing success of this convert whose name is called in Israel* (convert's Hebrew name) *daughter of Avraham Avinu and spread over her Your lovingkindness. Just as You have caused her to merit standing on the threshold and being protected under Your wings, so may You plant within her the love and awe of God, and open her heart in Your Torah. Guide her in the path of Your commandments and to actualize Your will in order to find favor in Your eyes. Amen — thus may it be God's will.*

It is fitting that following the completion of the conversion procedure, a male convert should don Tallit and Tefillin. Both male and female converts should recite the Shema (p. 67) faith affirmation.

The finalization of the conversion is a joyous event, and should be celebrated in an appropriate, religiously meaningful fashion, such as by a Kiddush in shul or at home, accompanied by fitting words of Torah by the convert and the supervising Rabbi.

## ◆ Bat Mitzvah

*When a Jewish girl reaches the stage of Bat-Mitzvah, at the age of twelve years and one day, there are many who celebrate this entry into Judaic responsibility with a meaningful ceremony reinforcing the significance of the Bat-Mitzvah.*

*There are a number of potential ingredients which can combine for a meaningful ceremony. What follows is but one suggested format from among a host of possibilities.*

## BAT-MITZVAH CEREMONY

Following an appropriate opening by the Rabbi, the Bat Mitzvah reads the following Psalms.

תהלים קכא

**שִׁיר לַמַּעֲלוֹת,** אֶשָּׂא עֵינַי אֶל הֶהָרִים, מֵאַיִן יָבֹא עֶזְרִי. עֶזְרִי מֵעִם יהוה, עֹשֵׂה שָׁמַיִם וָאָרֶץ. אַל יִתֵּן לַמּוֹט רַגְלֶךָ, אַל יָנוּם שֹׁמְרֶךָ. הִנֵּה לֹא יָנוּם וְלֹא יִישָׁן, שׁוֹמֵר יִשְׂרָאֵל. יהוה שֹׁמְרֶךָ, יהוה צִלְּךָ עַל יַד יְמִינֶךָ. יוֹמָם הַשֶּׁמֶשׁ לֹא יַכֶּכָּה וְיָרֵחַ בַּלָּיְלָה. יהוה יִשְׁמָרְךָ מִכָּל רָע, יִשְׁמֹר אֶת נַפְשֶׁךָ. יהוה יִשְׁמָר צֵאתְךָ וּבוֹאֶךָ, מֵעַתָּה וְעַד עוֹלָם.

תהלים קכב

**שִׁיר הַמַּעֲלוֹת,** לְדָוִד, שָׂמַחְתִּי בְּאֹמְרִים לִי, בֵּית יהוה נֵלֵךְ. עֹמְדוֹת הָיוּ רַגְלֵינוּ, בִּשְׁעָרַיִךְ יְרוּשָׁלָיִם. יְרוּשָׁלַיִם הַבְּנוּיָה, כְּעִיר שֶׁחֻבְּרָה לָּהּ יַחְדָּו. שֶׁשָּׁם עָלוּ שְׁבָטִים, שִׁבְטֵי יָהּ עֵדוּת לְיִשְׂרָאֵל, לְהוֹדוֹת לְשֵׁם יהוה. כִּי שָׁמָּה יָשְׁבוּ כִסְאוֹת לְמִשְׁפָּט, כִּסְאוֹת לְבֵית דָּוִד. שַׁאֲלוּ שְׁלוֹם יְרוּשָׁלָיִם, יִשְׁלָיוּ אֹהֲבָיִךְ. יְהִי שָׁלוֹם בְּחֵילֵךְ, שַׁלְוָה בְּאַרְמְנוֹתָיִךְ. לְמַעַן אַחַי וְרֵעָי, אֲדַבְּרָה נָּא שָׁלוֹם בָּךְ. לְמַעַן בֵּית יהוה אֱלֹהֵינוּ, אֲבַקְשָׁה טוֹב לָךְ.

תהלים קכו

**שִׁיר הַמַּעֲלוֹת,** בְּשׁוּב יהוה אֶת שִׁיבַת צִיּוֹן הָיִינוּ כְּחֹלְמִים.אָז יִמָּלֵא שְׂחוֹק פִּינוּ, וּלְשׁוֹנֵנוּ רִנָּה, אָז יֹאמְרוּ בַגּוֹיִם, הִגְדִּיל יהוה לַעֲשׂוֹת עִם אֵלֶּה. הִגְדִּיל יהוה לַעֲשׂוֹת עִמָּנוּ, הָיִינוּ שְׂמֵחִים. שׁוּבָה יהוה אֶת שְׁבִיתֵנוּ, כַּאֲפִיקִים בַּנֶּגֶב. הַזֹּרְעִים בְּדִמְעָה, בְּרִנָּה יִקְצֹרוּ. הָלוֹךְ יֵלֵךְ וּבָכֹה נֹשֵׂא מֶשֶׁךְ הַזָּרַע, בֹּא יָבֹא בְרִנָּה נֹשֵׂא אֲלֻמֹּתָיו.

The congregation is led in songs of joy. The Bat-Mitzvah then delivers a meaningful Devar Torah on the significance of her entry into responsibility. The Rabbi follows with fitting remarks for the occasion. Presentation of appropriate sefarim is then made to

## BAT-MITZVAH CEREMONY

Following an appropriate opening by the Rabbi, the Bat-Mitzvah reads the following Psalms.

Psalm 121

**שִׁיר לַמַּעֲלוֹת** *A song to ascents. I lift my eyes to the mountains, from where will my help come? My help comes from the Lord, Maker of heaven and earth. God will not let your foot falter, your Guardian will not slumber. Behold, the Guardian of Israel neither slumbers nor sleeps. The Lord is your Guardian, the Lord is your protection by your right side. By day the sun will not harm you, nor the moon by night. The Lord will guard you from all evil, the Lord will guard your life. The Lord will guard your going and coming from now and forever.*

Psalm 122

**שִׁיר הַמַּעֲלוֹת** *A song of ascents of David. I rejoiced when they said to me, 'Let us go to the House of the Lord.' Our feet stood inside your gates, Yerushalayim. The built-up Yerushalayim is like a city that is united together. To there the tribes would ascend, the tribes of God who are a testimony to Israel, to give thanks to the Name of the Lord. For there sat thrones of judgment, thrones for the house of David. Pray for the well-being of Yerushalayim, may those who love you be at peace. May there be peace in your ramparts, serenity within your citadels. For the sake of my kin and friends, I will speak peacefully in your midst. For the sake of the House of the Lord, our God, I will seek your good.*

Psalm 126

**שִׁיר הַמַּעֲלוֹת** *A song of ascents. When the Lord returns the captives of Zion, we will be like dreamers. Then our mouths will be filled with laughter and our tongues with song; then it will be said among the nations, 'The Lord has done great things for them.' The Lord did great things for us, we were happy. Lord, return our captives, like streams in the desert. Those who sow in tears shall reap in joy. The one who cries in carrying the bag of seed will return in joy, carrying the grain sheaves.*

The congregation is led in songs of joy. The Bat-Mitzvah then delivers a meaningful Devar Torah on the significance of her entry into responsibility. The Rabbi follows with fitting remarks for the occasion. Presentation of appropriate sefarim is then made to the Bat-Mitzvah, by the parents together with the Rabbi. The Bat-Mitzvah, through her recitation of the Shema, affirms her undertaking to live in accordance with the Torah.

דברים ו:ד-ט

**שְׁמַע יִשְׂרָאֵל, יהוה אֱלֹהֵינוּ, יהוה אֶחָד:**

בָּרוּךְ שֵׁם כְּבוֹד מַלְכוּתוֹ לְעוֹלָם וָעֶד. – In an undertone

**וְאָהַבְתָּ** אֵת יהוה אֱלֹהֶיךָ, בְּכָל־לְבָבְךָ, וּבְכָל־נַפְשְׁךָ, וּבְכָל־מְאֹדֶךָ. וְהָיוּ הַדְּבָרִים הָאֵלֶּה, אֲשֶׁר אָנֹכִי מְצַוְּךָ הַיּוֹם, עַל־לְבָבֶךָ. וְשִׁנַּנְתָּם לְבָנֶיךָ, וְדִבַּרְתָּ בָּם, בְּשִׁבְתְּךָ בְּבֵיתֶךָ, וּבְלֶכְתְּךָ בַדֶּרֶךְ, וּבְשָׁכְבְּךָ וּבְקוּמֶךָ. וּקְשַׁרְתָּם לְאוֹת עַל־יָדֶךָ, וְהָיוּ לְטֹטָפֹת בֵּין עֵינֶיךָ. וּכְתַבְתָּם עַל־מְזֻזוֹת בֵּיתֶךָ, וּבִשְׁעָרֶיךָ.

The parents then bestow the traditional parental blessing upon their Bat-Mitzvah daughter.

**יְשִׂמֵךְ** אֱלֹהִים כְּשָׂרָה רִבְקָה רָחֵל וְלֵאָה. יְבָרֶכְךָ יהוה וְיִשְׁמְרֶךָ. יָאֵר יהוה פָּנָיו אֵלֶיךָ וִיחֻנֶּךָּ. יִשָּׂא יהוה פָּנָיו אֵלֶיךָ, וְיָשֵׂם לְךָ שָׁלוֹם.

**וִיהִי רָצוֹן** מִלִּפְנֵי אָבִינוּ שֶׁבַּשָּׁמַיִם, שֶׁיִּתֵּן בְּלִבֵּךְ אַהֲבָתוֹ וְיִרְאָתוֹ; וְתִהְיֶה יִרְאַת יהוה עַל פָּנַיִךְ כָּל יָמַיִךְ, שֶׁלֹּא תֶחֱטָאִי. וִיהִי חֶשְׁקֵךְ בַּתּוֹרָה וּבַמִּצְוֹת. עֵינַיִךְ לְנֹכַח יַבִּיטוּ; פִּיךְ יְדַבֵּר חָכְמוֹת וְלִבֵּךְ יֶהְגֶּה אֵימוֹת; יָדַיִךְ יַעַסְקוּ בְמִצְוֹת, רַגְלַיִךְ יָרוּצוּ לַעֲשׂוֹת רְצוֹן אָבִיךְ שֶׁבַּשָּׁמַיִם. יִתֵּן לָךְ בָּנִים וּבָנוֹת, צַדִּיקִים וְצִדְקָנִיּוֹת, עוֹסְקִים בַּתּוֹרָה וּבְמִצְוֹת כָּל יְמֵיהֶם. וִיהִי מְקוֹרֵךְ בָּרוּךְ, וְיַזְמִין לָךְ פַּרְנָסָתֵךְ בְּהֶתֵּר בְּנַחַת וּבְרֶוַח, מִתַּחַת יָדוֹ הָרְחָבָה, וְלֹא עַל יְדֵי מַתְּנַת בָּשָׂר וָדָם; פַּרְנָסָה שֶׁתִּהְיִי פְּנוּיָה לַעֲבוֹדַת יהוה. וְתִתְבָּרְכִי לְחַיִּים טוֹבִים וַאֲרוּכִים, בְּתוֹךְ כָּל צַדִּיקֵי יִשְׂרָאֵל, אָמֵן.

Ceremony concludes as the assembled join in singing:

**סִמָּן טוֹב וּמַזָּל טוֹב יְהֵא לָנוּ וּלְכָל יִשְׂרָאֵל, אָמֵן.**

It is fitting to follow the Bat-Mitzvah ceremony with a celebrative meal.

the Bat-Mitzvah, by the parents together with the Rabbi. The Bat-Mitzvah, through her recitation of the Shema, affirms her undertaking to live in accordance with the Torah.

Deuteronomy 6:4-9

***Hear, O Israel, the Lord is our God, only the Lord.***

In an undertone— *Blessed is the Name of God's honored Dominion forever.*

**וְאָהַבְתָּ** *You shall love the Lord your God with all your heart and with all your soul and with all your might. These words, which I instruct you this day, take to heart. Teach them diligently to your children and make them your essential conversation when you are at home and when you are on the way, when you lie down and when you are awake. Bind them as a sign on your hand and make them as frontlets on your forehead. Inscribe them on the doorposts of your home and on your gates.*

The parents then bestow the traditional parental blessing upon their Bat-Mitzvah daughter.

**יְשִׂמֵךְ** *May God make you as Sarah, Rivkah, Rahel and Leah. May the Lord bless you and safeguard you. May the Lord shine the Godly countenance upon you and be gracious to you. May the Lord bestow favor upon you and grant you tranquility.*

**וִיהִי רָצוֹן** *May it be God's will that there be put in your heart the love and awe of God; may the awe of God be ever-present so that you do not sin, and may your yearning be for the Torah and its precepts. Your eyes should see straight; let your mouth speak wisdom and your heart mediate awe; your hands should be engaged in the performance of the precepts, your feet should run to fulfill the will of your Heavenly Parent. May you be granted righteous children who will be engaged in Torah study and good deeds all their lives. May your foundation be blessed, and may your livelihood come to you legitimately, with satisfaction and abundance, from God's wide hand, and not by the gift of mortals; a livelihood which will allow you to serve God. May you be blessed with a good and long life amongst all the righteous people of Israel, Amen.*

Ceremony concludes as the assembled join in singing:

***May there be a good sign and good fortune for us and for all Israel, Amen.***

It is fitting to follow the Bat-Mitzvah ceremony with a celebrative meal.

## ◆§ Pre-nuptial and Arbitration Agreements

*The two agreements appearing in the ensuing pages address issues of pressing concern, related to intransigence in the get process, behavior which is inexcusable.*

*It is essential that all Rabbis make the signing of these documents mandatory. Since the contents are delicate — a couple desiring to marry do not relish a conversation about divorce — it behooves the officiating Rabbi to discuss these matters well before the wedding, in a calm, relaxed, and sensitive manner. Every Rabbi is much better served if he is honestly able to tell the couple that the signing of this document is standard procedure, for their protection, and for the protection of people contemplating marriage.*

*The texts of the following agreements are the only ones approved by the Rosh Bet Din of the Bet Din of America. This Bet Din is affiliated with the Rabbinical Council of America.*

# ⊰ THE PRE-NUPTIAL AGREEMENT ⊱

This document, to be signed by the husband-to-be, is intended to avoid the problem of the husband's non-cooperation in the get process should the marriage disintegrate.

## Instructions for Husband's Obligation

A person can obligate himself to feed and support another individual, unconditionally, for a period of time. The Mishnah (Ketubot 101b) describes precisely such an obligation, made to one's stepdaughter for the duration of the marriage.

A similar obligation can be effected towards one's own halakhic wife, in the event that the couple no longer maintains domestic residence together and the normal family system of expenses and their defrayment is interrupted. This obligation, unlike the marital obligation mandated automatically by Halakhah, can be made unconditionally, e.g., even if the wife has abandoned her husband (moredet), and the wife has earnings (Even HaEzer 113; Bet Shmuel, 113:2). The husband can also waive his rights to his wife's earnings (Even HaEzer 134, Pithay Teshuvah 9).

In addition, the precise amount of the obligation can be specified. In order to conform with reasonable expectations of expenses — which include food, rent, clothing, insurance, etc. — the daily amount should not be exaggerated. Presently, $100 per day is considered reasonable, with adjustments to reflect the parties' financial situation. Indexing to the C.P.I. is appropriate to avoid subsequent trivialization of the sum.

While the obligation can be made totally unconditionally, principles of fairness and equity indicate a possibility of relief under certain circumstances. This should be determined by a Bet Din. Thus, if he summons her to Bet Din and she refuses to appear, or she refuses to comply with the decision or recommendation while he does comply, his obligation is terminated.

It must be emphasized that the obligation is not a penalty for not appearing in Bet Din or not obeying its decision. Rather, it is an estimate of the expenses which are incurred when a separate household is established. The Bet Din clause is a means of preventing abuse of the obligation by an unscrupulous wife.

To be certain that the husband understands the contents of the document, he must be given the opportunity to study it carefully and seek rabbinic and legal advice. Therefore, the document should be completed in advance of the wedding day. The document may include the name of the Rabbi and/or the attorney who was consulted (after Article III).

The husband should execute a kinyan sudar by taking hold of a utensil (e.g. handkerchief) belonging to one of the witnesses, and then write his name and address, date and place that the form is completed. He and two witnesses should then sign the document. Triplicate originals should be executed and given to the husband, wife and Rabbi.

# THE ARBITRATION AGREEMENT

This document, to be signed by the future husband and wife, is designed to avoid the jurisdictional disputes that often obstruct the get process.

## Instructions for Arbitration Agreement

To prevent disputes over the jurisdiction of the case, an arbitration agreement should designate the Bet Din. An institutional Bet Din may be chosen (e.g. RCA, Igud Harabonim, Agudas Harabonim). Alternatively, three rabbis may be named. In such a case, one should add — 'or their respective successors at [name of congregation or other position] or designees (if a rabbi disqualifies himself).' In either case, if the designated Bet Din cannot or will not judge the case, a different Bet Din, institutional or ad hoc (Zabla), of mutual consent, will arbitrate.

The Bet Din is empowered to deal with the issues of the get, the ketubah, and any written pre-nuptial obligation. In addition, the parties can authorize the Bet Din to decide all other monetary disputes. These can also include child support, visitation and custody. In this case, the secular courts reserve the right to review the decision as protectors of the interests of the children. If the parties exclude these disputes from the authority of the Bet Din, they can be brought to another Bet Din, or if a Bet Din allows, to a secular court.

In the event of the failure or refusal of either party to appear before it upon reasonable notice, the Bet Din may issue its decision in default of said party's appearance. Under such circumstances, or where a party refuses to comply with the order of the Bet Din, the Bet Din will then declare the defaulting party to be a Mesarev LaDin; thereby authorizing the parties to move, for enforcement, to any court of competent jurisdiction, and thereby making the defaulting party subject to all consequences of such status, appropriate according to Jewish Law and practice.

To be certain that the parties understand the contents of the document, they must be given the opportunity to study it carefully and seek rabbinic and legal advice. As such, the document should be completed in advance of the wedding day. The document may include the name of the Rabbi and/or the attorney who was consulted (after Article VII).

The parties should execute a kinyan sudar, and then write their respective names, addresses and the date and place where the form is completed. The parties and witnesses should then sign the document. Triplicate originals should be executed and given to the husband, wife and Rabbi.

## Pre-nuptial Agreement

## Husband's Assumption of Obligation

חתימת ידי תעיד עלי כמאה עדים שהתחייבתי בקגא״ס לזון ולפרנס את אשתי מרת ______________ כהלכות גוברין יהודאין דזנים ומפרנסים נשותיהם בקושטא. ואם ח״ו לא מיתדר לנו לקבוע דירתנו הקבועה ביחד בדירה אחת מאיזה טעם שיהיה, אני מתחייב לה מעכשיו סך ______________ דולר ליום עבור מזונותיה ופרנסתה כל זמן היותנו נשואים כדת משה וישראל, וחיוב מזונות ופרנסה בסך הנ״ל יהיה בתוקפו גם אם יש לאשתי פרנסה ו/או הכנסה ממקור אחר. ואני מוחל לה כל הזכויות והחיובים שזוכה בהם אדם כשנושא אשה מתשמיש ומעשי ידיה בזמן שחיוב סך הנ״ל בתוקפו. אולם אם אזמין אותה לדין תורה בנידון הפירוד בב״ד ______________ וב״ד יפסקו עליה שהיא לא צאית דינא בענין הפירוד, הן משום שתסרב להופיע לדין תורה, והן אם תבא לב״ד והב״ד יפסקו בינינו ואני אהיה מוכן לקיים פסק או הצעת הב״ד והיא תסרב לקיים פסק או הצעת הב״ד, יפסק חיובי זה. ואני מודה שההתחייבות שבשטר זה נעשה בקנין המועיל בדין תורה וכחומר כל שטרות בב״ד חשוב והתנאים נעשו כחומר כל התנאים. ולראיה באתי על החתום ב ______________ לחדש ______ שנת תש____ פה ______________ והכל שריר וקים.

נאום ______________________ עד

נאום ______________________ עד

## Pre-nuptial Agreement
## Husband's Assumption of Obligation

**I.** I, the undersigned, ______________________, husband-to-be, hereby obligate myself to support my wife-to-be, ______________________, in the manner of Jewish husbands who feed and support their wives loyally. If, God forbid, we do not continue domestic residence together for any reason, then I obligate myself, from now to pay to her $_____ per day, indexed annually to the Consumer Price Index for all Urban Consumers (CPI-U) as published by the U.S. Department of Labor, Bureau of Labor Statistics, beginning as of December 31st following the date of our marriage, for food and support (*parnasah*) from the day we no longer continue domestic residence together, and for the duration of our Jewish marriage, which is payable each week during the time due, under any circumstances, even if she has another source of income and earnings. Furthermore, I waive my *halakhic* rights to my wife's earnings for the period that she is entitled to the above-stipulated sum. However, this obligation (to provide food and support, *parnasah*) shall terminate if my wife refuses to appear upon due notice before the Bet Din of ____________ or any other Bet Din specified in writing by that Bet Din *before* proceedings commence, for purpose of a hearing concerning any outstanding disputes between us, or in the event that she fails to abide by the decision or recommendation of such Bet Din.

**II.** I execute this document as an inducement to the marriage between myself and my wife-to-be. The obligations and conditions contained herein are executed according to *all legal* and *halakhic* requirements. I acknowledge that I have effected the above obligation by means of a *kinyan* (formal Jewish transaction) in an esteemed (*hashuv*) Bet Din.

**III.** I have been given the opportunity, prior to executing this document, to consult with a rabbinic advisor and a legal advisor.

**IV.** I, the undersigned wife-to-be acknowledge the acceptance of this obligation by my husband-to-be, and in partial reliance on it agree to enter into our forthcoming marriage.

| **Groom** | **Bride** |
|---|---|
| Signature ______________________ | Signature ______________________ |
| Name ______________________ | Name ______________________ |
| Address ______________________ | Address ______________________ |

Signed at ______________________ Date ______________________

Witness ______________________ Witness ______________________

## Arbitration Agreement Between Husband and Wife

Memorandum of agreement made this ___ day of __________ 5___, which is the ___ day of ______, 20___, in the City of _________, State/Province of ________, between ______________, the husband-to-be, who presently lives at ____________ and _________________, the wife-to-be, who presently lives at _______________.

The parties are shortly going to be married.

**I.** Should a dispute arise between the parties after they are married, Heaven forbid, so that they do not live together as husband and wife, they agree to refer their marital dispute to an arbitration panel, namely, the Bet Din of ____________________ for a binding decision. Each of the parties agrees to appear in person before the Bet Din at the demand of the other party.

**II.** The decision of the panel, or a majority of them, shall be fully enforceable in any court of competent jurisdiction.

**III.** (a) The parties agree that the Bet Din is authorized to decide all issues relating to a *get* (Jewish divorce) as well as any issues arising from premarital agreements (e.g. *ketubah, tena'im*) entered into by the husband and the wife.

[The following three clauses (b,c,d) are optional, each to be separately included or excluded, by mutual consent, when signing this agreement.]

(b) The parties agree that the Bet Din is authorized to decide any other monetary disputes that may arise between them.

(c) The parties agree that the Bet Din is authorized to decide issues of child support, visitation and custody (if both parties consent to the inclusion of this provision in the arbitration at the time that the arbitration itself begins.)

(d) In deciding disputes pursuant to paragraph III b, the parties agree that the Bet Din shall apply the equitable distribution law of the Sate/Province of ____________________, as interpreted as of the date of this agreement, to any property disputes which may rise between them, the division of their property, and to questions of support. Notwithstanding any other provision of the equitable distribution law, the Bet Din may take into account the respective responsibilities of the parties for the end of the marriage, as an additional, but no exclusive factor, in determining the distribution of the marital property and support obligations.

**IV.** Failure of either party to perform his or her obligations under this agreement shall make that party liable for all costs awarded by either a Bet Din or a court of competent jurisdiction, including reasonable attorneys' fees, incurred by one side in order to obtain the other pary's performance of the terms of this agreement.

**V.** (a) In the event any of the Bet Din members are unwilling or unable to serve, then their successors shall serve in their place. If there are no successors, the parties will at the time of the arbitration choose a mutually acceptable Bet Din. If no such Bet Din can be agreed upon, the parties shall each choose one member of the Bet Din and the two members selected in this way shall choose a third member. The decision of the Bet Din shall be made in accordance with

Jewish Law (*halakhah*) and/or the general principles of arbitration and equity (*pesharah*) customarily employed by rabbinical tribunals.

(b) At any time, should there be a division of opinion among the members of the Bet Din, the decision of a majority of the members of the Bet Din shall be the decision of the Bet Din. Should any of the members of the Bet Din remain in doubt as to the proper decision, resign, withdraw, or refuse or become unable to perform duties, the remaining members shall render a decision. Their decision shall be that of the Bet Din for the purposes of this agreement.

(c) In the event of the failure of either party to appear before it upon reasonable notice, the Bet Din may issue its decision despite the defaulting party's failure to appear.

**VI.** This agreement may be signed in one or more copies, each one of which shall be considered an original.

**VII.** This agreement constitutes a fully enforceable arbitration agreement.

**VIII.** The parties acknowledge that each of them has been given the opportunity prior to signing this agreement to consult with their own rabbinic advisor and legal advisor.

In witness of all of the above, the Bride and Groom have entered into this Agreement in the City of ______________, State/Province of ______________,

| Groom | Bride |
|---|---|
| Signature ______________________ | Signature ______________________ |
| Name ______________________ | Name ______________________ |
| Address ______________________ | Address ______________________ |

Acknowledgements

State/Province of ____________ County of ____________ } ss.: ____________

On the ________ day of ____________ 20 ____, before me personally came ____________________, the groom, to me known and known to me to be the individual described in, and who executed the foregoing instrument, and duly acknowledged to me that he executed the same.

______________________________

Notary Public

State/Province of ____________ County of ____________ } ss.: ____________

On the ________ day of ____________ 20 ____, before me personally came ____________________, the bride, to me known and known to me to be the individual described in, and who executed the foregoing instrument, and duly acknowledged to me that she executed the same.

______________________________

Notary Public

## ◆§ Tenaim — Agreement to Marry

*It is an age-old custom to bind the couple in the commitment to marriage, via a document called* tenaim, *which literally means condtions. This document sets out the conditions of agreement between the couple as to some details of the impending marriage.*

*The prevailing contemporary custom regarding this* tenaim *document is that, if it is arranged at all, it is done just prior to the wedding.*

*The document is filled out by the officiating Rabbi as per below. Just prior to filling in the word v'kanina (וקנינא), one of the witnesses takes a handkerchief or other item that belongs to him, and gives it to the guarantors of the agreement on both sides, usually the fathers, for them to lift, to indicate their agreement with their respective undertakings as spelled out in the tenaim. If either hatan or kallah has no father, the mother can stand in for them.*

*The witnesses, having carefully watched all this, then sign the tenaim document. The completed* tenaim *document is then read aloud. A person acceptable to both sides holds on to the tenaim document till after the marriage ceremony.*

## THE TENAIM

# מזל טוב

יַעֲלֶה וְיִצְמַח כְּגַן רָטוֹב    מָצָא אִשָּׁה מָצָא טוֹב
וְיָפֵק רָצוֹן מֵהַשֵּׁם הַטּוֹב    הָאוֹמֵר לַדֶּבֶק טוֹב

הַמַּגִּיד מֵרֵאשִׁית אַחֲרִית הוּא יִתֵּן שֵׁם טוֹב וּשְׁאֵרִית לְדִבְרֵי הַתְּנָאִים וְהַבְּרִית שֶׁנִּדְבְּרוּ וְהוּתְנוּ בֵּין הֲנֵי שְׁנֵי הַצְּדָדִים, הַיְינוּ מִצַּד הָאֶחָד הר׳ (שם אבי החתן או מי שעומד מצד החתן) __________ הָעוֹמֵד מִצַּד (בְּנוֹ) הֶחָתָן (שם החתן) __________, וּמִצַּד הַשֵּׁנִי הר׳ (שם אבי הכלה, או מי שעומד מצד הכלה) __________ הָעוֹמֵד מִצַּד (בִּתּוֹ) הַכַּלָּה הַבְּתוּלָה מָרַת __________ (שם הכלה), אֲשֶׁר כְּבָר נִתְקַיְּמוּ כָּל הַחִיּוּבִים מִצַּד הֶחָתָן לַכַּלָּה וְכֵן נִתְקַיְּמוּ כָּל הַחִיּוּבִים מִצַּד הַכַּלָּה לֶחָתָן. וְאֵין לָהֶם זֶה עַל זֶה שׁוּם טְעָנוֹת וּתְבִיעוֹת, אֲבָל נִשְׁאַר עוֹד לְהִתְקַיֵּם מַה שֶּׁהֶחָתָן הנ״ל יִשָּׂא אֶת הַכַּלָּה הנ״ל בְּחוּפָּה וְקִדּוּשִׁין כְּדָת מֹשֶׁה וְיִשְׂרָאֵל, בְּיוֹם ______ לְחוֹדֶשׁ ____ שְׁנַת ____. וְאַל יַבְרִיחוּ וְאַל יַעֲלִימוּ לֹא זֶה מִזּוֹ וְלֹא זוֹ מִזֶּה שׁוּם הַבְרָחַת מָמוֹן בָּעוֹלָם; אֶלָּא יִשְׁלְטוּ בְּנִכְסֵיהוֹן שָׁוֶה בְּשָׁוֶה וּבְשָׁלוֹם וְשַׁלְוָה כְּדֶרֶךְ בְּנֵי תוֹרָה וְיִרְאֵי הַשֵּׁם יִתְבָּרַךְ. כָּל זֶה נַעֲשָׂה בְּדֵעָה שְׁלֵמָה וּמְיוּשֶּׁבֶת. (וְקָנִינָא — see instructions above) מִן שְׁנֵי הַצְּדָדִים עַל כָּל מַה דִּכְתוּב וּמְפוֹרָשׁ לְעֵיל, בְּמָנָא דְּכָשֵׁר לְמִקְנְיָא בֵּיהּ, **וְהַכֹּל שָׁרִיר וְקַיָּם.**

נְאוּם ____________________ עֵד

נְאוּם ____________________ עֵד

After the tenaim document is read, the mothers of the bride and groom break a plate, at which time the spontaneous outburst of 'Mazal Tov' and attendant lively singing ensue.

## THE TENAIM

### *To good fortune*

*May it come up and sprout forth like a green garden.*
*One who finds a wife finds a great good,*
*and obtains favor of God Who is good,*
*Who endorses this union*

*May the One Who determines the ultimate from the outset bestow a good name and lastingness to the obligations and conditions which were agreed upon by the two parties hereto, that is, as party of the first part,* (Groom's father's name, or whoever is representing the Groom) ______________, *who represents (his son), the groom* (Groom's name) ____________ *and as party of the second part,* (Bride's father's name, or whoever is representing the Bride) ________________, *who represents (his daughter), the bride* (Bride's name) ________________, *that all the obligations of the groom toward the bride have been fulfilled, and likewise the obligations of the bride toward the groom have been fulfilled. Neither has any claims or demands on the other, but there remains yet to fulfill that the above-named groom marries the above-named bride, through hupah and betrothal, in accordance with the Law of Mosheh and Yisrael, on the ______ day of __________ in the year ___________. They shall not run away nor conceal from each other anything with regard to their possessions; rather, they should equally share authority over their possessions, in peace and tranquility, as is the way of those who are children of the Torah and who are in awe of God. All this was done with perfect understanding and due deliberation. We have effected the legal formality of binding agreement (a kinyan) from both parties on all that is written and elaborated above, by an instrument that is legally appropriate for establishing a transaction,* AND EVERYTHING IS VALID AND CONFIRMED.

*Attested to* ______________________________________ *Witness*

*Attested to* ______________________________________ *Witness*

After the tenaim document is read, the mothers of the bride and groom break a plate, at which time the spontaneous outburst of 'Mazal Tov' and attendant lively singing ensue.

## ☙ The Wedding

*The day of the wedding is a joyous yet solemn occasion. Because bride and groom are starting a fresh life together, this is a Yom Kippur-like day for them, on which they should fast until after the ceremony, if that does not pose great physical problems.*

*Bride and groom do not fast on Isru Hag, Rosh Hodesh (except Rosh Hodesh Nisan, if they usually fast that day), Hanukah, Purim, Shushan Purim, Purim Katan, Shushan Purim Katan, 15th of Av, and Tu b'Shevat. Fasting can more easily be waived on other days when tahanun is not recited, in case of weakness.*

*Even when allowed to eat, bride and groom should not overdo it, and should avoid intoxicants. Their focus should be on the transcending importance of their coming together, expressed in meditation and special prayer.*

*Prior to the wedding, the officiating Rabbi, called the Mesader Kiddushin, prepares the ketubah document which will be given to the bride during the ceremony.*

*Before the signing of the ketubah, one of the witnesses gives the groom his own handkerchief, or other item. The groom picks it up and affirms his agreement with all his undertakings in the ketubah. The bottom part of the ketubah, starting from v'kanina, is then completed, and the ketubah is signed by the designated witnesses.*

# ◈ THE KETUBAH ◈

See pages 84-85 for charts corresponding to the numbers.

___[1]___ בְּשַׁבָּת ___[2]___ לְחֹדֶשׁ ___[3]___ שְׁנַת חֲמֵשֶׁת אֲלָפִים
___[4]___ מֵאוֹת ___[5]___ לְמִנְיָן שֶׁאָנוּ מוֹנִין כָּאן ___(שם המקום)___
אֵיךְ הֶחָתָן ___(שם החתן)___ בֶּן ___(שם אביו; אם מבחינה הלכתית אין להחתן אב,
קוראים לו על שם אמו)___ לְמִשְׁפַּחַת ___(פלוני)___ אָמַר לַהֲדָא ___[6]___
___(שם הכלה)___ בַּת ___(שם אביה; אם מבחינה הלכתית אין להכלה אב, קוראים לה על
שם אמה)___ לְמִשְׁפַּחַת ___(פלוני)___ הֲוִי לִי לְאִנְתּוּ כְּדַת משֶׁה וְיִשְׂרָאֵל וַאֲנָא
אֶפְלַח וְאוֹקִיר וְאֵיזוּן וַאֲפַרְנֵס יָתִיכִי לִיכִי כְּהִלְכוֹת גוּבְרִין יְהוּדָאִין דְּפָלְחִין
וּמוֹקְרִין וְזָנִין וּמְפַרְנְסִין לִנְשֵׁיהוֹן בְּקוּשְׁטָא וְיָהִיבְנָא לִיכִי מֹהַר ___[7]___ כֶּסֶף
זוּזֵי ___[8]___ דְּחָזֵי לִיכִי ___[9]___ וּמְזוֹנַיְכִי וּכְסוּתַיְכִי וְסִיפּוּקַיְכִי וּמֵיעַל
לְוָתַיְכִי כְּאוֹרַח כָּל אַרְעָא וּצְבִיאַת מָרַת ___(שם הכלה)___ ___ ___[6]___
דָא וַהֲוַת לֵיהּ לְאִנְתּוּ וְדֵן נְדוּנְיָא דְהַנְעֲלַת לֵיהּ מִבֵּי ___[10]___ בֵּין בְּכֶסֶף
בֵּין בְּזָהָב בֵּין בְּתַכְשִׁיטִין בְּמָאנֵי דִלְבוּשָׁא בְּשִׁימוּשֵׁי דִירָה וּבְשִׁימוּשָׁא דְעַרְסָא
הַכֹּל קִבֵּל עָלָיו ___(שם החתן)___ חֲתַן דְּנָן ___[11]___ זְקוּקִים כֶּסֶף צָרוּף
וּצְבִי ___(שם החתן)___ חֲתַן דְּנָן וְהוֹסִיף לָהּ מִן דִּילֵיהּ עוֹד ___[12]___ זְקוּקִים
כֶּסֶף צָרוּף אֲחֵרִים כְּנֶגְדָּן סַךְ הַכֹּל ___[13]___ זְקוּקִים כֶּסֶף צָרוּף וְכָךְ אָמַר
___(שם החתן)___ חֲתַן דְּנָן אַחֲרָיוּת שְׁטַר כְּתוּבְּתָא דָא נְדוּנְיָא דֵן וְתוֹסֶפְתָּא
דָא קַבְּלִית עָלַי וְעַל יָרְתַי בָּתְרַאי לְהִתְפָּרַע מִכָּל שְׁפַר אֲרַג נִכְסִין וְקִנְיָנִין דְּאִית לִי
תְּחוֹת כָּל שְׁמַיָּא דִּקְנָאִי וּדְעָתִיד אֲנָא לְמִקְנָא נִכְסִין דְּאִית לְהוֹן אַחֲרָיוּת וּדְלֵית
לְהוֹן אַחֲרָיוּת כֻּלְּהוֹן יְהוֹן אַחֲרָאִין וְעַרְבָאִין לִפְרוֹעַ מִנְהוֹן שְׁטַר כְּתוּבְּתָא דָא
נְדוּנְיָא דֵן וְתוֹסֶפְתָּא דָא מִנַּאי וַאֲפִילּוּ מִן גְּלִימָא דְּעַל כַּתְפַאי בְּחַיֵּי וּבָתַר חַיֵּי מִן
יוֹמָא דְנָן וּלְעָלַם וְאַחְרָיוּת שְׁטַר כְּתוּבְּתָא דָא נְדוּנְיָא דֵן וְתוֹסֶפְתָּא דָא קִבֵּל עָלָיו
___(שם החתן)___ חֲתַן דְּנָן כְּחוֹמֶר כָּל שְׁטָרֵי כְתוּבּוֹת וְתוֹסֶפְתּוֹת דְּנָהֲגִין בִּבְנוֹת
יִשְׂרָאֵל הָעֲשׂוּיִין כְּתִקּוּן חֲכָמֵינוּ זִכְרוֹנָם לִבְרָכָה דְּלָא כְּאַסְמַכְתָּא וּדְלָא כְּטוֹפְסֵי
דִשְׁטָרֵי ___[14]___ מִן ___(שם החתן)___ בֶּן ___(שם אביו; אם מבחינה הלכתית אין
להחתן אב, קוראים לו על שם אמו)___ לְמִשְׁפַּחַת ___(פלוני)___ חֲתַן דְּנָן
לְמָרַת ___(שם הכלה)___ בַּת ___(שם אביה; אם מבחינה הלכתית אין להכלה אב,
קוראים לה על שם אמה)___ לְמִשְׁפַּחַת ___(פלוני)___ ___ ___[6]___ דָא עַל
כָּל מַה דִּכְתוּב וּמְפוֹרָשׁ לְעֵיל בְּמָנָא דְּכָשֵׁר לְמִקְנְיָא בֵיהּ **וְהַכֹּל שָׁרִיר וְקַיָּם.**
נְאוּם ____________________ עֵד
נְאוּם ____________________ עֵד

## THE KETUBAH

*On the* ___[1]___ *day of the week, the* ___[2]___ *day of the month* ___[3]___, *in the year five thousand* ___[4]___ *hundred and* ___[5]___ *since the creation of the world, according to the reckoning which we are accustomed to employ here in the city of* ______ (city, state/province and country), *how* ______ *son of* ______ (father's name; if hatan has no father according to halakhah, mother's name is inserted) *of the family* _____ *said to* __[6]__, *daughter of* _____ (father's name; if kallah has no father according to halakhah, mother's name is inserted) *of the family* ________: *"Be my wife according to the law of Moses and Israel. I will cherish, honor, support and maintain you in accordance with the custom of Jewish husbands who honestly cherish, honor, support and maintain their wives. I herewith set aside for you the portion of* __[7]__ __[8]__, *silver zuzim, which accrues to you according to* ____[9]____ *law, together with your food, clothing and necessities, and undertake to live with you as husband and wife according to universal custom." And* _______, __[6]__ *consented and became his wife. Her belongings that she brought unto him (from her* __[10]__ *house), in silver, gold, valuables, wearing apparel, house furnishings, and bedclothes, all this* _______, *the said bridegroom, accepted in the sum of* ___[11]___ *silver pieces, with* ______, *the bridegroom adding from his own property the sum of* ___[12]___ *silver pieces, making in all* ___[13]___ *silver pieces. And thus said* __________ *the bridegroom: "The responsibility of this marriage contract, this wedding dowry, and this additional sum, I take upon myself and my heirs after me, so that they shall be paid from the best part of my property and possession that I have beneath the whole heaven, that which I now possess or may hereafter acquire. All my property, real and personal, even the mantle on my shoulders, shall be mortgaged to secure the payment of this marriage contract, the wedding dowry, and the addition made thereto, during my lifetime and after my lifetime, from the present day and forever."* __________, *the bridegroom, has taken upon himself the responsibility of this marriage contract, of the wedding dowry and the addition made thereto, according to the restrictive usages of all marriage contracts and the additions thereto made for the daughters of Israel, in accordance with the institution of our sages of blessed memory. It is not to be regarded as an indecisive contractual obligation or as a stereotyped form. We have effected the legal formality of binding agreement (kinyan)* ___[14]___ *between* _______, *the son of* _____, *the bridegroom, and* _____, *the daughter of* __________, *this* ___[6]___, *by an instrument that is legally appropriate for establishing a transaction, and everything is valid and confirmed.*

*Attested to* ______________________________ *(Witness)*
*Attested to* ______________________________ *(Witness)*

CHART 1

| DAYS OF THE WEEK | |
|---|---|
| SUNDAY | בְּאֶחָד |
| MONDAY | בַּשֵּׁנִי |
| TUESDAY | בַּשְּׁלִישִׁי |
| WEDNESDAY | בָּרְבִיעִי |
| THURSDAY | בַּחֲמִישִׁי |
| FRIDAY | בַּשִּׁשִּׁי |

Note: The days refer, of course, to the halakhic day of the week (i.e., Sunday night is considered as Monday).

CHART 2

| DAYS OF THE MONTH | |
|---|---|
| 1 | יוֹם אֶחָד |
| 2 | שְׁנֵי יָמִים |
| 3 | שְׁלֹשָׁה יָמִים |
| 4 | אַרְבָּעָה יָמִים |
| 5 | חֲמִשָּׁה יָמִים |
| 6 | שִׁשָּׁה יָמִים |
| 7 | שִׁבְעָה יָמִים |
| 8 | שְׁמֹנָה יָמִים |
| 9 | תִּשְׁעָה יָמִים |
| 10 | עֲשָׂרָה יָמִים |
| 11 | אַחַד עָשָׂר יוֹם |
| 12 | שְׁנֵים עָשָׂר יוֹם |
| 13 | שְׁלֹשָׁה עָשָׂר יוֹם |
| 14 | אַרְבָּעָה עָשָׂר יוֹם |
| 15 | חֲמִשָּׁה עָשָׂר יוֹם |
| 16 | שִׁשָּׁה עָשָׂר יוֹם |
| 17 | שִׁבְעָה עָשָׂר יוֹם |
| 18 | שְׁמֹנָה עָשָׂר יוֹם |
| 19 | תִּשְׁעָה עָשָׂר יוֹם |
| 20 | עֶשְׂרִים יוֹם |
| 21 | אֶחָד וְעֶשְׂרִים יוֹם |
| 22 | שְׁנַיִם וְעֶשְׂרִים יוֹם |
| 23 | שְׁלֹשָׁה וְעֶשְׂרִים יוֹם |
| 24 | אַרְבָּעָה וְעֶשְׂרִים יוֹם |
| 25 | חֲמִשָּׁה וְעֶשְׂרִים יוֹם |
| 26 | שִׁשָּׁה וְעֶשְׂרִים יוֹם |
| 27 | שִׁבְעָה וְעֶשְׂרִים יוֹם |
| 28 | שְׁמֹנָה וְעֶשְׂרִים יוֹם |
| 29 | תִּשְׁעָה וְעֶשְׂרִים יוֹם |
| 30 | יוֹם שְׁלֹשִׁים לְחֹדֶשׁ___*<br>שֶׁהוּא רֹאשׁ חֹדֶשׁ___* |

* In such a circumstance, these words would comprise #2 and #3 of the Ketubah.

CHART 3

| NAMES OF THE MONTHS |
|---|
| נִיסָן |
| אִיָּר |
| סִיוָן |
| תַּמּוּז |
| אָב |
| אֱלוּל |
| תִּשְׁרֵי |
| מַרְחֶשְׁוָן |
| כִּסְלֵו |
| טֵבֵת |
| שְׁבָט |
| אֲדָר |
| אֲדָר הָרִאשׁוֹן |
| אֲדָר הַשֵּׁנִי |

CHART 4

| CENTURIES |
|---|
| וּמֵאָה |
| וּמָאתַיִם |
| וּשְׁלֹשׁ מֵאוֹת |
| וְאַרְבַּע מֵאוֹת |
| וַחֲמֵשׁ מֵאוֹת |
| וְשֵׁשׁ מֵאוֹת |
| וּשְׁבַע מֵאוֹת |
| וּשְׁמֹנֶה מֵאוֹת |
| וּתְשַׁע מֵאוֹת |

CHART 6

| לבתולה | לאלמנה | לגרושה | לגיורת |
|---|---|---|---|
| בְּתוּלְתָּא | אַרְמַלְתָּא | מְתָרַכְתָּא | גִּיּוֹרְתָּא |

CHART 7

| לבתולה | לאלמנה | לגרושה | לגיורת |
|---|---|---|---|
| בְּתוּלַיְכִי | אַרְמְלוּתַיְכִי | מְתָרְכוּתַיְכִי | גִּיּוֹרוּתַיְכִי |

CHART 8

| לבתולה | לאלמנה | לגרושה | לגיורת |
|---|---|---|---|
| מָאתָן | מְאָה | מְאָה | מְאָה |

CHART 9

| לבתולה | לאלמנה | לגרושה | לגיורת |
|---|---|---|---|
| מִדְּאוֹרַיְיתָא | מִדְּרַבָּנָן | מִדְּרַבָּנָן | מִדְּרַבָּנָן |

CHART 10

לבתולה שיש לה אב – אֲבוּהָ
ליתומה, לאלמנה, ולגרושה – נָשָׁא
לגיורת כותבים – ,,דְהַנְעַלַּת לֵיהּ בֵּין . . .״

CHART 11

| לבתולה | לאלמנה | לגרושה | לגיורת |
|---|---|---|---|
| בְּמְאָה | בַּחֲמִשִּׁים | בַּחֲמִשִּׁים | בַּחֲמִשִּׁים |

CHART 12

| לבתולה | לאלמנה | לגרושה | לגיורת |
|---|---|---|---|
| מְאָה | חֲמִשִּׁים | חֲמִשִּׁים | חֲמִשִּׁים |

CHART 13

| לבתולה | לאלמנה | לגרושה | לגיורת |
|---|---|---|---|
| מָאתַיִם | מְאָה | מְאָה | מְאָה |

CHART 14

וְקָנִינָא is filled in – see instructions on p. 81.

CHART 5

| YEARS | |
|---|---|
| וְאַחַת | וּתְשַׁע עֶשְׂרֵה |
| וּשְׁתַּיִם | וְעֶשְׂרִים |
| וְשָׁלֹשׁ | וְעֶשְׂרִים וְאַחַת |
| וְאַרְבַּע | וְעֶשְׂרִים וּשְׁתַּיִם |
| וְחָמֵשׁ | וְעֶשְׂרִים וְשָׁלֹשׁ |
| וְשֵׁשׁ | וְעֶשְׂרִים וְאַרְבַּע |
| וְשֶׁבַע | וְעֶשְׂרִים וְחָמֵשׁ |
| וּשְׁמֹנֶה | וְעֶשְׂרִים וְשֵׁשׁ |
| וְתֵשַׁע | וְעֶשְׂרִים וְשֶׁבַע |
| וְעֶשֶׂר | וְעֶשְׂרִים וּשְׁמֹנֶה |
| וְאַחַת עֶשְׂרֵה | וְעֶשְׂרִים וְתֵשַׁע |
| וּשְׁתֵּים עֶשְׂרֵה | וּשְׁלֹשִׁים |
| וּשְׁלֹשׁ עֶשְׂרֵה | וְאַרְבָּעִים |
| וְאַרְבַּע עֶשְׂרֵה | וַחֲמִשִּׁים |
| וַחֲמֵשׁ עֶשְׂרֵה | וְשִׁשִּׁים |
| וְשֵׁשׁ עֶשְׂרֵה | וְשִׁבְעִים |
| וּשְׁבַע עֶשְׂרֵה | וּשְׁמֹנִים |
| וּשְׁמֹנֶה עֶשְׂרֵה | וְתִשְׁעִים |

After the signing, the groom and his entourage repair to the bride's chambers, where the groom covers his bride with her veil, amidst joy and dancing.
The Rabbi and the parents then bless the bride, thusly:

אֲחוֹתֵנוּ אַתְּ הֲיִי לְאַלְפֵי רְבָבָה.

יְשִׂמֵךְ אֱלֹהִים כְּשָׂרָה רִבְקָה רָחֵל וְלֵאָה.

יְבָרֶכְךְ יהוה וְיִשְׁמְרֶךְ.

יָאֵר יהוה פָּנָיו אֵלֶיךְ וִיחֻנֶּךְ.

יִשָּׂא יהוה פָּנָיו אֵלֶיךְ וְיָשֵׂם לְךְ שָׁלוֹם.

Just before the ceremony, some carry out the custom of placing ashes on the head of the groom, where tefillin would normally be placed. This is a reminder of the destruction of the Bet HaMikdash.

After the signing, the groom and his entourage repair to the bride's chambers, where the groom covers his bride with her veil, amidst joy and dancing.
The Rabbi and the parents then bless the bride, thusly:

*Our sister, may you grow into thousands of myriads.*

*May God make you as Sarah, Rivkah, Rahel and Leah.*

*May the Lord bless you and safeguard you.*

*May the Lord shine the Godly countenance upon you and be gracious to you.*

*May the Lord bestow favor upon you and grant you tranquility.*

Just before the ceremony, some carry out the custom of placing ashes on the head of the groom, where tefillin would normally be placed. This is a reminder of the destruction of the Bet HaMikdash.

## ☙ The Wedding Ceremony

*The ceremony uniting groom and bride is composed of two parts — erusin, or betrothal, and nisuin, or marriage. In the first part, the bride is consecrated to her beloved, for the purpose of soon uniting together. In the second part, the actual uniting is effected, through the seven blessings under the hupah, and the subsequent yihud (domicile) of the couple right after the ceremony.*

# THE WEDDING CEREMONY

## ERUSIN – ארוסין

The *hatan,* wearing a kittel symbolic of his personal Yom Kippur, is escorted to the hupah by his parents, who may enter with lit candles.
When the groom reaches the hupah, the hazzan sings:

**בָּרוּךְ הַבָּא.**

מִי אַדִּיר עַל הַכֹּל, מִי בָּרוּךְ עַל הַכֹּל, מִי גָּדוֹל עַל הַכֹּל, מִי דָּגוּל עַל הַכֹּל, הוּא יְבָרֵךְ אֶת הֶחָתָן וְאֶת הַכַּלָּה.

The bride approaches the hupah escorted by her parents, who also may hold lit candles. The bride circles the groom either three times or seven times, during which time the hazzan sings:

**בְּרוּכָה הַבָּאָה.**

מִי בָּן שִׂיחַ שׁוֹשַׁן חוֹחִים, אַהֲבַת כַּלָּה מְשׂוֹשׂ דּוֹדִים. הוּא יְבָרֵךְ אֶת הֶחָתָן וְאֶת הַכַּלָּה.

The bride and groom both should preferably face in the direction of where the Bet HaMikdash once stood, with the kallah on her hatan's right. It is appropriate for the officiating Rabbi to share some fitting remarks with the bride and groom. For all berakhot recited under the hupah, those reciting should intend to fulfil the obligation of the hatan and kallah to hear the berakhot. The hatan and kallah should listen attentively with the intent of thereby discharging their obligation.

The *Mesader Kiddushin* holds a full cup of wine and recites:

**בָּרוּךְ** אַתָּה יהוה אֱלֹהֵינוּ מֶלֶךְ הָעוֹלָם, בּוֹרֵא פְּרִי הַגָּפֶן.
(All– אָמֵן)

**בָּרוּךְ** אַתָּה יהוה אֱלֹהֵינוּ מֶלֶךְ הָעוֹלָם, אֲשֶׁר קִדְּשָׁנוּ בְּמִצְוֹתָיו, וְצִוָּנוּ עַל הָעֲרָיוֹת, וְאָסַר לָנוּ אֶת הָאֲרוּסוֹת, וְהִתִּיר לָנוּ אֶת הַנְּשׂוּאוֹת לָנוּ עַל יְדֵי חֻפָּה וְקִדּוּשִׁין. בָּרוּךְ אַתָּה יהוה, מְקַדֵּשׁ עַמּוֹ יִשְׂרָאֵל עַל יְדֵי חֻפָּה וְקִדּוּשִׁין.
(All– אָמֵן)

Groom and bride each drink some wine from the cup.

# THE WEDDING CEREMONY

## ERUSIN – BETROTHAL

The *hatan,* wearing a kittel symbolic of his personal Yom Kippur, is escorted to the hupah by his parents, who may enter with lit candles.
When the groom reaches the hupah, the hazzan sings:

### *Blessed is he who has come!*

*May the One Who is powerful above all, the One Who is blessed above all, the One Who is great above all, the One Who is supreme above all, bless the groom and bride.*

The bride approaches the hupah escorted by her parents, who also may hold lit candles. The bride circles the groom either three times or seven times, during which time the hazzan sings:

### *Blessed is she who has come!*

*May the One Who understands the speech of the rose among the thorns, the love of a bride, the joy of the beloved ones, bless the groom and bride.*

The bride and groom both should preferably face in the direction of where the Bet HaMikdash once stood, with the kallah on her hatan's right. It is appropriate for the officiating Rabbi to share some fitting remarks with the bride and groom. For all berakhot recited under the hupah, those reciting should intend to fulfil the obligation of the hatan and kallah to hear the berakhot. The hatan and kallah should listen attentively with the intent of thereby discharging their obligation.

The *Mesader Kiddushin* holds a full cup of wine and recites:

**בָּרוּךְ** *Blessed are You, Lord our God, Ruler of the Universe, Who creates the fruit of the vine.* (All – *Amen*)

**בָּרוּךְ** *Blessed are You, Lord our God, Ruler of the Universe, Who has sanctified us with the Godly commandments, and has commanded us regarding forbidden unions; Who forbade betrothed women to us, and permitted those who are married to us through canopy and consecration. Blessed are You, Lord, Who sanctifies God's people Israel through canopy and consecration.*

(All – *Amen*)

Groom and bride each drink some wine from the cup.

The groom holds the ring in his right hand ( a lefty holds it in his left hand) ready to place it upon the bride's right index finger. (If the bride wears her ring on her left hand, the ring should be placed on her left hand [Responsa Be'er Moshe 2:2].) The officiating Rabbi instructs the groom to designate two witnesses, to the exclusion of any others. The witnesses hear the officiating Rabbi verify that the ring belongs to the groom, and they ascertain that it is of sufficient value to effect betrothal. The ring should be made of a precious metal, preferably gold or silver, with no stones in it.

The witnesses watch as the groom says to the bride:

**הֲרֵי אַתְּ מְקֻדֶּשֶׁת לִי, בְּטַבַּעַת זוֹ, כְּדַת מֹשֶׁה וְיִשְׂרָאֵל.**

The ring is then immediately placed on the bride's index finger.

## INTERLUDE

The ketubah is read at this point. It serves to separate between the two components of the ceremony, the betrothal (*erusin* or *kiddushin* ) and the marriage (*nisuin* ).
The ketubah is then presented to the bride by the groom.

## MARRIAGE — נִישׂוּאִין

A second cup of wine is filled and seven blessings are recited aloud, only in the presence of a minyan. Failing a minyan, only the first and last berakhot are recited. In such a circumstance, the hatan and kallah should make sure to gather a minyan together as soon after the wedding as possible, to have the missing berakhot recited for them. If a mistake is made in the order of the berakhot, the missed berakhah is recited upon recall, followed by the other, yet unpronounced berakhot. There is no need to repeat any berakhot because of their being out of order.

The Berakhot (p. 94) are recited at this point.

After the Berakhot the hatan and kallah drink some wine from the cup. Then, the groom smashes a glass with his foot. The breaking of the glass serves as a reminder that the joy of the wedding is a serious joy, which the couple and those in attendance should experience in sobriety. This also symbolizes that until the Bet HaMikdash is rebuilt our joy cannot be complete.

This culminates the marriage ceremony. The hatan and kallah then repair to a completely private room, ideally belonging to or rented by the hatan. Two witnesses assure their privacy, as they spend time together, and have something to eat, before joining the festivities. This time together alone is yihud (domicile), and is essential to the finalization of the wedding ceremony.

The groom holds the ring in his right hand (a lefty holds it in his left hand) ready to place it upon the bride's right index finger. (If the bride wears her ring on her left hand, the ring should be placed on her left hand [Responsa Be'er Moshe 2:2].) The officiating Rabbi instructs the groom to designate two witnesses, to the exclusion of any others. The witnesses hear the officiating Rabbi verify that the ring belongs to the groom, and they ascertain that it is of sufficient value to effect betrothal. The ring should be made of a precious metal, preferably gold or silver, with no stones in it.

The witnesses watch as the groom says to the bride:

***Behold, you are consecrated to me via this ring, according to the law of Mosheh and Yisrael.***

The ring is then immediately placed on the bride's index finger.

## INTERLUDE

The ketubah is read at this point. It serves to separate between the two components of the ceremony, the betrothal (*erusin* or *kiddushin*) and the marriage (*nisuin*).

The ketubah is then presented to the bride by the groom.

## MARRIAGE — NISUIN

A second cup of wine is filled and seven blessings are recited aloud, only in the presence of a minyan. Failing a minyan, only the first and last berakhot are recited. In such a circumstance, the hatan and kallah should make sure to gather a minyan together as soon after the wedding as possible, to have the missing berakhot recited for them. If a mistake is made in the order of the berakhot, the missed berakhah is recited upon recall, followed by the other, yet unpronounced berakhot. There is no need to repeat any berakhot because of their being out of order.

The Berakhot (translated on p. 95) are recited at this point.

After the Berakhot the hatan and kallah drink some wine from the cup. Then, the groom smashes a glass with his foot. The breaking of the glass serves as a reminder that the joy of the wedding is a serious joy, which the couple and those in attendance should experience in sobriety. This also symbolizes that until the Bet HaMikdash is rebuilt our joy cannot be complete.

This culminates the marriage ceremony. The hatan and kallah then repair to a completely private room, ideally belonging to or rented by the hatan. Two witnesses assure their privacy, as they spend time together, and have something to eat, before joining the festivities. This time together alone is yihud (domicile), and is essential to the finalization of the wedding ceremony.

The person or persons reciting these berakhot hold the wine cup, and say:

**1. בָּרוּךְ** אַתָּה יהוה אֱלֹהֵינוּ מֶלֶךְ הָעוֹלָם, בּוֹרֵא פְּרִי הַגָּפֶן. (All – אָמֵן)

**2. בָּרוּךְ** אַתָּה יהוה אֱלֹהֵינוּ מֶלֶךְ הָעוֹלָם, שֶׁהַכֹּל בָּרָא לִכְבוֹדוֹ. (All – אָמֵן)

**3. בָּרוּךְ** אַתָּה יהוה אֱלֹהֵינוּ מֶלֶךְ הָעוֹלָם, יוֹצֵר הָאָדָם. (All – אָמֵן)

**4. בָּרוּךְ** אַתָּה יהוה אֱלֹהֵינוּ מֶלֶךְ הָעוֹלָם, אֲשֶׁר יָצַר אֶת הָאָדָם בְּצַלְמוֹ, בְּצֶלֶם דְּמוּת תַּבְנִיתוֹ, וְהִתְקִין לוֹ מִמֶּנּוּ בִּנְיַן עֲדֵי עַד. בָּרוּךְ אַתָּה יהוה, יוֹצֵר הָאָדָם. (All – אָמֵן)

**5. שׂוֹשׂ** תָּשִׂישׂ וְתָגֵל הָעֲקָרָה, בְּקִבּוּץ בָּנֶיהָ לְתוֹכָהּ בְּשִׂמְחָה. בָּרוּךְ אַתָּה יהוה, מְשַׂמֵּחַ צִיּוֹן בְּבָנֶיהָ. (All – אָמֵן)

**6. שַׂמֵּחַ** תְּשַׂמַּח רֵעִים הָאֲהוּבִים, כְּשַׂמֵּחֲךָ יְצִירְךָ בְּגַן עֵדֶן מִקֶּדֶם. בָּרוּךְ אַתָּה יהוה, מְשַׂמֵּחַ חָתָן וְכַלָּה. (All – אָמֵן)

**7. בָּרוּךְ** אַתָּה יהוה אֱלֹהֵינוּ מֶלֶךְ הָעוֹלָם, אֲשֶׁר בָּרָא שָׂשׂוֹן וְשִׂמְחָה, חָתָן וְכַלָּה, גִּילָה רִנָּה, דִּיצָה וְחֶדְוָה, אַהֲבָה וְאַחֲוָה, וְשָׁלוֹם וְרֵעוּת. מְהֵרָה יהוה אֱלֹהֵינוּ יִשָּׁמַע בְּעָרֵי יְהוּדָה וּבְחֻצוֹת יְרוּשָׁלָיִם, קוֹל שָׂשׂוֹן וְקוֹל שִׂמְחָה, קוֹל חָתָן וְקוֹל כַּלָּה, קוֹל מִצְהֲלוֹת חֲתָנִים מֵחֻפָּתָם, וּנְעָרִים מִמִּשְׁתֵּה נְגִינָתָם. בָּרוּךְ אַתָּה יהוה, מְשַׂמֵּחַ חָתָן עִם הַכַּלָּה. (All – אָמֵן)

The person or persons reciting these berakhot hold the wine cup, and say:

**1.** בָּרוּךְ *Blessed are You, Lord our God, Ruler of the Universe, Who creates the fruit of the vine.* (All— *Amen*)

**2.** בָּרוּךְ *Blessed are You, Lord our God, Ruler of the Universe, that all was created for God's glory.* (All— *Amen*)

**3.** בָּרוּךְ *Blessed are You, Lord our God, Ruler of the Universe, Who fashioned the human being.* (All— *Amen*)

**4.** בָּרוּךְ *Blessed are You, Lord our God, Ruler of the Universe, Who fashioned the human being in the Godly image, in the image of God's likeness, and prepared for the human being, from itself, an eternal structure. Blessed are You, Lord, Who fashioned the human being.* (All— *Amen*)

**5.** שׂוֹשׂ *Bring intense joy and exultation to the barren one through the ingathering of her children amidst her in gladness. Blessed are You, Lord, Who gladdens Zion through her children.* (All— *Amen*)

**6.** שַׂמֵּחַ *Gladden the beloved companions as You gladdened Your creature in the Garden of Eden from aforetime. Blessed are You, Lord, Who gladdens groom and bride.* (All— *Amen*)

**7.** בָּרוּךְ *Blessed are You, Lord our God, Ruler of the Universe, Who created joy and gladness, groom and bride, mirth, glad song, pleasure, delight, love, fellowship, harmony, and companionship. Lord our God, let there soon be heard in the cities of Judah and the streets of Yerushalayim, the sound of joy and the sound of gladness, the voice of the groom and the voice of the bride, the sound of the grooms' jubilance from their canopies and of youths from their song-filled feasts. Blessed are You, Lord, Who gladdens the groom with the bride.* (All— *Amen*)

# Birkat HaMazon and Sheva Berakhot

*After the meal, a special version of Birkat HaMazon is recited, culminating with Sheva Berakhot, the same seven blessings recited under the hupah, although in a slightly different order.*

*This Birkat HaMazon text is used for any other meal in the seven days following the wedding (the wedding day counts as the first day), in which a minyan is present, with one member of that minyan being a 'new face' who did not attend the wedding or a previous Sheva Berakhot meal. The new-face requirement is not operative on Shabbat and Yom Tov.*

*In a festive post-wedding meal with no minyan present, or in the absence of a new-face when required, only the "asher bara" (Who has created) blessing is recited.*

*If a widower or divorced man marries a widow or divorced woman, the Sheva Berakhot are recited only at the first meal after the wedding.*

**שִׁיר הַמַּעֲלוֹת,** בְּשׁוּב יהוה אֶת שִׁיבַת צִיּוֹן, הָיִינוּ כְּחֹלְמִים. אָז יִמָּלֵא שְׂחוֹק פִּינוּ וּלְשׁוֹנֵנוּ רִנָּה, אָז יֹאמְרוּ בַגּוֹיִם, הִגְדִּיל יהוה לַעֲשׂוֹת עִם אֵלֶּה. הִגְדִּיל יהוה לַעֲשׂוֹת עִמָּנוּ, הָיִינוּ שְׂמֵחִים. שׁוּבָה יהוה אֶת שְׁבִיתֵנוּ, כַּאֲפִיקִים בַּנֶּגֶב. הַזֹּרְעִים בְּדִמְעָה בְּרִנָּה יִקְצֹרוּ. הָלוֹךְ יֵלֵךְ וּבָכֹה נֹשֵׂא מֶשֶׁךְ הַזָּרַע, בֹּא יָבֹא בְרִנָּה, נֹשֵׂא אֲלֻמֹּתָיו.

Some add the following:

**תְּהִלַּת** יהוה יְדַבֶּר פִּי, וִיבָרֵךְ כָּל בָּשָׂר שֵׁם קָדְשׁוֹ לְעוֹלָם וָעֶד. וַאֲנַחְנוּ נְבָרֵךְ יָהּ, מֵעַתָּה וְעַד עוֹלָם, הַלְלוּיָהּ. הוֹדוּ לַיהוה כִּי טוֹב, כִּי לְעוֹלָם חַסְדּוֹ. מִי יְמַלֵּל גְּבוּרוֹת יהוה, יַשְׁמִיעַ כָּל תְּהִלָּתוֹ.

## THE INVITATION

Two cups of wine are filled, and the one leading the Birkat HaMazon takes one and begins (words in brackets are omitted in absence of a minyan):

המזומן– רַבּוֹתַי נְבָרֵךְ.

המסובין– יְהִי שֵׁם יהוה מְבֹרָךְ מֵעַתָּה וְעַד עוֹלָם.

המזמן– יְהִי שֵׁם יהוה מְבֹרָךְ מֵעַתָּה וְעַד עוֹלָם.
דְּוַי הָסֵר וְגַם חָרוֹן, וְאָז אִלֵּם בְּשִׁיר יָרוֹן, נְחֵנוּ בְּמַעְגְּלֵי צֶדֶק, שְׁעֵה בִּרְכַּת בְּנֵי אַהֲרֹן. בִּרְשׁוּת מָרָנָן וְרַבָּנָן וְרַבּוֹתַי, נְבָרֵךְ [אֱלֹהֵינוּ] שֶׁהַשִּׂמְחָה בִמְעוֹנוֹ, וְשֶׁאָכַלְנוּ מִשֶּׁלּוֹ.

המסובין– בָּרוּךְ [אֱלֹהֵינוּ] שֶׁהַשִּׂמְחָה בִמְעוֹנוֹ, וְשֶׁאָכַלְנוּ מִשֶּׁלּוֹ, וּבְטוּבוֹ חָיִינוּ.

המזמן– בָּרוּךְ [אֱלֹהֵינוּ] שֶׁהַשִּׂמְחָה בִמְעוֹנוֹ, וְשֶׁאָכַלְנוּ מִשֶּׁלּוֹ, וּבְטוּבוֹ חָיִינוּ.
בָּרוּךְ הוּא וּבָרוּךְ שְׁמוֹ.

**שִׁיר הַמַּעֲלוֹת** *A song of ascents. When the Lord returns the captives of Zion, we will be like dreamers. Then our mouths will be filled with laughter and our tongues with song; then it will be said among the nations, 'The Lord has done great things for them.' The Lord did great things for us, we were happy. Lord, return our captives, like streams in the desert. Those who sow in tears shall reap in joy. The one who cries in carrying the bag of seed will return in joy, carrying the grain sheaves.*

Some add the following:

**תְּהִלַּת** *Let my mouth declare the praise of the Lord, so that all humanity will bless God's holy Name for all eternity. And we will bless God, and henceforth and forever sing God's praises. Give thanks to the Lord, for the Lord is good; the Lord's lovingkindness is everlasting. Who can adequately express the mighty deeds of the Lord, or make known all the Lord's praise?*

## THE INVITATION

Two cups of wine are filled, and the one leading the Birkat HaMazon takes one and begins (words in brackets are omitted in absence of a minyan):

Leader – *Distinguished Assembled, let us bless.*

Assembled – *Blessed is the Name of the Lord henceforth and forever!*

Leader – *Blessed is the Name of the Lord henceforth and forever. Banish pain and also wrath, and then the mute will exult in song. Guide us in paths of righteousness, heed the blessing of the children of Aharon. With the permission of the distinguished people present let us bless [our God] in Whose abode is this celebration, and of Whose bounty we have eaten.*

Assembled – *Blessed is [our God] in Whose abode is this celebration, of Whose bounty we have eaten and through Whose goodness we live.*

Leader – *Blessed is [our God] in Whose abode is this celebration, of Whose bounty we have eaten, and through Whose goodness we live. Blessed is God and Blessed is God's Name.*

**בָּרוּךְ** אַתָּה יהוה אֱלֹהֵינוּ מֶלֶךְ הָעוֹלָם, הַזָּן אֶת הָעוֹלָם כֻּלּוֹ, בְּטוּבוֹ, בְּחֵן בְּחֶסֶד וּבְרַחֲמִים. הוּא נֹתֵן לֶחֶם לְכָל בָּשָׂר, כִּי לְעוֹלָם חַסְדּוֹ, וּבְטוּבוֹ הַגָּדוֹל, תָּמִיד לֹא חָסַר לָנוּ, וְאַל יֶחְסַר לָנוּ מָזוֹן לְעוֹלָם וָעֶד. בַּעֲבוּר שְׁמוֹ הַגָּדוֹל, כִּי הוּא אֵל זָן וּמְפַרְנֵס לַכֹּל, וּמֵטִיב לַכֹּל, וּמֵכִין מָזוֹן לְכָל בְּרִיּוֹתָיו אֲשֶׁר בָּרָא. ❖ בָּרוּךְ אַתָּה יהוה, הַזָּן אֶת הַכֹּל. (All– אָמֵן)

**נוֹדֶה** לְּךָ יהוה אֱלֹהֵינוּ, עַל שֶׁהִנְחַלְתָּ לַאֲבוֹתֵינוּ אֶרֶץ חֶמְדָּה טוֹבָה וּרְחָבָה. וְעַל שֶׁהוֹצֵאתָנוּ יהוה אֱלֹהֵינוּ מֵאֶרֶץ מִצְרַיִם, וּפְדִיתָנוּ מִבֵּית עֲבָדִים, וְעַל בְּרִיתְךָ שֶׁחָתַמְתָּ בִּבְשָׂרֵנוּ, וְעַל תּוֹרָתְךָ שֶׁלִּמַּדְתָּנוּ, וְעַל חֻקֶּיךָ שֶׁהוֹדַעְתָּנוּ, וְעַל חַיִּים חֵן וָחֶסֶד שֶׁחוֹנַנְתָּנוּ, וְעַל אֲכִילַת מָזוֹן שָׁאַתָּה זָן וּמְפַרְנֵס אוֹתָנוּ תָּמִיד, בְּכָל יוֹם וּבְכָל עֵת וּבְכָל שָׁעָה.

בחנוכה מוסיפים:

**(וְ)עַל** הַנִּסִּים וְעַל הַפֻּרְקָן וְעַל הַגְּבוּרוֹת וְעַל הַתְּשׁוּעוֹת וְעַל הַמִּלְחָמוֹת שֶׁעָשִׂיתָ לַאֲבוֹתֵינוּ בַּיָּמִים הָהֵם בַּזְּמַן הַזֶּה.

**בִּימֵי** מַתִּתְיָהוּ בֶּן יוֹחָנָן כֹּהֵן גָּדוֹל חַשְׁמוֹנָאִי וּבָנָיו, כְּשֶׁעָמְדָה מַלְכוּת יָוָן הָרְשָׁעָה עַל עַמְּךָ יִשְׂרָאֵל, לְהַשְׁכִּיחָם תּוֹרָתֶךָ, וּלְהַעֲבִירָם מֵחֻקֵּי רְצוֹנֶךָ. וְאַתָּה בְּרַחֲמֶיךָ הָרַבִּים, עָמַדְתָּ לָהֶם בְּעֵת צָרָתָם, רַבְתָּ אֶת רִיבָם, דַּנְתָּ אֶת דִּינָם, נָקַמְתָּ אֶת נִקְמָתָם. מָסַרְתָּ גִבּוֹרִים בְּיַד חַלָּשִׁים, וְרַבִּים בְּיַד מְעַטִּים, וּטְמֵאִים בְּיַד טְהוֹרִים, וּרְשָׁעִים בְּיַד צַדִּיקִים, וְזֵדִים בְּיַד עוֹסְקֵי תוֹרָתֶךָ. וּלְךָ עָשִׂיתָ שֵׁם גָּדוֹל וְקָדוֹשׁ בְּעוֹלָמֶךָ, וּלְעַמְּךָ יִשְׂרָאֵל עָשִׂיתָ תְּשׁוּעָה גְדוֹלָה וּפֻרְקָן כְּהַיּוֹם הַזֶּה. וְאַחַר כֵּן בָּאוּ בָנֶיךָ לִדְבִיר בֵּיתֶךָ, וּפִנּוּ אֶת הֵיכָלֶךָ, וְטִהֲרוּ אֶת מִקְדָּשֶׁךָ, וְהִדְלִיקוּ נֵרוֹת בְּחַצְרוֹת קָדְשֶׁךָ, וְקָבְעוּ שְׁמוֹנַת יְמֵי חֲנֻכָּה אֵלּוּ, לְהוֹדוֹת וּלְהַלֵּל לְשִׁמְךָ הַגָּדוֹל.

**בָּרוּךְ** *Blessed are You, Lord our God, Ruler of the Universe, Who sustains the entire world in Godly goodness, with grace, lovingkindness, and compassion. God gives sustenance to all flesh, for God's lovingkindness is everlasting, and in bountiful goodness God has never failed us, and may God never fail to sustain us for all eternity. For the sake of God's great Name, for God sustains and provides for all, and does good for all and prepares provision for all the creatures that God created. Blessed are You, Lord, Who sustains all.* (All – *Amen*)

**נוֹדֶה** *We extend thanks to You, Lord our God, for having given to our ancestors the heritage of a lovely, good, and spacious land; for Your having brought us out, Lord our God, from the land of Egypt, and having redeemed us from the house of bondage; for Your covenant that You sealed in our flesh; for Your Torah which You taught to us; for Your statutes which You made known to us; for the life, grace, and loving-kindness You have graciously bestowed upon us; and for the provision of food through which You sustain and provide for us constantly, every day, every occasion, and every hour.*

On Hanukah add:

**(וְ)עַל הַנִּסִּים** *(And) we thank You for the miracles, for the redemption, for the mighty deeds and deliverances, and for the battles which You carried out for our ancestors in those days, at this season.*

**בִּימֵי מַתִּתְיָהוּ** *In the days of the Hasmonean, Matityahu son of Yohanan, the Great Kohen, and his sons, when a wicked Hellenic government rose up against Your people Israel to make them forget Your Torah and divert them from fulfilling the laws of Your will. You in Your great mercy stood by them in the time of their distress; You championed their cause, defended their rights and avenged their wrong. You delivered the strong into the hands of the weak, the many into the hands of the few, the impure into the hands of the pure, the wicked into the hands of the righteous, and the arrogant into the hands of those who occupy themselves with Your Torah. You made a great and holy Name for Yourself in Your world, and for Your people Israel You performed a great deliverance unto this day. Thereupon Your children came to the shrine of Your House, cleansed Your Temple, purified Your Sanctuary, kindled lights in Your holy Courts, and designated these eight days of Hanukah for giving thanks and praise to Your great Name.*

בפורים מוסיפים:

**(וְ)עַל** הַנִּסִּים וְעַל הַפֻּרְקָן וְעַל הַגְּבוּרוֹת וְעַל הַתְּשׁוּעוֹת וְעַל הַמִּלְחָמוֹת שֶׁעָשִׂיתָ לַאֲבוֹתֵינוּ בַּיָּמִים הָהֵם בַּזְּמַן הַזֶּה.

**בִּימֵי** מָרְדְּכַי וְאֶסְתֵּר בְּשׁוּשַׁן הַבִּירָה, כְּשֶׁעָמַד עֲלֵיהֶם הָמָן הָרָשָׁע, בִּקֵּשׁ לְהַשְׁמִיד לַהֲרֹג וּלְאַבֵּד אֶת כָּל הַיְּהוּדִים, מִנַּעַר וְעַד זָקֵן, טַף וְנָשִׁים, בְּיוֹם אֶחָד, בִּשְׁלוֹשָׁה עָשָׂר לְחֹדֶשׁ שְׁנֵים עָשָׂר, הוּא חֹדֶשׁ אֲדָר, וּשְׁלָלָם לָבוֹז. וְאַתָּה בְּרַחֲמֶיךָ הָרַבִּים הֵפַרְתָּ אֶת עֲצָתוֹ, וְקִלְקַלְתָּ אֶת מַחֲשַׁבְתּוֹ, וַהֲשֵׁבוֹתָ לּוֹ גְּמוּלוֹ בְּרֹאשׁוֹ, וְתָלוּ אוֹתוֹ וְאֶת בָּנָיו עַל הָעֵץ.

**וְעַל הַכֹּל** יהוה אֱלֹהֵינוּ אֲנַחְנוּ מוֹדִים לָךְ, וּמְבָרְכִים אוֹתָךְ, יִתְבָּרַךְ שִׁמְךָ בְּפִי כָּל חַי תָּמִיד לְעוֹלָם וָעֶד. כַּכָּתוּב, וְאָכַלְתָּ וְשָׂבָעְתָּ, וּבֵרַכְתָּ אֶת יהוה אֱלֹהֶיךָ, עַל הָאָרֶץ הַטֹּבָה אֲשֶׁר נָתַן לָךְ. ❖ בָּרוּךְ אַתָּה יהוה, עַל הָאָרֶץ וְעַל הַמָּזוֹן. (All– אָמֵן)

**רַחֵם** יהוה אֱלֹהֵינוּ עַל יִשְׂרָאֵל עַמֶּךָ, וְעַל יְרוּשָׁלַיִם עִירֶךָ, וְעַל צִיּוֹן מִשְׁכַּן כְּבוֹדֶךָ, וְעַל מַלְכוּת בֵּית דָּוִד מְשִׁיחֶךָ, וְעַל הַבַּיִת הַגָּדוֹל וְהַקָּדוֹשׁ שֶׁנִּקְרָא שִׁמְךָ עָלָיו. אֱלֹהֵינוּ אָבִינוּ רְעֵנוּ זוּנֵנוּ פַּרְנְסֵנוּ וְכַלְכְּלֵנוּ וְהַרְוִיחֵנוּ, וְהַרְוַח לָנוּ יהוה אֱלֹהֵינוּ מְהֵרָה מִכָּל צָרוֹתֵינוּ. וְנָא אַל תַּצְרִיכֵנוּ יהוה אֱלֹהֵינוּ, לֹא לִידֵי מַתְּנַת בָּשָׂר וָדָם, וְלֹא לִידֵי הַלְוָאָתָם, כִּי אִם לְיָדְךָ הַמְּלֵאָה הַפְּתוּחָה הַקְּדוֹשָׁה (נ״א הַגְּדוּשָׁה) וְהָרְחָבָה, שֶׁלֹּא נֵבוֹשׁ וְלֹא נִכָּלֵם לְעוֹלָם וָעֶד.

On Purim add:

**(וְ)עַל הַנִסִּים** *(And) we thank You for the miracles, for the redemption, for the mighty deeds and deliverances, and for the battles which You carried out for our ancestors in those days, at this season.*

**בִּימֵי מָרְדְּכַי** *In the days of Mordekhai and Esther, in Shushan the Persian capital, when the evil Haman rose up against them and sought to destroy, slay and wipe out all the Jews, young and old, infants and women, in one day, the thirteenth of the twelfth month, which is Adar, and to plunder their possessions. You in Your great mercy nullified his counsel, blunted his plan, and rebounded his designs upon his own head, and they hanged him and his sons upon the gallows.*

**וְעַל הַכֹּל** *For all this, Lord, our God, we thank You and bless You; may Your Name be blessed in the mouths of all the living, constantly, for all eternity, according to that which is written: 'You shall eat and be satisfied, and shall bless the Lord, your God, for the good land that God gave to you.' Blessed are You, Lord, for the land and for the sustenance.* (All— *Amen*)

**רַחֵם** *Please have compassion, Lord our God, on Israel Your people, on Yerushalayim Your city, on Zion the dwelling of Your glory, on the royal house of David Your anointed one, and on the great and holy House through which Your Name is called. Our God, our Parent, our Shepherd, sustain us, provide for us, support us and relieve us, by granting us, Lord our God, speedy relief from all our troubles. Please, Lord our God, do not make us dependent on gifts of flesh and blood, nor upon their loans, but on Your hand — full, open, hallowed (abundant), and generous; that we not be shamed and not disgraced for all eternity.*

בשבת מוסיפים:

**רְצֵה** וְהַחֲלִיצֵנוּ יהוה אֱלֹהֵינוּ בְּמִצְוֹתֶיךָ, וּבְמִצְוַת יוֹם הַשְּׁבִיעִי הַשַּׁבָּת הַגָּדוֹל וְהַקָּדוֹשׁ הַזֶּה. כִּי יוֹם זֶה גָּדוֹל וְקָדוֹשׁ הוּא לְפָנֶיךָ, לִשְׁבָּת בּוֹ וְלָנוּחַ בּוֹ בְּאַהֲבָה כְּמִצְוַת רְצוֹנֶךָ. וּבִרְצוֹנְךָ הָנִיחַ לָנוּ יהוה אֱלֹהֵינוּ, שֶׁלֹּא תְהֵא צָרָה וְיָגוֹן וַאֲנָחָה בְּיוֹם מְנוּחָתֵנוּ. וְהַרְאֵנוּ יהוה אֱלֹהֵינוּ בְּנֶחָמַת צִיּוֹן עִירֶךָ, וּבְבִנְיַן יְרוּשָׁלַיִם עִיר קָדְשֶׁךָ, כִּי אַתָּה הוּא בַּעַל הַיְשׁוּעוֹת וּבַעַל הַנֶּחָמוֹת.

בראש חדש ויום טוב מוסיפים:

**אֱלֹהֵינוּ** וֵאלֹהֵי אֲבוֹתֵינוּ, יַעֲלֶה, וְיָבֹא, וְיַגִּיעַ, וְיֵרָאֶה, וְיֵרָצֶה, וְיִשָּׁמַע, וְיִפָּקֵד, וְיִזָּכֵר זִכְרוֹנֵנוּ וּפִקְדוֹנֵנוּ, וְזִכְרוֹן אֲבוֹתֵינוּ, וְזִכְרוֹן מָשִׁיחַ בֶּן דָּוִד עַבְדֶּךָ, וְזִכְרוֹן יְרוּשָׁלַיִם עִיר קָדְשֶׁךָ, וְזִכְרוֹן כָּל עַמְּךָ בֵּית יִשְׂרָאֵל לְפָנֶיךָ, לִפְלֵיטָה לְטוֹבָה לְחֵן וּלְחֶסֶד וּלְרַחֲמִים, לְחַיִּים וּלְשָׁלוֹם בְּיוֹם

| לראש חדש | לפסח | לשבועות |
|---|---|---|
| רֹאשׁ הַחֹדֶשׁ | חַג הַמַּצּוֹת | חַג הַשָּׁבֻעוֹת |
| **לראש השנה** | **לסוכות** | **לשמיני עצרת/שמחת תורה** |
| הַזִּכָּרוֹן | חַג הַסֻּכּוֹת | הַשְּׁמִינִי חַג הָעֲצֶרֶת |

הַזֶּה. זָכְרֵנוּ יהוה אֱלֹהֵינוּ בּוֹ לְטוֹבָה, וּפָקְדֵנוּ בוֹ לִבְרָכָה, וְהוֹשִׁיעֵנוּ בוֹ לְחַיִּים. וּבִדְבַר יְשׁוּעָה וְרַחֲמִים, חוּס וְחָנֵּנוּ וְרַחֵם עָלֵינוּ וְהוֹשִׁיעֵנוּ, כִּי אֵלֶיךָ עֵינֵינוּ, כִּי אֵל מֶלֶךְ חַנּוּן וְרַחוּם אָתָּה.

❖ **וּבְנֵה** יְרוּשָׁלַיִם עִיר הַקֹּדֶשׁ בִּמְהֵרָה בְיָמֵינוּ. בָּרוּךְ אַתָּה יהוה, בּוֹנֵה בְרַחֲמָיו יְרוּשָׁלָיִם. אָמֵן. (All – אָמֵן)

**בָּרוּךְ** אַתָּה יהוה אֱלֹהֵינוּ מֶלֶךְ הָעוֹלָם, הָאֵל אָבִינוּ מַלְכֵּנוּ אַדִּירֵנוּ בּוֹרְאֵנוּ גּוֹאֲלֵנוּ יוֹצְרֵנוּ קְדוֹשֵׁנוּ קְדוֹשׁ יַעֲקֹב, רוֹעֵנוּ רוֹעֵה יִשְׂרָאֵל, הַמֶּלֶךְ הַטּוֹב וְהַמֵּטִיב לַכֹּל, שֶׁבְּכָל יוֹם וָיוֹם הוּא הֵטִיב, הוּא מֵטִיב, הוּא יֵיטִיב

On Shabbat, the following paragraph is added:

**רְצֵה** *May it please You, Lord our God, to invigorate us through Your commandments, and through the commandment of the seventh day, this great and holy Shabbat. For this day is great and holy before You, to rest and relax thereon, in love, according to Your commanded desire. And by Your favor, allow for us, Lord our God, that there be no distress, grief, or lament on our day of rest. Let us experience, Lord our God, the consolation of Zion Your city, and the building of Yerushalayim the city manifesting Your holiness; for You are the Master of salvations and the Master of consolations.*

On Rosh Hodesh, the festivals, or Rosh HaShanah, the following paragraph is added:

**אֱלֹהֵינוּ** *God and the God of our ancestors, may there ascend, come, reach, be noted, favored, heard, acknowledged, and remembered before You the remembrance and recollection of us, the remembrance of our ancestors, the remembrance of the anointed, son of David Your servant, the remembrance of Yerushalayim the city manifesting Your holiness, and the remembrance of Your entire people the house of Israel; for deliverance, for goodness, for grace, lovingkindness and compassion, for life and tranquility,*

for Rosh Hodesh — *on this Rosh Hodesh day.*
for Pesah – *on this festival of Matzot.*
for Shavuot – *on this festival of Shavuot.*
for Sukkot – *on this festival of Sukkot.*
for Shemini Atzeret & Simhat Torah – *on the eighth day, this festival of Atzeret.*
for Rosh HaShanah – *on this day of Remembrance.*

*Remember us on it, Lord our God, for good; recall us on it for blessing; and save us on it for life. As to the matter of salvation and compassion, have pity and be gracious to us, have compassion on us and save us, as our eyes are directed toward You; for You are a gracious, compassionate God and Ruler.*

**וּבְנֵה** *And build Yerushalayim, the holy city, speedily, in our time. Blessed are You, Lord, Who in Godly compassion builds Yerushalayim. Amen.* (All – *Amen*)

**בָּרוּךְ** *Blessed are You, Lord our God, Ruler of the Universe, the God Who is our Parent, our Ruler, our Sovereign, our Creator, our Redeemer, our Fashioner, our Holy One, the Holy One of Yaakov; our Shepherd, the Shepherd of Israel, the Ruler Who is good and does good for all, Who every day has done good, does good, and will continue to do good for us. God was bountiful to us, is bountiful to us, and will forever be bountiful*

לָנוּ. הוּא גְמָלָנוּ הוּא גוֹמְלֵנוּ הוּא יִגְמְלֵנוּ לָעַד, לְחֵן וּלְחֶסֶד וּלְרַחֲמִים וּלְרֶוַח הַצָּלָה וְהַצְלָחָה, בְּרָכָה וִישׁוּעָה נֶחָמָה פַּרְנָסָה וְכַלְכָּלָה ❖ וְרַחֲמִים וְחַיִּים וְשָׁלוֹם וְכָל טוֹב, וּמִכָּל טוּב לְעוֹלָם אַל יְחַסְּרֵנוּ. (All – אָמֵן)

**הָרַחֲמָן** הוּא יִמְלוֹךְ עָלֵינוּ לְעוֹלָם וָעֶד. הָרַחֲמָן הוּא יִתְבָּרַךְ בַּשָּׁמַיִם וּבָאָרֶץ. הָרַחֲמָן הוּא יִשְׁתַּבַּח לְדוֹר דּוֹרִים, וְיִתְפָּאַר בָּנוּ לָעַד וּלְנֵצַח נְצָחִים, וְיִתְהַדַּר בָּנוּ לָעַד וּלְעוֹלְמֵי עוֹלָמִים. הָרַחֲמָן הוּא יְפַרְנְסֵנוּ בְּכָבוֹד. הָרַחֲמָן הוּא יִשְׁבּוֹר עֻלֵּנוּ מֵעַל צַוָּארֵנוּ, וְהוּא יוֹלִיכֵנוּ קוֹמְמִיּוּת לְאַרְצֵנוּ. הָרַחֲמָן הוּא יִשְׁלַח לָנוּ בְּרָכָה מְרֻבָּה בַּבַּיִת הַזֶּה, וְעַל שֻׁלְחָן זֶה שֶׁאָכַלְנוּ עָלָיו. הָרַחֲמָן הוּא יִשְׁלַח לָנוּ אֶת אֵלִיָּהוּ הַנָּבִיא זָכוּר לַטּוֹב, וִיבַשֶּׂר לָנוּ בְּשׂוֹרוֹת טוֹבוֹת יְשׁוּעוֹת וְנֶחָמוֹת.

If the meal is held in a private home, add the following (from Shulhan Arukh, Orah Hayyim 201:1). For a female, substitute the words in parentheses:

**יְהִי רָצוֹן** שֶׁלֹּא יֵבוֹשׁ (תֵבוֹשׁ) וְלֹא יִכָּלֵם (תִכָּלֵם) בַּעַל (בַּעֲלַת) הַבַּיִת הַזֶּה, לֹא בָעוֹלָם הַזֶּה וְלֹא בָעוֹלָם הַבָּא, וְיַצְלִיחַ (וְתַצְלִיחַ) בְּכָל נְכָסָיו (נְכָסֶיהָ), וְיִהְיוּ נְכָסָיו (נְכָסֶיהָ) מוּצְלָחִים וּקְרוֹבִים לָעִיר, וְאַל יִשְׁלוֹט שָׂטָן בְּמַעֲשֵׂה יָדָיו (יָדֶיהָ) , וְאַל יִזְדַּקֵּק לְפָנָיו (לְפָנֶיהָ) שׁוּם דְּבַר חֵטְא וְהִרְהוּר עָוֹן, מֵעַתָּה וְעַד עוֹלָם.

**הָרַחֲמָן** הוּא יְבָרֵךְ אֶת הֶחָתָן וְאֶת הַכַּלָּה וְאֶת הַשּׁוֹשְׁבִינִין, וְאֶת כָּל הַמְּסוּבִּין כָּאן, אוֹתָם וְאֶת כָּל אֲשֶׁר לָהֶם, אוֹתָנוּ וְאֶת כָּל אֲשֶׁר לָנוּ, כְּמוֹ שֶׁנִּתְבָּרְכוּ אֲבוֹתֵינוּ אַבְרָהָם יִצְחָק וְיַעֲקֹב, בַּכֹּל, מִכֹּל, כֹּל. כֵּן יְבָרֵךְ אוֹתָנוּ כֻּלָּנוּ יַחַד בִּבְרָכָה שְׁלֵמָה, וְנֹאמַר אָמֵן

**בַּמָּרוֹם** יְלַמְּדוּ עֲלֵיהֶם וְעָלֵינוּ זְכוּת, שֶׁתְּהֵא לְמִשְׁמֶרֶת שָׁלוֹם. וְנִשָּׂא בְרָכָה מֵאֵת יהוה, וּצְדָקָה מֵאֱלֹהֵי יִשְׁעֵנוּ. וְנִמְצָא חֵן וְשֵׂכֶל טוֹב בְּעֵינֵי אֱלֹהִים וְאָדָם.

*to us with grace, lovingkindness, compassion, and relief, rescue and success, blessing and salvation, comfort, provision and support, compassion, life, and tranquility, and all that is good; and may we never lack of all that is good.* (All – *Amen*)

**הָרַחֲמָן** *May the Compassionate One rule over us for all eternity. May the Compassionate One be blessed in the heavens and on earth. May the Compassionate One be praised for all generations, glorified through us forever, to ultimate times, and honored through us forever, to all eternity. May the Compassionate One provide for us in dignity. May the Compassionate One break off the oppressive yoke from our necks, and lead us proudly to our land. May the Compassionate One bestow abundant blessing on this home, and on this table, upon which we have eaten. May the Compassionate One send to us the prophet Eliyahu, who is remembered for good, and may he bring us good tidings of salvations and comforts.*

If the meal is held in a private home, add the following
(from Shulhan Arukh, Orah Hayyim 201:1):

**יְהִי רָצוֹן** *May it be God's will that our host not be shamed or humiliated in this world or in the world to come; may our host be successful in all dealings; may those dealings be successful and close to the city; may no untoward impediment have power over our host's handiwork, and may no semblance of sin or iniquitous thought attach itself to our host from this time on and forever.*

**הָרַחֲמָן** *May the Compassionate One bless the hatan and the kallah and the patrons, and all those gathered here, them and all that is theirs, ourselves and all that is ours, just as our patriarchs Avraham Yitzhak and Yaakov were blessed in all, from all, and with all. So may God bless us all together, with complete blessing, and let us respond, Amen.*

**בַּמָּרוֹם** *On high may they seek out merit for them and for us, that shall be a safeguard of tranquility. Let us obtain blessing from the Lord and charitableness from the God of our salvation. And let us find grace and true understanding in the eyes of God and humankind.*

לשבת

הָרַחֲמָן הוּא יַנְחִילֵנוּ יוֹם שֶׁכֻּלּוֹ שַׁבָּת וּמְנוּחָה לְחַיֵּי הָעוֹלָמִים.

לראש חודש

הָרַחֲמָן הוּא יְחַדֵּשׁ עָלֵינוּ אֶת הַחֹדֶשׁ הַזֶּה לְטוֹבָה וְלִבְרָכָה.

ליום טוב

הָרַחֲמָן הוּא יַנְחִילֵנוּ יוֹם שֶׁכֻּלּוֹ טוֹב.

לראש השנה (יש אומרים תפילה זו עד יום הכפורים)

הָרַחֲמָן הוּא יְחַדֵּשׁ עָלֵינוּ אֶת הַשָּׁנָה הַזֹּאת לְטוֹבָה וְלִבְרָכָה.

לסוכות

הָרַחֲמָן הוּא יָקִים לָנוּ אֶת סֻכַּת דָּוִיד הַנֹּפָלֶת.

**הָרַחֲמָן** הוּא יְזַכֵּנוּ לִימוֹת הַמָּשִׁיחַ וּלְחַיֵּי הָעוֹלָם הַבָּא. [בחול– מַגְדִּל] [בשבת, יו"ט ור"ח– מִגְדּוֹל] יְשׁוּעוֹת מַלְכּוֹ וְעֹשֶׂה חֶסֶד לִמְשִׁיחוֹ לְדָוִד וּלְזַרְעוֹ עַד עוֹלָם. עֹשֶׂה שָׁלוֹם בִּמְרוֹמָיו, הוּא יַעֲשֶׂה שָׁלוֹם עָלֵינוּ וְעַל כָּל יִשְׂרָאֵל, וְאִמְרוּ אָמֵן.

**יְראוּ** אֶת יהוה קְדֹשָׁיו, כִּי אֵין מַחְסוֹר לִירֵאָיו. כְּפִירִים רָשׁוּ וְרָעֵבוּ, וְדֹרְשֵׁי יהוה לֹא יַחְסְרוּ כָל טוֹב. הוֹדוּ לַיהוה כִּי טוֹב, כִּי לְעוֹלָם חַסְדּוֹ. פּוֹתֵחַ אֶת יָדֶךָ, וּמַשְׂבִּיעַ לְכָל חַי רָצוֹן. בָּרוּךְ הַגֶּבֶר אֲשֶׁר יִבְטַח בַּיהוה, וְהָיָה יהוה מִבְטַחוֹ. נַעַר הָיִיתִי גַּם זָקַנְתִּי, וְלֹא רָאִיתִי צַדִּיק נֶעֱזָב, וְזַרְעוֹ מְבַקֶּשׁ לָחֶם. יהוה עֹז לְעַמּוֹ יִתֵּן, יהוה יְבָרֵךְ אֶת עַמּוֹ בַשָּׁלוֹם.

After Birkat HaMazon, the second cup is employed for the first six of the Sheva Berakhot. These may be recited by one person or divided among several people. Whoever recites a blessing should do so seated, and with cup in hand.

CONTINUE WITH SHEVA BERAKHOT ON FOLLOWING PAGE

On Shabbat, the following sentence is added:
*May the Compassionate One bequeath to us a day of complete rest and contentedness in eternal life.*

On Rosh Hodesh, the following sentence is added:
*May the Compassionate One renew this month for us, for good and for blessing.*

On Festival days, the following sentence is added:
*May the Compassionate One bequeath to us a day that is wholly good.*

On Rosh HaShanah, the following sentence is added (some add this until Yom Kippur):
*May the Compassionate One renew this year for us, for good and for blessing.*

On the seven days of Sukkot, the following sentence is added:
*May the Compassionate One re-establish David's fallen tabernacle for us.*

**הָרַחֲמָן** *May the Compassionate One deem us worthy of the Messianic days and the life of the world to come.* [Weekdays – *God, Who magnifies the deliverances of God's king,*] [Shabbat, Yom Tov, and Rosh Hodesh – *God, Who is a tower of deliverances to God's king,*] *and does lovingkindness for God's anointed, for David and his posterity forever. The Effector of harmony in God's heights, may God effect harmony for us and for all Israel, and let us say, Amen.*

**יִרְאוּ** *Let the Lord's holy ones be in awe of the Lord, for those who are in awe of the Lord feel no deficiency. Young lions may experience poverty and hunger, but those who seek the Lord will not lack any good. Give thanks to the Lord, for the Lord is good; the Lord's lovingkindness is everlasting. You open Your hand, and satisfy the desire of all the living. Blessed is the person who trusts in the Lord, the Lord will be that one's security. I was once young and have also grown older, but have never seen a righteous person forlorn, with the offspring begging for sustenance. The Lord will give strength to the Lord's people, the Lord will bless the Lord's people with tranquility.*

After Birkat HaMazon, the second cup is employed for the first six of the Sheva Berakhot. These may be recited by one person or divided among several people. Whoever recites a blessing should do so seated, and with cup in hand.

CONTINUE WITH SHEVA BERAKHOT ON FOLLOWING PAGE

## SHEVA BERAKHOT

**בָּרוּךְ** אַתָּה יהוה אֱלֹהֵינוּ מֶלֶךְ הָעוֹלָם, שֶׁהַכֹּל בָּרָא לִכְבוֹדוֹ. (All– אָמֵן)

**בָּרוּךְ** אַתָּה יהוה אֱלֹהֵינוּ מֶלֶךְ הָעוֹלָם, יוֹצֵר הָאָדָם. (All– אָמֵן)

**בָּרוּךְ** אַתָּה יהוה אֱלֹהֵינוּ מֶלֶךְ הָעוֹלָם, אֲשֶׁר יָצַר אֶת הָאָדָם בְּצַלְמוֹ, בְּצֶלֶם דְּמוּת תַּבְנִיתוֹ, וְהִתְקִין לוֹ מִמֶּנּוּ בִּנְיַן עֲדֵי עַד. בָּרוּךְ אַתָּה יהוה, יוֹצֵר הָאָדָם. (All– אָמֵן)

**שׂוֹשׂ** תָּשִׂישׂ וְתָגֵל הָעֲקָרָה, בְּקִבּוּץ בָּנֶיהָ לְתוֹכָהּ בְּשִׂמְחָה. בָּרוּךְ אַתָּה יהוה, מְשַׂמֵּחַ צִיּוֹן בְּבָנֶיהָ. (All– אָמֵן)

**שַׂמֵּחַ** תְּשַׂמַּח רֵעִים הָאֲהוּבִים, כְּשַׂמֵּחֲךָ יְצִירְךָ בְּגַן עֵדֶן מִקֶּדֶם. בָּרוּךְ אַתָּה יהוה, מְשַׂמֵּחַ חָתָן וְכַלָּה. (All– אָמֵן)

**בָּרוּךְ** אַתָּה יהוה אֱלֹהֵינוּ מֶלֶךְ הָעוֹלָם, אֲשֶׁר בָּרָא שָׂשׂוֹן וְשִׂמְחָה, חָתָן וְכַלָּה, גִּילָה רִנָּה, דִּיצָה וְחֶדְוָה, אַהֲבָה וְאַחֲוָה, וְשָׁלוֹם וְרֵעוּת. מְהֵרָה יהוה אֱלֹהֵינוּ יִשָּׁמַע בְּעָרֵי יְהוּדָה וּבְחֻצוֹת יְרוּשָׁלָיִם, קוֹל שָׂשׂוֹן וְקוֹל שִׂמְחָה, קוֹל חָתָן וְקוֹל כַּלָּה, קוֹל מִצְהֲלוֹת חֲתָנִים מֵחֻפָּתָם, וּנְעָרִים מִמִּשְׁתֵּה נְגִינָתָם. בָּרוּךְ אַתָּה יהוה, מְשַׂמֵּחַ חָתָן עִם הַכַּלָּה. (All– אָמֵן)

The one who led the Birkat HaMazon now takes the first cup, and says:

**בָּרוּךְ** אַתָּה יהוה אֱלֹהֵינוּ מֶלֶךְ הָעוֹלָם, בּוֹרֵא פְּרִי הַגָּפֶן. (All– אָמֵן)

The leader drinks some wine of this cup. The wine from the two cups is then mixed together; one cup is given to the groom, the other to the bride. Wine from the hatan's cup may be shared with other men, and from the kallah's cup with other women.

## SHEVA BERAKHOT

בָּרוּךְ *Blessed are You, Lord our God, Ruler of the Universe, that all was created for God's glory.* (All – *Amen*)

בָּרוּךְ *Blessed are You, Lord our God, Ruler of the Universe, Who fashioned the human being.* (All – *Amen*)

בָּרוּךְ *Blessed are You, Lord our God, Ruler of the Universe, Who fashioned the human being in the Godly image, in the image of God's likeness, and prepared for the human being, from itself, an eternal structure. Blessed are You, Lord, Who fashioned the human being.* (All – *Amen*)

שׂוֹשׂ *Bring intense joy and exultation to the barren one through the ingathering of her children amidst her in gladness. Blessed are You, Lord, Who gladdens Zion through her children.* (All – *Amen*)

שַׂמֵּחַ *Gladden the beloved companions as You gladdened Your creature in the Garden of Eden from aforetime. Blessed are You, Lord, Who gladdens groom and bride.* (All – *Amen*)

בָּרוּךְ *Blessed are You, Lord our God, Ruler of the Universe, Who created joy and gladness, groom and bride, mirth, glad song, pleasure, delight, love, fellowship, harmony and companionship. Lord our God, let there soon be heard in the cities of Judah and the streets of Yerushalayim, the sound of joy and the sound of gladness, the voice of the groom and the voice of the bride, the sound of the grooms' jubilance from their canopies and of youths from their song-filled feasts. Blessed are You, Lord, Who gladdens the groom with the bride.* (All – *Amen*)

The one who led the Birkat HaMazon now takes the first cup, and says:

בָּרוּךְ *Blessed are You, Lord our God, Ruler of the Universe, Who creates the fruit of the vine.* (All – *Amen*)

The leader drinks some wine of this cup. The wine from the two cups is then mixed together; one cup is given to the groom, the other to the bride. Wine from the hatan's cup may be shared with other men, and from the kallah's cup with other women.

The leader, having consumed more than a revi'it (3.3 fluid ounces), then recites the following concluding blessing:

**בָּרוּךְ** אַתָּה יהוה אֱלֹהֵינוּ מֶלֶךְ הָעוֹלָם, עַל הַגֶּפֶן וְעַל פְּרִי הַגֶּפֶן, וְעַל תְּנוּבַת הַשָּׂדֶה, וְעַל אֶרֶץ חֶמְדָּה טוֹבָה וּרְחָבָה, שֶׁרָצִיתָ וְהִנְחַלְתָּ לַאֲבוֹתֵינוּ, לֶאֱכוֹל מִפִּרְיָהּ וְלִשְׂבּוֹעַ מִטּוּבָהּ. רַחֵם נָא יהוה אֱלֹהֵינוּ עַל יִשְׂרָאֵל עַמֶּךָ, וְעַל יְרוּשָׁלַיִם עִירֶךָ, וְעַל צִיּוֹן מִשְׁכַּן כְּבוֹדֶךָ, וְעַל מִזְבְּחֶךָ וְעַל הֵיכָלֶךָ. וּבְנֵה יְרוּשָׁלַיִם עִיר הַקֹּדֶשׁ בִּמְהֵרָה בְיָמֵינוּ, וְהַעֲלֵנוּ לְתוֹכָהּ, וְשַׂמְּחֵנוּ בְּבִנְיָנָהּ, וְנֹאכַל מִפִּרְיָהּ, וְנִשְׂבַּע מִטּוּבָהּ, וּנְבָרֶכְךָ עָלֶיהָ בִּקְדֻשָּׁה וּבְטָהֳרָה.

בשבת – וּרְצֵה וְהַחֲלִיצֵנוּ בְּיוֹם הַשַּׁבָּת הַזֶּה.

בראש חודש – וְזָכְרֵנוּ לְטוֹבָה בְּיוֹם רֹאשׁ הַחֹדֶשׁ הַזֶּה.

בפסח – וְשַׂמְּחֵנוּ בְּיוֹם חַג הַמַּצּוֹת הַזֶּה.

בשבועות – וְשַׂמְּחֵנוּ בְּיוֹם חַג הַשָּׁבֻעוֹת הַזֶּה.

בראש השנה – וְזָכְרֵנוּ לְטוֹבָה בְּיוֹם הַזִּכָּרוֹן הַזֶּה.

בסוכות – וְשַׂמְּחֵנוּ בְּיוֹם חַג הַסֻּכּוֹת הַזֶּה.

כִּי אַתָּה יהוה טוֹב וּמֵטִיב לַכֹּל,° וְנוֹדֶה לְּךָ עַל הָאָרֶץ וְעַל פְּרִי הַגָּפֶן. בָּרוּךְ אַתָּה יהוה, עַל הָאָרֶץ וְעַל פְּרִי הַגָּפֶן.

°If the wine used is from Israel, the blessing concludes as follows:

וְנוֹדֶה לְּךָ עַל הָאָרֶץ וְעַל פְּרִי גַפְנָהּ. בָּרוּךְ אַתָּה יהוה, עַל הָאָרֶץ וְעַל פְּרִי גַפְנָהּ.

The leader, having consumed more than a revi'it (3.3 fluid ounces), then recites the following concluding blessing:

**בָּרוּךְ** *Blessed are You, Lord our God, Ruler of the Universe, for the vine and for the fruit of the vine, for the produce of the field, and for the lovely, good, and spacious land that You desired and bequeathed to our ancestors, to eat of its fruits and to be sated from its goodness. Please have compassion, Lord our God, on Israel Your people, on Yerushalayim Your city, on Zion the dwelling of Your glory, on Your altar and on Your abode. And build Yerushalayim the holy city, speedily, in our time, bring us up into it, make us happy in its being built, let us eat of its fruits and be sated from its goodness, and let us bless You upon it in holiness and purity.*

On Shabbat— *And may it please You to invigorate us on this Shabbat day.*

On Rosh Hodesh— *And remember us for good on this Rosh Hodesh day.*

On Pesah— *And gladden us on this festival of Matzot.*

On Shavuot— *And gladden us on this festival of Shavuot.*

On Rosh HaShanah— *And remember us for good on this day of Remembering,*

On Sukkot— *And gladden us on this festival of Sukkot.*

*For You, God, are good and do good for all, °and we thank You for the land and for the fruit of the vine. Blessed are You, Lord, for the land and for the fruit of the vine.*

° If the wine used is from Israel, the blessing concludes as follows:

*and we thank You for the land and for the fruit of its vine. Blessed are You, Lord, for the land and for the fruit of its vine.*

# Illness

## ◆§ Visiting the Sick

*Visiting the sick is a great mitzvah. The key element of this mitzvah is to be alert to the needs of the one who is sick. Sometimes the sick person has a greater need for sleep or rest than for conversation. There is no mitzvah in making the one being visited even more unwell by overstaying the visit or by being insensitive.*

*Additionally, the mitzvah is fulfilled only if subsequent to the visit, one prays on behalf of the one who is not well.*

## ILLNESS

Two short-form prayers on behalf of the holeh are:

**הַמָּקוֹם** יְשַׁלַּח לְךָ רְפוּאָה שְׁלֵמָה בִּמְהֵרָה עִם שְׁאָר כָּל חוֹלֵי עַמּוֹ יִשְׂרָאֵל.

**הַמָּקוֹם** יְרַחֵם עָלֶיךָ בְּתוֹךְ שְׁאָר חוֹלֵי יִשְׂרָאֵל.

To this one may add the following:

**וְהֵסִיר** יהוה מִמְּךָ כָּל חוֹלִי, וְכָל מַדְוֵי מִצְרַיִם הָרָעִים אֲשֶׁר יָדַעְתָּ לֹא יְשִׂימָם בָּךְ, וּנְתָנָם בְּכָל שֹׂנְאֶיךָ.

וַיֹּאמֶר אִם שָׁמוֹעַ תִּשְׁמַע לְקוֹל יהוה אֱלֹהֶיךָ, וְהַיָּשָׁר בְּעֵינָיו תַּעֲשֶׂה וְהַאֲזַנְתָּ לְמִצְוֹתָיו וְשָׁמַרְתָּ כָּל חֻקָּיו, כָּל הַמַּחֲלָה אֲשֶׁר שַׂמְתִּי בְמִצְרַיִם לֹא אָשִׂים עָלֶיךָ כִּי אֲנִי יהוה רֹפְאֶךָ.

בּוֹרֵא נִיב שְׂפָתָיִם, שָׁלוֹם שָׁלוֹם לָרָחוֹק וְלַקָּרוֹב, אָמַר יהוה, וּרְפָאתִיו.

לֹא תְאֻנֶּה אֵלֶיךָ רָעָה, וְנֶגַע לֹא יִקְרַב בְּאָהֳלֶךָ.
כִּי מַלְאָכָיו יְצַוֶּה לָּךְ, לִשְׁמָרְךָ בְּכָל דְּרָכֶיךָ.
רְפָאֵנוּ יהוה וְנֵרָפֵא, הוֹשִׁיעֵנוּ וְנִוָּשֵׁעָה, כִּי תְהִלָּתֵנוּ אָתָּה:
יהוה יִסְעָדֶנּוּ עַל עֶרֶשׂ דְּוָי, כָּל מִשְׁכָּבוֹ הָפַכְתָּ בְחָלְיוֹ.

# ILLNESS

Two short-form prayers on behalf of the ill person are:

**הַמָּקוֹם** *May the Omnipresent speedily send you a complete recovery together with all the other sick of God's people Israel.*

**הַמָּקוֹם** *May the Omnipresent have compassion upon you among the other sick people of Israel.*

To this one may add the following:

**וְהֵסִיר** *The Lord will remove from you all sickness, and will not bring upon you any of the dreadful diseases of Egypt which you once knew, but will inflict them upon your enemies.*

*And God said: If you will diligently listen to the Lord your God, and will do that which is upright in God's eyes, and will be attentive to God's commandments and will keep all God's laws, then all the diseases which I brought upon the Egyptians I will not bring upon you, for I am the Lord your healer.*

*The Creator of the expression of the lips — it shall be very well with the far and the near, said the Lord, and I will heal them.*

*No evil shall befall you, nor affliction come near your dwelling.*
*For God will charge God's angels, to guard you in all your ways.*
*Lord, heal us and we will be healed, save us and we will be saved, for You are our praise.*
*The Lord will sustain the person on the bed of suffering; You have transformed the bed of sickness.*

## Changing of Name

*When an individual is seriously ill, it is customary to change that person's name, in the context of praying for that person's recovery. The name change signals a new reality, a new person, and hopefully with that newness will come renewed health.*

*The added name is placed before the other names the person already has. For males, new names such as Azriel, Eliezer, Hayyim, Yerahmiel, Paltiel and Refael are suggested. For females, new names such as Havah, Hayyah, Sarah and Yokheved are fitting.*

*The change of name should ideally take place with a minyan present, and following recitation of appropriate chapters from Tehilim.*

*The added name remains as official if the ill person recovered from the illness, even somewhat, and survived for at least thirty days. Otherwise, the added name is not used in recalling that person.*

# NAME CHANGING

The text of the name changing is as follows:

לזכר:

**וְאַף** אִם נִגְזַר עָלָיו בְּבֵית דִּינְךָ הַצֶּדֶק שֶׁ (שם הישן של החולה) בֶּן (שם אמו) יָמוּת מֵחוֹלִי זֶה, הִנֵּה רַבּוֹתֵינוּ הַקְּדוֹשִׁים אָמְרוּ, שְׁלֹשָׁה דְבָרִים קוֹרְעִים גְּזַר דִּינוֹ שֶׁל אָדָם, וְאֶחָד מֵהֶם שִׁנּוּי הַשֵּׁם, שֶׁיְּשַׁנּוּ הַשֵּׁם שֶׁל הַחוֹלֶה, וְקִיַּמְנוּ דִבְרֵיהֶם וְנִשְׁתַּנָּה שְׁמוֹ כִּי אַחֵר הוּא, וְאִם עַל (שם הישן) נִגְזַר הַגְּזַר דִּין, עַל (שם החדש) לֹא נִגְזַר, לָכֵן אַחֵר הוּא וְאֵינוֹ הוּא הַנִּקְרָא בַּשֵּׁם הָרִאשׁוֹן. וּכְשֵׁם שֶׁנִּשְׁתַּנָּה שְׁמוֹ, כֵּן יִשְׁתַּנֶּה הַגְּזַר דִּין מֵעָלָיו מִדִּין לְרַחֲמִים וּמִמִּיתָה לְחַיִּים, וּמִמַּחֲלָה לִרְפוּאָה שְׁלֵמָה לְ (שם החדש) בֶּן (שם אמו). (If the name is added by opening a Sefer Torah and choosing the first Patriarchal name that is found, add the words in brackets) – [בְּשֵׁם כָּל הַשֵּׁמוֹת הַכְּתוּבִים בְּסֵפֶר תּוֹרָה זֶה, וּ]בְשֵׁם כָּל הַשֵּׁמוֹת, וּבְשֵׁם כָּל הַמַּלְאָכִים הַמְּמוּנִים עַל כָּל הָרְפוּאוֹת וְהַצָּלוֹת, תִּשְׁלַח מְהֵרָה רְפוּאָה שְׁלֵמָה לְ (שם החדש) בֶּן (שם אמו). וְתַאֲרִיךְ יָמָיו וּשְׁנוֹתָיו בַּנְּעִימִים, וִיבַלֶּה בְּטוֹב יָמָיו בְּרוֹב עוֹז וְשָׁלוֹם, מֵעַתָּה וְעַד עוֹלָם, אָמֵן סֶלָה.

לנקבה:

**וְאַף** אִם נִגְזַר עָלֶיהָ בְּבֵית דִּינְךָ הַצֶּדֶק שֶׁ (שם הישן של החולה) בַּת (שם אמה) תָּמוּת מֵחוֹלִי זֶה, הִנֵּה רַבּוֹתֵינוּ הַקְּדוֹשִׁים אָמְרוּ, שְׁלֹשָׁה דְבָרִים קוֹרְעִים גְּזַר דִּינוֹ שֶׁל אָדָם, וְאֶחָד מֵהֶם שִׁנּוּי הַשֵּׁם, שֶׁיְּשַׁנּוּ הַשֵּׁם שֶׁל הַחוֹלֶה, וְקִיַּמְנוּ דִבְרֵיהֶם וְנִשְׁתַּנָּה שְׁמָהּ כִּי אַחֶרֶת הִיא, וְאִם עַל (שם הישן) נִגְזַר הַגְּזַר דִּין, עַל (שם החדש) לֹא נִגְזַר, לָכֵן אַחֶרֶת הִיא וְאֵינָהּ הִיא הַנִּקְרֵאת בַּשֵּׁם הָרִאשׁוֹן. וּכְשֵׁם שֶׁנִּשְׁתַּנָּה שְׁמָהּ, כֵּן יִשְׁתַּנֶּה הַגְּזַר דִּין מֵעָלֶיהָ מִדִּין לְרַחֲמִים וּמִמִּיתָה לְחַיִּים, וּמִמַּחֲלָה לִרְפוּאָה שְׁלֵמָה לְ (שם החדש) בַּת (שם אמה) (If the name is added by opening a Sefer Torah and

## NAME CHANGING

The text of the name changing is as follows:

For males:

**וְאַף** *Even if it were decreed against* (name of the sick person) *son of* (name of his mother) *by Your righteous Court that he die of his present illness, behold, our holy Rabbis said that three things cancel an evil decree passed on the person, one of them being a change of the name, that they change the sick person's name. We have fulfilled their words and his name has been changed, and he is a different person. If a decree was issued against* (old name), *it was not issued against* (new name) *for it is now someone else who is not called by the original name. As his name was changed, so may the decree issued against him be changed from justice to compassion, from death to life, from illness to a complete cure for* (new name), *son of* (mother's name). (If the name is added by opening a sefer Torah and choosing the first Patriarchal name that is found, add the words in brackets)— *[In the name of the persons mentioned in the Torah, and] In the name of all the names, and in the name of the angels appointed for all healing and relief, send speedily a complete cure to* (new name) *son of* (mother's name) *and prolong his days and years in pleasantness. May he spend his days in abundant vigor and tranquility, henceforth and forever, Amen, Selah.*

For females:

**וְאַף** *Even if it were decreed against* (name of the sick person) *daughter of* (name of her mother) *by Your righteous Court that she die of her present illness, behold, our holy Rabbis said that three things cancel an evil decree passed on the person, one of them being a change of the name, that they change the sick person's name. We have fulfilled their words and her name has been changed, and she is a different person. If a decree was issued against* (old name), *it was not issued against* (new name), *for it is now someone else who is not called by the original name. As her name was changed, so may the decree issued against her be changed from justice to compassion, from death to life, from illness to a complete cure for* (new name) *daughter of* (mother's name). (If the name is added by opening a Sefer Torah and

–(choosing the first Matriarchal name that is found, add the words in brackets

[בְּשֵׁם כָּל הַשֵּׁמוֹת הַכְּתוּבִים בְּסֵפֶר תּוֹרָה זֶה, וּ]בְשֵׁם כָּל הַשֵּׁמוֹת, וּבְשֵׁם כָּל הַמַּלְאָכִים הַמְּמוּנִים עַל כָּל הָרְפוּאוֹת וְהַצָּלוֹת, תִּשְׁלַח מְהֵרָה רְפוּאָה שְׁלֵמָה לְ (שם החדש) בַּת (שם אמה) וְתַאֲרִיךְ יָמֶיהָ וּשְׁנוֹתֶיהָ בַּנְּעִימִים, וּתְבַלֶּה בְּטוֹב יָמֶיהָ בְּרוֹב עוֹז וְשָׁלוֹם מֵעַתָּה וְעַד עוֹלָם, אָמֵן סֶלָה.

Following this prayer, the "Mee Shebayrakh" prayer is recited.

לזכר:

**מִי שֶׁבֵּרַךְ** אֲבוֹתֵינוּ אַבְרָהָם יִצְחָק וְיַעֲקֹב, מֹשֶׁה וְאַהֲרֹן דָּוִד וּשְׁלֹמֹה, הוּא יְבָרֵךְ וִירַפֵּא אֶת הַחוֹלֶה (שם החדש של החולה) בֶּן (שם אמו) בַּעֲבוּר שֶׁאֲנַחְנוּ מִתְפַּלְלִים בַּעֲבוּרוֹ. בִּשְׂכַר זֶה הַקָּדוֹשׁ בָּרוּךְ הוּא יִמָּלֵא רַחֲמִים עָלָיו לְהַחֲלִימוֹ וּלְרַפֹּאתוֹ וּלְהַחֲזִיקוֹ וּלְהַחֲיוֹתוֹ וְיִשְׁלַח לוֹ מְהֵרָה רְפוּאָה שְׁלֵמָה מִן הַשָּׁמַיִם לִרְמַ״ח אֵבָרָיו וּשְׁסָ״ה גִּידָיו בְּתוֹךְ שְׁאָר חוֹלֵי יִשְׂרָאֵל רְפוּאַת הַנֶּפֶשׁ וּרְפוּאַת הַגּוּף (בשבת או יום טוב מוסיפים – שַׁבָּת/יוֹם טוֹב/ הִיא מִלִּזְעוֹק וּרְפוּאָה קְרוֹבָה לָבוֹא) הַשְׁתָּא בַּעֲגָלָא וּבִזְמַן קָרִיב, וְנֹאמַר אָמֵן.

לנקבה:

**מִי שֶׁבֵּרַךְ** אֲבוֹתֵינוּ אַבְרָהָם יִצְחָק וְיַעֲקֹב, מֹשֶׁה וְאַהֲרֹן דָּוִד וּשְׁלֹמֹה, הוּא יְבָרֵךְ וִירַפֵּא אֶת הַחוֹלָה (שם החדש של החולה) בַּת (שם אמה) בַּעֲבוּר שֶׁאֲנַחְנוּ מִתְפַּלְלִים בַּעֲבוּרָהּ. בִּשְׂכַר זֶה הַקָּדוֹשׁ בָּרוּךְ הוּא יִמָּלֵא רַחֲמִים עָלֶיהָ לְהַחֲלִימָהּ וּלְרַפֹּאתָהּ וּלְהַחֲזִיקָהּ וּלְהַחֲיוֹתָהּ וְיִשְׁלַח לָהּ מְהֵרָה רְפוּאָה שְׁלֵמָה מִן הַשָּׁמַיִם לְכָל אֵבָרֶיהָ וּלְכָל גִּידֶיהָ בְּתוֹךְ שְׁאָר חוֹלֵי יִשְׂרָאֵל רְפוּאַת הַנֶּפֶשׁ וּרְפוּאַת הַגּוּף (בשבת או יום טוב מוסיפים – שַׁבָּת/יוֹם טוֹב/ הִיא מִלִּזְעוֹק וּרְפוּאָה קְרוֹבָה לָבוֹא) הַשְׁתָּא בַּעֲגָלָא וּבִזְמַן קָרִיב, וְנֹאמַר אָמֵן.

choosing the first Matriarchal name that is found, add the words in brackets)— *[In the name of the persons mentioned in the Torah, and] In the name of all the names, and in the name of the angels appointed for all healing and relief, send speedily a complete cure to* (new name) *daughter of* (mother's name), *and prolong her days and years in pleasantness. May she spend her days in abundant vigor and tranquility, henceforth and forever, Amen, Selah.*

Following this prayer, the "Mee Shebayrakh" prayer is recited.

For males:

**מִי שֶׁבֵּרַךְ** *May God Who has blessed our Patriarchs Avraham Yitzhak and Yaakov, Mosheh, Aharon, David and Shelomoh, bless and heal* (sick person's new name) *son of* (mother's name), *on whose behalf we are praying. In merit of this may the Holy One, Blessed is God, be filled with compassion for him, to restore his health, to heal him, to strengthen him, and to revitalize him. May God send him a complete recovery from heaven for all his 248 organs and 365 veins, among the other sick people in Israel, a recovery of the spirit and a recovery of the body (*on Shabbat or Yom Tov add – *because it is Shabbat/Yom Tov we cannot cry out, yet may the recovery be near) now, speedily and in due time, and let us respond, Amen.*

For a female:

**מִי שֶׁבֵּרַךְ** *May God Who has blessed our patriarchs Avraham Yitzhak and Yaakov, Mosheh, Aharon, David and Shelomoh, and our Matriarchs Sarah, Rivkah, Rahel and Leah, bless and heal* (sick person's new name) *daughter of* (mother's name), *on whose behalf we are praying. In merit of this may the Holy One, Blessed is God, be filled with compassion for her, to restore her health, to heal her, to strengthen her, and to revitalize her. May God send her a complete recovery from heaven for all her organs and veins, among the other sick people in Israel, a recovery of the spirit and a recovery of the body* (on Shabbat or Yom Tov add – *because it is Shabbat/Yom Tov we cannot cry out, yet may the recovery be near) now, speedily and in due time, and let us respond, Amen.*

# The Ultimate Passage

## ⸎ The Dying Person

*It is important to meaningfully confess by reciting viduy (confession) prior to passing from this world. It is a way to make amends, to put one's affairs in order prior to death.*

*This expression sharpens the focus on matters of critical importance at this most sensitive time in one's life.*

*Putting one's house in order includes paying back one's obligations and asking pardon from those against whom one has sinned.*

*Preparing one who is close to death for viduy is obviously a delicate matter that must be approached with exquisite care. Rabbis are uniquely positioned to offer this spiritual guidance at such a critical time.*

*If the person is unable to speak, viduy should be recited on their behalf.*

*Recitation of viduy does not mean that hope is abandoned. Viduy combines the request for forgiveness with hope for the future — either in this world or in Olam Haba. Many have confessed and lived; many who never confessed died. There is no cause-and-effect.*

*It is also customary that the dying person gives charity prior to reciting viduy. 26, 91, or 112 coins, all numbers symbolizing various combinations of the numerical equivalent of God's Name, are given.*

*The priority at this time is the well-being of the sick person. If saying much will further weaken the sick person, this is reason to avoid saying much. It is better to say less, with proper focus, than just to mouth words.*

If one is unable to recite the entire viduy, then this abbreviated phrase should be said. If even that is not possible, this phrase should be contemplated in one's thoughts.

**אִם** חַס וְשָׁלוֹם אָמוּת, תְּהֵא מִיתָתִי כַּפָּרָה עַל כָּל עֲוֹנוֹתָי.

A lengthier version is as follows:

**מוֹדֶה** אֲנִי לְפָנֶיךָ, יהוה אֱלֹהַי וֵאלֹהֵי אֲבוֹתַי, שֶׁרְפוּאָתִי וּמִיתָתִי בְּיָדֶךָ, עַל כָּל הַחַיִּים וְצָרְכֵי הַחַיִּים שֶׁנָּתַתָּ לִי. יְהִי רָצוֹן מִלְּפָנֶיךָ שֶׁתִּרְפָּאֵנִי רְפוּאָה שְׁלֵמָה; וְאִם חַס וְשָׁלוֹם אָמוּת תְּהֵא מִיתָתִי כַּפָּרָה עַל כָּל הַחֲטָאִים וְהָעֲוֹנוֹת וְהַפְּשָׁעִים שֶׁחָטָאתִי וְשֶׁעָוִיתִי וְשֶׁפָּשַׁעְתִּי לְפָנֶיךָ. וְתֵן חֶלְקִי בְּגַן עֵדֶן, וְזַכֵּנִי לָעוֹלָם הַבָּא הַצָּפוּן לַצַּדִּיקִים, אֵל נָא רְפָא נָא לִי.

אֲנִי מַאֲמִין בֶּאֱמוּנָה שְׁלֵמָה שֶׁאֱלֹהִים אֱמֶת וּשְׁמוֹ אֱמֶת, וּבִשְׁלֹשָׁה עָשָׂר הָעִקָּרִים. וְהִנְנִי מוֹחֵל לְכָל אָדָם וּמְבַקֵּשׁ שֶׁכּוּלָּם יִמְחֲלוּ לִי.

It is absolutely vital that the dying person not be left alone. In the last hours, if it is at all possible, the sick person should endeavor to recite or think the following:

**מִי** אֵל כָּמוֹךָ נֹשֵׂא עָוֹן וְעֹבֵר עַל פֶּשַׁע לִשְׁאֵרִית נַחֲלָתוֹ, לֹא הֶחֱזִיק לָעַד אַפּוֹ כִּי חָפֵץ חֶסֶד הוּא.

יָשׁוּב יְרַחֲמֵנוּ, יִכְבֹּשׁ עֲוֹנֹתֵינוּ, וְתַשְׁלִיךְ בִּמְצֻלוֹת יָם כָּל חַטֹּאתָם.

בְּיָדְךָ אַפְקִיד רוּחִי, פָּדִיתָה אוֹתִי יהוה, אֵל אֱמֶת.

יְבָרֶכְךָ יהוה וְיִשְׁמְרֶךָ. יָאֵר יהוה פָּנָיו אֵלֶיךָ וִיחֻנֶּךָּ. יִשָּׂא יהוה פָּנָיו אֵלֶיךָ וְיָשֵׂם לְךָ שָׁלוֹם.

לִישׁוּעָתְךָ קִוִּיתִי יהוה, קִוִּיתִי יהוה לִישׁוּעָתְךָ, יהוה לִישׁוּעָתְךָ קִוִּיתִי.

יהוה אֵל אֱמֶת, מֹשֶׁה אֱמֶת וְתוֹרָתוֹ אֱמֶת.

שְׁמַע יִשְׂרָאֵל, יהוה אֱלֹהֵינוּ, יהוה אֶחָד.

בָּרוּךְ שֵׁם כְּבוֹד מַלְכוּתוֹ לְעוֹלָם וָעֶד.

If one is unable to recite the entire viduy, then this abbreviated phrase should be said. If even that is not possible, this phrase should be contemplated in one's thoughts.

**אִם** *If Heaven forfend I will die, may my death be an atonement for all my sins.*

A lengthier version is as follows:

**מוֹדֶה** *I give thanks to You, Lord my God and the God of my ancestors, in Whose hands is my recovery and my death, for all the life and the necessities of life that You have provided for me. May it be Your will that You grant me a full recovery, and if Heaven forfend I will die, may my death be an atonement for all my sins, iniquities, and transgressions that I have perpetrated before You. Place my portion in the Garden of Eden and allow me to merit the world to come, that is reserved for the righteous. God, please heal me.*

*I believe with complete faith in the true Lord God, Whose Name is Truth, and in the thirteen basic principles. I forgive everyone and ask that everyone forgive me.*

It is absolutely vital that the dying person not be left alone. In the last hours, if it is at all possible, the sick person should endeavor to recite or think the following:

**מִי** *Who is like You, God, pardoning iniquity and overlooking transgression for the remnant of God's people, Who has not retained wrath forever for God desires mercifulness.*

*God will return us in compassion, God will suppress our iniquities, and will cast all their sins into the sea-depths.*

*In Your hand I entrust my spirit, You redeem me, Lord, true God.*

*May the Lord bless you and safeguard you. May the Lord shine the Godly countenance upon you and be gracious to you. May the Lord bestow favor upon you and grant you tranquility.*

*For your salvation I long, God; I long, God, for your salvation; God, for your salvation I long.*

*The Lord is the true God, Mosheh is true, as is his Torah.*

*Hear, O Israel, the Lord is our God, only the Lord.*

*Blessed is the name of God's honored Dominion forever.*

If there is time, the following three Tehillim selections should be recited in the presence of the dying person by those present. If there is not sufficient time for this, the Tehillim are skipped and those present go straight to Yigdal.

תהלים קכא

**שִׁיר לַמַּעֲלוֹת,** אֶשָּׂא עֵינַי אֶל הֶהָרִים, מֵאַיִן יָבֹא עֶזְרִי. עֶזְרִי מֵעִם יהוה, עֹשֵׂה שָׁמַיִם וָאָרֶץ. אַל יִתֵּן לַמּוֹט רַגְלֶךָ, אַל יָנוּם שֹׁמְרֶךָ. הִנֵּה לֹא יָנוּם וְלֹא יִישָׁן, שׁוֹמֵר יִשְׂרָאֵל. יהוה שֹׁמְרֶךָ, יהוה צִלְּךָ עַל יַד יְמִינֶךָ. יוֹמָם הַשֶּׁמֶשׁ לֹא יַכֶּכָּה וְיָרֵחַ בַּלָּיְלָה. יהוה יִשְׁמָרְךָ מִכָּל רָע, יִשְׁמֹר אֶת נַפְשֶׁךָ. יהוה יִשְׁמָר צֵאתְךָ וּבוֹאֶךָ, מֵעַתָּה וְעַד עוֹלָם.

תהלים קל

**שִׁיר הַמַּעֲלוֹת,** מִמַּעֲמַקִּים קְרָאתִיךָ יהוה. אֲדֹנָי שִׁמְעָה בְקוֹלִי, תִּהְיֶינָה אָזְנֶיךָ קַשֻּׁבוֹת לְקוֹל תַּחֲנוּנָי. אִם עֲוֹנוֹת תִּשְׁמָר יָהּ, אֲדֹנָי מִי יַעֲמֹד. כִּי עִמְּךָ הַסְּלִיחָה, לְמַעַן תִּוָּרֵא. קִוִּיתִי יהוה קִוְּתָה נַפְשִׁי, וְלִדְבָרוֹ הוֹחָלְתִּי. נַפְשִׁי לַאדֹנָי, מִשֹּׁמְרִים לַבֹּקֶר, שֹׁמְרִים לַבֹּקֶר. יַחֵל יִשְׂרָאֵל אֶל יהוה, כִּי עִם יהוה הַחֶסֶד, וְהַרְבֵּה עִמּוֹ פְדוּת. וְהוּא יִפְדֶּה אֶת יִשְׂרָאֵל, מִכֹּל עֲוֹנוֹתָיו.

תהלים צא

**יֹשֵׁב** בְּסֵתֶר עֶלְיוֹן, בְּצֵל שַׁדַּי יִתְלוֹנָן. אֹמַר לַיהוה, מַחְסִי וּמְצוּדָתִי, אֱלֹהַי אֶבְטַח בּוֹ. כִּי הוּא יַצִּילְךָ מִפַּח יָקוּשׁ, מִדֶּבֶר הַוּוֹת. בְּאֶבְרָתוֹ יָסֶךְ לָךְ, וְתַחַת כְּנָפָיו תֶּחְסֶה, צִנָּה וְסֹחֵרָה אֲמִתּוֹ. לֹא תִירָא מִפַּחַד לָיְלָה, מֵחֵץ יָעוּף יוֹמָם. מִדֶּבֶר בָּאֹפֶל יַהֲלֹךְ, מִקֶּטֶב יָשׁוּד צָהֳרָיִם. יִפֹּל מִצִּדְּךָ אֶלֶף, וּרְבָבָה מִימִינֶךָ, אֵלֶיךָ לֹא יִגָּשׁ. רַק בְּעֵינֶיךָ תַבִּיט, וְשִׁלֻּמַת רְשָׁעִים תִּרְאֶה. כִּי אַתָּה יהוה מַחְסִי, עֶלְיוֹן שַׂמְתָּ מְעוֹנֶךָ. לֹא תְאֻנֶּה אֵלֶיךָ רָעָה, וְנֶגַע לֹא יִקְרַב בְּאָהֳלֶךָ. כִּי

If there is time, the following three Tehilim selections should be recited in the presence of the dying person by those present. If there is not sufficient time for this, the Tehilim are skipped and those present go straight to Yigdal.

Psalm 121

**שִׁיר לַמַּעֲלוֹת** *A song to ascents. I lift my eyes to the mountains, from where will my help come? My help comes from the Lord, Maker of heaven and earth. God will not let your foot falter, your Guardian will not slumber. Behold, the Guardian of Israel neither slumbers nor sleeps. The Lord is your Guardian, the Lord is your protection by your right side. By day the sun will not harm you, nor the moon by night. The Lord will guard you from all evil; the Lord will guard your life. The Lord will guard your going and coming from now and forever.*

Psalm 130

**שִׁיר לַמַּעֲלוֹת** *A song of ascents. Out of the depths I call you, Lord. Lord, listen to my cry, let your ears be attentive to my supplicative plea. If You preserve the account of sins, God, Lord who can survive? Pardon resides with You, so that You are held in awe. I hope for the Lord, my soul hopes, I await God's word. I yearn more for the Lord than guards for the morning, guards for the morning. Israel, wait for the Lord, for with the Lord is kindness and great redemption. And it is God Who will redeem Israel from all its iniquities.*

Psalm 91

**יֹשֵׁב** *You who dwell in the shelter of the Most High, abiding in the shadow of the Almighty. I say of the Lord, my refuge and my stronghold, my God in whom I trust, That God will deliver you from the ensnaring net, from destructive plague. With God's pinion will God shelter you, and under God's wings shall you find refuge; faith in God shall be your shield and protector. Fear not the terror of night, the arrow that flies by day, the plague that stalks in the darkness, the destruction that ravages at noon. Though a thousand may fall at your left side, and ten thousand at your right, it shall not reach you. Look but clearly, and you shall see the retribution against the wicked. Because [you said] 'You, Lord, are my trust,' you set the Most High as your dwelling. No harm shall befall you, nor disease come near your tent. For*

מַלְאָכָיו יְצַוֶּה לָּךְ, לִשְׁמָרְךָ בְּכָל דְּרָכֶיךָ. עַל כַּפַּיִם יִשָּׂאוּנְךָ, פֶּן תִּגֹּף בָּאֶבֶן רַגְלֶךָ. עַל שַׁחַל וָפֶתֶן תִּדְרֹךְ, תִּרְמֹס כְּפִיר וְתַנִּין. כִּי בִי חָשַׁק וַאֲפַלְּטֵהוּ, אֲשַׂגְּבֵהוּ כִּי יָדַע שְׁמִי. יִקְרָאֵנִי וְאֶעֱנֵהוּ, עִמּוֹ אָנֹכִי בְצָרָה, אֲחַלְּצֵהוּ וַאֲכַבְּדֵהוּ. אֹרֶךְ יָמִים אַשְׂבִּיעֵהוּ, וְאַרְאֵהוּ בִּישׁוּעָתִי. אֹרֶךְ יָמִים אַשְׂבִּיעֵהוּ, וְאַרְאֵהוּ בִּישׁוּעָתִי.

**יִגְדַּל** אֱלֹהִים חַי וְיִשְׁתַּבַּח, נִמְצָא וְאֵין עֵת אֶל מְצִיאוּתוֹ. אֶחָד וְאֵין יָחִיד כְּיִחוּדוֹ, נֶעְלָם וְגַם אֵין סוֹף לְאַחְדּוּתוֹ. אֵין לוֹ דְּמוּת הַגּוּף וְאֵינוֹ גוּף, לֹא נַעֲרוֹךְ אֵלָיו קְדֻשָּׁתוֹ. קַדְמוֹן לְכָל דָּבָר אֲשֶׁר נִבְרָא, רִאשׁוֹן וְאֵין רֵאשִׁית לְרֵאשִׁיתוֹ. הִנּוֹ אֲדוֹן עוֹלָם לְכָל נוֹצָר, יוֹרֶה גְדֻלָּתוֹ וּמַלְכוּתוֹ. שֶׁפַע נְבוּאָתוֹ נְתָנוֹ, אֶל אַנְשֵׁי סְגֻלָּתוֹ וְתִפְאַרְתּוֹ. לֹא קָם בְּיִשְׂרָאֵל כְּמֹשֶׁה עוֹד, נָבִיא וּמַבִּיט אֶת תְּמוּנָתוֹ. תּוֹרַת אֱמֶת נָתַן לְעַמּוֹ אֵל, עַל יַד נְבִיאוֹ נֶאֱמַן בֵּיתוֹ. לֹא יַחֲלִיף הָאֵל וְלֹא יָמִיר דָּתוֹ, לְעוֹלָמִים לְזוּלָתוֹ. צוֹפֶה וְיוֹדֵעַ סְתָרֵינוּ, מַבִּיט לְסוֹף דָּבָר בְּקַדְמָתוֹ. גּוֹמֵל לְאִישׁ חֶסֶד כְּמִפְעָלוֹ, נוֹתֵן לְרָשָׁע רָע כְּרִשְׁעָתוֹ. יִשְׁלַח לְקֵץ הַיָּמִין מְשִׁיחֵנוּ, לִפְדּוֹת מְחַכֵּי קֵץ יְשׁוּעָתוֹ. מֵתִים יְחַיֶּה אֵל בְּרֹב חַסְדּוֹ, בָּרוּךְ עֲדֵי עַד שֵׁם תְּהִלָּתוֹ.

**אֲדוֹן עוֹלָם** אֲשֶׁר מָלַךְ, בְּטֶרֶם כָּל יְצִיר נִבְרָא. לְעֵת נַעֲשָׂה בְחֶפְצוֹ כֹּל, אֲזַי מֶלֶךְ שְׁמוֹ נִקְרָא. וְאַחֲרֵי כִּכְלוֹת הַכֹּל, לְבַדּוֹ יִמְלוֹךְ נוֹרָא. וְהוּא הָיָה וְהוּא הֹוֶה, וְהוּא יִהְיֶה בְּתִפְאָרָה. וְהוּא אֶחָד וְאֵין שֵׁנִי, לְהַמְשִׁיל לוֹ לְהַחְבִּירָה. בְּלִי רֵאשִׁית בְּלִי תַכְלִית, וְלוֹ הָעֹז וְהַמִּשְׂרָה. וְהוּא אֵלִי וְחַי גֹּאֲלִי, וְצוּר חֶבְלִי בְּעֵת צָרָה. וְהוּא נִסִּי וּמָנוֹס לִי, מְנָת כּוֹסִי בְּיוֹם אֶקְרָא. בְּיָדוֹ אַפְקִיד רוּחִי, בְּעֵת אִישַׁן וְאָעִירָה. וְעִם רוּחִי גְּוִיָּתִי, יהוה לִי וְלֹא אִירָא.

*God will give God's angels charge concerning you, to guard you in all your ways. They shall carry you on their hands, lest you injure your foot against a stone. You shall tread on the lion and viper, you shall trample the young lion and serpent. Because he yearned for Me I will deliver him; I will be his refuge, for having known My Name. He will call upon Me and I will answer, I will be with him in distress; I will rescue him and give him honor. With length of days will I satisfy him, and reveal to him My salvation. With length of days will I satisfy him, and reveal to him My salvation.*

**יִגְדַּל** *Exalted and praised be the living God; God exists, God's existence transcends time. God is One, there is no unity like God's Oneness; God is unknowable, God's Oneness is infinite. God has no semblance of body, and is not corporeal; God's holiness is beyond estimation. God preceded all that was created; First, with nothing preceding God's firstness. God is the Master of the Universe; to every creature God shows greatness and majesty. God's abundant prophecy was granted; to God's treasured and glorified people. Never has there arisen in Israel another like Moses; a prophet, beholding God's likeness. The Torah of truth God gave to God's people; through God's prophet, the most trusted in God's abode. God will not amend or change God's Law; forever, for any other law. God gazes and knows all our secret thoughts; God foresees the end of things at their origin. God bestows kindness to the person according to the deed; and sends harm to the wicked one for evil. At the end of days God will send our Messiah, to redeem all who wait for God's final salvation. God, in great kindness, will revive the dead; Blessed is God's glorious Name forever.*

**אֲדוֹן עוֹלָם** *Master of the Universe Who reigned, before any form was created. At the time when all was made by God's will, then as Ruler was God's Name proclaimed. After all shall cease to be, the revered One alone shall still be Ruler. God was, God is, and God shall be, in glorious eternity. God is One, and there is no other, to compare to God, to be God's equal. God is without beginning, without end; power and dominion belong to God. God is my Lord, my living Redeemer, Rock for my pain in time of distress. God is my banner and my refuge, the portion of my cup on the day I call. Into God's hand I entrust my spirit, when I sleep and when I awaken. As long as my soul is with my body, the Lord is with me, I will not fear.*

**אָנָּא** בְּכֹחַ גְּדֻלַּת יְמִינְךָ תַּתִּיר צְרוּרָה. קַבֵּל רִנַּת עַמְּךָ שַׂגְּבֵנוּ טַהֲרֵנוּ נוֹרָא. נָא גִבּוֹר דּוֹרְשֵׁי יִחוּדְךָ כְּבָבַת שָׁמְרֵם. בָּרְכֵם טַהֲרֵם רַחֲמֵם צִדְקָתְךָ תָּמִיד גָּמְלֵם. חֲסִין קָדוֹשׁ בְּרוֹב טוּבְךָ נַהֵל עֲדָתֶךָ. יָחִיד גֵּאֶה לְעַמְּךָ פְּנֵה זוֹכְרֵי קְדֻשָּׁתֶךָ. שַׁוְעָתֵנוּ קַבֵּל וּשְׁמַע צַעֲקָתֵנוּ יוֹדֵעַ תַּעֲלֻמוֹת. בָּרוּךְ שֵׁם כְּבוֹד מַלְכוּתוֹ לְעוֹלָם וָעֶד.

**עַל כֵּן** נְקַוֶּה לְּךָ יהוה אֱלֹהֵינוּ לִרְאוֹת מְהֵרָה בְּתִפְאֶרֶת עֻזֶּךָ, לְהַעֲבִיר גִּלּוּלִים מִן הָאָרֶץ, וְהָאֱלִילִים כָּרוֹת יִכָּרֵתוּן, לְתַקֵּן עוֹלָם בְּמַלְכוּת שַׁדַּי. וְכָל בְּנֵי בָשָׂר יִקְרְאוּ בִשְׁמֶךָ, לְהַפְנוֹת אֵלֶיךָ כָּל רִשְׁעֵי אָרֶץ. יַכִּירוּ וְיֵדְעוּ כָּל יוֹשְׁבֵי תֵבֵל, כִּי לְךָ תִּכְרַע כָּל בֶּרֶךְ, תִּשָּׁבַע כָּל לָשׁוֹן. לְפָנֶיךָ יהוה אֱלֹהֵינוּ יִכְרְעוּ וְיִפֹּלוּ, וְלִכְבוֹד שִׁמְךָ יְקָר יִתֵּנוּ. וִיקַבְּלוּ כֻלָּם אֶת עוֹל מַלְכוּתֶךָ, וְתִמְלֹךְ עֲלֵיהֶם מְהֵרָה לְעוֹלָם וָעֶד. כִּי הַמַּלְכוּת שֶׁלְּךָ הִיא וּלְעוֹלְמֵי עַד תִּמְלוֹךְ בְּכָבוֹד, כַּכָּתוּב בְּתוֹרָתֶךָ: יהוה יִמְלֹךְ לְעֹלָם וָעֶד. וְנֶאֱמַר: וְהָיָה יהוה לְמֶלֶךְ עַל כָּל הָאָרֶץ, בַּיּוֹם הַהוּא יִהְיֶה יהוה אֶחָד וּשְׁמוֹ אֶחָד.

As the soul departs, the following is recited:

שְׁמַע יִשְׂרָאֵל, יהוה אֱלֹהֵינוּ, יהוה אֶחָד.

בָּרוּךְ שֵׁם כְּבוֹד מַלְכוּתוֹ לְעוֹלָם וָעֶד. (ג׳ פעמים)

יהוה הוּא הָאֱלֹהִים. (ז׳ פעמים)

יהוה מֶלֶךְ יהוה מָלָךְ יהוה יִמְלֹךְ לְעוֹלָם וָעֶד.

If possible, the last words recited in the presence of the dying person should be the Shema. At the moment of death, those present should say the following:

יהוה נָתַן ויהוה לָקַח. יְהִי שֵׁם יהוה מְבֹרָךְ מֵעַתָּה וְעַד עוֹלָם.

הַצּוּר תָּמִים פָּעֳלוֹ כִּי כָל דְּרָכָיו מִשְׁפָּט,<br>
אֵל אֱמוּנָה וְאֵין עָוֶל, צַדִּיק וְיָשָׁר הוּא.

**אָנָּא** *Please, by the great power of Your right hand, set the captive free. Accept Your people's prayer; strengthen us, purify us, Revered One. Almighty One, please guard as the apple of the eye those who seek You. Bless them, purify them, show them compassion; always bestow upon them through Your righteousness. Mighty, Holy One, in Your abundant goodness, guide Your people. One and Only exalted One, turn to Your people who proclaim Your holiness. Accept our plea and hear our cry, You who know secret thoughts. Blessed is the Name of God's honored dominion forever.*

**עַל כֵּן** *Therefore we hope for You, Lord our God, soon to behold Your majestic glory, to remove idols from the earth, and the false gods totally eliminated, to perfect the world through the reign of the Almighty. And all humanity will call in Your Name, to turn toward You all the earth's wicked. All the world's inhabitants will recognize and know that to You every knee must bend, every tongue must vow allegiance. Before You, Lord our God, they will bend and prostrate, and give homage to Your honored Name. They will all accept upon themselves the yoke of Your dominion, and You will reign over them speedily forever. For the dominion is Yours, and to all eternity You will reign in glory, as it is written in your Torah: The Lord shall reign forever. And it is said: The Lord shall be Ruler over all the world; on that day the Lord shall be One, and God's Name One.*

As the soul departs, the following is recited:

*Hear, O Israel, the Lord is our God, only the Lord.*

*Blessed is the Name of God's honored Dominion forever.* (3 times)

*The Lord is God.* (7 times)

*The Lord rules, the Lord has ruled, the Lord will rule forever.*

If possible, the last words recited in the presence of the dying person should be the Shema. At the moment of death, those present should say the following:

*The Lord has given, and the Lord has taken away.*
*Blessed is the Name of the Lord from now and forever.*

*The Rock, perfect is God's work, for all God's paths are just;*
*God of faith without iniquity, righteous and fair is God.*

## ☙ Dayan Ha'Emet and Rending the Garments

*The berakhah, Dayan Ha'Emet, should be recited at the moment of death, if one is present, or immediately upon hearing of the death. Common practice is to wait until the rending of the garment, and to pronounce this berakhah at that time.*

***For a child who died before thirty days, in which instance there is no mandated rending of the garment or shiv'ah, this berakhah may still be recited.***

*The rending is done in a standing position, with the tear being vertical and a little less than four inches.*

*The tear should be of a basic garment, such as a shirt or blouse. For the loss of anyone other than a parent, only one basic garment is rent, and the rent is made on the right side.*

*For parents, the tear is on the left side, to literally expose the heart. Thus, when rending for a parent, all garments aside from coats and undergarments are rent. This includes sweaters and jackets, shirts and blouses. A woman's garment is torn in a way which does not compromise the dictates of modesty.*

*Ribbons, it is obvious, should never be used to fulfill this kriyah obligation, which signifies that someone vital has been torn away.*

*The rending of the garment should be done at a time of passion, when the loss is felt most intensely. Aside from the actual moment of death, some such moments are right after the funeral, when the deceased is being escorted out to burial. Another moment of passion is right after burial.*

*The moment of passion most frequently used for rending the garment or garments is just before the funeral, when the family is gathered together, and is gently guided through this procedure by the officiating Rabbi.*

*Each mourner pronounces the berakhah prior to the rending, and does not rely on any of the other mourners pronouncing the berakhah.*

*When death occurs on Hol HaMoed and shiv'ah is delayed until the conclusion of the Yom Tov, there are varying customs regarding the rending procedure. The most common practice is to rend the garment on Hol HaMoed only for a deceased parent, and to defer any other rending till after the Yom Tov. In such instance of deferral, the berakhah Dayan Ha'Emet is recited on Hol HaMoed. If one failed to do so, then one should not recite said berakhah when rending the garment at the later date, if the funeral had already taken place on Hol HaMoed.*

*Although there are varying regulations regarding sewing the tear after shiv'ah, the garment or garments are not worn after the conclusion of shiv'ah in their torn state.*

## DAYAN HA'EMET AND RENDING THE GARMENTS

Son, daughter, brother, sister, father, mother and spouse are the seven basic relatives who observe mourning following death. If any of these relatives are present at the time of passing, they should recite the following blessing:

בָּרוּךְ אַתָּה יהוה אֱלֹהֵנוּ מֶלֶךְ הָעוֹלָם, דַּיַּן הָאֱמֶת.

*Blessed are You, Lord our God, Ruler of the Universe, Who is the true Judge.*

After that, they rend their garments.
Others present at the moment of death should simply say:

בָּרוּךְ דַּיַּן הָאֱמֶת.

*Blessed is the true Judge.*

## ☙ Funeral Service

*The funeral service is usually but not always divided into two components; the gathering at the chapel for eulogizing, and the burial at the cemetery.*

*At the chapel, the service includes Scriptural readings, a eulogy, recitation of the Memorial Prayer, and escorting the deceased to the words of Yoshev B'Seter.*

*If the entire service is at the cemetery, Yoshev B'Seter and the accompanying seven stops would be first, followed by Scriptural readings, a eulogy, the memorial prayer, interment, rending of garments (if this has not yet been done), Tziduk HaDin, a Scriptural reading, and the appropriate Kaddish.*

***Tziduk HaDin is recited for a child who lives for at least thrity days. The Memorial Prayer, and Kaddish, may be recited for a child who has lived for thirty or more days.***

*On days when Tahanun is not recited, and from noon of the day before Shabbat or Yom Tov (excluding Erev Rosh Hodesh, Erev Hanukah or Purim, and Erev Tish'ah B'Av), the regular Memorial Prayer is not recited, and a mournful eulogy not delivered. However, even then words of praise for the deceased are in order.*

*It is of particular importance to emphasize that the eulogy not be a long and involved Talmudic discourse. It must be a heartfelt lament of the great loss that is felt by family and friends, through conveying a true reflection of the deeds and virtues of the deceased.*

*The Rabbi has a sacred obligation to eulogize out of knowledge of the deceased, rather than giving a 'universal recipient' speech. Proper preparation takes time and often painstaking work, especially when due to circumstance the Rabbi did not know the deceased that well. But it means so much to the surviving family, and is often the key to how well the Rabbi helps the family through the trying times.*

# FUNERAL SERVICE

Some fitting readings at the outset of the funeral follow.

תהלים א

**אַשְׁרֵי** הָאִישׁ אֲשֶׁר לֹא הָלַךְ בַּעֲצַת רְשָׁעִים, וּבְדֶרֶךְ חַטָּאִים לֹא עָמָד, וּבְמוֹשַׁב לֵצִים לֹא יָשָׁב. כִּי אִם בְּתוֹרַת יהוה חֶפְצוֹ, וּבְתוֹרָתוֹ יֶהְגֶּה יוֹמָם וָלָיְלָה. וְהָיָה כְּעֵץ שָׁתוּל עַל פַּלְגֵי מָיִם; אֲשֶׁר פִּרְיוֹ יִתֵּן בְּעִתּוֹ, וְעָלֵהוּ לֹא יִבּוֹל, וְכֹל אֲשֶׁר יַעֲשֶׂה יַצְלִיחַ. לֹא כֵן הָרְשָׁעִים, כִּי אִם כַּמֹּץ אֲשֶׁר תִּדְּפֶנּוּ רוּחַ. עַל כֵּן לֹא יָקֻמוּ רְשָׁעִים בַּמִּשְׁפָּט, וְחַטָּאִים בַּעֲדַת צַדִּיקִים. כִּי יוֹדֵעַ יהוה דֶּרֶךְ צַדִּיקִים, וְדֶרֶךְ רְשָׁעִים תֹּאבֵד.

תהלים טו

**מִזְמוֹר** לְדָוִד, יהוה מִי יָגוּר בְּאָהֳלֶךָ, מִי יִשְׁכֹּן בְּהַר קָדְשֶׁךָ. הוֹלֵךְ תָּמִים וּפֹעֵל צֶדֶק, וְדֹבֵר אֱמֶת בִּלְבָבוֹ. לֹא רָגַל עַל לְשֹׁנוֹ, לֹא עָשָׂה לְרֵעֵהוּ רָעָה, וְחֶרְפָּה לֹא נָשָׂא עַל קְרֹבוֹ. נִבְזֶה בְּעֵינָיו נִמְאָס, וְאֶת יִרְאֵי יהוה יְכַבֵּד, נִשְׁבַּע לְהָרַע וְלֹא יָמִר. כַּסְפּוֹ לֹא נָתַן בְּנֶשֶׁךְ, וְשֹׁחַד עַל נָקִי לֹא לָקָח; עֹשֵׂה אֵלֶּה לֹא יִמּוֹט לְעוֹלָם.

תהלים כג

**מִזְמוֹר** לְדָוִד, יהוה רֹעִי, לֹא אֶחְסָר. בִּנְאוֹת דֶּשֶׁא יַרְבִּיצֵנִי, עַל מֵי מְנֻחוֹת יְנַהֲלֵנִי. נַפְשִׁי יְשׁוֹבֵב, יַנְחֵנִי בְמַעְגְּלֵי צֶדֶק לְמַעַן שְׁמוֹ. גַּם כִּי אֵלֵךְ בְּגֵיא צַלְמָוֶת, לֹא אִירָא רָע כִּי אַתָּה עִמָּדִי; שִׁבְטְךָ וּמִשְׁעַנְתֶּךָ הֵמָּה יְנַחֲמֻנִי. תַּעֲרֹךְ לְפָנַי שֻׁלְחָן נֶגֶד צֹרְרָי; דִּשַּׁנְתָּ בַשֶּׁמֶן רֹאשִׁי, כּוֹסִי רְוָיָה. אַךְ טוֹב וָחֶסֶד יִרְדְּפוּנִי כָּל יְמֵי חַיָּי, וְשַׁבְתִּי בְּבֵית יהוה לְאֹרֶךְ יָמִים.

# FUNERAL SERVICE

Some fitting readings at the outset of the funeral follow.

Psalm 1

**אַשְׁרֵי** *Happy is the one who has not followed the counsel of the wicked, nor stood in the path of sinners, nor sat in the company of the scornful. Rather, that one's delight is in the Torah of the Lord, meditating in God's Torah day and night. And will be like a tree planted by streams of water, that yields its fruit in season, whose leaf will not wither, and whatever that one does prospers. Not so the wicked, who are like chaff that the wind drives away. Therefore the wicked shall not survive judgment, nor sinners in the assembly of the righteous. For the Lord loves the way of the righteous, but the way of the wicked is doomed.*

Psalm 15

**מִזְמוֹר** *A song of David: Lord, who may sojourn in Your tent,who may dwell on Your holy mountain? One who walks in purity, does what is righteous, and speaks the truth from the heart. Who has no slander on the tongue, nor has done harm to a fellow, nor casts disgrace toward a neighbor. In whose eyes a contemptible person is repulsive, but who honors those who are in awe of the Lord; who swears truthfully even to personal hurt, and never retracts. Who does not lend money on interest, nor takes a bribe against the innocent; one who does these things shall never falter.*

Psalm 23

**מִזְמוֹר** *A song of David: The Lord is my shepherd, I shall not lack. God causes me to lie down in lush pastures, God leads me beside tranquil waters. God restores my soul, and guides me in righteous paths for God's Name's sake. Though I walk through the valley of the shadow of death, I will fear no evil, for You are with me; Your scepter and staff, they comfort me. You prepare a table before me in full view of my adversaries; You have anointed my head with oil, my cup overflows. May only goodness and kindness pursue me all the days of my life, and I shall dwell in the House of the Lord for length of days.*

For Ladies:

משלי לא:י-לא

**אֵשֶׁת חַיִל** מִי יִמְצָא, וְרָחֹק מִפְּנִינִים מִכְרָהּ.
בָּטַח בָּהּ לֵב בַּעְלָהּ, וְשָׁלָל לֹא יֶחְסָר.
גְּמָלַתְהוּ טוֹב וְלֹא רָע, כֹּל יְמֵי חַיֶּיהָ.
דָּרְשָׁה צֶמֶר וּפִשְׁתִּים, וַתַּעַשׂ בְּחֵפֶץ כַּפֶּיהָ.
הָיְתָה כָּאֳנִיּוֹת סוֹחֵר, מִמֶּרְחָק תָּבִיא לַחְמָהּ.
וַתָּקָם בְּעוֹד לַיְלָה, וַתִּתֵּן טֶרֶף לְבֵיתָהּ, וְחֹק לְנַעֲרֹתֶיהָ.
זָמְמָה שָׂדֶה וַתִּקָּחֵהוּ, מִפְּרִי כַפֶּיהָ נָטְעָה כָּרֶם.
חָגְרָה בְעוֹז מָתְנֶיהָ, וַתְּאַמֵּץ זְרוֹעֹתֶיהָ.
טָעֲמָה כִּי טוֹב סַחְרָהּ, לֹא יִכְבֶּה בַלַּיְלָה נֵרָהּ.
יָדֶיהָ שִׁלְּחָה בַכִּישׁוֹר, וְכַפֶּיהָ תָּמְכוּ פָלֶךְ.
כַּפָּהּ פָּרְשָׂה לֶעָנִי, וְיָדֶיהָ שִׁלְּחָה לָאֶבְיוֹן.
לֹא תִירָא לְבֵיתָהּ מִשָּׁלֶג, כִּי כָל בֵּיתָהּ לָבֻשׁ שָׁנִים.
מַרְבַדִּים עָשְׂתָה לָּהּ, שֵׁשׁ וְאַרְגָּמָן לְבוּשָׁהּ.
נוֹדָע בַּשְּׁעָרִים בַּעְלָהּ, בְּשִׁבְתּוֹ עִם זִקְנֵי אָרֶץ.
סָדִין עָשְׂתָה וַתִּמְכֹּר, וַחֲגוֹר נָתְנָה לַכְּנַעֲנִי.
עוֹז וְהָדָר לְבוּשָׁהּ, וַתִּשְׂחַק לְיוֹם אַחֲרוֹן.
פִּיהָ פָּתְחָה בְחָכְמָה, וְתוֹרַת חֶסֶד עַל לְשׁוֹנָהּ.
צוֹפִיָּה הֲלִיכוֹת בֵּיתָהּ, וְלֶחֶם עַצְלוּת לֹא תֹאכֵל.
קָמוּ בָנֶיהָ וַיְאַשְּׁרוּהָ, בַּעְלָהּ וַיְהַלְלָהּ.
רַבּוֹת בָּנוֹת עָשׂוּ חָיִל, וְאַתְּ עָלִית עַל כֻּלָּנָה.
שֶׁקֶר הַחֵן וְהֶבֶל הַיֹּפִי, אִשָּׁה יִרְאַת יהוה הִיא תִתְהַלָּל.
תְּנוּ לָהּ מִפְּרִי יָדֶיהָ, וִיהַלְלוּהָ בַשְּׁעָרִים מַעֲשֶׂיהָ.

For Ladies:

Proverbs 31:10-31

**אֵשֶׁת חַיִל** *A gallant woman, who can find? Far beyond pearls is her worth.*

**ב** *Her husband's heartfelt trust is in her, and he shall lack for nothing.*

**ג** *She bestows good upon him, and never harm, all the days of her life.*

**ד** *She seeks out wool and linen, and her hands work willingly.*

**ה** *She is like a merchant fleet, bringing her sustenance from afar.*

**ו** *She arises while it is yet night, and gives provision to her household and direction to her maidens.*

**ז** *She envisions a field and acquires it, from the fruit of her handiwork she plants a vineyard.*

**ח** *With vigor she girds her loins, and strengthens her arms.*

**ט** *She discerns that her enterprise is good, her lamp does not go out by night.*

**י** *Her hands she stretches out to the distaff, and her palms support the spindle.*

**כ** *She spreads out her palm to the poor, and extends her hands to the destitute.*

**ל** *She fears not snow for her household, for her entire household is clothed with scarlet wool.*

**מ** *Fine covers she made herself, linen and purple wool are her clothing.*

**נ** *Prominent in the gates is her husband, as he sits with the elders of the land.*

**ס** *She makes a cloak and sells it, and deals a belt to the peddler.*

**ע** *Strength and splendor are her raiment, she cheerfully awaits the last day.*

**פ** *Her mouth is opened with wisdom, and the teaching of kindness is on her tongue.*

**צ** *She oversees the ways of her household, and partakes not of the bread of laziness.*

**ק** *Her children arise and praise her; her husband, and he lauds her.*

**ר** *'Many daughters have accomplished well, but you surpass them all.'*

**ש** *Grace is false and beauty is vain; a woman in awe of God — she should be praised.*

**ת** *Give her the fruits of her own hand, and let her deeds praise her in the gathering places.*

The following is traditionally recited on days when Tahanun is not recited:

תהלים טז

**מִכְתָּם** לְדָוִד, שָׁמְרֵנִי אֵל כִּי חָסִיתִי בָךְ. אָמַרְתְּ לַיהוה, אֲדֹנָי אָתָּה, טוֹבָתִי בַּל עָלֶיךָ. לִקְדוֹשִׁים אֲשֶׁר בָּאָרֶץ הֵמָּה, וְאַדִּירֵי כָּל חֶפְצִי בָם. יִרְבּוּ עַצְּבוֹתָם אַחֵר מָהָרוּ; בַּל אַסִּיךְ נִסְכֵּיהֶם מִדָּם, וּבַל אֶשָּׂא אֶת שְׁמוֹתָם עַל שְׂפָתָי. יהוה מְנָת חֶלְקִי וְכוֹסִי, אַתָּה תּוֹמִיךְ גּוֹרָלִי. חֲבָלִים נָפְלוּ לִי בַּנְּעִמִים, אַף נַחֲלָת שָׁפְרָה עָלָי. אֲבָרֵךְ אֶת יהוה אֲשֶׁר יְעָצָנִי, אַף לֵילוֹת יִסְּרוּנִי כִלְיוֹתָי. שִׁוִּיתִי יהוה לְנֶגְדִּי תָמִיד, כִּי מִימִינִי, בַּל אֶמּוֹט. לָכֵן שָׂמַח לִבִּי וַיָּגֶל כְּבוֹדִי, אַף בְּשָׂרִי יִשְׁכֹּן לָבֶטַח. כִּי לֹא תַעֲזֹב נַפְשִׁי לִשְׁאוֹל, לֹא תִתֵּן חֲסִידְךָ לִרְאוֹת שָׁחַת. תּוֹדִיעֵנִי אֹרַח חַיִּים, שֹׂבַע שְׂמָחוֹת אֶת פָּנֶיךָ, נְעִמוֹת בִּימִינְךָ נֶצַח.

Here the officiating Rabbi delivers a meaningful eulogy.
Other people close to the deceased may add their words of tribute, as well.

## MEMORIAL PRAYER

### FOR MALES

The assembled rise for the memorial prayer.

**אֵל** מָלֵא רַחֲמִים, שׁוֹכֵן בַּמְּרוֹמִים, הַמְצֵא מְנוּחָה נְכוֹנָה עַל כַּנְפֵי הַשְּׁכִינָה, בְּמַעֲלוֹת קְדוֹשִׁים וּטְהוֹרִים כְּזֹהַר הָרָקִיעַ מַזְהִירִים, אֶת נִשְׁמַת (שם הנפטר) בֶּן (שם אביו; אם מבחינה הלכתית לא היה לנפטר אב, קוראים אותו על שם אמו) שֶׁהָלַךְ לְעוֹלָמוֹ, בַּעֲבוּר שֶׁאֲנַחְנוּ מִתְפַּלְּלִים בְּעַד הַזְכָּרַת נִשְׁמָתוֹ. בְּגַן עֵדֶן תְּהֵא מְנוּחָתוֹ. לָכֵן בַּעַל הָרַחֲמִים יַסְתִּירֵהוּ בְּסֵתֶר כְּנָפָיו לְעוֹלָמִים, וְיִצְרוֹר בִּצְרוֹר הַחַיִּים אֶת נִשְׁמָתוֹ. יהוה הוּא נַחֲלָתוֹ; וְיָנוּחַ בְּשָׁלוֹם עַל מִשְׁכָּבוֹ, וְנֹאמַר אָמֵן.

The following is traditionally recited on days when Tahanun is not recited:

Psalm 16

**מִכְתָּם** *Mikhtam L'David: Guard me, God, for in You I have taken refuge. You have said to the Lord, 'You are my Lord; I have no good beyond You.' As for the holy ones who are in the earth, and the mighty in whom is all my desire. Their sorrows will multiply, those that run to other gods; their blood libations will I not pour out, nor take their names upon my lips. The Lord is my allotted portion and my share; You sustain my fate. Portions have fallen to me in pleasant places; lovely indeed is my estate. I will bless the Lord Who has given me counsel; my conscience admonishes me at night. I have set the Lord before me always; because God is at my right hand, I shall not falter. Therefore my heart rejoices and my entire being exults; also my body will rest secure. For You will not abandon me to the grave, nor will You let Your devout one see destruction. You will make known to me the path of life; in Your presence is fullness of joy; there is delight at Your right hand for eternity.*

Here the officiating Rabbi delivers a meaningful eulogy.
Other people close to the deceased may add their words of tribute, as well.

## MEMORIAL PRAYER

### FOR MALES

The assembled rise for the memorial prayer.

**אֵ‑ל** *God, full of compassion, Who dwells on high, grant proper repose on the sheltering wings of Your presence, in the lofty levels of the holy and pure who shine as the brightness of the firmament, unto the soul of* (name of deceased) *son of* (father's name; if deceased had no halakhic father, he is called by his mother's name), *who has gone to his world, and for whose memory we pray. May his repose be in Paradise. May the Master of compassion bring him under the cover of God's wings, and bind his soul in the bond of life. May the Lord be his heritage, and may he repose on his resting place in peace, and let us respond, Amen.*

## FOR FEMALES

**אֵל** מָלֵא רַחֲמִים, שׁוֹכֵן בַּמְּרוֹמִים, הַמְצֵא מְנוּחָה נְכוֹנָה עַל כַּנְפֵי הַשְּׁכִינָה, בְּמַעֲלוֹת קְדוֹשִׁים וּטְהוֹרִים כְּזֹהַר הָרָקִיעַ מַזְהִירִים, אֶת נִשְׁמַת (שם הנפטרת) בַּת (שם אביה; אם מבחינה הלכתית לא היה לנפטרת אב, קוראים אותה על שם אמה) שֶׁהָלְכָה לְעוֹלָמָהּ, בַּעֲבוּר שֶׁאֲנַחְנוּ מִתְפַּלְּלִים בְּעַד הַזְכָּרַת נִשְׁמָתָהּ. בְּגַן עֵדֶן תְּהֵא מְנוּחָתָהּ. לָכֵן בַּעַל הָרַחֲמִים יַסְתִּירֶהָ בְּסֵתֶר כְּנָפָיו לְעוֹלָמִים, וְיִצְרוֹר בִּצְרוֹר הַחַיִּים אֶת נִשְׁמָתָהּ. יהוה הוּא נַחֲלָתָהּ; וְתָנוּחַ בְּשָׁלוֹם עַל מִשְׁכָּבָהּ, וְנֹאמַר אָמֵן.

On days when tahanun is not said, and from noon on the day prior to Shabbat or Yom Tov, additional Tehillim should be recited in the absence of the memorial prayer. A few appropriate Tehillim readings are herein suggested.

תהלים קכא

**שִׁיר לַמַּעֲלוֹת,** אֶשָּׂא עֵינַי אֶל הֶהָרִים, מֵאַיִן יָבֹא עֶזְרִי. עֶזְרִי מֵעִם יהוה, עֹשֵׂה שָׁמַיִם וָאָרֶץ. אַל יִתֵּן לַמּוֹט רַגְלֶךָ, אַל יָנוּם שֹׁמְרֶךָ. הִנֵּה לֹא יָנוּם וְלֹא יִישָׁן, שׁוֹמֵר יִשְׂרָאֵל. יהוה שֹׁמְרֶךָ, יהוה צִלְּךָ עַל יַד יְמִינֶךָ. יוֹמָם הַשֶּׁמֶשׁ לֹא יַכֶּכָּה וְיָרֵחַ בַּלָּיְלָה. יהוה יִשְׁמָרְךָ מִכָּל רָע, יִשְׁמֹר אֶת נַפְשֶׁךָ. יהוה יִשְׁמָר צֵאתְךָ וּבוֹאֶךָ, מֵעַתָּה וְעַד עוֹלָם.

תהלים קל

**שִׁיר הַמַּעֲלוֹת,** מִמַּעֲמַקִּים קְרָאתִיךָ יהוה. אֲדֹנָי שִׁמְעָה בְקוֹלִי, תִּהְיֶינָה אָזְנֶיךָ קַשֻּׁבוֹת לְקוֹל תַּחֲנוּנָי. אִם עֲוֹנוֹת תִּשְׁמָר יָהּ, אֲדֹנָי מִי יַעֲמֹד. כִּי עִמְּךָ הַסְּלִיחָה, לְמַעַן תִּוָּרֵא. קִוִּיתִי יהוה קִוְּתָה נַפְשִׁי, וְלִדְבָרוֹ הוֹחָלְתִּי. נַפְשִׁי לַאדֹנָי, מִשֹּׁמְרִים לַבֹּקֶר, שֹׁמְרִים לַבֹּקֶר. יַחֵל יִשְׂרָאֵל אֶל יהוה, כִּי עִם יהוה הַחֶסֶד, וְהַרְבֵּה עִמּוֹ פְדוּת. וְהוּא יִפְדֶּה אֶת יִשְׂרָאֵל, מִכֹּל עֲוֹנוֹתָיו.

## FOR FEMALES

**אֵל** *God, full of compassion, Who dwells on high, grant proper repose on the sheltering wings of Your presence, in the lofty levels of the holy and pure who shine as the brightness of the firmament, unto the soul of* (name of deceased) *daughter of* (father's name; if deceased had no halakhic father, she is called by her mother's name)*, who has gone to her world, and for whose memory we pray. May her repose be in Paradise. May the Master of compassion bring her under the cover of God's wings, and bind her soul in the bond of life. May the Lord be her heritage, and may she repose on her resting place in peace, and let us respond Amen.*

On days when tahanun is not said, and from noon on the day prior to Shabbat or Yom Tov, additional Tehillim should be recited in the absence of the memorial prayer. A few appropriate Tehillim readings are herein suggested.

Psalm 121

**שִׁיר לַמַּעֲלוֹת** *A song to ascents. I lift my eyes to the mountains, from where will my help come? My help comes from the Lord, Maker of heaven and earth. God will not let your foot falter, your Guardian will not slumber. Behold, the Guardian of Israel neither slumbers nor sleeps. The Lord is your Guardian, the Lord is your protection by your right side. By day the sun will not harm you, nor the moon by night. The Lord will guard you from all evil; the Lord will guard your life. The Lord will guard your going and coming from now and forever.*

Psalm 130

**שִׁיר הַמַּעֲלוֹת** *A song of ascents. Out of the depths I call you, Lord. Lord, listen to my cry, let your ears be attentive to my supplicative plea. If You preserve the account of sins, God, Lord who can survive? Pardon resides with You, so that You are held in awe. I hope for the Lord, my soul hopes, I await God's word. I yearn more for the Lord than guards for the morning, guards for the morning. Israel, wait for the Lord, for with the Lord is kindness and great redemption. And it is God Who will redeem Israel from all its iniquities.*

The deceased is escorted to these words:

תהלים צ״א

**יֹשֵׁב** בְּסֵתֶר עֶלְיוֹן, בְּצֵל שַׁדַּי יִתְלוֹנָן. אֹמַר לַיהוה, מַחְסִי וּמְצוּדָתִי, אֱלֹהַי אֶבְטַח בּוֹ. כִּי הוּא יַצִּילְךָ מִפַּח יָקוּשׁ, מִדֶּבֶר הַוּוֹת. בְּאֶבְרָתוֹ יָסֶךְ לָךְ, וְתַחַת כְּנָפָיו תֶּחְסֶה, צִנָּה וְסֹחֵרָה אֲמִתּוֹ. לֹא תִירָא מִפַּחַד לָיְלָה, מֵחֵץ יָעוּף יוֹמָם. מִדֶּבֶר בָּאֹפֶל יַהֲלֹךְ, מִקֶּטֶב יָשׁוּד צָהֳרָיִם. יִפֹּל מִצִּדְּךָ אֶלֶף, וּרְבָבָה מִימִינֶךָ, אֵלֶיךָ לֹא יִגָּשׁ. רַק בְּעֵינֶיךָ תַבִּיט, וְשִׁלֻּמַת רְשָׁעִים תִּרְאֶה. כִּי אַתָּה יהוה מַחְסִי, עֶלְיוֹן שַׂמְתָּ מְעוֹנֶךָ. לֹא תְאֻנֶּה אֵלֶיךָ רָעָה, וְנֶגַע לֹא יִקְרַב בְּאָהֳלֶךָ. כִּי מַלְאָכָיו יְצַוֶּה לָּךְ, לִשְׁמָרְךָ בְּכָל דְּרָכֶיךָ. עַל כַּפַּיִם יִשָּׂאוּנְךָ, פֶּן תִּגֹּף בָּאֶבֶן רַגְלֶךָ. עַל שַׁחַל וָפֶתֶן תִּדְרֹךְ, תִּרְמֹס כְּפִיר וְתַנִּין. כִּי בִי חָשַׁק וַאֲפַלְּטֵהוּ, אֲשַׂגְּבֵהוּ כִּי יָדַע שְׁמִי. יִקְרָאֵנִי וְאֶעֱנֵהוּ, עִמּוֹ אָנֹכִי בְצָרָה, אֲחַלְּצֵהוּ וַאֲכַבְּדֵהוּ. אֹרֶךְ יָמִים אַשְׂבִּיעֵהוּ, וְאַרְאֵהוּ בִּישׁוּעָתִי. אֹרֶךְ יָמִים אַשְׂבִּיעֵהוּ, וְאַרְאֵהוּ בִּישׁוּעָתִי.

## AT THE CEMETERY

Those, aside from the mourners, who have not been in a cemetery for thirty days recite the following when arriving there:

**בָּרוּךְ** אַתָּה יהוה אֱלֹהֵינוּ מֶלֶךְ הָעוֹלָם, אֲשֶׁר יָצַר אֶתְכֶם בַּדִּין, וְזָן וְכִלְכֵּל אֶתְכֶם בַּדִּין, וְהֵמִית אֶתְכֶם בַּדִּין, וְיוֹדֵעַ מִסְפַּר כֻּלְּכֶם בַּדִּין, וְהוּא עָתִיד לְהַחֲיוֹתְכֶם וּלְקַיֵּם אֶתְכֶם בַּדִּין. בָּרוּךְ אַתָּה יהוה, מְחַיֵּה הַמֵּתִים.

**אַתָּה** גִּבּוֹר לְעוֹלָם אֲדֹנָי, מְחַיֵּה מֵתִים אַתָּה, רַב לְהוֹשִׁיעַ. מְכַלְכֵּל חַיִּים בְּחֶסֶד, מְחַיֵּה מֵתִים בְּרַחֲמִים רַבִּים, סוֹמֵךְ נוֹפְלִים, וְרוֹפֵא חוֹלִים, וּמַתִּיר אֲסוּרִים, וּמְקַיֵּם אֱמוּנָתוֹ

The deceased is escorted to these words:

Psalm 91

**יֹשֵׁב** *You who dwell in the shelter of the Most High, abiding in the shadow of the Almighty. I say of the Lord, my refuge and my stronghold, my God in whom I trust, That God will deliver you from the ensnaring net, from destructive plague. With God's pinion will God shelter you, and under God's wings shall you find refuge; faith in God shall be your shield and protector. Fear not the terror of night, the arrow that flies by day, the plague that stalks in the darkness, the destruction that ravages at noon. Though a thousand may fall at your left side, and ten thousand at your right, it shall not reach you. Look but clearly, and you shall see the retribution against the wicked. Because [you said] 'You, Lord, are my trust,' you set the Most High as your dwelling. No harm shall befall you, nor disease come near your tent. For God will give God's angels charge concerning you, to guard you in all your ways. They shall carry you on their hands, lest you injure your foot against a stone. You shall tread on the lion and viper; you shall trample the young lion and serpent. Because he yearned for Me I will deliver him; I will be his refuge, for having known My Name. He will call upon Me and I will answer, I will be with him in distress; I will rescue him and give him honor. With length of days will I satisfy him, and reveal to him My salvation. With length of days will I satisfy him, and reveal to him My salvation.*

## AT THE CEMETERY

Those, aside from the mourners, who have not been in a cemetery for thirty days recite the following when arriving there:

**בָּרוּךְ** *Blessed are You, Lord our God, Ruler of the Universe, Who fashioned you with justice, nourished and sustained you with justice, took your lives with justice, knows the sum total of you all in justice, and will restore and resuscitate you in justice. Blessed are You, Lord, Who revives the dead.*

**אַתָּה** *You are eternally mighty, Lord, the Reviver of the dead are You; abundantly to save. God sustains the living with kindness, revives the dead with abundant compassion, supports the fallen, heals the sick, releases the confined, and maintains faith*

לִישֵׁנֵי עָפָר. מִי כָמוֹךָ בַּעַל גְּבוּרוֹת, וּמִי דוֹמֶה לָּךְ, מֶלֶךְ מֵמִית וּמְחַיֶּה וּמַצְמִיחַ יְשׁוּעָה. וְנֶאֱמָן אַתָּה לְהַחֲיוֹת מֵתִים.

The deceased is carried to the burial site, and from outside about fifty feet of that site, the *Yoshev B'Seter* is recited seven times, each time concluding with one more of the numbered, bold words, and stopping the procession at those words. This is not done on days when Tahanun is not recited, and from noon prior to *Shabbat* or *Yom Tov*.

**יֹשֵׁב** בְּסֵתֶר עֶלְיוֹן, בְּצֵל שַׁדַּי יִתְלוֹנָן. אֹמַר לַיהוה, מַחְסִי וּמְצוּדָתִי, אֱלֹהַי אֶבְטַח בּוֹ. כִּי הוּא יַצִּילְךָ מִפַּח יָקוּשׁ, מִדֶּבֶר הַוּוֹת. בְּאֶבְרָתוֹ יָסֶךְ לָךְ, וְתַחַת כְּנָפָיו תֶּחְסֶה, צִנָּה וְסֹחֵרָה אֲמִתּוֹ. לֹא תִירָא מִפַּחַד לָיְלָה, מֵחֵץ יָעוּף יוֹמָם. מִדֶּבֶר בָּאֹפֶל יַהֲלֹךְ, מִקֶּטֶב יָשׁוּד צָהֳרָיִם. יִפֹּל מִצִּדְּךָ אֶלֶף, וּרְבָבָה מִימִינֶךָ, אֵלֶיךָ לֹא יִגָּשׁ. רַק בְּעֵינֶיךָ תַבִּיט, וְשִׁלֻּמַת רְשָׁעִים תִּרְאֶה. כִּי אַתָּה יהוה מַחְסִי, עֶלְיוֹן שַׂמְתָּ מְעוֹנֶךָ. לֹא תְאֻנֶּה אֵלֶיךָ רָעָה, וְנֶגַע לֹא יִקְרַב בְּאָהֳלֶךָ. **1) כִּי 2) מַלְאָכָיו 3) יְצַוֶּה 4) לָּךְ, 5) לִשְׁמָרְךָ 6) בְּכָל 7) דְּרָכֶיךָ.**

Upon reaching the burial site, the deceased is gently lowered, and then covered by earth till the burial site is mounded, forming a *tzurat ha'kever* that encompasses the burial place. Prior to commencing this mitzvah, it is appropriate to ask forgiveness from the deceased. The first three shovels of earth that one puts in are done with the shovel turned upside-down, and the shovel is never given from hand to hand. After one person has completed their share of the burial mitzvah, the shovel should be placed in the ground, for the next person to take it.

After burial, the garments are rent, if they have not as yet been rent, following the mourners pronouncing the *Dayan Ha'Emet berakhah.*

**בָּרוּךְ** אַתָּה יהוה אֱלֹהֵינוּ מֶלֶךְ הָעוֹלָם, דַּיַּן הָאֱמֶת.

## ACCEPTANCE OF JUDGMENT

Upon completion of the burial, the following *Tziduk HaDin* is recited by the mourners, and by those involved in preparing the deceased for burial. However, it is omitted when *tahanun* is not recited, and from noon prior to *Shabbat* and *Yom Tov,* and as well is not recited at night.

Those mourners who do not go to the burial recite *Tziduk HaDin* at home.

*to those asleep in the earth. Who is like You, Master of mighty deeds, and who is comparable to You, the Ruler Who causes death and restores life and makes salvation sprout. And You are trustworthy to revive the dead.*

The deceased is carried to the burial site, and from outside about fifty feet of that site, the *Yoshev B'Seter* is recited seven times, each time concluding with one more of the numbered, bold words, and stopping the procession at those words. This is not done on days when Tahanun is not recited, and from noon prior to *Shabbat* or *Yom Tov.*

**יֹשֵׁב** *You who dwell in the shelter of the Most High, abiding in the shadow of the Almighty. I say of the Lord, my refuge and my stronghold, my God in whom I trust, That God will deliver you from the ensnaring net, from destructive plague. With God's pinion will God shelter you, and under God's wings shall you find refuge; faith in God shall be your shield and protector. Fear not the terror of night, the arrow that flies by day, the plague that stalks in the darkness, the destruction that ravages at noon. Though a thousand may fall at your left side, and ten thousand at your right, it shall not reach you. Look but clearly, and you shall see the retribution against the wicked. Because [you said] 'You, Lord, are my trust,' you set the Most High as your dwelling. No harm shall befall you, nor disease come near your tent.* ***1) For God 2) will give God's angels 3) charge 4) concerning you, 5) to guard you 6) in all 7) your ways.***

Upon reaching the burial site, the deceased is gently lowered, and then covered by earth till the burial site is mounded, forming a *tzurat ha'kever* that encompasses the burial place. Prior to commencing this mitzvah, it is appropriate to ask forgiveness from the deceased. The first three shovels of earth that one puts in are done with the shovel turned upside-down, and the shovel is never given from hand to hand. After one person has completed their share of the burial mitzvah, the shovel should be placed in the ground, for the next person to take it.

After burial, the garments are rent, if they have not as yet been rent, following the mourners pronouncing the *Dayan Ha'Emet berakhah.*

**בָּרוּךְ** *Blessed are You, Lord our God, Ruler of the Universe, Who is the true Judge.*

## ACCEPTANCE OF JUDGMENT

Upon completion of the burial, the following *Tziduk HaDin* is recited by the mourners, and by those involved in preparing the deceased for burial. However, it is omitted when *tahanun* is not recited, and from noon prior to *Shabbat* and *Yom Tov,* and as well is not recited at night.

Those mourners who do not go to the burial recite *Tziduk HaDin* at home.

**הַצּוּר** תָּמִים פָּעֳלוֹ, כִּי כָל דְּרָכָיו מִשְׁפָּט, אֵל אֱמוּנָה וְאֵין עָוֶל, צַדִּיק וְיָשָׁר הוּא.

הַצּוּר תָּמִים בְּכָל פֹּעַל, מִי יֹאמַר לוֹ מַה תִּפְעָל, הַשַּׁלִּיט בְּמַטָּה וּבְמַעַל, מֵמִית וּמְחַיֶּה, מוֹרִיד שְׁאוֹל וַיָּעַל.

הַצּוּר תָּמִים בְּכָל מַעֲשֶׂה, מִי יֹאמַר אֵלָיו מַה תַּעֲשֶׂה, הָאוֹמֵר וְעֹשֶׂה, חֶסֶד חִנָּם לָנוּ תַעֲשֶׂה, וּבִזְכוּת הַנֶּעֱקַד כְּשֶׂה, הַקְשִׁיבָה וַעֲשֵׂה.

צַדִּיק בְּכָל דְּרָכָיו הַצּוּר תָּמִים, אֶרֶךְ אַפַּיִם וּמָלֵא רַחֲמִים, חֲמָל נָא וְחוּס נָא עַל אָבוֹת וּבָנִים, כִּי לְךָ אָדוֹן הַסְּלִיחוֹת וְהָרַחֲמִים.

צַדִּיק אַתָּה יהוה לְהָמִית וּלְהַחֲיוֹת, אֲשֶׁר בְּיָדְךָ פִּקְדוֹן כָּל רוּחוֹת, חָלִילָה לְּךָ זִכְרוֹנֵנוּ לִמְחוֹת, וְיִהְיוּ נָא עֵינֶיךָ בְּרַחֲמִים עָלֵינוּ פְקוּחוֹת, כִּי לְךָ אָדוֹן הָרַחֲמִים וְהַסְּלִיחוֹת.

אָדָם אִם בֶּן שָׁנָה יִהְיֶה, אוֹ אֶלֶף שָׁנִים יִחְיֶה, מַה יִּתְרוֹן לוֹ, כְּלֹא הָיָה יִהְיֶה, בָּרוּךְ דַּיַּן הָאֱמֶת, מֵמִית וּמְחַיֶּה.

בָּרוּךְ הוּא, כִּי אֱמֶת דִּינוֹ, וּמְשׁוֹטֵט הַכֹּל בְּעֵינוֹ, וּמְשַׁלֵּם לְאָדָם חֶשְׁבּוֹנוֹ וְדִינוֹ, וְהַכֹּל לִשְׁמוֹ הוֹדָיָה יִתֵּנוּ.

יָדַעְנוּ יהוה כִּי צֶדֶק מִשְׁפָּטֶךָ, תִּצְדַּק בְּדָבְרֶךָ וְתִזְכֶּה בְּשָׁפְטֶךָ, וְאֵין לְהַרְהֵר אַחַר מִדַּת שָׁפְטֶךָ, צַדִּיק אַתָּה יהוה, וְיָשָׁר מִשְׁפָּטֶיךָ.

דַּיַּן אֱמֶת, שׁוֹפֵט צֶדֶק וֶאֱמֶת, בָּרוּךְ דַּיַּן הָאֱמֶת, שֶׁכָּל מִשְׁפָּטָיו צֶדֶק וֶאֱמֶת.

נֶפֶשׁ כָּל חַי בְּיָדֶךָ, צֶדֶק מָלְאָה יְמִינְךָ וְיָדֶךָ, רַחֵם עַל פְּלֵיטַת צֹאן יָדֶךָ, וְתֹאמַר לַמַּלְאָךְ הֶרֶף יָדֶךָ.

גְּדֹל הָעֵצָה וְרַב הָעֲלִילִיָּה, אֲשֶׁר עֵינֶיךָ פְקֻחוֹת עַל כָּל דַּרְכֵי בְּנֵי אָדָם, לָתֵת לְאִישׁ כִּדְרָכָיו וְכִפְרִי מַעֲלָלָיו.

לְהַגִּיד כִּי יָשָׁר יהוה, צוּרִי וְלֹא עַוְלָתָה בּוֹ.

יהוה נָתַן, וַיהוה לָקָח, יְהִי שֵׁם יהוה מְבֹרָךְ.

וְהוּא רַחוּם, יְכַפֵּר עָוֹן וְלֹא יַשְׁחִית, וְהִרְבָּה לְהָשִׁיב אַפּוֹ, וְלֹא יָעִיר כָּל חֲמָתוֹ.

הַצּוּר *The Rock, perfect is God's work, for all God's paths are just; God of faith without iniquity, righteous and fair is God.*

*The Rock, perfect in every work, who can tell God what to do? God rules below and above, causes death and restores life, lowers down to the grave and raises up.*

*The Rock, perfect in every action, who can tell God how to act? God Whose word generates deed, do undeserved kindness with us. In the merit of him (Yitzhak) who was bound like a lamb, hearken and act.*

*Righteous One in all ways, the Rock Who is perfect, slow to anger and full of compassion, please have mercy and spare parents and children, for Yours, Master, are forgiveness and compassion.*

*Righteous are You, Lord, to cause death and to restore life, for in Your hand is the safekeeping of all spirits. Far be it from You to erase our memory. May Your eyes compassionately take cognizance of us, for Yours, Master, are compassion and forgiveness.*

*For a person, whether a year old, or whether living a thousand years, of what profit is it? As if having never been shall that person be. Blessed is the true Judge, Who engenders death and revives.*

*Blessed is God, for God's judgment is true, God scans everything with God's eye, and recompenses the person according to the account and the just sentence, and all must give God's Name acknowledgment.*

*We know, Lord, that Your judgment is righteous, You are righteous when You speak and pure when You judge; there is no complaining about the manner of Your judgment. Righteous are You, Lord, and Your judgments are fair.*

*True Judge, Judge of righteousness and truth; blessed is the true Judge, for all of God's judgments are righteous and true.*

*The soul of all the living is in Your hand, righteousness fills Your right hand and Your power. Have mercy on the remnant of the sheep of Your hand, and say to the Angel {of Death}, 'Hold back your hand!'*

*Great in counsel and abundant in deed, Your eyes are open upon all the ways of the children of humankind, to give to each one according to their ways and according to the fruit of their deeds.*

*To declare that the Lord is just; my Rock, in Whom there is no wrong.*

*The Lord has given and the Lord has taken away; blessed is the Name of the Lord.*

*And God, the Merciful One, will forgive iniquity and not destroy, frequently withdrawing anger, not arousing the entirety of God's rage.*

## KADDISH AFTER BURIAL

The following Burial Kaddish is now recited. Like Tziduk HaDin, it is omitted on days when Tahanun is not recited, and from noon prior to Shabbat and Yom Tov. On these occasions, the regular Kaddish is recited. If there is no mourner to recite the Burial Kaddish, it is recited by the officiating Rabbi or head of the Hevra Kadisha.

**A transliteration of this Kaddish appears on page 188**

**יִתְגַּדַּל** וְיִתְקַדַּשׁ שְׁמֵהּ רַבָּא (קהל– אָמֵן), בְּעָלְמָא דְּהוּא עָתִיד לְאִתְחַדְתָּא, וּלְאַחֲיָא מֵתַיָּא, וּלְאַסָּקָא לְחַיֵּי עָלְמָא, וּלְמִבְנֵי קַרְתָּא דִירוּשְׁלֵם, וּלְשַׁכְלֵל הֵיכָלֵהּ בְּגַוָּהּ, וּלְמֶעֱקַר פּוּלְחָנָא נוּכְרָאָה מֵאַרְעָא, וּלְאָתָבָא פּוּלְחָנָא דִשְׁמַיָּא לְאַתְרָהּ, וְיַמְלִיךְ קוּדְשָׁא בְּרִיךְ הוּא בְּמַלְכוּתֵהּ וִיקָרֵהּ, בְּחַיֵּיכוֹן וּבְיוֹמֵיכוֹן וּבְחַיֵּי דְכָל בֵּית יִשְׂרָאֵל, בַּעֲגָלָא וּבִזְמַן קָרִיב. וְאִמְרוּ אָמֵן.

(קהל– אָמֵן. יְהֵא שְׁמֵהּ רַבָּא מְבָרַךְ לְעָלַם וּלְעָלְמֵי עָלְמַיָּא).

**יְהֵא שְׁמֵהּ רַבָּא מְבָרַךְ לְעָלַם וּלְעָלְמֵי עָלְמַיָּא.**

יִתְבָּרַךְ וְיִשְׁתַּבַּח וְיִתְפָּאַר וְיִתְרוֹמַם וְיִתְנַשֵּׂא וְיִתְהַדָּר וְיִתְעַלֶּה וְיִתְהַלָּל שְׁמֵהּ דְּקוּדְשָׁא בְּרִיךְ הוּא (קהל– בְּרִיךְ הוּא). לְעֵלָּא מִן כָּל (בעשרת ימי תשובה– °לְעֵלָּא לְעֵלָּא מִכָּל) — ° בִּרְכָתָא וְשִׁירָתָא תֻּשְׁבְּחָתָא וְנֶחֱמָתָא, דַּאֲמִירָן בְּעָלְמָא. וְאִמְרוּ אָמֵן. (קהל– אָמֵן)

יְהֵא שְׁלָמָא רַבָּא מִן שְׁמַיָּא, וְחַיִּים עָלֵינוּ וְעַל כָּל יִשְׂרָאֵל. וְאִמְרוּ אָמֵן. (קהל– אָמֵן)

Take three steps back. Bow left and say . . . עֹשֶׂה; bow right and say . . . הוּא; bow forward and say . . . וְעַל כָּל.

עֹשֶׂה °°שָׁלוֹם (יש אומרים בעשרת ימי תשובה – °°הַשָּׁלוֹם) בִּמְרוֹמָיו, הוּא יַעֲשֶׂה שָׁלוֹם עָלֵינוּ וְעַל כָּל יִשְׂרָאֵל. וְאִמְרוּ אָמֵן. (קהל– אָמֵן)

Remain standing in place for a few seconds, then take three steps forward.

On days when *Tahanun* is omitted, and from noon prior to *Shabbat* or *Yom Tov*, *Mikhtam L'David* is recited, followed by the regular *Kaddish*.

## KADDISH AFTER BURIAL

The following Burial Kaddish is now recited. Like Tziduk HaDin, it is omitted on days when Tahanun is not recited, and from noon prior to Shabbat and Yom Tov. On these occasions, the regular Kaddish is recited. If there is no mourner to recite the Burial Kaddish, it is recited by the officiating Rabbi or head of the Hevra Kadisha.

**A transliteration of this Kaddish appears on page 188.**

**יִתְגַּדַּל** *May God's great Name grow exalted and sanctified* (All– *Amen*), *in the world which will be renewed, and where God will revive the dead and raise them up to eternal life, and rebuild the city of Yerushalayim and complete its Sanctuary within it, and uproot alien worship from the earth, and return the service of Heaven to its place, and where the Holy One, Blessed is God, will reign in sovereignty and splendor, in your lifetimes and in your days, and in the lifetimes of the entire Family of Israel, swiftly and in due time. And we respond, Amen.*

(All— *Amen. May God's great Name be blessed forever and ever*).

*May God's great Name be blessed forever and ever.*

*Blessed, praised, glorified, exalted, extolled, beautified, upraised, and lauded be the Name of the Holy One, Blessed is God.* (All– *Blessed is God);* (From Rosh HaShanah to Yom Kippur add: *Exceedingly)* *Beyond any blessing and song, praise and consolation that are uttered in the world. And we respond, Amen.* (All– *Amen)*

*May there be abundant tranquility from Heaven, and life, upon us and upon all Israel. And we respond, Amen.* (All– *Amen)*

Take three steps back. Bow left and say . . . עֹשֶׂה; bow right and say . . . הוּא; bow forward and say . . . וְעַל כָּל.

*The Effector of harmony* (some, in the Ten Days of Repentance, say – *the harmony)* *in God's heights, may God effect tranquility for us, and for all Israel. And we respond, Amen.* (All– *Amen)*

Remain standing in place for a few seconds, then take three steps forward.

On days when *tahanun* is omitted, and from noon prior to *Shabbat* or *Yom Tov, Mikhtam L'David* is recited, followed by the regular *Kaddish*.

תהלים טז

**מִכְתָּם** לְדָוִד, שָׁמְרֵנִי אֵל כִּי חָסִיתִי בָךְ. אָמַרְתְּ לַיהוה, אֲדֹנָי אָתָּה, טוֹבָתִי בַּל עָלֶיךָ. לִקְדוֹשִׁים אֲשֶׁר בָּאָרֶץ הֵמָּה, וְאַדִּירֵי כָּל חֶפְצִי בָם. יִרְבּוּ עַצְּבוֹתָם אַחֵר מָהָרוּ; בַּל אַסִּיךְ נִסְכֵּיהֶם מִדָּם, וּבַל אֶשָּׂא אֶת שְׁמוֹתָם עַל שְׂפָתָי. יהוה מְנָת חֶלְקִי וְכוֹסִי, אַתָּה תּוֹמִיךְ גּוֹרָלִי. חֲבָלִים נָפְלוּ לִי בַּנְּעִמִים, אַף נַחֲלָת שָׁפְרָה עָלָי. אֲבָרֵךְ אֶת יהוה אֲשֶׁר יְעָצָנִי, אַף לֵילוֹת יִסְּרוּנִי כִלְיוֹתָי. שִׁוִּיתִי יהוה לְנֶגְדִּי תָמִיד, כִּי מִימִינִי, בַּל אֶמּוֹט. לָכֵן שָׂמַח לִבִּי וַיָּגֶל כְּבוֹדִי, אַף בְּשָׂרִי יִשְׁכֹּן לָבֶטַח. כִּי לֹא תַעֲזֹב נַפְשִׁי לִשְׁאוֹל, לֹא תִתֵּן חֲסִידְךָ לִרְאוֹת שָׁחַת. תּוֹדִיעֵנִי אֹרַח חַיִּים, שֹׂבַע שְׂמָחוֹת אֶת פָּנֶיךָ, נְעִמוֹת בִּימִינְךָ נֶצַח.

## THE MOURNER'S KADDISH

A transliteration of this Kaddish appears on page 189

**יִתְגַּדַּל** וְיִתְקַדַּשׁ שְׁמֵהּ רַבָּא (קהל– אָמֵן), בְּעָלְמָא דִּי בְרָא כִרְעוּתֵהּ, וְיַמְלִיךְ מַלְכוּתֵהּ, בְּחַיֵּיכוֹן וּבְיוֹמֵיכוֹן וּבְחַיֵּי דְכָל בֵּית יִשְׂרָאֵל, בַּעֲגָלָא וּבִזְמַן קָרִיב, וְאִמְרוּ אָמֵן.

(קהל– אָמֵן. יְהֵא שְׁמֵהּ רַבָּא מְבָרַךְ לְעָלַם וּלְעָלְמֵי עָלְמַיָּא.)

**יְהֵא שְׁמֵהּ רַבָּא מְבָרַךְ לְעָלַם וּלְעָלְמֵי עָלְמַיָּא.**

יִתְבָּרַךְ וְיִשְׁתַּבַּח וְיִתְפָּאַר וְיִתְרוֹמַם וְיִתְנַשֵּׂא וְיִתְהַדָּר וְיִתְעַלֶּה וְיִתְהַלָּל שְׁמֵהּ דְּקֻדְשָׁא בְּרִיךְ הוּא (קהל– בְּרִיךְ הוּא). °לְעֵלָּא מִן כָּל (בעשרת ימי תשובה– °לְעֵלָּא לְעֵלָּא מִכָּל) בִּרְכָתָא וְשִׁירָתָא תֻּשְׁבְּחָתָא וְנֶחֱמָתָא, דַּאֲמִירָן בְּעָלְמָא. וְאִמְרוּ אָמֵן. (קהל– אָמֵן)

יְהֵא שְׁלָמָא רַבָּא מִן שְׁמַיָּא, וְחַיִּים עָלֵינוּ וְעַל כָּל יִשְׂרָאֵל. וְאִמְרוּ אָמֵן. (קהל– אָמֵן)

Take three steps back. Bow left and say . . . עֹשֶׂה; bow right and say . . . הוּא; bow forward and say . . . וְעַל כָּל.

עֹשֶׂה °שָׁלוֹם (יש אומרים בעשרת ימי תשובה– °הַשָּׁלוֹם) בִּמְרוֹמָיו, הוּא יַעֲשֶׂה שָׁלוֹם עָלֵינוּ, וְעַל כָּל יִשְׂרָאֵל. וְאִמְרוּ אָמֵן. (קהל– אָמֵן)

Remain standing in place for a few seconds, then take three steps forward.

Psalm 16

**מִכְתָּם** *Mikhtam L'David: Guard me, God, for in You I have taken refuge. You have said to the Lord, 'You are my Lord; I have no good beyond You.' As for the holy ones who are in the earth, and the mighty in whom is all my desire. Their sorrows will multiply, those that run to other gods; their blood libations will I not pour out, nor take their names upon my lips. The Lord is my allotted portion and my share; You sustain my fate. Portions have fallen to me in pleasant places; lovely indeed is my estate. I will bless the Lord Who has given me counsel: my conscience admonishes me at night. I have set the Lord before me always; because God is at my right hand, I shall not falter. Therefore my heart rejoices and my entire being exults; also my body will rest secure. For You will not abandon me to the grave, nor will You let your devout one see destruction. You will make known to me the path of life; in Your presence is fullness of joy; there is delight at Your right hand for eternity.*

## THE MOURNER'S KADDISH

**A transliteration of this Kaddish appears on page 189.**

**יִתְגַּדַּל** *May God's great Name grow exalted and sanctified* (All – *Amen), in the world which God created according to God's will, and may God rule over that dominion in your lifetimes and in your days, and in the lifetimes of the entire Family of Israel, swiftly and in due time. And we respond, Amen.*

(All – *Amen. May God's great Name be blessed forever and ever*).

*May God's great Name be blessed forever and ever.*

*Blessed, praised, glorified, exalted, extolled, beautified, upraised, and lauded be the Name of the Holy One, Blessed is God.* (All – *Blessed is God*). (From Rosh HaShanah to Yom Kippur add: *Exceedingly) Beyond any blessing and song, praise and consolation that are uttered in the world. And we respond, Amen.* (All – *Amen)*

*May there be abundant tranquility from Heaven, and life, upon us and upon all Israel. And we respond, Amen.* (All – *Amen)*

Take three steps back. Bow left and say . . . עֹשֶׂה; bow right and say . . . הוּא; bow forward and say . . . וְעַל כָּל.

*The Effector of harmony* (some, in the Ten Days of Repentance, say – *the harmony) in God's heights, may God effect tranquility for us, and for all of Israel. And we respond, Amen.* (All – *Amen)*

Remain standing in place for a few seconds, then take three steps forward.

When taking leave of the deceased, one says (based on *Berakhot* 64a, *Daniel* 12:13):

For a Male:

**לֵךְ** בְּשָׁלוֹם, וְתָנוּחַ בְּשָׁלוֹם, וְתַעֲמוֹד לְגוֹרָלְךָ לְקֵץ הַיָּמִין.

For a Female:

**לְכִי** בְּשָׁלוֹם, וְתָנוּחִי בְּשָׁלוֹם, וְתַעַמְדִי לְגוֹרָלֵיךְ לְקֵץ הַיָּמִין.

Those present at the burial form two rows through which the mourners walk. As the mourners pass through, those forming the rows recite the traditional prayer of consolation.

**הַמָּקוֹם יְנַחֵם**

for one male mourner — אוֹתְךָ

for one female mourner — אוֹתָךְ

for several mourners — אֶתְכֶם

for several mourners, if all are female — אֶתְכֶן

בְּתוֹךְ שְׁאָר אֲבֵלֵי צִיּוֹן וִירוּשָׁלָיִם.

As the participants leave the cemetery, they tear out some blades of grass and toss them over their right shoulders as they recite:

**וְיָצִיצוּ** מֵעִיר כְּעֵשֶׂב הָאָרֶץ. זָכוּר כִּי עָפָר אֲנָחְנוּ.

Upon leaving the cemetery, one washes the hands left on right, right on left, three times and recites:

**בִּלַּע** הַמָּוֶת לָנֶצַח, וּמָחָה אֲדֹנָי יֱהוִֹה דִּמְעָה מֵעַל כָּל פָּנִים, וְחֶרְפַּת עַמּוֹ יָסִיר מֵעַל כָּל הָאָרֶץ, כִּי יהוה דִּבֵּר.

When taking leave of the deceased, one says
(based on *Berakhot* 64a, *Daniel* 12:13):

**לֵךְ** *Go in peace, repose in peace, and arise to your ultimate destiny at the end of the days.*

Those present at the burial form two rows through which the mourners walk. As the mourners pass through, those forming the rows recite the traditional prayer of consolation.

**הַמָּקוֹם** *May the Omnipresent console you among the other mourners of Zion and Yerushalayim.*

As the participants leave the cemetery,
they tear out some blades of grass
and toss them over their right shoulders as they recite:

**וְיָצִיצוּ** *May they blossom forth from the city like the earth's grass. Remember that we are but dust.*

Upon leaving the cemetery, one washes the hands left on right, right on left, three times and recites:

**בִּלַּע** *May death be swallowed up forever, and may the Lord God wipe away tears from every face and remove the mocking of God's people from throughout the world, for the Lord has spoken.*

## ◆§ *Birkat HaMazon in a House of Mourning*

*Birkat HaMazon in a house of mourning differs from the regular text. The call to bless is different, as are some of the blessings. As per Arukh HaShulhan to Yoreh De'ah, 379, this special Birkat HaMazon is the mandatory text for a house of mourning, even without a minyan.*

*This amended Birkat HaMazon is also recited on Shabbat, if the mourners are among themselves only. However, if others have joined the mourners on Shabbat, the standard Birkat HaMazon is employed, since reciting the special Birkat HaMazon in the company of non-mourners would constitute public mourning on Shabbat.*

## BIRKAT HAMAZON IN A HOUSE OF MOURNING

[The bracketed words are added if a *minyan* is present].

המזומן– רַבּוֹתַי נְבָרֵךְ.

המסובין– יְהִי שֵׁם יהוה מְבֹרָךְ מֵעַתָּה וְעַד עוֹלָם.

המזומן– יְהִי שֵׁם יהוה מְבֹרָךְ מֵעַתָּה וְעַד עוֹלָם. בִּרְשׁוּת מָרָנָן וְרַבָּנָן וְרַבּוֹתַי, נְבָרֵךְ [אֱלֹהֵינוּ] מְנַחֵם אֲבֵלִים שֶׁאָכַלְנוּ מִשֶּׁלּוֹ.

המסובין– בָּרוּךְ [אֱלֹהֵינוּ] מְנַחֵם אֲבֵלִים שֶׁאָכַלְנוּ מִשֶּׁלּוֹ וּבְטוּבוֹ חָיִינוּ.

המזומן– בָּרוּךְ [אֱלֹהֵינוּ] מְנַחֵם אֲבֵלִים שֶׁאָכַלְנוּ מִשֶּׁלּוֹ וּבְטוּבוֹ חָיִינוּ.
בָּרוּךְ הוּא וּבָרוּךְ שְׁמוֹ.

**בָּרוּךְ** אַתָּה יהוה אֱלֹהֵינוּ מֶלֶךְ הָעוֹלָם, הַזָּן אֶת הָעוֹלָם כֻּלּוֹ, בְּטוּבוֹ, בְּחֵן בְּחֶסֶד וּבְרַחֲמִים. הוּא נֹתֵן לֶחֶם לְכָל בָּשָׂר, כִּי לְעוֹלָם חַסְדּוֹ, וּבְטוּבוֹ הַגָּדוֹל, תָּמִיד לֹא חָסַר לָנוּ, וְאַל יֶחְסַר לָנוּ מָזוֹן לְעוֹלָם וָעֶד. בַּעֲבוּר שְׁמוֹ הַגָּדוֹל, כִּי הוּא אֵל זָן וּמְפַרְנֵס לַכֹּל, וּמֵטִיב לַכֹּל, וּמֵכִין מָזוֹן לְכָל בְּרִיּוֹתָיו אֲשֶׁר בָּרָא. ❖ בָּרוּךְ אַתָּה יהוה, הַזָּן אֶת הַכֹּל.
(All– אָמֵן)

**נוֹדֶה** לְּךָ יהוה אֱלֹהֵינוּ, עַל שֶׁהִנְחַלְתָּ לַאֲבוֹתֵינוּ אֶרֶץ חֶמְדָּה טוֹבָה וּרְחָבָה. וְעַל שֶׁהוֹצֵאתָנוּ יהוה אֱלֹהֵינוּ מֵאֶרֶץ מִצְרַיִם, וּפְדִיתָנוּ מִבֵּית עֲבָדִים, וְעַל בְּרִיתְךָ שֶׁחָתַמְתָּ בִּבְשָׂרֵנוּ, וְעַל תּוֹרָתְךָ שֶׁלִּמַּדְתָּנוּ, וְעַל חֻקֶּיךָ שֶׁהוֹדַעְתָּנוּ, וְעַל חַיִּים חֵן וָחֶסֶד שֶׁחוֹנַנְתָּנוּ, וְעַל אֲכִילַת מָזוֹן שָׁאַתָּה זָן וּמְפַרְנֵס אוֹתָנוּ תָּמִיד, בְּכָל יוֹם וּבְכָל עֵת וּבְכָל שָׁעָה.

## BIRKAT HAMAZON IN A HOUSE OF MOURNING

[The bracketed words are added if a *minyan* is present].

Leader– *Distinguished Assembled, let us bless.*

Assembled– *Blessed is the Name of the Lord henceforth and forever!*

Leader– *Blessed is the Name of the Lord henceforth and forever! With the permission of the distinguished people present let us bless [our God] Who comforts mourners, of Whose bounty we have eaten.*

Assembled– *Blessed is [our God] Who comforts mourners, of Whose bounty we have eaten, and through Whose goodness we live.*

Leader– *Blessed is [our God] Who comforts mourners, of Whose bounty we have eaten, and through Whose goodness we live.*
*Blessed is God and Blessed is God's Name.*

**בָּרוּךְ** *Blessed are You, Lord our God, Ruler of the Universe, Who sustains the entire world in Godly goodness, with grace, lovingkindness, and compassion. God gives sustenance to all flesh, for God's lovingkindness is everlasting, and in bountiful goodness God has never failed us, and may God never fail to sustain us for all eternity. For the sake of God's great Name, for God sustains and provides for all, and does good for all and prepares provision for all the creatures that God created. Blessed are You, Lord, Who sustains all.* (All– *Amen)*

**נוֹדֶה** *We extend thanks to You, Lord our God, for having given to our ancestors the heritage of a lovely, good, and spacious land; for Your having brought us out, Lord our God, from the land of Egypt, and having redeemed us from the house of bondage; for Your covenant that You sealed in our flesh; for Your Torah which You taught to us; for Your statutes which You made known to us; for the life, grace, and loving-kindness You have graciously bestowed upon us; and for the provision of food through which You sustain and provide for us constantly, every day, every occasion, and every hour.*

בחנוכה מוסיפים:

**(וְ)עַל** הַנִּסִּים וְעַל הַפֻּרְקָן וְעַל הַגְּבוּרוֹת וְעַל הַתְּשׁוּעוֹת וְעַל הַמִּלְחָמוֹת שֶׁעָשִׂיתָ לַאֲבוֹתֵינוּ בַּיָּמִים הָהֵם בַּזְּמַן הַזֶּה.

**בִּימֵי** מַתִּתְיָהוּ בֶּן יוֹחָנָן כֹּהֵן גָּדוֹל חַשְׁמוֹנָאִי וּבָנָיו, כְּשֶׁעָמְדָה מַלְכוּת יָוָן הָרְשָׁעָה עַל עַמְּךָ יִשְׂרָאֵל, לְהַשְׁכִּיחָם תּוֹרָתֶךָ, וּלְהַעֲבִירָם מֵחֻקֵּי רְצוֹנֶךָ. וְאַתָּה בְּרַחֲמֶיךָ הָרַבִּים, עָמַדְתָּ לָהֶם בְּעֵת צָרָתָם, רַבְתָּ אֶת רִיבָם, דַּנְתָּ אֶת דִּינָם, נָקַמְתָּ אֶת נִקְמָתָם. מָסַרְתָּ גִבּוֹרִים בְּיַד חַלָּשִׁים, וְרַבִּים בְּיַד מְעַטִּים, וּטְמֵאִים בְּיַד טְהוֹרִים, וּרְשָׁעִים בְּיַד צַדִּיקִים, וְזֵדִים בְּיַד עוֹסְקֵי תוֹרָתֶךָ. וּלְךָ עָשִׂיתָ שֵׁם גָּדוֹל וְקָדוֹשׁ בְּעוֹלָמֶךָ, וּלְעַמְּךָ יִשְׂרָאֵל עָשִׂיתָ תְּשׁוּעָה גְדוֹלָה וּפֻרְקָן כְּהַיּוֹם הַזֶּה. וְאַחַר כֵּן בָּאוּ בָנֶיךָ לִדְבִיר בֵּיתֶךָ, וּפִנּוּ אֶת הֵיכָלֶךָ, וְטִהֲרוּ אֶת מִקְדָּשֶׁךָ, וְהִדְלִיקוּ נֵרוֹת בְּחַצְרוֹת קָדְשֶׁךָ, וְקָבְעוּ שְׁמוֹנַת יְמֵי חֲנֻכָּה אֵלּוּ, לְהוֹדוֹת וּלְהַלֵּל לְשִׁמְךָ הַגָּדוֹל.

בפורים מוסיפים:

**(וְ)עַל** הַנִּסִּים וְעַל הַפֻּרְקָן וְעַל הַגְּבוּרוֹת וְעַל הַתְּשׁוּעוֹת וְעַל הַמִּלְחָמוֹת שֶׁעָשִׂיתָ לַאֲבוֹתֵינוּ בַּיָּמִים הָהֵם בַּזְּמַן הַזֶּה.

**בִּימֵי** מָרְדְּכַי וְאֶסְתֵּר בְּשׁוּשַׁן הַבִּירָה, כְּשֶׁעָמַד עֲלֵיהֶם הָמָן הָרָשָׁע, בִּקֵּשׁ לְהַשְׁמִיד לַהֲרֹג וּלְאַבֵּד אֶת כָּל הַיְּהוּדִים, מִנַּעַר וְעַד זָקֵן, טַף וְנָשִׁים, בְּיוֹם אֶחָד, בִּשְׁלוֹשָׁה עָשָׂר לְחֹדֶשׁ שְׁנֵים עָשָׂר, הוּא חֹדֶשׁ אֲדָר, וּשְׁלָלָם לָבוֹז. וְאַתָּה בְּרַחֲמֶיךָ הָרַבִּים הֵפַרְתָּ אֶת עֲצָתוֹ, וְקִלְקַלְתָּ אֶת מַחֲשַׁבְתּוֹ, וַהֲשֵׁבוֹתָ לּוֹ גְּמוּלוֹ בְּרֹאשׁוֹ, וְתָלוּ אוֹתוֹ וְאֶת בָּנָיו עַל הָעֵץ.

**וְעַל הַכֹּל** יהוה אֱלֹהֵינוּ אֲנַחְנוּ מוֹדִים לָךְ, וּמְבָרְכִים אוֹתָךְ, יִתְבָּרַךְ שִׁמְךָ בְּפִי כָּל חַי תָּמִיד לְעוֹלָם וָעֶד. כַּכָּתוּב, וְאָכַלְתָּ וְשָׂבָעְתָּ, וּבֵרַכְתָּ אֶת יהוה אֱלֹהֶיךָ, עַל הָאָרֶץ הַטֹּבָה אֲשֶׁר נָתַן לָךְ. ❖ בָּרוּךְ אַתָּה יהוה, עַל הָאָרֶץ וְעַל הַמָּזוֹן. (All – אָמֵן)

On Hanukah add:

**(וְ)עַל הַנִּיסִים** *(And) we thank You for the miracles, for the redemption, for the mighty deeds and deliverances, and for the battles which You performed for our ancestors in those days, at this season.*

**בִּימֵי מַתִּתְיָהוּ** *In the days of the Hasmonean, Matityahu son of Yohanan, the Great Kohen, and his sons, when a wicked Hellenic government rose up against Your people Israel to make them forget Your Torah and divert them from fulfilling the laws of Your will. You in Your great mercy stood by them in the time of their distress; You championed their cause, defended their rights and avenged their wrong. You delivered the strong into the hands of the weak, the many into the hands of the few, the impure into the hands of the pure, the wicked into the hands of the righteous, and the arrogant into the hands of those who occupy themselves with Your Torah. You made a great and holy Name for Yourself in Your world, and for Your people Israel You performed a great deliverance unto this day. Thereupon Your children came to the shrine of Your House, cleansed Your Temple, purified Your Sanctuary, kindled lights in Your holy Courts, and designated these eight days of Hanukah for giving thanks and praise to Your great Name.*

On Purim add:

**(וְ)עַל הַנִּסִּים** *(And) we thank You for the miracles, for the redemption, for the mighty deeds and deliverances, and for the battles which You performed for our ancestors in those days, at this season.*

**בִּימֵי מָרְדְּכַי** *In the days of Mordekhai and Esther, in Shushan the Persian capital, when the evil Haman rose up against them and sought to destroy, slay and wipe out all the Jews, young and old, infants and women, in one day, the thirteenth of the twelfth month, which is Adar, and to plunder their possessions. You in Your great mercy nullified his counsel, blunted his plan, and rebounded his designs upon his own head, and they hanged him and his sons upon the gallows.*

**וְעַל הַכֹּל** *For all this, Lord our God, we thank You and bless You; may Your Name be blessed in the mouths of all the living, constantly, for all eternity, according to that which is written: 'You shall eat and be satisfied, and shall bless the Lord, your God, for the good land that God gave to you.' Blessed are You, Lord, for the land and for the sustenance.* (All— *Amen*)

**רַחֵם** יהוה אֱלֹהֵינוּ עַל יִשְׂרָאֵל עַמֶּךָ, וְעַל יְרוּשָׁלַיִם עִירֶךָ, וְעַל צִיּוֹן מִשְׁכַּן כְּבוֹדֶךָ, וְעַל מַלְכוּת בֵּית דָּוִד מְשִׁיחֶךָ, וְעַל הַבַּיִת הַגָּדוֹל וְהַקָּדוֹשׁ שֶׁנִּקְרָא שִׁמְךָ עָלָיו. אֱלֹהֵינוּ אָבִינוּ רְעֵנוּ זוּנֵנוּ פַּרְנְסֵנוּ וְכַלְכְּלֵנוּ וְהַרְוִיחֵנוּ, וְהַרְוַח לָנוּ יהוה אֱלֹהֵינוּ מְהֵרָה מִכָּל צָרוֹתֵינוּ. וְנָא אַל תַּצְרִיכֵנוּ יהוה אֱלֹהֵינוּ, לֹא לִידֵי מַתְּנַת בָּשָׂר וָדָם, וְלֹא לִידֵי הַלְוָאָתָם, כִּי אִם לְיָדְךָ הַמְּלֵאָה הַפְּתוּחָה הַקְּדוֹשָׁה (נ״א– הַגְּדוּשָׁה) וְהָרְחָבָה, שֶׁלֹּא נֵבוֹשׁ וְלֹא נִכָּלֵם לְעוֹלָם וָעֶד.

בשבת מוסיפים:

**רְצֵה** וְהַחֲלִיצֵנוּ יהוה אֱלֹהֵינוּ בְּמִצְוֹתֶיךָ, וּבְמִצְוַת יוֹם הַשְּׁבִיעִי הַשַּׁבָּת הַגָּדוֹל וְהַקָּדוֹשׁ הַזֶּה. כִּי יוֹם זֶה גָּדוֹל וְקָדוֹשׁ הוּא לְפָנֶיךָ, לִשְׁבָּת בּוֹ וְלָנוּחַ בּוֹ בְּאַהֲבָה כְּמִצְוַת רְצוֹנֶךָ. וּבִרְצוֹנְךָ הָנִיחַ לָנוּ יהוה אֱלֹהֵינוּ, שֶׁלֹּא תְהֵא צָרָה וְיָגוֹן וַאֲנָחָה בְּיוֹם מְנוּחָתֵנוּ. וְהַרְאֵנוּ יהוה אֱלֹהֵינוּ בְּנֶחָמַת צִיּוֹן עִירֶךָ, וּבְבִנְיַן יְרוּשָׁלַיִם עִיר קָדְשֶׁךָ, כִּי אַתָּה הוּא בַּעַל הַיְשׁוּעוֹת וּבַעַל הַנֶּחָמוֹת.

בראש חדש מוסיפים:

**אֱלֹהֵינוּ** וֵאלֹהֵי אֲבוֹתֵינוּ, יַעֲלֶה, וְיָבֹא, וְיַגִּיעַ, וְיֵרָאֶה, וְיֵרָצֶה, וְיִשָּׁמַע, וְיִפָּקֵד, וְיִזָּכֵר זִכְרוֹנֵנוּ וּפִקְדוֹנֵנוּ, וְזִכְרוֹן אֲבוֹתֵינוּ, וְזִכְרוֹן מָשִׁיחַ בֶּן דָּוִד עַבְדֶּךָ, וְזִכְרוֹן יְרוּשָׁלַיִם עִיר קָדְשֶׁךָ, וְזִכְרוֹן כָּל עַמְּךָ בֵּית יִשְׂרָאֵל לְפָנֶיךָ, לִפְלֵיטָה לְטוֹבָה לְחֵן וּלְחֶסֶד וּלְרַחֲמִים, לְחַיִּים וּלְשָׁלוֹם בְּיוֹם רֹאשׁ הַחֹדֶשׁ הַזֶּה. זָכְרֵנוּ יהוה אֱלֹהֵינוּ בּוֹ לְטוֹבָה, וּפָקְדֵנוּ בוֹ לִבְרָכָה, וְהוֹשִׁיעֵנוּ בוֹ לְחַיִּים. וּבִדְבַר יְשׁוּעָה וְרַחֲמִים, חוּס וְחָנֵּנוּ וְרַחֵם עָלֵינוּ וְהוֹשִׁיעֵנוּ, כִּי אֵלֶיךָ עֵינֵינוּ, כִּי אֵל מֶלֶךְ חַנּוּן וְרַחוּם אָתָּה.

**רַחֵם** *Please have compassion, Lord our God, on Israel Your people, on Yerushalayim Your city, on Zion the dwelling of Your glory, on the royal house of David Your anointed one, and on the great and holy House through which Your Name is called. Our God, our Parent, our Shepherd, sustain us, provide for us, support us and relieve us, by granting us, Lord our God, speedy relief from all our troubles. Please, Lord our God, do not make us dependent on gifts of flesh and blood, nor upon their loans, but on Your hand — full, open, hallowed (abundant), and generous; that we not be shamed and not disgraced for all eternity.*

On Shabbat, the following paragraph is added:

**רְצֵה** *May it please You, Lord our God, to invigorate us through Your commandments, and through the commandment of the seventh day, this great and holy Shabbat. For this day is great and holy before You, to rest and relax thereon, in love, according to Your commanded desire. And by Your favor, allow for us, Lord our God, that there be no distress, grief, or lament on our day of rest. Let us experience, Lord our God, the consolation of Zion Your city, and the building of Yerushalayim the city manifesting Your holiness; for You are the Master of salvations and the Master of consolations.*

On Rosh Hodesh, the following paragraph is added:

**אֱלֹהֵינוּ** *God and the God of our ancestors, may there ascend, come, reach, be noted, favored, heard, acknowledged, and remembered before You the remembrance and recollection of us, the remembance of our ancestors, the remembrance of the anointed, son of David Your servant, the remembrance of Yerushalayim the city manifesting Your holiness, and the remembrance of Your entire people the house of Israel; for deliverance, for goodness, for grace, lovingkindness and compassion, for life and tranquillity, on this Rosh Hodesh day; Remember us on it, Lord our God, for good; recall us on it for blessing; and save us on it for life. As to the matter of salvation and compassion, have pity and be gracious to us, have compassion on us and save us, as our eyes are directed toward You; for You are a gracious, compassionate God and Ruler.*

**נַחֵם** יהוה אֱלֹהֵינוּ אֶת אֲבֵלֵי יְרוּשָׁלַיִם וְאֶת הָאֲבֵלִים הַמִּתְאַבְּלִים בָּאֵבֶל הַזֶּה. נַחֲמֵם מֵאֶבְלָם וְשַׂמְּחֵם מִיגוֹנָם, כָּאָמוּר: כְּאִישׁ אֲשֶׁר אִמּוֹ תְּנַחֲמֶנּוּ, כֵּן אָנֹכִי אֲנַחֶמְכֶם וּבִירוּשָׁלַיִם תְּנֻחָמוּ. בָּרוּךְ אַתָּה יהוה, מְנַחֵם צִיּוֹן בְּבִנְיַן יְרוּשָׁלָיִם. אָמֵן. (All– אָמֵן)

**בָּרוּךְ** אַתָּה יהוה אֱלֹהֵינוּ מֶלֶךְ הָעוֹלָם, הָאֵל אָבִינוּ מַלְכֵּנוּ אַדִּירֵנוּ בּוֹרְאֵנוּ גֹּאֲלֵנוּ יוֹצְרֵנוּ קְדוֹשֵׁנוּ קְדוֹשׁ יַעֲקֹב, רוֹעֵנוּ רוֹעֵה יִשְׂרָאֵל, הַמֶּלֶךְ הַטּוֹב וְהַמֵּטִיב לַכֹּל, שֶׁבְּכָל יוֹם וָיוֹם הוּא הֵטִיב, הוּא מֵטִיב, הוּא יֵיטִיב לָנוּ. הַמֶּלֶךְ הַחַי הַטּוֹב וְהַמֵּטִיב, אֵל אֱמֶת, דַּיַּן אֱמֶת, שׁוֹפֵט בְּצֶדֶק, לוֹקֵחַ נְפָשׁוֹת בְּמִשְׁפָּט, וְשַׁלִּיט בְּעוֹלָמוֹ לַעֲשׂוֹת בּוֹ כִּרְצוֹנוֹ, כִּי כָל דְּרָכָיו מִשְׁפָּט, וַאֲנַחְנוּ עַמּוֹ וַעֲבָדָיו. וְעַל הַכֹּל אֲנַחְנוּ חַיָּבִים לְהוֹדוֹת לוֹ וּלְבָרְכוֹ. גּוֹדֵר פִּרְצוֹת יִשְׂרָאֵל, הוּא יִגְדּוֹר אֶת הַפִּרְצָה הַזֹּאת, מֵעָלֵינוּ וּמֵעַל הָאָבֵל הַזֶּה, לְחַיִּים וּלְשָׁלוֹם וְכָל טוֹב, וּמִכָּל טוּב לְעוֹלָם אַל יְחַסְּרֵנוּ. (All– אָמֵן.)

**הָרַחֲמָן** הוּא יִמְלוֹךְ עָלֵינוּ לְעוֹלָם וָעֶד. הָרַחֲמָן הוּא יִתְבָּרַךְ בַּשָּׁמַיִם וּבָאָרֶץ. הָרַחֲמָן הוּא יִשְׁתַּבַּח לְדוֹר דּוֹרִים, וְיִתְפָּאַר בָּנוּ לָעַד וּלְנֵצַח נְצָחִים, וְיִתְהַדַּר בָּנוּ לָעַד וּלְעוֹלְמֵי עוֹלָמִים. הָרַחֲמָן הוּא יְפַרְנְסֵנוּ בְּכָבוֹד. הָרַחֲמָן הוּא יִשְׁבּוֹר עֻלֵּנוּ מֵעַל צַוָּארֵנוּ, וְהוּא יוֹלִיכֵנוּ קוֹמְמִיּוּת לְאַרְצֵנוּ. הָרַחֲמָן הוּא יִשְׁלַח לָנוּ בְּרָכָה מְרֻבָּה בַּבַּיִת הַזֶּה, וְעַל שֻׁלְחָן זֶה שֶׁאָכַלְנוּ עָלָיו. הָרַחֲמָן הוּא יִשְׁלַח לָנוּ אֶת אֵלִיָּהוּ הַנָּבִיא זָכוּר לַטּוֹב, וִיבַשֶּׂר לָנוּ בְּשׂוֹרוֹת טוֹבוֹת יְשׁוּעוֹת וְנֶחָמוֹת.

**נַחֵם** *Lord our God, comfort the mourners of Yerushalayim and those who mourn in this sad circumstance. Console them from their mourning and gladden them from their grief, as it is said, 'Like one who is consoled by the mother, so I will console you, and in Yerushalayim you will be consoled.' Blessed are You, Lord, Comforter of Zion through the rebuilding of Yerushalayim. Amen.*
(All – *Amen)*

**בָּרוּךְ** *Blessed are You, Lord our God, Ruler of the Universe, the God Who is our Parent, our Ruler, our Sovereign, our Creator, our Redeemer, our Maker, our Holy One, the Holy One of Yaakov; our Shepherd, the Shepherd of Israel, the Ruler Who is good and does good for all, Who every day has done good, does good, and will continue to do good for us. The living Ruler, Who is good and does good, God of truth, Judge of truth, Who judges with righteousness, Who takes souls with justice, Who rules the Godly universe to do with it as God wishes, for all God's ways are with justice and we are God's nation and God's servants. For everything, we are obliged to thank God and bless God. God Who repairs the breaches of Israel, may God repair this breach from us and from this mourning, for life, tranquility, and all that is good; and of all that is good may we never lack.*
(All – *Amen)*

**הָרַחֲמָן** *May the Compassionate One rule over us for all eternity. May the Compassionate One be blessed in the heavens and on earth. May the Compassionate One be praised for all generations, glorified through us forever, to ultimate times, and honored through us forever, to all eternity. May the Compassionate One provide for us in dignity. May the Compassionate One break off the oppressive yoke from our necks, and lead us proudly to our land. May the Compassionate One bestow abundant blessing on this home, and on this table, upon which we have eaten. May the Compassionate One send to us the prophet Eliyahu, who is remembered for good, and may he bring us good tidings of salvations and comforts.*

Guests recite the following.
Children at their parents' table also include the words in brackets.

הָרַחֲמָן הוּא יְבָרֵךְ אֶת (אָבִי מוֹרִי) בַּעַל הַבַּיִת הַזֶּה, וְאֶת (אִמִּי מוֹרָתִי) בַּעֲלַת הַבַּיִת הַזֶּה, אוֹתָם וְאֶת בֵּיתָם וְאֶת זַרְעָם וְאֶת כָּל אֲשֶׁר לָהֶם (אם יש שם אחרים חוץ מההורים, מוסיפים — וְאֶת כָּל הַמְּסֻבִּין כָּאן).

Those eating at their own table say the following,
adding the choice in brackets that is appropriate to them.

הָרַחֲמָן הוּא יְבָרֵךְ אוֹתִי (וְאֶת אִשְׁתִּי / בַּעְלִי, וְאֶת זַרְעִי) וְאֶת כָּל אֲשֶׁר לִי (אם יש שם אחרים, מוסיפים – וְאֶת כָּל הַמְּסֻבִּין כָּאן).

אוֹתָנוּ וְאֶת כָּל אֲשֶׁר לָנוּ, כְּמוֹ שֶׁנִּתְבָּרְכוּ אֲבוֹתֵינוּ אַבְרָהָם יִצְחָק וְיַעֲקֹב בַּכֹּל, מִכֹּל, כֹּל. כֵּן יְבָרֵךְ אוֹתָנוּ כֻּלָּנוּ יַחַד בִּבְרָכָה שְׁלֵמָה, וְנֹאמַר אָמֵן.

**בַּמָּרוֹם** יְלַמְּדוּ עֲלֵיהֶם וְעָלֵינוּ זְכוּת, שֶׁתְּהֵא לְמִשְׁמֶרֶת שָׁלוֹם. וְנִשָּׂא בְרָכָה מֵאֵת יהוה, וּצְדָקָה מֵאֱלֹהֵי יִשְׁעֵנוּ. וְנִמְצָא חֵן וְשֵׂכֶל טוֹב בְּעֵינֵי אֱלֹהִים וְאָדָם.

לשבת

הָרַחֲמָן הוּא יַנְחִילֵנוּ יוֹם שֶׁכֻּלּוֹ שַׁבָּת וּמְנוּחָה לְחַיֵּי הָעוֹלָמִים.

לראש חודש

הָרַחֲמָן הוּא יְחַדֵּשׁ עָלֵינוּ אֶת הַחֹדֶשׁ הַזֶּה לְטוֹבָה וְלִבְרָכָה.

**הָרַחֲמָן** הוּא יְזַכֵּנוּ לִימוֹת הַמָּשִׁיחַ וּלְחַיֵּי הָעוֹלָם הַבָּא. [בחול– מַגְדִּל] [בשבת, יו"ט ור"ח– מִגְדּוֹל] יְשׁוּעוֹת מַלְכּוֹ וְעֹשֶׂה חֶסֶד לִמְשִׁיחוֹ לְדָוִד וּלְזַרְעוֹ עַד עוֹלָם. עֹשֶׂה שָׁלוֹם בִּמְרוֹמָיו, הוּא יַעֲשֶׂה שָׁלוֹם עָלֵינוּ וְעַל כָּל יִשְׂרָאֵל, וְאִמְרוּ אָמֵן.

Guests recite the following.
Children at their parents' table also include the words in brackets.

*May the Compassionate One bless (my father, my mentor) the master of this house, and (my mother, my mentor) the lady of this house, they, their home, their family, and all that is theirs* (if there are people other than the aforementioned family members present, add — *and all those assembled here).*

Those eating at their own table say the following,
adding the choice in brackets that is appropriate to them.

*May the Compassionate One bless me, (my wife/husband and my offspring), and all that is mine* (if there are people other than the aforementioned family members present, add — *and all those assembled here),*

*ourselves and all that is ours, just as our patriarchs Avraham Yitzhak and Yaakov were blessed in all, from all, and with all. So may God bless us all together with complete blessing, and let us respond, Amen.*

**בַּמָּרוֹם** *On high may they seek out merit for them and for us, that shall be a safeguard of tranquility. Let us obtain blessing from the Lord and charitableness from the God of our salvation. And let us find grace and true understanding in the eyes of God and humankind.*

On Shabbat add:
*May the Compassionate One bequeath to us a day of complete rest and contentedness in eternal life.*

On Rosh Hodesh add:
*May the Compassionate One renew this month for us, for good and for blessing.*

**הָרַחֲמָן** *May the Compassionate One deem us worthy of the Messianic days and the life of the world to come.* [Weekdays – *God Who magnifies the deliverances of God's king,*] [Shabbat, Yom Tov, and Rosh Hodesh – *God Who is a tower of deliverances to God's king,*] *and does lovingkindness for God's anointed, for David and his posterity forever. The Effector of harmony in God's heights, may God effect tranquility for us and for all Israel, and let us say, Amen.*

**יְראוּ** אֶת יהוה קְדֹשָׁיו, כִּי אֵין מַחְסוֹר לִירֵאָיו. כְּפִירִים רָשׁוּ וְרָעֵבוּ, וְדֹרְשֵׁי יהוה לֹא יַחְסְרוּ כָל טוֹב. הוֹדוּ לַיהוה כִּי טוֹב, כִּי לְעוֹלָם חַסְדּוֹ. פּוֹתֵחַ אֶת יָדֶךָ, וּמַשְׂבִּיעַ לְכָל חַי רָצוֹן. בָּרוּךְ הַגֶּבֶר אֲשֶׁר יִבְטַח בַּיהוה, וְהָיָה יהוה מִבְטַחוֹ. נַעַר הָיִיתִי גַּם זָקַנְתִּי, וְלֹא רָאִיתִי צַדִּיק נֶעֱזָב, וְזַרְעוֹ מְבַקֶּשׁ לָחֶם. יהוה עֹז לְעַמּוֹ יִתֵּן, יהוה יְבָרֵךְ אֶת עַמּוֹ בַשָּׁלוֹם.

The leader recites:

**בָּרוּךְ** אַתָּה יהוה אֱלֹהֵינוּ מֶלֶךְ הָעוֹלָם, בּוֹרֵא פְּרִי הַגָּפֶן.

(All – אָמֵן)

The leader, having consumed more than a revi'it (3.3 fluid ounces), then recites the following concluding blessing:

**בָּרוּךְ** אַתָּה יהוה אֱלֹהֵינוּ מֶלֶךְ הָעוֹלָם, עַל הַגֶּפֶן וְעַל פְּרִי הַגֶּפֶן, וְעַל תְּנוּבַת הַשָּׂדֶה, וְעַל אֶרֶץ חֶמְדָּה טוֹבָה וּרְחָבָה, שֶׁרָצִיתָ וְהִנְחַלְתָּ לַאֲבוֹתֵינוּ, לֶאֱכוֹל מִפִּרְיָהּ וְלִשְׂבּוֹעַ מִטּוּבָהּ. רַחֵם נָא יהוה אֱלֹהֵינוּ עַל יִשְׂרָאֵל עַמֶּךָ, וְעַל יְרוּשָׁלַיִם עִירֶךָ, וְעַל צִיּוֹן מִשְׁכַּן כְּבוֹדֶךָ, וְעַל מִזְבְּחֶךָ וְעַל הֵיכָלֶךָ. וּבְנֵה יְרוּשָׁלַיִם עִיר הַקֹּדֶשׁ בִּמְהֵרָה בְיָמֵינוּ, וְהַעֲלֵנוּ לְתוֹכָהּ, וְשַׂמְּחֵנוּ בְּבִנְיָנָהּ, וְנֹאכַל מִפִּרְיָהּ, וְנִשְׂבַּע מִטּוּבָהּ, וּנְבָרֶכְךָ עָלֶיהָ בִּקְדֻשָּׁה וּבְטָהֳרָה.

בשבת – וּרְצֵה וְהַחֲלִיצֵנוּ בְּיוֹם הַשַּׁבָּת הַזֶּה.

בראש חודש – וְזָכְרֵנוּ לְטוֹבָה בְּיוֹם רֹאשׁ הַחֹדֶשׁ הַזֶּה.

כִּי אַתָּה יהוה טוֹב וּמֵטִיב לַכֹּל,° וְנוֹדֶה לְּךָ עַל הָאָרֶץ וְעַל פְּרִי הַגָּפֶן. בָּרוּךְ אַתָּה יהוה, עַל הָאָרֶץ וְעַל פְּרִי הַגָּפֶן.

°If the wine used is from Israel, the blessing concludes as follows:

וְנוֹדֶה לְּךָ עַל הָאָרֶץ וְעַל פְּרִי גַפְנָהּ. בָּרוּךְ אַתָּה יהוה, עַל הָאָרֶץ וְעַל פְּרִי גַפְנָהּ.

**יִרְאוּ** *Let the Lord's holy ones be in awe of the Lord, for those who are in awe of the Lord feel no deficiency. Young lions may experience poverty and hunger, but those who seek the Lord will not lack any good. Give thanks to the Lord, for the Lord is good; the Lord's lovingkindness is everlasting. You open Your hand, and satisfy the desire of all the living. Blessed is the person who trusts in the Lord, the Lord will be that one's security. I was once young and have also grown older, but have never seen a righteous person forlorn, with the offspring begging for sustenance. The Lord will give strength to the Lord's people, the Lord will bless the Lord's people with tranquility.*

The leader recites:

**בָּרוּךְ** *Blessed are You, Lord our God, Ruler of the Universe, Who creates the fruit of the vine.* (All— *Amen*)

The leader, having consumed more than a revi'it (3.3 fluid ounces), then recites the following concluding blessing:

**בָּרוּךְ** *Blessed are You, Lord our God, Ruler of the Universe, for the vine and for the fruit of the vine, for the produce of the field, and for the lovely, good, and spacious land that You desired and bequeathed to our ancestors, to eat of its fruits and to be sated from its goodness. Please have compassion, Lord our God, on Israel Your people, on Yerushalayim Your city, on Zion the dwelling of Your glory, on Your altar and on Your abode. And build Yerushalayim, the holy city, speedily, in our time; bring us up into it, make us happy in its being built, let us eat of its fruits and be sated from its goodness, and let us bless You upon it in holiness and purity.*

On Shabbat – *And may it please You to invigorate us on this Shabbat day.*
On Rosh Hodesh – *And remember us for good on this Rosh Hodesh day.*

*For You, God, are good and do good for all, °and we thank You for the land and for the fruit of the vine. Blessed are You, Lord, for the land and for the fruit of the vine.*

° If the wine used is from Israel, the blessing concludes as follows:
*and we thank You for the land and for the fruit of its vine. Blessed are You, Lord, for the land and for the fruit of its vine.*

## ⸙ *Hakamat Matzayvah*

*There are varying customs concerning the dedication of the* matzayvah *(memorial monument).*

*The obligation to set this up devolves upon the family, and is considered a component of the honor one must accord the deceased.*

*Some attend to this immediately after* shiv'ah. *That is certainly the preferable practice, although there are those who wait twelve months for this.*

*The* matzayvah *should contain the name of the deceased and the name of the deceased's halakhic father, the Hebrew date of death, and the Hebrew abbreviation* T'N'Z'B'H' *(ת.נ.צ.ב.ה.).*

*The monument should not contain a proliferation of praise. Rather, it should be short and modest.*

*The important matter is to erect the memorial. The timing of any gathering to recite prayers at the site is not as pressing an issue.*

*Also, it is important to know that this gathering is* **not** *an unveiling, and the placing of a sheet on the monument, to be unveiled, is pure nonsense.*

## HAKAMAT MATZAYVAH

The service at the establishing of a memorial monument begins with appropriate readings, of which a few examples follow.

תהלים א

**אַשְׁרֵי** הָאִישׁ אֲשֶׁר לֹא הָלַךְ בַּעֲצַת רְשָׁעִים, וּבְדֶרֶךְ חַטָּאִים לֹא עָמָד, וּבְמוֹשַׁב לֵצִים לֹא יָשָׁב. כִּי אִם בְּתוֹרַת יהוה חֶפְצוֹ, וּבְתוֹרָתוֹ יֶהְגֶּה יוֹמָם וָלָיְלָה. וְהָיָה כְּעֵץ שָׁתוּל עַל פַּלְגֵי מָיִם; אֲשֶׁר פִּרְיוֹ יִתֵּן בְּעִתּוֹ, וְעָלֵהוּ לֹא יִבּוֹל, וְכֹל אֲשֶׁר יַעֲשֶׂה יַצְלִיחַ. לֹא כֵן הָרְשָׁעִים, כִּי אִם כַּמֹּץ אֲשֶׁר תִּדְּפֶנּוּ רוּחַ. עַל כֵּן לֹא יָקֻמוּ רְשָׁעִים בַּמִּשְׁפָּט, וְחַטָּאִים בַּעֲדַת צַדִּיקִים. כִּי יוֹדֵעַ יהוה דֶּרֶךְ צַדִּיקִים, וְדֶרֶךְ רְשָׁעִים תֹּאבֵד.

תהלים טז

**מִכְתָּם** לְדָוִד, שָׁמְרֵנִי אֵל כִּי חָסִיתִי בָךְ. אָמַרְתְּ לַיהוה, אֲדֹנָי אָתָּה, טוֹבָתִי בַּל עָלֶיךָ. לִקְדוֹשִׁים אֲשֶׁר בָּאָרֶץ הֵמָּה, וְאַדִּירֵי כָּל חֶפְצִי בָם. יִרְבּוּ עַצְּבוֹתָם אַחֵר מָהָרוּ; בַּל אַסִּיךְ נִסְכֵּיהֶם מִדָּם, וּבַל אֶשָּׂא אֶת שְׁמוֹתָם עַל שְׂפָתָי. יהוה מְנָת חֶלְקִי וְכוֹסִי, אַתָּה תּוֹמִיךְ גּוֹרָלִי. חֲבָלִים נָפְלוּ לִי בַּנְּעִמִים, אַף נַחֲלָת שָׁפְרָה עָלָי. אֲבָרֵךְ אֶת יהוה אֲשֶׁר יְעָצָנִי, אַף לֵילוֹת יִסְּרוּנִי כִלְיוֹתָי. שִׁוִּיתִי יהוה לְנֶגְדִּי תָמִיד, כִּי מִימִינִי, בַּל אֶמּוֹט. לָכֵן שָׂמַח לִבִּי וַיָּגֶל כְּבוֹדִי, אַף בְּשָׂרִי יִשְׁכֹּן לָבֶטַח. כִּי לֹא תַעֲזֹב נַפְשִׁי לִשְׁאוֹל, לֹא תִתֵּן חֲסִידְךָ לִרְאוֹת שָׁחַת. תּוֹדִיעֵנִי אֹרַח חַיִּים, שֹׂבַע שְׂמָחוֹת אֶת פָּנֶיךָ, נְעִמוֹת בִּימִינְךָ נֶצַח.

For Ladies:

משלי לא:י-לא

**אֵשֶׁת חַיִל** מִי יִמְצָא, וְרָחֹק מִפְּנִינִים מִכְרָהּ.
בָּטַח בָּהּ לֵב בַּעְלָהּ, וְשָׁלָל לֹא יֶחְסָר.
גְּמָלַתְהוּ טוֹב וְלֹא רָע, כֹּל יְמֵי חַיֶּיהָ.

# HAKAMAT MATZAYVAH

The service at the establishing of a memorial monument begins with appropriate readings, of which a few examples follow.

Psalm 1

**אַשְׁרֵי** *Happy is the one who has not followed the counsel of the wicked, nor stood in the path of sinners, nor sat in the company of the scornful. Rather, that one's delight is in the Torah of the Lord, meditating in God's Torah day and night. And will be like a tree planted by streams of water, that yields its fruit in season, whose leaf will not wither, and whatever that one does prospers. Not so the wicked, who are like chaff that the wind drives away. Therefore the wicked shall not survive judgment, nor sinners in the assembly of the righteous. For the Lord loves the way of the righteous, but the way of the wicked is doomed.*

Psalm 16

**מִכְתָּם** *Mikhtam L'David: Guard me, God, for in You I have taken refuge. You have said to the Lord, 'You are my Lord; I have no good beyond You.' As for the holy ones who are in the earth, and the mighty in whom is all my desire. Their sorrows will multiply, those that run to other gods; their blood libations will I not pour out, nor take their names upon my lips. The Lord is my allotted portion and my share; You sustain my fate. Portions have fallen to me in pleasant places; lovely indeed is my estate. I will bless the Lord Who has given me counsel; my conscience admonishes me at night. I have set the Lord before me always; because God is at my right hand, I shall not falter. Therefore my heart rejoices and my entire being exults; also my body will rest secure. For You will not abandon me to the grave, nor will You let Your devout one see destruction. You will make known to me the path of life; in Your presence is fullness of joy; there is delight at Your right hand for eternity.*

For Ladies:

Proverbs 31:10-31

**אֵשֶׁת חַיִל** *A gallant woman, who can find? Far beyond pearls is her worth.*

ב *Her husband's heartfelt trust is in her, and he shall lack for nothing.*

ג *She bestows good upon him, and never harm, all the days of her life.*

דָּרְשָׁה צֶמֶר וּפִשְׁתִּים, וַתַּעַשׂ בְּחֵפֶץ כַּפֶּיהָ.
הָיְתָה כָּאֳנִיּוֹת סוֹחֵר, מִמֶּרְחָק תָּבִיא לַחְמָהּ.
וַתָּקָם בְּעוֹד לַיְלָה, וַתִּתֵּן טֶרֶף לְבֵיתָהּ,
וְחֹק לְנַעֲרֹתֶיהָ.
זָמְמָה שָׂדֶה וַתִּקָּחֵהוּ, מִפְּרִי כַפֶּיהָ נָטְעָה כָּרֶם.
חָגְרָה בְּעוֹז מָתְנֶיהָ, וַתְּאַמֵּץ זְרוֹעֹתֶיהָ.
טָעֲמָה כִּי טוֹב סַחְרָהּ, לֹא יִכְבֶּה בַלַּיְלָה נֵרָהּ.
יָדֶיהָ שִׁלְּחָה בַכִּישׁוֹר, וְכַפֶּיהָ תָּמְכוּ פָלֶךְ.
כַּפָּהּ פָּרְשָׂה לֶעָנִי, וְיָדֶיהָ שִׁלְּחָה לָאֶבְיוֹן.
לֹא תִירָא לְבֵיתָהּ מִשָּׁלֶג,
כִּי כָל בֵּיתָהּ לָבֻשׁ שָׁנִים.
מַרְבַדִּים עָשְׂתָה לָּהּ, שֵׁשׁ וְאַרְגָּמָן לְבוּשָׁהּ.
נוֹדָע בַּשְּׁעָרִים בַּעְלָהּ, בְּשִׁבְתּוֹ עִם זִקְנֵי אָרֶץ.
סָדִין עָשְׂתָה וַתִּמְכֹּר, וַחֲגוֹר נָתְנָה לַכְּנַעֲנִי.
עוֹז וְהָדָר לְבוּשָׁהּ, וַתִּשְׂחַק לְיוֹם אַחֲרוֹן.
פִּיהָ פָּתְחָה בְחָכְמָה, וְתוֹרַת חֶסֶד עַל לְשׁוֹנָהּ.
צוֹפִיָּה הֲלִיכוֹת בֵּיתָהּ,
וְלֶחֶם עַצְלוּת לֹא תֹאכֵל.
קָמוּ בָנֶיהָ וַיְאַשְּׁרוּהָ, בַּעְלָהּ וַיְהַלְלָהּ.
רַבּוֹת בָּנוֹת עָשׂוּ חָיִל, וְאַתְּ עָלִית עַל כֻּלָּנָה.
שֶׁקֶר הַחֵן וְהֶבֶל הַיֹּפִי,
אִשָּׁה יִרְאַת יהוה הִיא תִתְהַלָּל.
תְּנוּ לָהּ מִפְּרִי יָדֶיהָ, וִיהַלְלוּהָ בַשְּׁעָרִים מַעֲשֶׂיהָ.

The officiating Rabbi here expounds on the life of the lamented departed, eulogizing and sensitively pointing the way toward integrating the virtues of the one whose stone is being established, effectively toward creating a living monument. After this, the memorial prayer is recited.

ד *She seeks out wool and linen, and her hands work willingly.*
ה *She is like a merchant fleet, bringing her sustenance from afar.*
ו *She arises while it is yet night, and gives provision to her household and direction to her maidens.*
ז *She envisions a field and acquires it, from the fruit of her handiwork she plants a vineyard.*
ח *With vigor she girds her loins, and strengthens her arms.*
ט *She discerns that her enterprise is good, her lamp does not go out by night.*
י *Her hands she stretches out to the distaff, and her palms support the spindle.*
כ *She spreads out her palm to the poor, and extends her hands to the destitute.*
ל *She fears not snow for her household, for her entire household is clothed with scarlet wool.*
מ *Fine covers she made herself, linen and purple wool are her clothing.*
נ *Prominent in the gates is her husband, as he sits with the elders of the land.*
ס *She makes a cloak and sells it, and deals a belt to the peddler.*
ע *Strength and splendor are her raiment, she cheerfully awaits the last day.*
פ *Her mouth is opened with wisdom, and the teaching of kindness is on her tongue.*
צ *She oversees the ways of her household, and partakes not of the bread of laziness.*
ק *Her children arise and praise her; her husband, and he lauds her.*
ר *'Many daughters have accomplished well, but you surpass them all.'*
ש *Grace is false and beauty is vain; a woman in awe of God — she should be praised.*
ת *Give her the fruits of her own hand, and let her deeds praise her in the gathering places.*

The officiating Rabbi here expounds on the life of the lamented departed, eulogizing and sensitively pointing the way toward integrating the virtues of the one whose stone is being established, effectively toward creating a living monument. After this, the memorial prayer is recited.

## MEMORIAL PRAYER

For males:

**אֵל** מָלֵא רַחֲמִים, שׁוֹכֵן בַּמְּרוֹמִים, הַמְצֵא מְנוּחָה נְכוֹנָה עַל כַּנְפֵי הַשְּׁכִינָה, בְּמַעֲלוֹת קְדוֹשִׁים וּטְהוֹרִים כְּזֹהַר הָרָקִיעַ מַזְהִירִים, אֶת נִשְׁמַת (שם הנפטר) בֶּן (שם אביו; אם מבחינה הלכתית לא היה להנפטר אב, קוראים אותו על שם אמו) שֶׁהָלַךְ לְעוֹלָמוֹ, בַּעֲבוּר שֶׁאֲנַחְנוּ מִתְפַּלְּלִים בְּעַד הַזְכָּרַת נִשְׁמָתוֹ. בְּגַן עֵדֶן תְּהֵא מְנוּחָתוֹ. לָכֵן בַּעַל הָרַחֲמִים יַסְתִּירֵהוּ בְּסֵתֶר כְּנָפָיו לְעוֹלָמִים, וְיִצְרוֹר בִּצְרוֹר הַחַיִּים אֶת נִשְׁמָתוֹ. יהוה הוּא נַחֲלָתוֹ; וְיָנוּחַ בְּשָׁלוֹם עַל מִשְׁכָּבוֹ, וְנֹאמַר אָמֵן.

For females:

**אֵל** מָלֵא רַחֲמִים, שׁוֹכֵן בַּמְּרוֹמִים, הַמְצֵא מְנוּחָה נְכוֹנָה עַל כַּנְפֵי הַשְּׁכִינָה, בְּמַעֲלוֹת קְדוֹשִׁים וּטְהוֹרִים כְּזֹהַר הָרָקִיעַ מַזְהִירִים, אֶת נִשְׁמַת (שם הנפטרת) בַּת (שם אביה; אם מבחינה הלכתית לא היה לנפטרת אב, קוראים אותה על שם אמה) שֶׁהָלְכָה לְעוֹלָמָהּ, בַּעֲבוּר שֶׁאֲנַחְנוּ מִתְפַּלְּלִים בְּעַד הַזְכָּרַת נִשְׁמָתָהּ. בְּגַן עֵדֶן תְּהֵא מְנוּחָתָהּ. לָכֵן בַּעַל הָרַחֲמִים יַסְתִּירֶהָ בְּסֵתֶר כְּנָפָיו לְעוֹלָמִים, וְיִצְרוֹר בִּצְרוֹר הַחַיִּים אֶת נִשְׁמָתָהּ. יהוה הוּא נַחֲלָתָהּ; וְתָנוּחַ בְּשָׁלוֹם עַל מִשְׁכָּבָהּ, וְנֹאמַר אָמֵן.

A reading from *Tehillim* should precede the recitation of *Kaddish*.

תהלים טו

**מִזְמוֹר** לְדָוִד; יהוה מִי יָגוּר בְּאָהֳלֶךָ, מִי יִשְׁכֹּן בְּהַר קָדְשֶׁךָ. הוֹלֵךְ תָּמִים וּפֹעֵל צֶדֶק, וְדֹבֵר אֱמֶת בִּלְבָבוֹ. לֹא רָגַל עַל לְשֹׁנוֹ, לֹא עָשָׂה לְרֵעֵהוּ רָעָה, וְחֶרְפָּה לֹא נָשָׂא עַל קְרֹבוֹ. נִבְזֶה בְּעֵינָיו נִמְאָס, וְאֶת יִרְאֵי יהוה יְכַבֵּד, נִשְׁבַּע לְהָרַע וְלֹא יָמִר. כַּסְפּוֹ לֹא נָתַן בְּנֶשֶׁךְ, וְשֹׁחַד עַל נָקִי לֹא לָקָח; עֹשֵׂה אֵלֶּה לֹא יִמּוֹט לְעוֹלָם.

## ◈ MEMORIAL PRAYER ◈

For males:

**אֵל** *God, full of compassion, Who dwells on high, grant proper repose on the sheltering wings of Your presence, in the lofty levels of the holy and pure who shine as the brightness of the firmament, unto the soul of* (name of deceased) *son of* (father's name; if deceased had no halakhic father, he is called by his mother's name), *who has gone to his world, and for whose memory we pray. May his repose be in Paradise. May the Master of compassion bring him under the cover of God's wings, and bind his soul in the bond of life. May the Lord be his heritage, and may he repose on his resting place in peace, and let us respond, Amen.*

For females:

**אֵל** *God, full of compassion, Who dwells on high, grant proper repose on the sheltering wings of Your presence, in the lofty levels of the holy and pure who shine as the brightness of the firmament, unto the soul of* (name of deceased) *daughter of* (father's name; if deceased had no halakhic father, she is called by her mother's name) *who has gone to her world, and for whose memory we pray. May her repose be in Paradise. May the Master of compassion bring her under the cover of God's wings, and bind her soul in the bond of life. May the Lord be her heritage, and may she repose on her resting place in peace, and let us respond, Amen.*

A reading from *Tehillim* should precede the recitation of *Kaddish*.

Psalm 15.

**מִזְמוֹר** *A song of David. Lord, who may sojourn in Your tent, who may dwell on Your holy mountain? One who walks in purity, does what is righteous, and speaks the truth from the heart. Who has no slander on the tongue, nor has done harm to a fellow, nor casts disgrace toward a neighbor. In whose eyes a contemptible person is repulsive, but who honors those who are in awe of the Lord; who swears truthfully even to personal hurt, and never retracts. Who does not lend money on interest, nor takes a bribe against the innocent; one who does these things shall never falter.*

# ⊰ THE MOURNER'S KADDISH ⊱

**A transliteration of this Kaddish appears on page 189.**

**יִתְגַּדַּל** וְיִתְקַדַּשׁ שְׁמֵהּ רַבָּא (קהל– אָמֵן), בְּעָלְמָא דִּי בְרָא כִרְעוּתֵהּ, וְיַמְלִיךְ מַלְכוּתֵהּ, בְּחַיֵּיכוֹן וּבְיוֹמֵיכוֹן וּבְחַיֵּי דְכָל בֵּית יִשְׂרָאֵל, בַּעֲגָלָא וּבִזְמַן קָרִיב, וְאִמְרוּ אָמֵן.

(קהל– אָמֵן. יְהֵא שְׁמֵהּ רַבָּא מְבָרַךְ לְעָלַם וּלְעָלְמֵי עָלְמַיָּא).

**יְהֵא שְׁמֵהּ רַבָּא מְבָרַךְ לְעָלַם וּלְעָלְמֵי עָלְמַיָּא.**

יִתְבָּרַךְ וְיִשְׁתַּבַּח וְיִתְפָּאַר וְיִתְרוֹמַם וְיִתְנַשֵּׂא וְיִתְהַדָּר וְיִתְעַלֶּה וְיִתְהַלָּל שְׁמֵהּ דְּקֻדְשָׁא בְּרִיךְ הוּא (קהל– בְּרִיךְ הוּא). °לְעֵלָּא מִן כָּל (בעשרת ימי תשובה– °לְעֵלָּא לְעֵלָּא מִכָּל) בִּרְכָתָא וְשִׁירָתָא תֻּשְׁבְּחָתָא וְנֶחֱמָתָא, דַּאֲמִירָן בְּעָלְמָא. וְאִמְרוּ אָמֵן. (קהל– אָמֵן)

יְהֵא שְׁלָמָא רַבָּא מִן שְׁמַיָּא, וְחַיִּים עָלֵינוּ וְעַל כָּל יִשְׂרָאֵל. וְאִמְרוּ אָמֵן. (קהל– אָמֵן)

Take three steps back. Bow left and say . . . עֹשֶׂה; bow right and say . . . הוּא; bow forward and say . . . וְעַל כָּל.

עֹשֶׂה °שָׁלוֹם (יש אומרים בעשרת ימי תשובה– °הַשָּׁלוֹם) בִּמְרוֹמָיו, הוּא יַעֲשֶׂה שָׁלוֹם עָלֵינוּ, וְעַל כָּל יִשְׂרָאֵל. וְאִמְרוּ אָמֵן. (קהל– אָמֵן)

Remain standing in place for a few seconds, then take three steps forward.

The service concludes with the officiating Rabbi offering some comforting wishes to the family, including that they be granted the strength to endure, that they be inspired by the memory of the departed, and that they gather in the future for happy occasions.

Those in attendance should place a pebble or some grass on the monument upon taking leave of the gravesite.

## THE MOURNER'S KADDISH

**A transliteration of this Kaddish appears on page 189.**

**יִתְגַּדַּל** *May God's great Name grow exalted and sanctified (*All– *Amen), in the world which God created according to God's will, and may God rule over that dominion in your lifetimes and in your days, and in the lifetimes of the entire Family of Israel, swiftly and in due time. And we respond, Amen.*

(All– *Amen. May God's great Name be blessed forever and ever*).

*May God's great Name be blessed forever and ever.*

*Blessed, praised, glorified, exalted, extolled, beautified, upraised, and lauded be the Name of the Holy One, Blessed is God. (*All– *Blessed is God). (*From Rosh HaShanah to Yom Kippur add: *Exceedingly) Beyond any blessing and song, praise and consolation that are uttered in the world. And we respond, Amen. (*All– *Amen)*

*May there be abundant tranquility from Heaven, and life, upon us and upon all Israel. And we respond, Amen. (*All– *Amen)*

Take three steps back. Bow left and say . . . עֹשֶׂה; bow right and say . . . הוּא; bow forward and say . . . וְעַל כָּל.

*The Effector of harmony* (some in the Ten Days of Repentance, say – *the harmony) in God's heights, may God effect tranquility for us, and for all Israel. And we respond, Amen. (*All– *Amen)*

Remain standing in place for a few seconds, then take three steps forward.

The service concludes with the officiating Rabbi offering some comforting wishes to the family, including that they be granted the strength to endure, that they be inspired by the memory of the departed, and that they gather in the future for happy occasions.

Those in attendance should place a pebble or some grass on the monument upon taking leave of the gravesite.

# ⸨ TRANSLITERATION OF KADDISH FOLLOWING BURIAL ⸩

*Yit-ga-dal ve-yit-ka-dash She-may raba.* (All— *Amen*)
*b'al-ma dee Hoo a-tid le-it-ha-da-ta*
*ool-le-a-ha-ya may-ta-ya*
*oo-le-a-sa-ka le-ha-yay al-ma,*
*oo-le-miv-nay kar-ta dee ye-rush-laim*
*oo-le-shakh-lale hay-khe-lay be-ga-vah*
*oo-le-me'e-kar pul-ha-na nookh-ra'ah may-ar'a*
*oo-le-a-ta-va pul-ha-na dee-she-ma-ya le-at-ra*
*Ve-yam-likh kood-sha b'rikh Hoo be-mal-khu-tay vee-ka-ray*
*be-ha-yay-khon oo-ve-yo-may-khon oo-ve-ha-yay de-khol bayt Yis-ra-el*
*ba'a-ga-la oo-viz-man ka-riv.*
*Ve-ee-me-roo Amen.*
(All— *Amen. Ye-hay She-may rab-ba me-va-rakh le-a-lam oo-le-al-may al-ma-ya.)*

**Ye-hay She-may rab-ba me-va-rakh**
**le-a-lam oo-le-al-may al-ma-ya.**

*Yit-ba-rakh ve-yish-ta-bakh ve-yit-pa'ar ve-yit-ro-mam*
*ve-yit-na-say ve-yit-ha-dar ve-yit-a-leh ve-yit-ha-lal*
*She-may de-kood-sha b'rikh Hoo.* (All— *B'rikh Hoo)*
*Le-ay-la min kol* (from *Rosh HaShanah* to *Yom Kippur* substitute *Le-ay-la le-ay-la mee-kol) bir-kha-ta ve-shee-ra-ta*
*toosh-be-ha-ta ve-ne-he-ma-ta*
*da-a-mee-ran b'al-ma.*
*Ve-ee-me-roo Amen.* (All— *Amen*)
*Ye-hay she-la-ma rab-ba min she-ma-ya ve-ha-yyim*
*a-lay-noo ve-al kol Yis-ra-el.*
*Ve-ee-me-roo Amen.* (All— *Amen*)

Take three steps back. Bow left and say *O-seh . . .*; bow right and say *Hoo . . .*; bow forward and say *ve-al kal . . . .*

*O-seh sha-lom (*some, in Ten Days of Repentance, say: *ha-sha-lom) bim-ro-mav*
*Hoo ya-a-seh sha-lom a-lay-noo*
*ve-al kal Yis-ra-el.*
*Ve-ee-me-roo Amen.* (All— *Amen*)

Remain standing in place for a few seconds, then take three steps forward.

## TRANSLITERATION OF MOURNER'S KADDISH

*Yit-ga-dal ve-yit-ka-dash She-may raba.* (All – *Amen*)
*b'al-ma dee ve-ra khee-re-oo-tay*
*ve-yam-likh mal-khoo-tay*
*be-ha-yay-khon oo-ve-yo-may-khon oo-ve-ha-yay de-khol bayt Yis-ra-el ba'a-ga-la oo-viz-man ka-riv.*
*Ve-ee-me-roo Amen.*
(All – *Amen. Ye-hay She-may rab-ba meva-rakh le-a-lam oo-le-al-may al-may-ya.)*

***Ye-hay She-may rab-ba me-va-rakh***
***le-a-lam oo-le-al-may al-may-ya.***

*Yit-ba-rakh ve-yish-ta-bakh ve-yit-pa'ar ve-yit-ro-mam*
*ve-yit-na-say ve-yit-ha-dar ve-yit-a-leh ve-yit-ha-lal*
*She-may de-kood-sha b'rikh Hoo.* (All – *B'rikh Hoo)*
*Le-ay-la min kol* (from *Rosh Hashanah* to *Yom Kippur* substitute: *Le-ayla le-ay-la mee-kol) bir-kha-ta ve-shee-ra-ta*
*toosh-be-ha-ta ve-ne-he-ma-ta*
*da-a-mee-ran b'al-ma.*
*Ve-ee-me-roo Amen.* (All – *Amen*)
*Ye-hay she-la-ma rab-ba min she-ma-ya ve-ha-yyim a-lay-nu ve-al kol Yis-ra-el. Ve-ee-me-roo Amen.* (All – *Amen*)

Take three steps back. Bow left and say *O-seh . . .*; bow right and say *Hoo . . .*; bow forward and say *ve-al kal . . .*.

*O-seh sha-lom* (some, in Ten Days of Repentance, say: *ha-sha-lom) bim-ro-mav*
*Hoo ya-a-seh sha-lom a-lay-noo*
*ve-al kal Yis-ra-el . . .*
*Ve-ee-me-roo Amen.* (All – *Amen*)

Remain standing in place for a few seconds, then take three steps forward.